the
further
adventures of
SHERLOCK HOLMES
THE GENTLEMAN BURGLAR

the further adventures of
SHERLOCK HOLMES
THE GENTLEMAN BURGLAR

SAM SICILIANO

TITAN BOOKS

THE FURTHER ADVENTURES OF SHERLOCK HOLMES:
THE GENTLEMAN BURGLAR

Print edition ISBN: 9781803369440
E-book edition ISBN: 9781803369457

Published by Titan Books
A division of Titan Publishing Group Ltd
144 Southwark Street, London SE1 0UP
www.titanbooks.com

First edition: May 2024
10 9 8 7 6 5 4 3 2 1

A CIP catalogue record for this title is available from the British Library.

Printed and bound by CPI Group (UK) Ltd, Croydon, CR0 4YY.

To Maurice Leblanc, creator of Arsène Lupin, a character still going strong over a century after his first appearance

Author's Note

ↄ

Two iconic French characters, both masters of disguise, first appeared in print early in the twentieth century: the lovable rogue and gentleman burglar Arsène Lupin, and the evil and cruel Fantômas. Both would go on to appear in many novels, plays, and films throughout the century.

Maurice Leblanc published his first story featuring Lupin in 1905 and made a good living off the character for the remaining thirty-six years of his life. Lupin starts out as a clever thief, but over time becomes a wily detective, solving countless crimes and puzzles, and also rescuing unfortunate couples in distress from various monstrous villains. He also distinguishes himself during an interlude in the French Foreign Legion and even spends time working in the French Sûreté trying to catch himself! During his career, he assumes countless identities, often of foreign noblemen.

This novel was inspired by *L'Aiguille creuse* (*The Hollow Needle*, 1909), and uses some of the settings, the paraphernalia, and the plot mechanisms, including a mysterious coded document. However, all of Part 3 is my own invention.

Sherlock Holmes appeared as antagonist early on in the Lupin stories, but because of rights issues and the disapproval of Conan Doyle and his publishers, the name was changed to Herlock Sholmès, and Watson became Wilson. Sholmès is older than Lupin and rather cold-blooded. He shows up briefly later in *The Hollow Needle* and acts almost as the villain of the piece, accidentally killing someone close to Lupin at the conclusion.

I, however, see Holmes and Lupin more as kindred spirits and speculate on what might happen if the two chose to work together on the same enigma, the one portrayed in *The Hollow Needle*: a search for the great hidden treasure of the kings of France. Readers who know that novel will have a surprise at the end, for the treasure is not where it is to be expected.

My backstory for Lupin comes mostly from Leblanc, but I think my explanation of his prodigious childish exploits is more believable.

I hope my readers will enjoy this encounter between the Gallic and the British titans of detection!

Part 1

LE CHÂTEAU DE L'AIGUILLE, CREUSE

Chapter 1

O n a typical late March afternoon in Paris, cold and rainy with dark clouds, the weather more reminiscent of winter than spring, my cousin Sherlock Holmes and I walked along a narrow street on the Île Saint-Louis. The island was in the oldest part of the city, at its very heart, next to the other small island where the church of Notre-Dame stood. We were on our way to the mansion or *hôtel particulier* of the Baron Frédéric Chamerac to discuss some mysterious business.

Ahead of us, a shadowy figure came out of a side street: a monstrously large black overcoat hid his bent body, a cane tapped at the pavement, and a black country cleric's hat with a wide brim cast a shadow over two odd smears of blue—the colored glass lenses of his spectacles. Around his neck, a narrow band of white with a notch at the center marked him as a Catholic priest. His tortoise-like shuffle and labored gait were those of a very old man. As he came closer, a mangy white beard and long wisps of white hair curling from under the hat were evident, and on his right cheek was a reddish-brown blotch, either a blemish from birth or from his extreme age.

He came toward us, glanced up, then stopped. Holmes nodded. "*Bonjour, monsieur l'abbé.*"

"*Bonjour*, Monsieur Sherlock Holmes," croaked the old man. His hoarseness had a husky crackle like that of a crow or raven.

"Have we met before?" Holmes asked him in French, and the man replied in kind.

"No, but I know you. And I come with a warning: beware the treasure of the Needle. It swims in centuries of blood, and the grievous crimes of the French monarchs have poisoned it. No good can ever come of such tainted wealth. It is cursed. And do not trust the baron! Greed is one of the seven deadly sins, and his greed has swallowed him up entirely."

Holmes gave him a curious glance, his blue-gray eyes faintly puzzled. We both wore the requisite gentleman's garb: long black woolen frock coats with striped gray trousers, shiny shoes, gray leather gloves, and black silken top hats. Holmes held the silver handle of an elegant walking stick of ebony wood.

The corners of his mouth rose slightly. "You seem singularly well informed, *mon ami.*"

The old man nodded. His thin nose had an odd sort of curve at the end, and his long white mustache hid his lips. He raised his cane shakily. "*Remember.*"

He lowered the cane, then resumed his shuffling walk, passing us by. Holmes and I watched him go. Holmes glanced at me, still smiling faintly. "Quite a remarkable performance."

I was frowning slightly. "Did you tell anyone that you were coming to see the baron?"

"No, but obviously someone has heard about it."

We had nearly reached the end of Rue Saint-Louis en l'Île, a street which bisected the tiny island, and we started through a small park. The wooden benches were wet and barren, the tall, pruned plane trees just beginning to leaf out. The sandy gravel underfoot was darkened by moisture. Something made a noise in the bushes, and I turned in time to catch sight of a gray form with a long curving pink tail.

"Lord!" I exclaimed. "How I hate a rat." Looking more closely amidst the greenery I could make out many more small forms. "This place is crawling with them!"

"No doubt the water of the Seine attracts them."

We stepped out of the park onto another street which curved round the island, and the gray waters of the river were before and round us. A coal barge puffing smoke was lumbering by, kicking up a white wake in the dark water. To our left rose the facade of the mansion, one of those spectacular old Parisian buildings of tan-colored limestone, probably built in the seventeenth or eighteenth century. Four stories high, with dormers higher still in the dark gray slate roof, the building had many tall white-framed and paneled windows. Across the cobbled way was a curving stone wall with, at intervals, openings to the steps which led down to the walkway along the Seine.

The house's entrance had huge doors of cast bronze with an elaborate design, and above the curving top was an impressive smiling sun god in relief with some strange dragon-like, fish-like, creatures on either side, winged and yet with odd curving tails. Holmes had to look about to find the small button of the bell on the left side. He pressed it. We waited briefly. Unlike a more common sort of dwelling, you certainly could not hear any sounds coming from behind the thick barrier of those doors.

They opened at last, and a thin elderly man in black formal dress peered warily out at us.

Holmes nodded. "*Je suis* Sherlock Holmes. *Le baron m'attend.*"

"*Ah, oui, monsieur.*" He gazed rather sternly at me. "*Et ce n'est pas encore un* Watson *?*"

I sighed, wishing again I had a shilling for every time I had been mistaken for Watson. "*Mon nom est Vernier,*" I said.

"*Ah, très bien,* Monsieur Vernier. *Venez, venez.*"

We followed him into the vestibule, and he took our hats, gloves, and Holmes's stick, setting them aside. We followed him up an incredible stone staircase and down a hallway. The opulence and ornamentation were spectacular, somewhat akin to Versailles or the Vatican palaces. There were no simple bare walls or ceilings. Statuesque maidens in relief lined the hallway; there were framed circular mirrors, curves, and arabesques everywhere of gold, and overhead on the ceiling, painted gods and goddesses lolled about pastures and woods, blue sky occasionally showing through. The floor was an elaborate wooden parquet of different hues of brown, varying from the yellow of oak to the dark shade of walnut.

We came into a sitting room filled with plush furniture of a crimson velvet, chairs and sofas all with carved curving legs, as well as small tables with bronze candelabras or brass lamps. Overhead hung two chandeliers with a myriad of dangling spangles of cut crystal. A young woman sat in a corner near a window with a book on her lap, the blue of her dress clashing with all the red.

She stood up and nodded. She appeared only about twenty and was one of those women whose remarkable beauty made it difficult for a normal red-blooded man not to stare. Her skin was very fair, with a hint of pink at her cheeks, her eyes a clear light blue, and her tightly bound hair was a silvery blond. Her nose was slight, but again, most men's eyes would be drawn to those full, sensual lips, so warmly and darkly colored for someone of such a pale, cool complexion. Her dress would have cost far more than what a typical lady's maid earned in a year. It was the latest fashionable cut, with leg-of-mutton style sleeves which narrowed about her slender wrists, and the beautiful azure silk shimmered under the gray-white light coming from the tall window. She looked only about five feet tall, and she had tiny, delicate white hands.

She nodded. "Messieurs."

Holmes did the same. "Mademoiselle." He gave a questioning look at the old servant.

The man's face was carefully neutral, but a couple of vertical creases showed above his nose. "Mademoiselle Chamerac, the baron's niece. This way, gentlemen. The baron is waiting for you in the library."

He opened the doors to perhaps the most magnificent library I have ever seen. Rows of leather-backed tomes of different heights lined tall shelves along the walls, and the ceiling was partitioned off into ornately framed sections with paintings within them, while on the floor was a splendid multicolored oriental rug. A massive table stained a dark brown-black dominated the room. Three tall windows bathed the interior with gray-white light. Two men sat at the far end of the table, and they rose to greet us.

A certain haughty air, as well as the finely tailored cut of his double-breasted frock coat, made the identity of Frédéric Chamerac, the Baron de Creuse, obvious enough. He was the shorter of the two, slightly stocky but broad-shouldered, and he had long wavy chestnut hair shiny with pomade and a big mustache waxed to points. His coat had striking ivory buttons, and the soft-looking blackish wool which was probably genuine cashmere, had a hint of blue in it. The coat's extravagant style and the swooping curve of the skirts made it clearly the work of a French tailor, rather than an English one.

His taller companion might have been younger, but his large, pale, shining cranium–emphasized by the contrasting black hair over his ears and two thick, black, mustache-like eyebrows–made him appear old. Rather than trying to comb his scanty hair forward to hide his baldness, he had swept it defiantly back, and his full but meticulously trimmed black beard and mustache dominated his face. His thin lips were set in a taut line, and he wore a dark gray suit, probably bought off the rack at one of the grand Parisian department stores.

The baron had piercing blue eyes, and his forehead was creased. Staring at Holmes, he seemed to relax ever so slightly. "I see Dr. Watson is not with you."

My cousin is very fluent in French, and it is my mother tongue, so the conversation that followed was in that language.

"No, this is my cousin and associate Dr. Henry Vernier."

The baron hesitated, his brow furrowed ominously, his eyes showing a seething anger. "I– I must tell you that I have rarely been so insulted in my life! If we are to do business, I must have your word that I shall never see him again."

Holmes stared at him, obviously flummoxed. "Of whom are you speaking?"

"Who else? Watson."

Holmes opened his mouth, then closed it. "I don't understand."

"You do not? He was here yesterday on your behalf, and he demanded an exorbitant sum–twenty-five thousand francs–for you to even consider my case. Twenty-five thousand francs! Is that your usual fee, Monsieur Holmes, or are you merely trying to take advantage of my wealth and position?" The baron's face had grown quite red.

Holmes raised both hands, spreading his long thin fingers. "Calm yourself, monsieur le baron. I think there is a misunderstanding here. You say Watson was here yesterday, and spoke to you on my behalf?"

"He did."

Holmes gave his head a slight shake. "And did he speak in French or English?"

"French—with a most abominable English accent."

Holmes's smile showed no trace of humor. "That settles it. Someone has deceived you. Watson is no doubt at home, in London. I have not seen him in a very long time. And he speaks no French at all. You saw someone else entirely."

The baron stared at him. "Is this true?"

"I assure you that it is. He was an impostor. I would never demand such a sum before taking on case." He shook his head. "Twenty-five thousand francs. That's a thousand pounds. A tidy sum indeed!"

The baron eased his breath out in a great sigh. He looked relieved, but still slightly suspicious. "This is a relief, Mr. Holmes. I had thought… No matter."

"I take it you refused such a payment. And what did this supposed Watson do?"

"I did refuse it, in no uncertain terms, and I said perhaps it would be better if we did not meet at all. This seemed to worry him, and he said we two might, after all, discuss your fee at our meeting the next day. I told him he would most certainly not be welcome again under my roof, and that, indeed, I would not meet with you if he were present."

Holmes's sardonic smile flickered over his lips. "Well, since that condition has been met, perhaps you can tell me now why you have called upon my services?"

"So I shall. And you may be seated." He pointed at two of the sturdy wooden chairs by the table and pulled out one for himself. He gestured toward the tall man at his side who was clasping a brown paper folder against his torso. "This is my personal secretary, Monsieur Louis Massier."

We all nodded, and Massier said, "It is a great honor to meet you, Monsieur Holmes. Your exploits and abilities are well known."

Holmes smiled again. "Messieurs, I hope your appraisal of my abilities is not based solely upon Watson's writings. They are... exaggerated, to say the least."

"You are too modest," the baron said. "Besides, I spoke with an acquaintance in the Sûreté, a commissaire, and he was lavish in your praise."

"I am glad to hear it. The detectives in the Sûreté are first-rate, quite the equal of the best of Scotland Yard."

The baron unbuttoned his coat before he sat, then withdrew a silver case and took out a cigarette. "You may smoke if you wish, gentlemen." Holmes reached inside his jacket, but the baron offered him his case. "Try one of mine, monsieur. I pride myself on the quality of my tobacco." Holmes nodded and took one. The secretary withdrew some matches, struck one, then lit first the baron's cigarette, then Holmes's.

"*Merci bien,*" Holmes said to Massier.

The baron said nothing and exhaled a huge cloud of smoke. Before him on the table was a thick glass ashtray the size of a soup bowl, which looked to weigh about five pounds. The baron's hands were sturdy and compact, strong-looking, with brown hair showing below the knuckles. A thick gold band was on the ring finger of his left hand. He peered thoughtfully at Holmes.

"Tell me, monsieur. Have you ever heard tell of a royal French treasure, a secret one, hidden for centuries? That of the Needle of Creuse?"

Holmes gave him a puzzled look. "That of the hollow needle?"

The baron had said "l'Aiguille de Creuse," the "Needle of Creuse," but *creuse* has two main meanings in French. Holmes must have heard *l'aiguille creuse*, creuse being the feminine variant of the adjective *creux* which means "hollow."

I touched Holmes's elbow lightly. "He said *'de* Creuse.' Creuse is the name of a river and a *département* in the midlands of France."

"Ah. I am not familiar with Creuse. Thank you for enlightening me." He turned to the baron. "Henry was born and raised in France, so he knows your country far better than I."

The baron nodded. "That explains why he has no English accent whatsoever. Regardless, do you know of this treasure, Monsieur Holmes?"

He shook his head. "I do not. You are, of course, the Baron de Creuse, so you must be quite familiar with the Creuse region. Is there some formation or landmark called the Needle there?"

"Yes, certainly. Le Château de l'Aiguille, constructed in the seventeenth century, is the family seat of the Chameracs."

"Ah, and you suspect a vast treasure may be hidden there?"

"Yes. Its existence is a secret which has been passed down from generation to generation."

"So your father must have told you?"

"No, I don't think my father even knew about it. My uncle was the prior baron, not my father."

"But you inherited the title and the estate?"

The baron nodded. "Yes. My uncle had no male heirs, so the title passed to me when he died three years ago. Oh, even as a boy, I had heard vague rumors about a hoard of golden louis and spectacular jewels, but I always thought it was romantic nonsense until I found a certain letter amongst my uncle's estate papers."

"Ah!" Holmes sat up very straight. "I trust you brought it along?"

"Of course. Louis." At a glance from the baron, Massier opened the folder and withdrew a suitably yellowed and ancient-looking sheet of parchment, which he pushed across the table toward us. It was rather old-fashioned French, but I could make it out easily enough:

Within the Chameracs flows the royal blood of France, that shared with the Bourbon kings, and for this reason, the Baron de Creuse has been entrusted with the most sacred duty of watching over the grand treasure of the Needle. Indeed, our good king Louis the Fourteenth has built for us the Castle of the Needle to conceal that secret, and he has made us its guardian. A foul traitor wanted to reveal everything, and for his crime, he must wear a mask of iron and remain in prison for the rest of his miserable life. Begun by our ancestors, the Gauls, continued by the good Count Rollo, the treasure has grown over the centuries and become the legacy of the monarchs of France, passed on from generation to generation, but the true Needle itself is ancient, older than time. The Maiden of Orléans went to the fire rather than tell the English the secret. The treasure may be hidden, but the key is ours to watch over. Whenever the next heir to the barony reaches the age of reason, explain to him the meaning of st. s. 138.

It was signed with a grand flourish, *Louis-Philippe Chamerac, Baron de Creuse*, and dated July 12, 1699.

I frowned. "*St. s.*? I wonder… saint something? Saint Sebastian? The one shot with arrows?"

Holmes grimaced slightly. "I think not. Nothing so obvious." He looked over at the baron. "And have you any idea what *st. s. 138* refers to?"

The baron tapped his cigarette in the ashtray and gave his head a brusque shake. "None whatsoever."

"I see. I would suspect, too, that the 'key' is not a literal one of metal. And I suppose you have looked for this treasure?"

"I certainly have. I have had every square inch of that castle searched without success. Louis was in charge, and he was very thorough. Since then I have…" He hesitated.

"Yes?" Holmes said.

He shrugged. "It is not, after all, a great secret. I recently employed someone else to help me with this matter, a supposed young genius by the name of Isidore Beautrelet. He has had some well-publicized successes as a sort of amateur detective who helped solve some mysterious crimes, some spectacular thefts by an infamous, so-called gentleman burglar, name of Arsène Lupin. However, I have dismissed Beautrelet, and everyone says you are the best, so—"

"Why exactly did you dismiss him? Because he failed to find the treasure?"

"There was more to it than that."

Holmes shrugged. "Meaning?"

The baron eased his breath out slowly. "I supposed it would not hurt anything to tell you. He became quite familiar with my niece and made certain… unwanted advances toward her. I warned him that she was only a young girl, and he was not to trouble her. He would not listen."

Holmes nodded slowly. "I believe we just saw your niece in the sitting room next door. She is visiting with you?"

"It is more than a visit. My younger brother joined the French Foreign Legion as a youth, and we went our separate ways. He was out of the country, mostly in Algeria, and I never heard from him, not a letter in years. Then the Legion notified me of his death two years ago. You can imagine my surprise when Angelique–his daughter–wrote to me last year. I had not even known he was married! Her mother had also died, and she was destitute. I felt a familial obligation to look after her, and so I have taken her in." He regarded us sternly, even as he drew in slowly on his cigarette. "I should warn you both to take heed from Beautrelet's example: Angelique is not to be trifled with."

It took me a second or two to realize what he was saying. "I assure you," I said, "I am a married man!"

Holmes eased out some cigarette smoke, smiling faintly. "She is certainly far too young for my consideration."

The baron shrugged. "Perhaps I am being overly cautious, but Beautrelet took me by surprise. My wife and I have no children of our own, and Angelique has become like a daughter to me."

"It was very generous of you to take in your niece. You said you have only been a baron for three years. Was your family well enough off before, that you might...?"

"Not in the least, I assure you! But I have worked hard for many years, with success, I might add. I made my own fortune long before the barony became mine. As the letter notes, the bloodline of the Chameracs is royal: in fact, one of my ancestors had a certain claim to the French throne. Nevertheless, I do not consider my labor an abasement, but rather a worthwhile usage of my natural intellectual endowments."

"What type of work did you do?"

"I trained as an engineer, and I have spent twenty-five years at one of the leading ship-building companies in France. I started as an engineer, but advanced to the upper ranks of the company. All the same, I continued to interest myself in all the technical details of our constructions."

Holmes smiled and pointed at a lone book which lay to one side of the table next to the folder. "That would explain your choice of reading matter."

Holmes had good eyes to discern the small print of the title on the spine. The baron smiled back, and turned over the book to reveal the cover embossed elaborately in gold, red, and brown. *VOYAGES EXTRAORDINAIRES* and JULES VERNE were at the top, each block of text forming an arc, and below was the smaller title, *Vingt Mille Lieues sous les mers–Twenty Thousand Leagues under the Seas.*

"I have read it so many times, and for me, it is almost a sort of... Bible."

"It is one of Verne's best." Holmes glanced at me. "I suppose you must have read it in French, Henry?"

"So I have."

He noticed a certain lack of enthusiasm on my part. "And yet you did not care for it?"

"Parts were very exciting, but all those descriptions of fish, crustaceans, the ocean flora and fauna... It grew tedious."

Holmes nodded. "I must confess I skimmed over certain parts. Regardless, it is a favorite of mine as well. And is your shipyard working on a submarine, monsieur le baron?"

The baron smiled. "I'm afraid not, although we have built some ironclad naval warships. The book came out in 1870, more than twenty years ago now, but alas, I fear we are not much closer to Captain Nemo's submarine than we were when the book first appeared."

"Yes, but the French have always been at the forefront of submarine research. *Le Plongeur* built in the sixties was supposed to be Verne's inspiration for the *Nautilus*, and one of the latest French submarines, le *Gymnote*, uses batteries for propulsion, as did the *Nautilus*."

The baron stared at him, creases again appearing in his forehead. "Your naval knowledge surprises me, Monsieur Holmes! I would not have expected it. However, those two French submarines— what absolutely feeble efforts, in the end! The batteries on le *Gymnote* are the right idea, but the actual technology used in their construction is still quite primitive. Neither submarine can begin to compare with Nemo's magnificent *Nautilus*. But we are not here to talk about my niece or submarines, but rather the lost treasure of France." He stubbed out the remnants of his cigarette and left the butt in the ashtray.

Holmes nodded. "What exactly would you like me to do?"

"I want you to go to the Château de l'Aiguille and see if you can get to the bottom of this. If the treasure is not actually at the château, perhaps you can discover the secret of where it is hidden."

"With little more to go on than *st. s. 138*. You said you had no clue what that might refer to?"

The baron shook his head. "None whatsoever. I was hoping you could discern its significance."

Holmes took a final draw on his cigarette, then crushed it into the ashtray. "I suspect the secret meaning which was to be passed on orally amongst the Chamerac heirs was lost a long time ago. All it would take would be a sudden death to break the chain. And of course, with the fall of Louis Napoleon in 1870, there have been no French kings or emperors for over two decades, but only your Third Republic. Your uncle never discussed this treasure or this letter with you before his death?"

"No."

Holmes set his palms and fingers together, then leaned forward. "Perhaps now would be an opportune time to stress that I am not a miracle worker. However…" He lowered his hands. "I shall do my best. And will you accompany us to the château?"

"No, I am afraid I have some urgent business. I cannot spare the time. I shall, of course, pay you for your efforts, whether you succeed or not in unraveling this mystery. I trust your fee will not be twenty-five thousand francs!" He smiled, but did not appear much amused.

"No, we might begin with perhaps a tenth that sum."

The baron nodded. "Done! Much more reasonable."

Holmes tapped lightly at the table with his long fingers. "But tell me, monsieur le baron: I am curious. Should we find the treasure… what exactly do you intend to do with it?"

The baron's gaze shifted briefly to Massier, then back to Holmes. "Monsieur, I am first and foremost a Frenchman and a patriot. True, we have no king now, but I would return the treasure to the Republic and the people of France. However, I would naturally insist upon some reward for my efforts, a certain commission for finding it, a percentage. You, too, would have your share, your commission. It would not surprise me if the sum greatly exceeded that mentioned by the false Watson."

Holmes smiled. "Well, that is certainly an incentive to do my best. However…" His fingers drummed again at the table. "You used the term 'romantic nonsense' earlier. Your story certainly has all the elements worthy of a romance by, say, Alexandre Dumas—and indeed, Dumas did write a volume about the Man in the Iron Mask. At least, hopefully, your treasure does not involve a secret twin of Louis the Fourteenth, although there in your letter, is the man in the mask himself!—as well as references to Joan of Arc and the ancient

Gauls. You must realize that the whole story may be poppycock–that no such treasure exists–that it is indeed, only fiction."

The baron shrugged. "I realize it is fantastical. However, I wish to be certain. After all, if such a treasure does exist it could be worth millions of francs. There would be nothing even remotely comparable."

Holmes frowned faintly. "There is something else I should tell you. On our way here, an old man, a priest, accosted us. He warned us to beware of the treasure of the Needle."

The baron was just preparing to light another cigarette, but it toppled from his fingers and landed on the table. "*What?*"

"I take it you do not know who this old priest could be."

The baron shook his head angrily. "Damnation! This must be Beautrelet's work. I should have known he could not keep a secret, or perhaps he did this to spite me. But an old priest? Why an old priest?"

Holmes raised his shoulders. "I cannot say."

"I certainly don't want the Church involved in this." The baron eased out his breath, took up the cigarette between his lips, and let Massier light it. "There is something I, too, should let you know, although I do not exactly trust Beautrelet. He said he feared that Arsène Lupin had gotten wind of the treasure of the Needle."

"Who is this Arsène Lupin? The name is not familiar to me."

"He is a so-called *gentleman-cambrioleur*, a burglar, who was first heard of three or four years ago. He specializes in thefts of expensive jewels or works of art. However, no one really knows for certain if he exists or not. The thefts attributed to him may be committed by some gang that wishes to confuse the police. Do you know Inspector Ganimard of the Sûreté?"

"I have heard tell of him, but I have never actually met him."

"He has been investigating the crimes of Arsène Lupin, and he is convinced that the man does exist. Of course, if Lupin did hear about this, such a treasure would be irresistible to him! However, I am not convinced. I think Beautrelet was only trying to drive up the cost of his services."

Holmes smiled. "He does sound a very enterprising young man."

A scowl twisted the baron's face. "I suppose I must grant that. And he is a clever devil, that one. Perhaps too clever for his own good."

"How old is Beautrelet?"

"He must be about twenty now, but his name first appeared in the newspapers a couple of years ago when he managed to restore the Countess de Gesvres's diamond necklace."

"You said Monsieur Massier has searched the Château de l'Aiguille?"

"Systematically, from top to bottom."

"And was Beautrelet at all involved in the search?"

"No. He has not been to the château. Even early on, I felt a certain wariness. I did not want him there. I entrusted Louis with the search, and a thorough job he did, indeed."

Massier nodded gratefully. "I can state categorically that there is no treasure at the château."

The baron smiled faintly. "Of course, if Louis had his way, I would not be employing your services."

Massier's eyes narrowed. "That does not mean I do not have the greatest respect for you, Monsieur Holmes! I assure you… All the same, I think I could do a better job investigating this matter than an adolescent prodigy like Beautrelet—a mere puppy! I am not convinced it requires some… wizardry."

The baron glanced at Massier, his lips still curving upward. "Louis does have a formidable intellect. And he, too, trained as an engineer. All the same, I absolutely cannot spare him just now. The case is yours, Monsieur Holmes."

"But to sum up, then, the search of the Château de l'Aiguille found nothing?"

The baron gestured at Massier, who answered. "Nothing at all—as concerns the treasure. We did find a secret chamber, and nearby, a secret passageway which led from the castle to a spot in the woods, but nothing was there except cobwebs, spiders, and rats. It must not have been used for centuries."

"Would you happen to have the plans of the château?"

"Indeed I do. Louis." The baron nodded toward Massier, who withdrew a large brown envelope from the folder. "You may take them with you. There is also a copy of the letter from my ancestor."

"Are the rooms…? Could there be some numbering scheme which relates to the 138?"

"That is possible. There are over eighty bedrooms in the castle. Perhaps you can discern something."

My eyes widened. "Eighty bedrooms? Good Lord."

Holmes reached across the table for the big envelope. "I shall have a look at them. And I suppose you would like me to go to the château as soon as possible? Very good. I want to make some inquiries here in Paris, and then we can take the train the day after tomorrow." He must have noticed the subtle change in my expression, for he smiled and grasped my arm. "Don't worry, Henry, I promise we will get you back to Paris in time to meet with Michelle! If need be, I can carry on by myself."

I smiled. "Thank you." I looked at the baron. "My wife is back in London laboring at her medical practice, but she is to join me late next week for a brief Parisian holiday."

The baron looked faintly wary. "I hope we can rely on your utter discretion, Dr. Vernier. No one must know of this treasure—no one at all."

I nodded. "My lips are sealed."

"I can vouch for his trustworthiness," Holmes said. "You need not fear. He has assisted me in many of my cases."

"I hope it is understood there are not to be any future volumes of the further adventures of Sherlock Holmes, nor one entitled 'the Mystery of the Needle.'"

Holmes shook his head in mock dismay. "God forbid!"

"You need not fear that," I said.

"Very well. All is settled, I believe." He turned to Massier. "Checkbook, *s'il te plaît.*"

Massier withdrew a leather checkbook with an embossed fleur-de-lis and handed it, as well as a wooden fountain pen to the baron. The baron squinted slightly as he filled out the check, then scribbled his signature, and gave it to Holmes.

"Thank you." Holmes folded the check and put it in his inside jacket pocket.

The baron stood first, by way of dismissal, and we all rose. "A great pleasure, Monsieur Holmes. And Dr. Vernier." Again I was struck by how immaculately groomed and tailored the baron was. His compact hand felt massive, his grip fierce, while Massier's more slender fingers were moist and faintly limp. "Please see them out, Louis. If you have any news, Monsieur Holmes, telegraph me at once. If it is truly urgent—especially if you were to actually find the treasure—I can dispense with my business and come immediately."

Holmes nodded. "As you wish. I shall do my best, but there is not a great deal to go on."

We went through the doorway into the sitting room with its crystal chandeliers, its abundance of furniture, its gilt decor and painted ceilings, and again the beautiful woman seated near the window rose and nodded toward us. She hesitated, then stepped forward. Massier ignored her and went round her, but Holmes stopped. She walked right up to him and stood with her back to Massier. I was just behind them.

Holmes said, "Mademoiselle Chamerac, I believe."

"Yes. And you must be Monsieur Sherlock Holmes."

"Indeed I am."

She stepped to the side and gave me a questioning glance. "And you, Monsieur?"

"I am Dr. Henry Vernier."

She nodded, "*Bonjour, Docteur.*" She turned again to Holmes. "I wish you luck in your quest, monsieur."

"So you know what I am looking for?"

"Yes. A treasure, a grand treasure." Lines appeared in the perfectly smooth white skin of her brow. "I hope, though… I hope my uncle did not speak too harshly of Monsieur Beautrelet. He meant no harm. And he is, after all, hardly more than a boy." I reflected that this seemed to be the pot calling the kettle black.

"So you do not share your uncle's outrage?"

"Not exactly." Her full lips rose in a faintly ironic smile. "He meant well."

"I see." He nodded. "Good afternoon, mademoiselle."

On the way down the hallway, we passed the doorway to a smaller, plainer sitting room, where on a chair in the corner sat a thin, dour-looking woman all in black. She was staring out of a window, her long white fingers with swollen knuckles resting upon her lap. Her long hair was bound up, and a flame of white amidst the darker brown showed above her temples. The set of her mouth and forehead somehow suggested both weariness and a sort of dull anger. Holmes and I had both halted before the doorway, and she glanced briefly at us, but did not budge from her seat, turning again toward the window, as if to dismiss us. Upon a small table were a beautiful lamp and an antique rococo-style clock of sculpted gold and a face with roman numerals, which ticked loudly.

As we proceeded down the hallway, Holmes said to Massier. "Who was that woman?"

"That was the Madame Chamerac, the baroness."

"Ah. She must be in mourning?"

"Yes, her mother died some time ago. All the same–" Massier's smile showed a certain contempt "–she has a great fondness for black."

We descended the stone staircase and went to the vestibule. Massier's gaze had changed, his eyes inquisitive.

"Have you something to say to me, Monsieur Massier?"

He shrugged. "Only that I fear it will be as you suspected: you will be wasting your time at the Castle of the Needle, Monsieur Holmes. If the treasure were there, I certainly would have found it. All the same, I suppose since you have been paid twenty-five hundred francs you must earn your fee. There's little point in trying to dissuade you." His thick black eyebrows shot briefly upward, and his smile became ironical. "Nor would I wish to contradict my employer's wishes! May you have better luck than I did."

"Thank you, monsieur."

The old servant in black brought us our top hats, gloves, and Holmes's stick, and Massier opened the massive doors for us. The gray light of day set his bald head all aglow. "Good day, messieurs, and, Monsieur Holmes, it has been a great honor to meet you!"

We stepped out in the fading gray light of afternoon, the misty drizzle cold and damp on my face, and I shivered slightly, wishing I had worn my greatcoat. Holmes put on his hat, but not his gloves.

He took an envelope out of his pocket, opened it, and unfolded a piece of paper. "Interesting," he murmured.

"What is that?"

"It is a note from Mademoiselle Chamerac. She hopes to meet with me tomorrow at 11 A.M. at the small café across the street from the Galeries Lafayette. If I cannot possibly come, she asks that I send her word of another possible time."

"What! But...? She just gave that note to you?"

He laughed. "It was nicely done. Neither you nor Massier noticed. Something of a risk, though, on her part."

"Why does she want to see you?"

"She says it is urgent but does not explain herself."

I shook my head. "Skillfully done indeed! She must have been prepared in advance."

"Yes." Holmes stroked his chin. "The baron may have told her I was coming. There is another possibility. Perhaps Beautrelet got wind of our appointment." He shrugged. "Someone obviously knew about our visit—hence that ancient priest and his warning." He finished pulling on his gray leather gloves, smiling. "Everyone seems to know Sherlock Holmes is in France looking for the great treasure of the kings! Yes, Henry, all quite preposterous—truly the makings of another novel by Dumas, but I fear, decidedly one of the second rank."

Chapter 2

Holmes and I went through the vast lobby of the *Maison d'Or* hotel with its comfortable leather furniture and giant potted ferns lavishly leafing, and stopped before the front desk to fetch our key. A large wall clock showed that the time was six thirty. The black-suited attendant set an old-fashioned key and an envelope on the marble counter.

"*Une lettre pour vous*, Monsieur Holmes."

"*Merci, monsieur.*"

I took the key, while Holmes examined the envelope, frowning slightly. He opened it and removed the folded paper. His gray eyes peered intently, even as his brows scrunched together. A smile flickered across his lips. "Better and better," he murmured.

"What is it?" I asked.

"Have a look."

It was brief and to the point:

Dear Mr. Sherlock Holmes, as one of your most fervent admirers, I was delighted to hear that you are taking on the case of the long lost treasure of the Needle! A little competition is always good, is it not? Nothing better than a contest to sharpen one's wits and stir the blood! I wonder which of us will find the treasure first? If it were anyone else but yourself, I would give considerable odds on my being the victor, but with Sherlock Holmes, I would say the chances are fifty–fifty. Forward then, and as you English say, may the best man win!

Cordially,
Arsène Lupin, gentleman-cambrioleur

I shook my head. "You were certainly right that everyone in Paris seems to know you are here looking for the treasure. Interesting that he calls himself a *gentleman-cambrioleur* and not a *gentilhomme-cambrioleur*. Granted the French have adopted the English word into their language, but the English variant does seem a trifle pretentious."

"A forceful handwriting this, and his English is quite good. Of course, he may have had a friend write it for him." Holmes folded the letter and put it back in the envelope. "I think we shall stop at the Sûreté headquarters tomorrow and see if we can speak with Inspector Ganimard. I am most curious about this Lupin, especially now that he has so forcefully thrust himself into our business. But come, Henry, I think we have more than earned a before-dinner drink. Normally I might have a whiskey and soda, but in Paris, one must emulate the natives—only a Cognac or Armagnac will do."

We started toward the adjoining restaurant. A young man in a big leather chair was watching us, and he leaped up and bounded forward to cross our path before we reached the doorway. He was of medium height, with a slight stoop, the typical bad posture one sees in the young. His hair was a nondescript light brown, cut very short, and his brownish suit of coarse wool was ill-cut, obviously cheap. Behind the thick lenses of his wire-rimmed spectacles, his dark amber eyes were opened very wide, which gave him a perpetually startled or apprehensive look. He seemed to stiffen, his face contorting briefly.

"Mr. Sherlock Holmes?" His tenor voice had a kind of awkward quaver.

"Yes?"

"You do not know me. That is to say, I do not think you know me, but perhaps, perhaps by some chance, you have indeed heard of me–I hope you have!–although if it was through the baron…" He gave his head a quick shake. "In that case, it is doubtful you have heard the truth. Who knows what calumnies he may be spreading! I beg you to let me defend myself." He spoke a very proper, formal French.

Holmes and I stared at him, but Holmes spoke first. "Your name, monsieur?"

"Beautrelet. Isidore Beautrelet."

Holmes smiled. "Of course."

Beautrelet raised his hands, his fingers spread wide apart. "You have no idea what a great honor it is to see you–to speak with you–to be under the same roof with you. I have followed your career with such interest, and I have tried, with my feeble efforts, to emulate your work! And to actually meet Dr. Vernier as well! That, too, is an honor."

I stared at him incredulously. Always, I was mistaken for Watson, and to have someone actually acknowledge me! "How did you know my name?"

"Oh, I have done my research, I assure you! As soon as I heard that Sherlock Holmes was coming, I made certain inquiries. John Watson craves the spotlight, but you are obviously a much more modest man."

I shook my head, smiling. "You certainly know how to flatter a person, Monsieur Beautrelet."

He was staring at Holmes. "I have only one desire, monsieur: to work with you, the master. Together, our forces united, it should be child's play to find the treasure of the Needle!"

"Your zeal is admirable, Monsieur Beautrelet, but I believe the Baron of Creuse decided to dispense with your services."

Beautrelet stiffened slightly, his upper lip curling. "What do I care for his approval or disapproval? He is the worst sort of aristocratic snob! Nor do I care for his dirty money! My only wish is to work with Sherlock Holmes—and I shall gladly do it gratis. I have made some discoveries which I wish to share. Together, what might we not accomplish!"

Holmes sighed softly. "I'm afraid it is quite out of the question, Monsieur Beautrelet. I always work alone."

He glanced at me. "But is not Dr. Vernier your frequent companion and collaborator?"

"Yes, but Henry—"

"Why not two companions instead of one!"

Holmes shook his head. "Again, I'm afraid that is not possible, but—" he gestured toward the doorway "—why don't you join us for an aperitif, Monsieur Beautrelet?"

A broad smile transformed the young man's face. "Gladly, gladly! But you should know, I never give up. I can help you—I promise I can help you."

We went into the dining area, which was mostly empty as the

French didn't generally sup for another two hours or so; closer to nine than seven. The waiter in his black suit and black vest nodded and told us to seat ourselves. Holmes went to a small table in the corner with a view of the entire room and the bar. He sat, then glanced at Beautrelet. "What will you have?"

Beautrelet looked briefly puzzled. "Whatever you and the good doctor are drinking."

The waiter had arrived at our table. Holmes raised the fingers of his right hand. "*Trois Armagnacs, s'il vous plaît.*"

"*Bien sûr, monsieur.*"

Beautrelet was sprawled in the chair, hands clasped before him, a certain lunatic grin on his face. "I cannot believe I am actually sitting here with Sherlock Holmes himself! It is something I have dreamed of, in certain idle moments, but I never imagined my wish could really come true. Let me explain to you, Monsieur Holmes, why you should accept my assistance. I have been working on the case for nearly a month and have uncovered a great deal. I suppose the baron gave you a copy of his predecessor's letter?"

Holmes stared closely at him, but did not reply.

Beautrelet shrugged. "That, of course, is a given, and I'll wager you have the plans for the château as well. However, while digging about ancient tomes in various libraries, I came across reference to a certain brochure written during the reign of Louis the Fourteenth. The author printed one hundred copies which were immediately seized by the king and destroyed, and the writer was imprisoned and forced to wear—" he paused, his eyes opening wider even as a twitch of a smile appeared "—a mask of iron! The booklets were all thrown onto a bonfire, but the head of the king's guard was an enterprising fellow, and he swiped one, which was passed down in his family. He used it, apparently, to find the treasure and snitch a few jewels, but he was set upon by robbers and died under mysterious circumstances. I could not find the actual copy, but I discovered a pamphlet published early in this century discussing the contents. The author was a royalist during the time of Napoleon who longed for the return of a Bourbon king. Once we have an agreement, I shall be happy to share it with you."

I could see that Holmes was tempted. "And are you certain it is genuine?"

"Yes, I had it looked at by an expert, and he said the paper, the binding, and the ink were consistent with those of the empire."

The waiter arrived with a small circular tray and set the three glasses before us. Each had a short stubby stem and a wide bowl. The Armagnac was a warm reddish-brown color, different from the paler amber of most Cognacs.

Beautrelet eagerly seized his glass, took a big swallow, gasped, coughed several times even as he clapped his hand over his chest. He gave his head a shake. "I'm afraid I am not used to strong drink."

"It is meant to be sipped." Holmes gave a brief demonstration, then set down his glass. "It is very good, as one might expect of a hotel of this quality. It has a certain age."

I had a swallow. It was more pungent than Cognac and burned slightly on the way down, but delicious all the same. "Excellent indeed."

Beautrelet took a very small sip. "Yes, it's better this way, rather than gulping." He set down the glass, curved the fingers of his right hand lightly about the bowl. "And what reason did the baron give you for my dismissal?"

Holmes shook his head. "I really do not feel I can discuss a private conversation with you."

Beautrelet scowled. "It was about Angelique, wasn't it?" Holmes's face remained strictly neutral, but I had less self-control than him. "Oh, you don't need to tell me. I am certain enough about it." His lips formed a seething angry smile. "Ironic, isn't it? He has only been a baron for three years, and that, because he was lucky enough to have his uncle die with no male heir, and already he puts on airs and considers those not of noble blood unworthy of his precious niece! Shouldn't it be up to Angelique, I ask you? Shouldn't she be allowed to choose her own husband, rather than have some blue-blooded nitwit forced upon her?" Holmes remained impassive, so Beautrelet turned to me. "And what do you think, Dr. Vernier? I know your wife is a physician, and I can only imagine what trials she must have undergone to become one. Surely she would argue that a woman should be allowed to choose her own husband!"

I could not restrain a laugh. "She certainly would!"

"And you would agree with her, I know! I can see it in your face."

"Yes, I suppose I would."

"Then you can understand why I would not kowtow and submit to outrageous commands from a pompous nobleman with an inflated sense of self-worth. No, no—if Angelique wishes to reject me, I shall submit—with a heavy heart, yes—but she and she alone has the power to command me! I am no slave that the baron can order about, or rather, I am a slave only to Angelique! Her wish is truly my command. Were she to ask it, I would gladly hurl myself from a parapet and dash out my brains."

The corners of Holmes's mouth had risen. "Let us hope it does not come to that."

"No, indeed. I think now you understand my position, Monsieur Holmes. I could not accede to the baron's demands. I simply could not. I was *not* dismissed because of incompetence, most assuredly not. Indeed, if the baron had sent me to the Château de l'Aiguille—which you will, no doubt, soon be visiting—I am certain that I could soon find the key to the treasure. As for *st. s. 138.*" He smiled. "A tantalizing mystery, that! But I have some ideas—I've always been good at puzzles. And with two of us in pursuit... I'll wager we have it figured out within twenty-four hours of our arrival!"

Holmes swirled the liquid in his glass, then took a sip. "I admire your enthusiasm, Monsieur Beautrelet."

"It is settled, then—we shall go together!"

"I'm afraid not. If it were up to me, I might take you along, but—"

"Then do so!"

"I must honor the wishes of my employer."

Beautrelet slouched in his chair, folding his arms. "I don't see why. I warn you: do not trust him. He is not an honorable man. I make it a rule to find out whatever I can about the people I work for. He has a terrible reputation in his nautical company and is known for his towering rages. Also, there is something you should really ask yourself, Monsieur Holmes."

"What might that be?"

"What do you think he will do if he finds the treasure?"

Holmes stroked his chin lightly. "He told me what he plans to do."

"Yes—supposedly, he will turn over the treasure to the Republic. And you believed him?"

Holmes merely shrugged.

"You have good reason to be skeptical! He is a greedy, miserly sort of man. I've heard that said of him, universally, and have seen it first-hand. There are rumors that he has squandered the wealth of the barony. If he finds that treasure, he will never willingly hand it over to anyone—certainly not to the Republic! These aristocrats are all the same. They despise the Republic. They want to bring back one king or another. The baron thinks he has the blood of the Bourbons, so he must have been rooting for Henri, the Duke of Bordeaux, but now that Henri is dead, he has probably switched his allegiance to the Orléans candidate."

Holmes nodded. "Very impressive, young man. Keeping up with all the various contenders for the French monarchy is a complicated affair. All the same…"

"Yes, yes—forgive me, I digress. The point is that, should we find it, he would definitely keep the treasure for himself. In fact, I would not be surprised if he packed up and fled the country with it."

Holmes sipped his brandy. "Attacking the baron is not going to make me change my mind."

"What then? What will change your mind?"

"Nothing. I'm afraid I take my professional obligations seriously. And if the baron were to hear that you were accompanying me…"

Beautrelet jerked upright, smiling broadly. "I have it all figured out! I shall come along as your valet! And I shall be disguised. A false mustache, some spectacles, perhaps a wig… They should do the trick!"

Holmes smiled. "Your zeal is most commendable. I wish I could oblige you, but again, it is simply not possible."

Beautrelet grew quite stern. "I shall not take no for answer. Promise me—promise me you will at least think it over."

Holmes shrugged. "As you wish, but I shall not change my mind. However, there is another topic I should like to discuss with you: Arsène Lupin."

Beautrelet scowled. "Ah, the villain—the great villain!"

"I hear you and he have crossed swords on more than one occasion."

Beautrelet nodded. "We have indeed. I am one of the few people to have actually seen him."

"Have you now? And what did he look like?"

"Oh, he is of medium height, with thick black hair and a black mustache, and a little scar over his right cheek. Just here." Beautrelet touched his face. "He must be about thirty. He seems to take his role as a gentleman very seriously. He is immaculately groomed, and his tailor is first-rate, no off-the-rack clothing for him! He sometimes sports a monocle. He has a shrewd gaze, and his usual mien is rather ironical. And of course, he is known for writing long florid letters to the police, the newspapers, and his victims, a rather silly occupation, if you ask me."

Holmes sipped his Armagnac thoughtfully. "Interesting. I had not heard about that. He must enjoy his notoriety and wishes to cultivate it."

"Without a doubt!" Beautrelet took a sip, then coughed twice.

"I must admit I have received one of his missives. I suppose it would not hurt…" He took out the envelope, withdrew the paper, unfolded it, and gave it to Beautrelet.

The young man scanned it, then shook his head. "Yes, very typical. All the same—if there were two of us working against him to find the treasure… we could not possibly fail! That would greatly increase the odds he speaks of in your favor! And at the risk of being immodest, I have already bested him on two occasions."

"Tell me about that, monsieur."

Beautrelet again sat back in the chair, folding his arms. "Well, I had some small success as an informal detective after finishing my education, but it was the case of the Count de Perron, which was written up in the newspapers, that made my reputation.

"In a typical fashion, Lupin sent the count a letter telling him how much he admired his two excellent Rubens paintings and warning that he would be taking them the following Friday night. The count, of course, took precautions. Not content with the local police, he hired special guards whom he locked in the sitting room where the paintings were hung. He used two special combination padlocks to secure the doors. That Friday evening, he settled in with the two guardians for the night, and the house was completely surrounded by other men whom he had employed. The last thing he remembers is drinking some coffee with the guards to keep them all vigilant. When he awoke early the next morning in a sort of stupor, the two paintings were gone, the doors still locked. The three of them had drunk drugged coffee and the dozen men outside the château swore that no one could have entered or departed on their watch.

"I read of the theft in the afternoon papers and rushed there at once, suspecting that the paintings—and Lupin himself—might still be nearby. That was when I first met Inspector Ganimard of the Sûreté. I pretended to be a newspaper reporter, and he allowed me to see the scene of the crime. In searching the sitting room, I discovered something suspicious amongst the painted portraits. The eye of a certain ancestor looked strange, and when we took down the painting, spyholes in the canvas and in the wall were revealed. I knew there must be a secret passage to get back there. It took me an hour or two, but I finally found the lever behind a thick volume in one of the bookshelves.

"A section below the wainscoting swung open, and Ganimard and I were soon following a narrow passageway. The exit was near the garden in back, and we found one of the Rubens, but not the other. Lupin had made off with it and probably hoped to return for the second one during the night. We laid a trap for him, but he never reappeared."

Holmes nodded thoughtfully. "So the matter ended in a draw."

"Exactly!"

"And the next encounter?"

Beautrelet frowned sternly. "I know you can be trusted to keep a secret, Monsieur Holmes. You must promise never to reveal what I am about to tell you." Holmes nodded, and when Beautrelet looked at me, I did the same.

"Very well. The newspaper said I had miraculously retrieved the diamond necklace of Madame Dussolier from Lupin, but that in the process, he had given me something of a beating. The last part is certainly true! I'm afraid I sported a black eye for a week or two after our encounter. I am, regrettably perhaps, more a man of brain than brawn." He smiled weakly. "I am very bad at fisticuffs. Anyway, what really happened was rather complicated. It involved Madame Dussolier and some compromising letters, as well as her maid Mademoiselle Chaudin."

He leaned forward to touch Holmes lightly on the wrist. "Lupin does have a weakness, one real weakness—his fondness for the ladies. As part of his scheme, Lupin began by ingratiating himself with the maid. Most likely this began as a game for him, but over time, he became genuinely fond of her. She was, after all, a very beautiful young woman with black hair and black eyes. The poor girl had no idea who her suitor really was, or what he was up to, but he was laying the groundwork for a theft. However—" Beautrelet grinned broadly "—someone else beat him to the necklace!

"A former suitor of the Madame Dussolier, a genuine blackguard, had incriminating letters, and he threatened to show them to her husband, a wealthy financier, unless she were to leave two doors unlocked on a particular night. She did so, and he entered and absconded with the necklace. Suspicion immediately fell upon the maid, who vehemently protested her innocence.

"I read about this in the paper, and my intuition told me that Lupin was involved. I watched the house in disguise as a peddler, and one day, when Mademoiselle Chaudin left, I followed her. She met in a café with a dark-haired gentleman with a mustache whom I described earlier." He peered intently at Holmes. "I cannot explain it, really, but a thrill shot through me, shaking me to my very core—somehow, I *knew* this was Arsène Lupin!

"I waited until they were finished, then I followed the man back to an old apartment building. After he had gone inside, I told the concierge I believed my old friend Valmont had just gone inside and could she give me his room number so I could talk with him. She told me I was mistaken, this was Monsieur Punil." He grinned triumphantly. "That, of course, clinched it!"

Holmes gave an appreciative nod, but I stared at Beautrelet. "How so?"

Holmes turned to me. "A rather obvious anagram of Lupin, the letters only slightly rearranged."

"I followed Lupin whenever he went out. On the second day, in the afternoon, he went to a house in one of the seedier parts of Paris. He was inside a long while, then came out with a packet under his arm. I was about to follow him when a shot rang out from inside. Lupin hustled away. I was torn, but in the end I went to the house and hammered upon the door. No one answered, but it was unlocked. I went inside, and in the hallway I discovered an ashen-faced valet. His master Monsieur Malroux had just shot himself in the head and lay dead in his study.

"I rushed back outside and started back in the direction of Lupin's dwelling, and sure enough, I managed to catch up to him halfway there. I closed in on him near a small park, when suddenly, he whirled around. 'Good day, Monsieur Beautrelet,' he said. 'I have something for you.' I was rather uneasy, but he moved very swiftly and struck me in the face, knocking me down. 'That is for following me for the last few days!' he said. Then he helped me up.

"He gave me the packet and explained that it contained both the diamond necklace and the compromising letters. Malroux had been both bankrupt and ill. Lupin had found out about him from the maid, and he had threatened to turn him over to the police. Using both persuasion and threats, Lupin forced him to give up both the necklace and the letters. Shortly thereafter, in despair, Malroux had killed himself. Lupin did not want Mademoiselle Chaudin to be arrested for a crime she did not commit, nor did he want the countess to suffer from a blackmailer. Hence, he told me I could tell Ganimard and the press that, he, Lupin was the thief. He would take the blame to ensure that the two women were troubled no more. And I could take the credit for recovering the necklace."

Holmes's sardonic smile appeared. "Ah, a gentleman burglar indeed!"

Beautrelet scowled. "That's easy for you to say—he didn't hit you in the face! I think it was more vanity than chivalry. Anyway, I also did not want the women to suffer, so I did as he said. I told Ganimard I had reclaimed the necklace after a struggle with Lupin at his apartment. I said nothing of the compromising letters."

"You are another gentleman," I said.

Beautrelet frowned ever so slightly. "I certainly hope so. But you must not give Lupin too much credit, Monsieur Holmes. I still think he is the very devil, and it is most troubling to think he may be involved in this case. Again, you must have my assistance! I can recognize him. I can help you. I have battled with him twice now, rather successfully both times."

Holmes shrugged. "I'm not so sure about the second time. He simply handed over the necklace."

"There was nothing simple about it—the villain might have blinded me with that blow! And he warned me that if we were to meet a third time, he might just put a bullet through my brain."

Holmes swished the small amount of liquid left in his glass, then took a swallow. "This has been quite interesting, Monsieur Beautrelet."

"So you will let me help you, then? Again, you need pay me nothing. I only want to work with Sherlock Holmes more than anything in the world." He spoke with a fervent intensity.

Holmes eased out his breath and shook his head. "I'm sorry."

Beautrelet's face was an open book, his dismay manifest in his eyes and mouth. He touched Holmes on the wrist with long wiry hand. "*Please*... Promise me you'll consider it! And as a sign of my good faith..." He took a large brown envelope out of an inside jacket pocket and set it before Holmes. "Here is the brochure I told you about. It is yours to examine." He took a final swallow of his drink, grimacing, and coughing once, then stood. "And then we shall talk again!"

Holmes and I also stood.

"Do not give yourself false hopes, monsieur," Holmes said.

"They cannot be false. *They cannot.*" He shook both our hands, smiled awkwardly, and then strode out of the restaurant.

Holmes glanced at me, and then we both sat back down. "A rather remarkable young man," Holmes said.

"I think he could be helpful to us. But of course I understand why you must refuse him. All the same, he strikes me as somehow more trustworthy than the baron."

Holmes frowned, but he did not speak.

Holmes spent much of the evening examining Beautrelet's pamphlet. The paper was brownish and blotchy. On the front was printed the title, *Le Vrai Histoire du Grand Trésor de France, le Trésor Royal de l'Aiguille*, along with an elaborate depiction of angels and hounds gathered round a shield with fleur-de-lis on it.

It had been a long day, and I went to bed early. The next morning I was up first and went down to the restaurant for my classic French *petit-déjeuner*. The Maison d'Or was the sort of grand hotel which would prepare a traditional substantial English breakfast if that was what you wanted, but when in Rome... Hence the waiter set before me a small cup of coffee and a *pain au chocolat*. I took a bite from the golden-brown crust of this puffy creation, tasting the chocolate within, and reflected that the English just couldn't make anything close to proper French patisserie.

I had polished it off and was considering another when Holmes appeared in his black frock coat, his thin face freshly shaven, and his black hair combed neatly back. He sat down and ordered a similar breakfast from the waiter, even as I asked for more coffee and a *pain aux raisins*, by way of variety.

"Well," I said, "did you discover any great hidden secrets in the pamphlet about the treasure?"

"No, I'm afraid not. It was all very fanciful and convinced me, more than ever, that we are most likely dealing with fiction rather than fact. What a hodgepodge! All the high points of French history are there: the ancient Gauls, Julius Caesar, Count Rollo, William the Conqueror, Joan of Arc, and all the Bourbon Loui. Those printed booklets which Louis the Fourteenth had burned are mentioned, along with the Man in the Iron Mask. Supposedly, the single booklet that escaped the fire was the source of much of the author's information. He also claims that Louis the Fourteenth and Louis the Fifteenth borrowed heavily from the treasure, squandering many gold louis to finance their various wars and building projects. Louis the Sixteenth supposedly sent information about its secret hiding place to Marie Antoinette before he went to the guillotine, but she was imprisoned and was executed only a few months after her husband."

The waiter set a small plate before each of us. "Thank you," Holmes said, and smiled at me. "A well-made croissant is truly a work of art, is it not?"

"Yes, indeed." I took a bite of my own pastry. "It is hard for me to choose between the *pain au chocolat* and the *pain aux raisin*. The ideal solution is one of each."

Holmes chewed thoughtfully, then dabbed at his mouth with his napkin. "The pamphlet did make me think we are unlikely to find the treasure at the Château de l'Aiguille. For one thing, the document suggests the château was built by Louis the Fourteenth as a kind of decoy, a false Needle. The true Needle may be something else altogether, something that has existed all through the long history of France."

"A needle? What could that possibly be?"

"I have... some ideas. We must have a good look around the château. Even if we cannot find the treasure, we may discover some sort of key which will guide us to the true hiding place. We have a busy day ahead of us! There is Mademoiselle Chamerac at eleven, but first we shall stop at the Sûreté headquarters to see if Inspector Ganimard has time to meet with us."

Once we had finished, we left the hotel. The gray wintery dampness of the prior day was gone, and one felt that spring and April were drawing near. Our umbrellas were left behind, but Holmes's gloved hand held the silver knob of his long ebony stick. A cool fresh breeze and the warm rays of the sun, which had just broken through the clouds, caressed our faces.

Ahead of us at the end of the narrow street was the busy Rue de Rivoli, where a carriage and a heavily laden cart drawn by massive horses rumbled by, and further still, were the tall plane trees lining the Jardin des Tuileries. We started in that direction. Since the day was so fine, we thought we would take the half-hour or so stroll to the Île de la Cité, the small central island home to both Notre-Dame and the headquarters of the Paris police.

Ahead of us, a well-dressed couple came around the corner, a black-bearded man in a navy suit and bowler hat, the lady at his arm in a mauve silk dress with a flamboyant hat of the same color. Something about the set of her lips reminded me of Michelle.

I smiled faintly, even as something orange and green flashed briefly before me, and then came a deafening crash, which sprayed us with debris. My eyes jerked shut for an instant. Simultaneously someone cried *"Attention!"* in French, and the woman in purple screamed even as Holmes seized my arm with a fierce grip and pulled us both back and against the brick wall of the hotel building.

I gazed down dumbly at shattered, brownish-orange fragments of terracotta, black dirt, and crumpled green leaves and vegetation scattered on the sidewalk–sad remnants of a potted plant! "My God," I murmured as I realized what a narrow miss it had been.

Holmes's stern gray eyes below the brim of his top hat, were before me. "Are you all right, Henry?"

"Yes, I think so." I was aware that my hands felt very cold, and a shiver went up my spine.

"Stay where you are." Holmes looked about, then darted across the street. He spoke with a portly man who had shouted the warning, and both of them gazed up at the building behind me, our hotel, the man pointing.

Just then, something white caught my vision, something floating and fluttering slowly downward—a sheet of paper. It landed on the sidewalk before me, and I stared warily down at the white rectangle, then bent over to pick it up.

The other man, the one with the black beard and bowler hat, had come forward, making a wide detour into the street well away from the shattered pot, while the woman remained safely distant. He grasped my arm: "*Vous êtes blessé, monsieur?*"

"*No, no. Tout va bien.*"

He shook his head. "*Quel accident affreux! Je suis soulagé.*" He let go, nodded, then went back to his companion, again going well round the broken fragments. He spoke briefly with the woman, then they turned and went back in the opposite direction.

"That cannot have been an accident," I murmured. "You cannot accidentally drop a huge potted fern from the window!"

"No, you cannot." Holmes had come back across the street and joined me. I held up the sheet of paper where we could both see the writing: *This is your only warning, Sherlock Holmes. Go back to London and leave the treasures of France to the French.*

Holmes took the paper from me and stuffed it into his jacket pocket. "Come along, Henry." He started back toward the hotel entrance at a rapid pace.

I was hard pressed to keep up with him. "Where are you going?"

"The fourth floor, one of the rooms near the end." We went through the lobby, and Holmes took the stairs at a gallop, then strode down the hallway. He stopped before the last door to our right, seized the crystal and brass doorknob, hesitated, then turned it. The door swung open, and he went inside.

The big bed was neatly made, the heavy red and gold spread without a wrinkle, but the sash window was pushed up, a cool breeze stirring gauzy white drapes. Holmes went to the sill and looked down at the street below. "Yes, obvious enough." He pointed at the gap of wooden floor between the carpet and the wall. "You can see, too, where some of the dirt spilled out."

He went past me back into the hall, and I followed. He stopped, and his raised right hand formed a fist. "Damnation," he muttered. "This is pointless, but all the same…"

"Did the man you spoke to on the street see anything?" I asked.

"He noticed the window was open, and he saw a person appear with a potted plant, which he set on upon the sill."

"Did he notice his face?"

"No, the person was wearing a black hood which, of course, was suspicious. And he could hardly believe that someone would deliberately drop something onto people below. He pointed out, rightly so, that we might have been killed, but of course, the note indicates it was meant to scare us, not to actually harm us."

I felt faintly dizzy, my vision somehow hyper-clear. "It was not so bad while it was happening, but when I think what might have been…"

"What makes me angriest is that you could have been hurt, Henry! I know the risks I run and expect danger, but for someone to have put your life at risk… That I cannot forgive. But come, I am sure it will be a waste of time, but we might ask some of the guests at this end of the hotel if they heard or saw anything unusual."

Only two people were in their rooms, and they could tell us nothing. I did notice on peering past one gentleman, that a large potted fern on a stand was a common feature of the decor, and I realized that there was one in our sitting room. They had always seemed harmless and innocuous, but now I fully realized their lethal potential from an upper floor.

When we had finished, Holmes looked carefully at me. "You are still rather pale, Henry."

"I am not used to so much excitement this early in the morning."

"Come along, back to our room. Unlike some of the French who consume white wine first thing in the morning, I do not normally drink so early, but this is a special case."

When we reached the sitting room of our suite, he went to the decanter of brandy on the mahogany sideboard and poured a small amount of Cognac into two glasses, gave me one, then raised his own. "To your good health—and may the rest of our stay in France be less exciting!"

We clinked glasses, then each drank some brandy. My nerves were still awry, but it did help calm me. After we had finished, we went down to the front desk, and Holmes explained what had happened to the hotel manager. He was horrified and very apologetic, and he insisted that it must have been a rogue guest and not any of his employees. All the same, Holmes told him to tell the staff that he would give a two-hundred-franc reward to anyone who could provide information.

Nearly an hour later, we started back down the narrow street before the hotel, but this time we walked on the other side, well away from the building!

Chapter 3

When Holmes and I walked into the small café around ten forty-five, only two of the round wooden tables had occupants as it was the slack time between breakfast and lunch. A bald man with a black mustache stood behind the long gray counter of the zinc bar. He wore what was a quintessential Parisian uniform: long-sleeved white shirt, black vest and trousers, and a white apron tied around his waist.

Holmes ordered two coffees, then we went to a corner table. Soon the man came our way with a small tray and placed two coffees in fat white china cups on matching saucers before us. Next came two glasses of water. I took a sip of coffee, then scowled.

Holmes's dark eyebrows rose. "Is something the matter?"

"I'm not sure how well Cognac and coffee mix. I have something of a sour stomach."

"Perhaps with a touch of milk?"

I added some from a white pitcher and took another sip. "That is better." I sighed. "What a morning! I wonder who arranged for that vivid warning with the plant."

"I too am wondering about that, Henry. Arsène Lupin would be one candidate, but he seemed to be looking forward to a contest of wits between us."

"At least..." My voice faded away.

"At least what?" Holmes asked.

"Well, it is bad luck to say it..." I rapped twice on the wooden surface with my knuckles. "At least no one has been murdered yet. Somehow the bodies always seem to stack up when we are working on a case together."

Holmes gave a brusque dry laugh. "Well, there is that to be thankful for!"

I was looking out of the huge plate-glass windows fronting the sidewalk, when Angelique Chamerac went by. The door swung open, she stepped inside, glanced about, then gave us a radiant smile and headed our way. The men at the other two tables were watching her. She wore a vibrant purple silk dress with a jacket of black velvet and a hat matching the dress. She removed the hat revealing bound-up blond hair, gave her head a shake, and pulled off her white leather gloves, one by one. Her hands were small, white, and perfectly shaped.

"*Bonjour*, mademoiselle." Holmes and I had risen, and we spoke in unison.

"Thank you so much for meeting with me, Monsieur Holmes." A bald man had appeared near our table and was giving her a certain male gaze. "*Bonjour*, monsieur. *Un café, s'il vous plaît.*"

He nodded. "*Certainement.*"

We all sat down. Angelique smiled rather awkwardly. "The weather is so much better today, is it not? Perhaps spring will arrive after all."

Holmes nodded, his gray eyes inquisitive. "Why did you want to see me, Mademoiselle Chamerac?"

Her shoulders rose ever so slightly. "Well, it is this business with Isidore, monsieur. You have not met him, but…"

Holmes hesitated only an instant. "Ah, but I have met him."

"What? How is that possible?"

"He stopped by yesterday evening at the hotel. He wants to work with me."

"Oh, that would be wonderful–a thing he has dreamed of!–but my uncle would never allow it."

"That was what I told Monsieur Beautrelet."

"Well, so much the better, then, that you have met him. It is true he is hardly more than a boy…" Again, I reflected that this seemed to be the kettle calling the pot black. "All the same, he has a certain charm, and we have become… friends, and I feel very bad that I have ruined things between him and my uncle. He is quite clever–I know that much–and I think he might have been able to find the treasure, but now my uncle wants nothing to do with him." She shook her head. "It is all my fault."

Holmes watched her carefully. "So your uncle does not consider him a worthy suitor?"

"No. Definitely not." She was staring down at the table, where her right hand rested, palm down.

"And why is that?"

She raised her pale blue eyes. "Isn't obvious? He thinks he is unworthy because he is not of noble blood." Her lips formed a brief, bitter smile. "I *will* say it. My uncle is a frightful snob. He wants me to marry a count or a marquis."

"But this lack of noble blood doesn't matter to you?" I asked.

She shook her head. "Not in the least. After all, my father was hardly wealthy—the Legion pays only a pittance. I certainly was not showered with luxuries when I was growing up—to the contrary, we were quite poor at times, and after my father died it was very hard. And then my mother…" Her gaze was somehow stern rather than sorrowful, and I suspected she was a much stronger young woman than she first appeared.

"Why are you telling me this, mademoiselle?" Holmes asked.

"Because I do not wish to go back to that life—never, not again! You are a detective. Can a man make a decent living as a detective?"

Holmes smiled, then laughed. "A very practical sort of question."

"You are mocking me!"

"Not really. A decent living? Yes, I suppose so, after one is established. It is an occupation of feast and famine, especially at the beginning, and some clients certainly pay better than others."

"Isidore does admire you, Monsieur Holmes. He takes you as his model, and he hopes to become the greatest detective on the continent."

I hesitated. "Does money mean so much to you, mademoiselle?"

Her eyes went icy. "Have you ever lived in real squalor, Dr. Vernier? Do you know what it is like to lie in bed at night, crammed in a room with others, and to hear the sounds of roaches and rats scuttling about? I assure you, they each make their own distinctive sound."

I shook my head. "I have not. I'm sorry. I certainly didn't mean to imply… I have visited enough patients in the slums of London to know that it is wretched to live in poverty. No one chooses it deliberately. And no one deserves it."

"Then you do understand." She took a quick sip of her coffee, then drew in her breath slowly and eased it out in a sigh. "I wish… I wish life were not always so complicated. The day will come, I fear, when I must choose between my uncle's wishes and my regard for another–but how I dread it! If only I could please them both."

I could not restrain myself. "The choice seems obvious enough. You would not want to stay forever with your uncle."

The corners of her full lips rose, something ironical briefly showing. "No, I suppose not."

Holmes smiled. "You must not mind Henry. He is a hopeless romantic."

I shrugged. "I suppose that's true."

Angelique briefly touched Holmes on the wrist, making his brow furrow. "If only you could let Isidore work with you. As I said, it would be the dream of a lifetime come true for him. Even though it meant his dismissal, he was delighted to hear that my uncle wanted to hire you in his stead."

"As I said, mademoiselle, I am certain your uncle would forbid it."

"That, too, is true enough," she said sadly. "All the same, if he did assist you... Perhaps, then, you could help me decide."

Holmes's sardonic smile reappeared. "I doubt I would be in a position to act as your advisor–nor would I ever presume to do so. I am a consulting detective, not a matrimonial guide for young ladies."

She smiled back. "Now you are indeed mocking me! But I suppose I deserve it." She set her hand lightly on my wrist. "And you, Dr. Vernier, would you give me your counsel?"

I shrugged. "I'm afraid I lack my cousin's discretion. I am only too willing to give advice."

"Excellent! Then I shall know whom to ask."

"However, I certainly do not have enough to go on, at this point. One brief meeting is not enough to allow for a character evaluation in so grave a matter." I saw that she understood that I was being ironical.

"That was why I hoped Isidore might work with Mr. Holmes. It would give you both the chance to know him better. All the same, I can certainly understand your reluctance to let him assist you." Her face grew rather grave. "I know my uncle well enough. I have seen his rages firsthand, although luckily I have never been the recipient. But my poor Isidore…!" She shook her head sadly and swallowed the last of her coffee. "But I have taken enough of your time, gentlemen."

We all stood. "Thank you for meeting with me, messieurs."

Holmes made a slight bow. "It was my pleasure, mademoiselle."

"And mine also," I said.

Her smile to me was playful. She hesitated, then said, "Should I decide to elope with Isidore and live in an unheated Parisian garret, I shall know whom to turn to for approbation."

"And I shall gladly give it."

She had pulled on her gloves, and she picked up her hat. "Good day."

She walked toward the door, nodding toward the server behind the counter. The vibrant purple silk of her skirts stood out in the dimly lighted room. Again, all the men present seemed to be watching her.

Holmes and I sat back down, and I shook my head. "There is something disconcerting about that sort of beauty in a woman."

Holmes stroked his jaw lightly. "Yes, there is. However, in my case, it always puts me on my guard."

"Why is that?"

"In the Platonic realm of philosophy and the abstract, great beauty and great virtue may be united, but in our hard practical world, they often go their separate ways."

"Not in her case, I hope."

He shrugged. "Perhaps not, but I have not known the young lady long enough to judge. I still do not understand exactly why she wanted to see me."

"That seems obvious enough. She is interested in young Beautrelet and wants to know whether we think she should obey her uncle's strictures or pursue her romantic inclinations."

Holmes was smiling at me. "Henry, Henry."

"What?"

"On one level, that is certainly true, but her motivation—her true state of mind—that is the mystery."

Given our narrow escape that morning (and the generous check the baron had given him), Holmes decided we deserved a true Parisian lunch at a first-class restaurant. He had *coq au vin* and I *gigot d'agneau*, accompanied by an excellent Bordeaux, and for dessert, we finished the meal with delicious *baba au rhum* swimming in sweet syrup.

After that, we strolled about the center of Paris, making a brief stop at Notre-Dame to take in the splendor of the old cathedral, but by three we arrived at the Parisian police headquarters by the Seine, the French equivalent of Scotland Yard. We stopped at the front counter where we had inquired earlier that morning about Inspector Ganimard's availability, then took the stairs to the second floor and went down the corridor with its gray and white marble-covered floor. Holmes rapped at a door with the large number 23 in bronze and a smaller plate with M. JUSTIN GANIMARD, INSPECTEUR.

"*Entrez.*"

We stepped inside. A small man sat behind a big desk cluttered with papers and a huge ashtray filled with butts. He sprang up and raised both his hands in a greeting. His thick old-fashioned mutton-chop sideburns and bushy graying mustache contrasted with the few strands of dark hair crossing his balding pate. His smile made creases at the outside of his dark eyes, and he strode around the desk. He wore an old-fashioned frock coat rather than a regular suit, the fabric a very odd olive-greenish hue.

"Ah, Monsieur Sherlock Holmes, at last! What a great honor, what a great honor." He took Holmes's hand, then clasped it round with his other hand, and shook both enthusiastically. "I recognize you from your pictures." I suspected he was referring to Sidney Paget's drawings, which I knew Holmes disliked.

He turned to me. "And this must be, Dr. Watson."

I was certainly accustomed to this, and it had been quite amazing that Beautrelet knew who I was. "No, the name is Vernier. Dr. Henry Vernier." We shook hands.

"Henry is my cousin, *inspecteur.*"

"A pleasure, *Docteur.*" Ganimard bustled about, pulling two stout oaken chairs with substantial armrests over to his desk. "*Asseyez-vous, messieurs. Asseyez-vous, s'il vous plaît.*"

We both sat down, and Ganimard stepped back around his desk. He also sat, then opened a silver cigarette case and took out a cigarette. "What brings you to Paris, Monsieur Holmes? Some spectacular case, no doubt." He lit his cigarette, drew in and released a quick puff. "Ah, forgive me!" He struck his head with his free hand, then took the case and pushed it toward us, offering its contents. "Would you care for a smoke, messieurs?"

Holmes had removed his top hat, and I saw his eyes narrow ever so slightly. "Thank you, but I have my own." His face did not really give him away, but I knew that Ganimard's cigarettes must be of inferior quality, nothing so fine as the baron's. Holmes withdrew his own cigarette case.

Ganimard shoved first a box of matches, then a second big

crystal ashtray toward us. "Now then, Monsieur Holmes, I was asking what brings you to Paris."

"I am investigating a certain matter for the Baron de Chamerac."

Ganimard's brow furrowed. "The Baron de Chamerac. Now where have I heard that name? He lives in Paris, does he not? And close by."

"Yes. On Île Saint-Louis."

"Oh yes, of course." He was still frowning, but then he smiled. "Ah, is this perhaps the same case that young Beautrelet told me about? Something to do with a mysterious treasure?"

Holmes hesitated, then smiled wryly. "Yes, it is."

"Ah, then you will be working with Beautrelet?"

"No, I'm afraid not."

"What? Can the baron have dismissed him?"

Holmes hesitated again. "I suppose it is not exactly a secret, especially as he has employed me in his stead."

Ganimard shook his head, then flicked some ash into his ashtray. "A pity. Beautrelet is a very enterprising young man, and I must admit, very shrewd, very intelligent. I took him at first for one of these annoying busybodies, these would-be detectives, who think they know more than the police. They have read some detective stories, and so–" He gave a sharp explosive laugh. "Often, they have read of *your* adventures, Monsieur Holmes!"

Holmes grimaced ever so slightly.

"For them, our years in the force and experience with multiple actual cases count for nothing. Amateurs, rank amateurs all of them! Except for Beautrelet. He is the genuine article. He has the makings of a real detective. Of course, he cannot match me with all my years of experience, but he is naturally gifted. Have you met him, monsieur?"

"Yes. We have had that pleasure."

"He is unprepossessing, to say the least. At first glance, he seems only a gawky yokel." He used the words *maladroit plouc*, which can be translated as "clumsy yokel" or "bumpkin." "Did he tell you about the case with the Count de Perron and his stolen Rubens?"

"Yes."

Ganimard drew in his cigarette. "He may wear spectacles, but with them he has the eyes of an eagle! That is one way in which youth has the advantage. He spotted the flaw in the portrait—my men and I had missed the spyhole entirely, but once we found it, we were certain of a secret passage behind the wall, and in fairness, it was also Beautrelet who discovered the hidden lever. He is very thorough that one, meticulous in the extreme. Yes, he has the makings of a first-class detective, but I fear he will not consider the police." Ganimard shook his head sadly. "Those stories of Watson are very bad for our profession! These young men all dream of being consulting detectives, not inspectors or commissaires!"

Holmes fiercely squashed his cigarette into the ashtray. "I cannot be responsible for Watson's feeble literary efforts."

Ganimard regarded him thoughtfully. "No, I suppose not."

Holmes drew in his breath slowly. "Clearly Monsieur Beautrelet has impressed you. I gather he has your highest recommendation?"

Ganimard nodded. "He does indeed. The very highest."

"I shall keep that in mind. I also wanted to inquire about Arsène Lupin."

"Ah!" Now it was Ganimard's turn to savagely extinguish the remnant of his cigarette. "That clever devil! One of these days I shall land him in my net, I promise you—you will see."

"What can you tell me about him?"

"Well, first and foremost, he is... he is like some annoying insect—like a mosquito buzzing about your ears when you are trying to fall asleep!" Holmes and I smiled at the comparison.

"He is always writing letters—letters to me, to his victims, to the newspapers. If he does retire from thievery, I am certain he could have a career as an author."

"And when did this all begin?"

Ganimard drew in on a fresh cigarette, shook the match to put out the flame, then inhaled. "The first letter I received was about three years ago. I have collected them all. In fact…" He turned to a stack of brownish folders on his desk, ran his forefinger down along the edges, and pulled one out. It was the sort that fastened shut by way of a piece of string wrapped round a small paper circle, and he opened it and took out a sheaf of papers. A pair of spectacles was hidden behind another stack, and he put them on, letting them rest low on his long thin nose, then scanned a sheet. "He was nice enough to date them. This brief one was first he sent me, almost exactly three years ago."

Ganimard read aloud: "'Cher Monsieur l'Inspecteur Justin Ganimard, let me present myself. I am Arsène Lupin, a *gentleman-cambrioleur*, and I am, so to speak, about to set up shop here in Paris. I hope you are not currently terribly busy, because I intend to provide you and your fellow policemen with several new crimes for your consideration. These will involve the thefts of valuable jewels, paintings, and even the occasional exquisite piece of period furniture or sculpture, whatever captures my fancy! However, I can assure you of one thing: I do not kill, so you need not worry about any homicides on my part. However, I shall try to commit the most daring and ostentatious crimes, so as to keep us both well employed and well entertained. Please excuse any inconvenience this may cause you, and accept my sentiments of respectful admiration. Your humble servant, Arsène Lupin.'"

Holmes looked amused. "I cannot recall a thief equally flamboyant and literate."

"Nor can I, Monsieur Holmes. Nor can I. Lupin is definitely *sui generis*. I have also clippings here of his letters to the newspapers."

"That, too, is unique. As is his referring to himself as a gentleman. Gentleman and burglar are generally considered mutually exclusive. It is interesting, too, that he says he does not kill." He gave me a brief sideways glance, then looked again at Ganimard. "I don't suppose, then, that he has ever dropped a heavy potted fern upon someone's head?"

Ganimard gave him a curious look. "No. Definitely not. Why do you ask?"

"Henry and I had a narrow miss this morning with such a pot. And have you ever actually met Lupin?"

Ganimard removed his spectacles, then sat back in his chair and drummed at a bare patch of desk with his small fingers. "I am not certain. If so, I think he was disguised. There have been witnesses to some of his crimes, but the description of the actual thief is never the same. Either he has a gang working for him, or he successfully changes his appearance."

"Beautrelet said he had seen him."

"Ah, yes! He is the only one to have had a good look at the man. He gave us the description we distributed to the police force: dark hair and mustache, brown eyes, a scar on the right cheek, medium height, perhaps a monocle, very well dressed and groomed."

Holmes sat back in his chair and placed the fingertips of his hands together. "At this point, I must admit that I am finding it difficult to take Lupin seriously. His behavior is so theatrical, so audacious, so buffoonish."

Ganimard leaned forward. "Take him seriously, monsieur—I beg you, take him seriously. I felt the same way when I received this absurd letter, but grand theft is no laughing matter, and that crime he has committed, again and again. He acknowledges some of his offenses, but there have been other mysterious cases where we have no clues, almost perfect crimes, in which I sense Lupin's touch. He may act the clown, but he is no joke, I promise you!"

Holmes nodded. "That is well worth knowing. I shall indeed take him seriously. It is troublesome that he has thrust himself into this affair with the baron." His eyes shifted to Ganimard's folder. "I do not suppose you could briefly part with those letters of his? I should like to have a look through them."

Ganimard's cigarette drooped from the side of his mouth as he shook his head. I noticed that the fingertips of his right hand had a brownish-yellow tint, no doubt tobacco stains. "I'm afraid not. They are official police documents. However, if you want to take a few moments to examine them here in the building, there is a small study room nearby."

"Excellent! I shall gladly do so. Given the thickness of that folder... It may take me an hour or two." He turned to me. "You need not stay, Henry, unless you are really curious."

I shook my head. "Thus far Monsieur Lupin's boastful style does not much appeal to me."

"Then why don't you walk about the neighborhood, and meet me..." He withdrew his watch from his waistcoat pocket. "You could meet me at six in front of Notre-Dame."

"Very good. I can stroll about and see if the booksellers on the Left Bank have any interesting offerings."

We stood, and Ganimard came round his desk and shook hands with us. Holmes and I were both over half a foot taller than him, but he had a formidable grip. A few freckles spotted the skin up over his forehead, between thin strands of black hair.

"Again, Monsieur Holmes, this has been a great honor."

"It has been my pleasure, Monsieur Ganimard. I may call upon you again to discuss Lupin."

"Any time you wish. And now, let me show you to that study room." He picked up the folder with the letters and handed it to Holmes.

I went down the corridor, passing two French policemen in their distinctive blue uniforms with the short capes and the distinctive kepi hats with the narrow brim in front and cleanly truncated cylinder over the head. By the front desk a stout man was arguing with two more policemen, but I went round them and stepped outside.

The sun had come out through the clouds and warmed my face. It felt wonderful, and I cautiously crossed the street and went to the concrete embankment overlooking the Seine. One of the big pleasure boats, a *bateau-mouche*, was just passing by, the stack belching smoke as it churned through gray-blue waters. The open upper deck was packed with people, both tourists and ordinary Parisians who used it as a cheap form of transportation. Unlike London, Paris still had no underground trains. A woman and a small boy waved at me, and I waved back. The boat soon passed under one of the arches of the nearby Pont Saint-Michel.

I drew in my breath deeply and smiled. Especially after what had happened that morning, I felt content just to be alive–and with my skull intact. The only thing missing was Michelle at my side. Unlike some men who were only too happy to go off alone on expeditions for weeks at a time, I did not like being apart from Michelle. I started missing her almost immediately–especially at night, when her nearby presence in our bed was always a comfort.

I strolled along the promenade overlooking the Seine, heading for the far end of the Île de la Cité. I passed two more bridges on my right, and soon the spire and towers of Notre-Dame were to my left. Finally, I took the last bridge, the Pont de l'Archevêché, over to the Left Bank, then turned almost immediately to the left, again following the Seine in a southeast direction.

There along the sidewalk off the Quai de la Tournelle were the stands of the *bouquinistes* or booksellers. Stacks of old volumes were piled up on tables and stands, along with magazines, newspapers, and drawings. There was something for every taste. Many of the vendors were bearded old men in rough woolens and cloth caps, who sat on their stool or chair, pipes in hand. Many of the stacked books gave off a faint musty smell which mingled with the fresh spring air.

At last I withdrew my watch, saw the time, and realized I would need to rush to make it back to Notre-Dame by six. I set off at a good clip, retracing my earlier path to return to the island. In the square before the cathedral, I saw a tall slender figure in a black frock coat and top hat, one hand held behind his back, the other tracing some pattern in the concrete with the brass tip of his stick. As I approached him, he looked up, smiled, and started forward.

I had done enough walking that when Holmes suggested we take a cab back to the hotel, I was tempted, but in the end, it seemed a shame to waste such a splendid evening inside a cab. We strolled slowly back, following the Rue de Rivoli once we had crossed the Seine to the north. As we turned at last onto the street of our hotel, we saw two men talking to each other by the entrance. One wore elaborate formal dress, the other a dark suit. As we drew nearer, the formal one noticed us, set his hand on the other man's shoulder, and they turned toward us.

Both appeared about thirty and were of medium height, but one looked ready to depart for the opera or some grand ball. His clothes were very well cut and expensive-looking. The silk of his top hat gleamed faintly from the streetlight, and his bow tie, shirt, and waistcoat were an immaculate white. He also wore white gloves, and he rested his ebony stick on his shoulder, his right hand grasping the shaft just above the silver handle. His coat with its satin lapels was a contrasting black, but a long black formal cape hid most of it. The cape had a certain sheen and fell below his knees. He had a thin black mustache and wore a monocle over his right eye. He smiled at us we drew nearer. On his cheek was a reddish line—a scar—and I knew who this must be.

"Sherlock Holmes and Dr. Vernier—what a pleasure to meet you," he said.

His companion nodded eagerly. "Indeed, indeed."

Holmes smiled ever so faintly. "The pleasure is mine, Monsieur Lupin."

Lupin had a certain rakish grin, the corners of his mouth rising into the mustache. "Very good, Monsieur Holmes—although I suppose it's obvious enough. Young Beautrelet and Inspector Ganimard must have given you my description." His voice was a resonant baritone, so much so that I wondered if he had ever trained as an actor.

Holmes was staring very closely at him, and turned his head as if to examine him better.

"This is my friend Maurice, Maurice Leblanc."

Leblanc wore a black bowler hat, and his face was dominated by an enormous reddish-brown sprouting sort of mustache, which completely hid his mouth and curled up to stick out on either side of his face. He eagerly shook hands with Holmes and me. "I have heard so much about you both. What a great privilege to meet you!"

Lupin had brought down his stick, and both his gloved hands were set on the silver handle, the shaft set before him, the tip resting between his two glossy black evening shoes. "Could you spare a few minutes of your time, Monsieur Holmes?"

"Gladly."

"Perhaps you could join us for an aperitif? There is a cozy bar nearby, Le Dragon Vert, less than five minutes away."

"Lead the way."

I glanced closely at Holmes. "Is that a good idea?" I murmured. Lupin may have written *I do not kill*, but I still wondered if he had dropped that plant before us as a warning.

"I am sure we can count on Monsieur Lupin's genteel hospitality."

"Certainly, messieurs. Certainly!"

The streets off the Rue de Rivoli were all of a piece: very narrow, lined with shops and an occasional restaurant or bar. Lupin was whistling softly. We went down a block, then over two more, and before us a small bar took up the corner, big plate-glass windows forming an L and opening out on either side. The weather was still fairly decent, and a few hardy souls sat at the outdoor tables.

Lupin went inside and walked up to the long zinc countertop. The bartender had thinning hair, but a mustache which rivaled Leblanc's. "Ah, Monsieur Punil! Bonsoir! How good to see you."

"Bonsoir, Andre. Maurice and I will have the usual." He turned to Holmes. "They have an excellent absinthe here, messieurs, the best in Paris."

The bartender smiled. "You are too kind."

Holmes nodded. "I shall be happy to sample it."

Although the metaphorical juxtaposition may seem ridiculous, absinthe is not my cup of tea! I do not like licorice flavor, whether it is candies, liquors, or anything else. And of course, besides the taste, there is its extreme potency to worry about. The alcohol content of undiluted absinthe varies between fifty and seventy-five percent. "I would prefer a Cognac."

"As you wish. Seat yourselves, messieurs."

The vast main room of the bar was so large it would have been difficult to fill, and there were still many empty tables. Lupin headed straight for one in the corner. We sat down and Holmes and I pulled off our gloves and removed our hats; Lupin left his on. He did unfasten his cape and remove it, letting it flop back over the chair. He had let his monocle drop while we were walking, but now he grasped the lens and placed it again over his right eye. A thin black ribbon provided a cord, which was looped around his neck. He gazed about the room, smiling broadly.

"Yes, this is perhaps my favorite bar in all of Paris. I have often imagined what it would be like to have Sherlock Holmes as my guest here! I had not planned on meeting you so soon, but after this morning's sinister events, I decided it could not wait."

Holmes stared at him. "The potted fern, you mean?"

"Exactly. What a crash that made! I wanted to personally assure you that I had absolutely nothing to do with the deed. You may think it an exaggeration, an affectation, for me to call myself a *gentleman-cambrioleur*, but I take the 'gentleman' part very seriously, and you have my word of honor that I was not involved. In fact, I wanted to ask if you know of anyone else besides myself and young Beautrelet who is aware you have come to France to work for the baron and seek the treasure of the Needle?"

Holmes shook his head. "No one."

"Blast it—that means there is another, unknown, player in the game. Ah well, as I said in my note, a little competition can be most stimulating."

The bartender came to our table with a huge tray. On it were four glasses and a tall metal stand with an ornate glass bowl up top and four small spouts, a so-called absinthe fountain. There was also a small cup with sugar cubes in it and three silver utensils. The smallest glass had a curved bowl and contained an amber-brown fluid. That was my Cognac, which the bartender set before me. The other three glasses were larger and more ornate, and each had an inch or two of greenish-yellow liquid in them. The man distributed these glasses, along with the utensils—so-called absinthe spoons. They had a long flat part with a leafy pattern of holes, their shape more like a pie server than a spoon.

Lupin picked up the fountain which was full of ice water and set it before Holmes. "After you, monsieur."

"Thank you." Holmes put the "spoon" on top of his glass, set a sugar cube on the spoon, then slowly opened the handle to the spout, letting cold water trickle out onto the sugar. The cube gradually dissolved, even as the glass filled with the water. The greenish liquid changed color, clouding up, becoming whitish and more opaque. When the glass was nearly full, Holmes turned off the spout, then put the spoon in the liquid and stirred, blending the sugar, water, and absinthe together.

Lupin took the fountain and handed it over to Leblanc. When Leblanc was done, Lupin finally prepared his own drink. When the elaborate absinthe ritual was finished, Lupin raised his glass and we all followed suit. "To your very good health, gentlemen—and to no further accidents with potted plants!" We all clinked glasses, then sipped our drinks.

Holmes turned to Leblanc. "We know something about Monsieur Lupin and his enterprises, but nothing of you, monsieur. Are you, so to speak, an accomplice, or only a friend?"

Leblanc smiled. "The latter! I haven't the stomach for crime. If a policeman even glances at me, I break into a cold sweat. No, it is not the life for me."

I nodded. "I understand your sentiments, Monsieur Leblanc. What is your profession, then?"

"I am a journalist and a writer. I hope to have a novel published within a year or two."

Lupin looked amused. "I think he also wishes to emulate Watson and become my chronicler."

Holmes scowled in a comic and exaggerated manner. "For heaven's sake, *forbid it!* You will be sorry if he does so."

"I shall keep that in mind, Monsieur Holmes. I wonder, would it be too much to ask you to share your impressions of the baron and young Beautrelet?"

Holmes regarded him silently.

"Of course, if you do not wish to…"

Holmes shrugged. "I do not exactly trust the baron."

Lupin took a quick sip of absinthe. "Ah! That is wise. And why not?"

"Let us just say there are… discrepancies, some of which I shall not discuss. However, he told me he does not plan to keep the treasure, but would give it to the Republic. That I find very difficult to believe."

I was surprised. "Why is that?"

"First of all, he is an aristocrat, and in general they have no use for the Republic, they want a king or emperor back, but more than that, is simple greed or avarice. He does not strike me as the kind of man who could have a huge treasure set before him, and then willingly turn it over to anyone else."

Lupin clapped his hands gently together. "Bravo, Monsieur Holmes–bravo. I concur with you completely. And Monsieur Beautrelet?"

Holmes's smile was ironic. "What can I say? He is certainly a zealous lad. He wants to work with me. I am still considering it."

I stared at him. "But you told him you that wouldn't be possible—and Mademoiselle Chamerac said the baron would never stand for it."

Holmes sighed wearily, shaking his head in dismay, while Lupin smiled. "So you have met the fair Angelique, messieurs? A vision of loveliness, is she not? Rare and hard-hearted indeed would be the red-blooded man who did not fall at her feet to worship such divine beauty! Who can blame young Beautrelet for being smitten?"

I bit my lower lip. "Forgive me," I said to Holmes. "I should have kept my mouth shut."

Lupin shook his head. "Don't trouble yourself, Dr. Vernier. You didn't tell me anything I didn't already know."

Holmes was smiling at Lupin. "Beautrelet said something about you which I suspect must be true."

"He did? And what was that?"

"That you had one weakness—a weakness for the ladies."

Lupin's rakish grin returned. "A clever and observant lad, young Beautrelet. I must admit that is my one foible. While I have a rather cynical and suspicious attitude toward men, with the fair sex I am far too trusting. I never seem to have quite outgrown the awkward infatuations of adolescence."

Holmes glanced at me, his lips flickering upward at the corners. "You remind me of someone else I know."

I shrugged faintly. "I am far too trustful of women, granted, but of men, also. I do not like to think the worst of people."

Holmes gave my wrist a squeeze. "And I respect you for it, Henry."

"Ah, but if one expects the worst of people, one is never disappointed!" Lupin smiled at Holmes. "Isn't that true, monsieur?"

"Indeed it is."

Lupin sat back in his chair, his gloved hand holding the stem of his glass lightly. "Do you think you will find a treasure at the Château de l'Aiguille?"

Holmes shrugged. "I doubt it. I hope to find the secret of its real location."

Lupin nodded. "Very good! We are of like minds, you and I. And *st. s. 138*—what do you think it signifies?"

"I have a few ideas, but nothing worth mentioning. I hope to find the answer somewhere in the castle."

"Again, we are of one mind, Monsieur Holmes. Well, it will be most interesting to see who finds the treasure first. As I said in my note, I think the odds are about fifty–fifty, and it is a great compliment, I assure you, for me to acknowledge as much."

Holmes smiled. "Now it is my turn to be honored."

Lupin swished the liquid in his glass. "I know you consider me only a thief, but some day, when I have sufficient funds… I don't plan on spending the rest of my life as a *gentleman-cambrioleur.*"

"No?" Holmes asked.

"No. Someday, I too, would like to be a detective. Someone must give you and Beautrelet some real competition." He pulled a gold watch out of his waistcoat pocket. "Ah, but I must be running along. They should be here momentarily, and I don't wish to demonstrate my physical prowess with my stick." He put back the watch and swallowed the last of his drink.

"Give my regards to young Beautrelet and the police." He stood up and glanced at Leblanc. "You needn't be in a rush, Maurice. Keep Monsieur Holmes and Dr. Vernier company." He bowed very formally from the waist. "*À bientôt,* messieurs! I hope to see you at Creuse. And be careful: I may not kill, but most thieves do not share my scruples, as you have already discovered." He strolled idly toward the door, nodding to the bartender on the way out.

Holmes sipped his drink. "Rather impressive, I must confess." He turned to Leblanc. "I suppose such sangfroid is typical."

"Oh yes. We may be the best of friends, but we are opposites in nearly every way. However, his predictions are never wrong, and I do not wish to remain here and answer questions from the police, so I too shall be on my way. *Au revoir.* Finish your drinks at your leisure."

He downed his absinthe, then pulled on his gloves as he stood. He also acknowledged the bartender on his way out. Holmes and I stared at one another. Our drinks were only half-finished.

"I think we should eat somewhere else tonight, Henry. The restaurant at the hotel is excellent, but I have a craving for a plate of *choucroute* in the Alsatian style. I know of a place near the baron's hotel on the Île Saint-Louis."

I shrugged. "As you wish. Sauerkraut, sausages, and potatoes is certainly more German than French, but it does sound agreeable." I frowned. "I wonder…?"

"Oh, without a doubt, Monsieur Lupin knows what he is talking about."

And sure enough, the front doors were abruptly flung open, and the police in their blue uniforms with short capes and their distinctive hats swarmed in. With them was Beautrelet, looking rather distraught. He came directly to our table. "Monsieur Holmes, are you all right?" He had grasped his bowler in both hands, and he peered down at us through the thick lenses of his spectacles.

Holmes took a quick sip of absinthe. "Never better."

"When I saw you go off with Lupin, I feared the worst! Did he threaten you?"

"No, he was quite the gentlemen."

A burly policeman who wore the insignia of a brigadier came up to us. "Where is he, messieurs? Where is Lupin?"

"I'm afraid you missed him, gentlemen. He left a few minutes ago. He can't have gone far if you wish to search the area."

The policeman gave a quick nod. "*Venez, venez!*" he exclaimed, gesturing toward the door, and they all rushed out as quickly as they had come in.

Holmes was smiling faintly, and he gestured at an empty chair. "Have a seat, Monsieur Beautrelet."

The young man ran his fingers back through his short hair, then set the bowler on the table. "So I shall." He sank down into the chair. "I am greatly relieved. I… I feared the worst."

Holmes was staring at him. "So you were near the hotel, and you saw us leave with Lupin?"

"Yes. I followed you here, and then I summoned the police."

"Most enterprising. You know, Monsieur Beautrelet, I think I have changed my mind. Your zeal has impressed me. Perhaps it would be useful to have you accompany us to the château. We shall take the early train for Creuse in the morning. Meet us at the hotel lobby promptly at 6:30 A.M., and we can leave for the Gare d'Austerlitz together."

Beautrelet sprang eagerly to his feet. "You will not regret it, Monsieur Holmes—I promise you will not regret it! I shall repay your kindness, I swear it." He smiled at us, then seized his hat. "I must go—I must pack—I must… I shall see you tomorrow morning, at six thirty *promptly*! *Au revoir!*" He went out at almost a gallop.

I gave Holmes a puzzled look, my forehead creased. "Are you certain about this, Sherlock?"

His smile faded. "Yes, I am."

"But the baron…"

"Leave the baron to me."

Chapter 4

The train ride from Austerlitz station to Guéret in the department of Creuse took a few hours, with a stop in Vierzon to change trains. Paris is well known for its cold and dreary weather—and the morning had certainly started that way with the pleasant sunshine from the prior day only history. However, as we went south, the dark skies cleared, and from the windows of the train we could see the full splendor of a French spring beginning. We passed orchards with the fruit trees in blossom, and many other trees had small light yellow-green leaves coming out. Each village had their stone buildings with tile or slate roofs, and inevitably, an old church with a spire.

All morning long, Beautrelet chatted at great length, his high-pitched voice modulating enthusiastically upward, as he asked Holmes and me questions about virtually everything, but especially our professions and our various prior cases, some of which he already knew a great deal about. He also wanted to talk about women, a subject upon which Holmes was most reticent, but when he saw I was receptive, he quizzed me at length about Michelle. He insisted he must meet her when she arrived in Paris. A beautiful redhead who was also a woman doctor was not to be missed! His enthusiasm made me smile.

After eating baguette sandwiches for lunch, we all grew quiet. Holmes was studying the plans of the castle, Beautrelet was immersed in a guidebook about Creuse, and I stared indolently out the window, enjoying the views which swept by. Growing up, I had spent many summers in the French countryside, and after the teeming streets, the noise and squalor of Paris and London, it was a relief to return to its calm beauty.

When we got off at Guéret before the station house of red brick, a small man in rough woolen garments and a cloth cap was waiting. He looked about fifty, his face brown and wizened, and he was missing teeth. He shook Holmes's hand eagerly and introduced himself as Pierre Legrand. Close by stood the French equivalent of a dogcart, an open carriage which could seat four passengers. Despite his age and slender build, Legrand quickly hoisted our luggage aboard, and then we were off on the final part of our journey. A narrow dirt road wound through pastoral valleys where sheep and cattle grazed, the air marvelously fresh and clean, the sun pleasantly warm.

Beautrelet was wearing his somewhat crumpled brown suit and a tweedy cloth cap of a matching fabric. He pointed toward a herd of reddish-brown cattle grazing, a monstrous bull standing protectively before his dames. The short horns above his head thrust out straight and horizontal to either side.

"Those are the Limousin breed named after another department of France, close by. According to my guidebook, this is one of the main agricultural regions of France, with more cows than people. The local pork is also supposed to be very tasty, and the pigs… Well, they have a vulgar name."

"What is that?" I asked.

"*Les porcs cul noir.*"

Holmes and I both smiled.

"I've heard that translated as 'black bottom pigs' in English," I said. "Rather more polite, if not so literal."

Legrand glanced over his shoulder, grinning. "That will be your supper this evening, messieurs. Madame Tambourin has put on a joint to roast. I promise you will never taste better!"

Holmes gave an appreciative nod. "I do not doubt it. Roast pork fresh from the countryside is always the best."

We went through sparsely wooded valleys with long sloping green meadows and occasionally passed solitary stone farmhouses which must have stood for decades, even centuries. A young woman wearing an apron was hanging her washing out to dry and waved at us. She and Legrand exchanged polite greetings.

At last the curving road emerged through thick woods of oak, beech, and evergreens, and there above us on a hill stood the Château de l'Aiguille. And indeed, its main feature was the tall central tower of gray stone which tapered to an exaggerated point, a reddish-brown spire worthy of a cathedral, a "needle" indeed! Around it were four lower turrets, each with conical roofs. The châteaux might have been built in the late seventeenth century, but clearly the architect had wanted to suggest something older, a medieval fortress, and indeed, a wall of matching gray stonework surrounded the castle.

We went upward through a park of trees and scraggly rhododendrons and came to a large rusty iron gate in the wall which stood open. Once inside the courtyard, Legrand stopped before some steps leading up to high oaken doors. He stepped out. "I shall fetch Monsieur Tambourin. He will want to welcome you." He sprang quickly up the steps and pulled open one of the doors. Holmes, Beautrelet, and I got out of the carriage.

Holmes was wearing gray herringbone tweed for the country, and a crumpled sort of hat with a large wavy brim. He went to the horse and touched it gently on the cheek, murmuring something, then turned to stare up at the château walls. We were close enough that we had to crane our necks back to see the spire set against blue sky and white clouds.

"Le Château de l'Aiguille—at last!" Beautrelet exclaimed.

Two bald old men with extravagantly bushy white beards came outside, followed by Legrand. They both wore black formal morning coats which had seen better days, along with white wingtip collars and black cravats. They were obviously related: if not twins, brothers at least.

The slightly taller one came forward and bowed. "Good day, gentleman. I am Jacques Tambourin, the head steward of le Château de l'Aiguille." He smiled with genuine warmth, his mouth mostly hidden by his exuberant white mustache. "I am very pleased to meet you, Mr. Holmes! I have read every one of your adventures, along with everything else I could find about crime and criminals, both fiction and nonfiction. You are clearly the grand master! Lecoq himself could never compare with you."

Holmes nodded, his gray eyes faintly wary, as was always the case when someone mentioned they had read all his adventures. "The pleasure is mine, Monsieur Tambourin." They shook hands. "And this is my companion, Dr. Henry Vernier, and Isidore Beautrelet, my... valet." His sardonic smile appeared briefly.

Tambourin's bushy eyebrows came together as he turned to me, and I knew he had been expecting Watson. His grip was quite firm.

He gestured toward his companion. "And this is my brother, Antoine, the horologist of the château."

I gave Antoine a puzzled look. "Horologist?" The French word he used was *horloger*, a word I knew well enough, but one which didn't make sense to me in the context of the château.

Holmes nodded. "Ah, of course. And how many clocks are there in the castle, monsieur?"

"There are eighty-nine rooms, but one hundred and three clocks, Monsieur Holmes, all of them from the late seventeenth century."

"Good Lord," I murmured. "*One hundred and three* clocks?"

Holmes glanced at me. "They would need oiling every two or three years, and disassembling, cleaning, and reassembling every seven years or so. And of course, they must be wound and the time adjusted regularly."

Antoine beamed, a dimple showing above his beard on the left side. "Ah, very good, Monsieur Holmes! What a pleasure to meet someone who understands. I know the baron dreams of gold and jewels, but these clocks are the real treasure of the château. The decree granting the château to the family Chamerac required that they were all to be maintained and passed down from generation to generation. My father was also the horologist, and he taught me everything, as did his father before him. It is the tradition in our family. Always a Tambourin has been horologist."

Jacques was also smiling. "And often a Tambourin has been majordomo as well." His smile faded. "But all that is changing now. My son lives in Paris and wants nothing to do with service."

Antoine also looked dejected. "And I have only daughters."

I recalled that there was a feminine form of the word—*horlogère*—for a female clockmaker. I knew Michelle would have pointed out that Antoine could pass on his trade to a daughter, but I kept silent. Both men looked to be in their seventies, and they would be the last generation of Tambourins to serve at the château.

Beautrelet's brown eyes behind the lenses of his spectacles had an odd gleam, and the corner of his mouth had risen in a sort of half-smile. "So many clocks. Most interesting, is it not, Mr. Holmes?"

Holmes smiled faintly. "Indeed it is, Monsieur Beautrelet. One can study from afar, but an actual visit always has its surprises."

Jacques gestured toward the doorway. "Come along, gentlemen, and I shall show you to your rooms."

Legrand took out two of the bags and followed us. It seemed ridiculous to me that the shortest man, by far, should be carrying our luggage, but I knew Jacques would never allow us to help. However, as valet, Beautrelet could do so, and he seized the two remaining bags.

We went through the entry way with its black-and-white tiled floor, and into a great hall. Despite the faintly medieval exterior appearance, the inside was decorated in the monumental style of Louis the Fourteenth, with ornately painted ceilings and massive chandeliers, the walls with many flourishes in gold and white. Tapestries ten feet tall in muted colors hung here and there. However, I noticed that some of the elegant furniture appeared slightly worn or tattered, and dust was obvious on the various surfaces of dark wood.

We went through a tall arching entryway into another wing, a long hallway lit by open doorways and occasional lamps. Each door had a number in bronze, starting with 1 and working upwards in sequence. A few of these stout wooden doors were open, and inside I glimpsed white cloths covering the beds and furnishings. At the far end of the hall were two rooms across from one another, numbers 24 and 25, with their doors wide open.

"These are two of our best rooms, the gold one for you, Monsieur Holmes, and the silver for the doctor," Jacques said. He stared at Beautrelet, biting briefly at his lower lip. "The telegram did not mention your valet. I shall have a room prepared for him close by."

Holmes nodded. "I suspect that although the clocks are kept in tip-top shape, the same cannot be said for much of the castle."

Above his beard, Jacques's cheeks flushed. "Ah, you noticed that! But it is not my fault. If you could only have come when the old baron was still alive. Everything was so well maintained, so splendid. He was willing to pay what it takes to keep up a castle. He was not a…" Jacques seemed to snap off and swallow the last word, and he gave his head a shake. "But what do I know? I am only a servant and an old man. The glory of the past is gone. I shall not see its like again."

"Was the word you wanted to say 'miser'?" Holmes asked.

Jacques stared at him, his brow furrowed. He would not speak it aloud, but gave a faint shrug of his shoulder, the answer obvious enough.

Holmes's eyes were thoughtful. "And has this miserliness by any chance grown worse over time?"

Jacques was surprised. "How could you know that?"

"Just a guess."

Beautrelet did not speak, but he was watching intently with an appreciative smile.

Jacques shook his head. "I have only a quarter of the staff I had when the old baron was alive. I've had to dismiss them, one by one—like a sort of slow death, drip by drip. But you don't want to hear my troubles. Come! You must be weary from your long train ride. You can rest up, if you wish. Dinner will not be served for another hour or two."

"We have been sitting all day," Holmes said. "I would rather have a brief look about the castle."

Jacques smiled. "And I should be happy to show it to you." He glanced at Legrand. "Leave the luggage in their rooms, and then tell Sandrine to prepare room 18 for Monsieur Beautrelet."

We started down the hall, Jacques in the lead, but Holmes stopped before the door marked with a "12." "Pardon, Monsieur Tambourin," Holmes said. The old man turned. "Might I have a quick look at this room? I am curious about something."

Beautrelet laughed softly, even as I frowned.

Jacques nodded, puzzled. "As you wish. There is nothing very remarkable about it—your room is far superior." He turned the knob and pushed open the door. "After you."

The room had clearly not been used in a long while. As was typical for the seventeenth century, the bed was pathetically short—my legs would have stuck out almost to my knees! A thick beige canvas covering hid the mattress and two chairs. Two tall arching windows with wavy panes of glass set in metal frames had wispy white drapery which obscured the golden light, and between them was a bureau with a beautiful table clock of bronze and ebony wood, ticking loudly.

Holmes went straight to the clock, and Beautrelet followed, his hands raised and fingers outspread, as if in anticipation. Holmes bent over slightly, peering at the clockface with its roman numerals, then glanced back at Jacques. "May I?"

The old majordomo looked puzzled. "As you wish—but be careful. The room is nothing special, but the clock is another matter."

A tiny key was set in a lock on the right side. Holmes turned it, then opened up the small glass door which protected the face. The ticking grew even louder. Holmes peered intently at the clock, then gently turned it. On the side was a glass window which revealed the teethed circular gearwork of its internal mechanism. He turned it again, and we could see the metal back, also covered by a glass door, and the pendulum within swinging back and forth. Holmes turned it a last time and stared for a long while at the face. At last, he shut the glass door and turned the key.

"Truly a beautiful piece of work. One would be hard pressed to find its equal nowadays."

"That is certainly true," Beautrelet said. He too had been closely gazing at the clock.

Holmes's eyes swept briefly round the room. "Thank you, Monsieur Tambourin. We can continue with our tour now."

We left the room, and Jacques did not close the door all the way. "This wing of the castle has most of the bedrooms, three floors of them, all much the same."

Holmes nodded. "Yes, I recall the layout from the castle plans."

"There is little to see here, little to distinguish the rooms. But you do have two of the best—and among the few which have had newer beds brought in. A good thing, indeed, given your height, Monsieur Holmes and Dr. Vernier! Let us have a look at the main hall."

"Pardon me," Holmes said, "but could you humor another fancy of mine? Could we just briefly have a look at the upper two floors?"

Jacques shrugged. "Of course. As you wish." He started down the hall, then glanced back. "I suppose you will also want to see the secret passageway off the main bedroom?"

"Eventually, I suppose." Holmes's sardonic smile briefly appeared. "Although if you have seen one secret passage you have seen them all."

I nodded. "I agree—and I do not care for the inevitable cobwebs in one's face."

Beautrelet smiled. "And there are the spiders lurking in the corners!"

We took the stairway up to another ornate hallway virtually identical to the first. Holmes peered closely at each door, and I had the impression that he was counting to himself. "None of these doors are locked, are they?" he asked.

"No, of course not. What would be the point?"

The third-floor hallway was much plainer than the other two, the walls of unfinished stone; these must be rooms for the servants. "How many of you live on this floor?" Holmes asked.

"All the remaining staff reside up here. Madame Tambourin and I are in number 72, the largest and finest room on the floor. Antoine and his wife are close by. Then there is Legrand, Sabine, Lucy—perhaps a dozen of us in all. The gardener Pierre has his own cottage." He sighed softly. "I remember when every room up here was occupied, many with two or three people."

Holmes pushed open the door to 75, took a quick look. It was much more modest, but the same sort of cover was over the beds and furniture. "And I suppose each room up here has its clock, too?"

"Yes, of course."

"Rather unusual for servants' quarters."

"I suppose so, but it is part of the patrimony of the château."

Beautrelet did not speak, but he seemed to be watching with the utmost concentration.

"Have you seen enough, Monsieur Holmes? Good, let us go then to the main hall. Creuse has been known for centuries for its tapestries, and we have some of the finest. Then, if you are up to it, we can also take the stairs up to the top of the central tower. It is a climb, but the view is well worth it."

Holmes nodded. "I look forward to it."

We strolled about the vast hall, gazing up at the tapestries hanging upon the stone walls, while Jacques related their history and the fine points of their depictions. The *pièce de résistance* showed the château itself on its hilltop, in the distance, with stylized trees and other vegetation in the foreground, as well as two large birds, either storks or swans. The colors appeared somewhat faded with age. Jacques also explained that the tapestries served a practical purpose, helping to mute the cold radiating from the thick stone walls.

Afterwards we visited the library, which had quite a collection of old volumes, along with more period furniture, and then came a brief visit to the kitchens, filled with the fragrant smell of roast pork. It set my mouth watering, and I realized how hungry I was. Jacques introduced us to his wife, Madame Tambourin, a small plump woman wearing a black dress and a white apron. Among her many duties, she was queen of the kitchen, and did much of the cooking. She had a rosy complexion, white hair, but with a few black hairs sprouting to one side of her mouth. She too was honored to meet Sherlock Holmes.

Finally we trudged up a winding stone staircase interrupted periodically by small windows which I avoided looking through, and came out at last onto a circular floor with a wooden door at each of the four corners. Holmes was breathing hard. Jacques opened a door, and we stepped out onto a rampart which went completely around the tower. There was a gap of about six feet between the tower itself and a stone parapet, and the others stepped eagerly forward to lean on it and admire the view below.

I, instead, pressed myself against the tower, my back and the palms of my hand pinned to the rough stones, even as a surge of nausea rose up my throat, almost making me gag. I had always suffered from vertigo, and while it was better than in the past, my reaction to this sudden height was a visceral reminder of my sensitivity.

Holmes gave me a sympathetic look. He had left his hat behind, and the sun gleamed on the pale skin of his high forehead and his slicked-back black hair. "Poor Henry." He explained my affliction to the others, who murmured their sympathy. "Have just a quick look, Henry. You need not come up to the wall itself, but just have a glance." He gripped my arm tightly. "Perhaps if I have hold of you…"

"That does help."

I stepped nearer the wall, and before me I could see the rolling green fields and the darker patches of the woodlands, as well as a glowing incandescent gold surface which wound like some ribbon through the idyllic landscape. "That must be the Creuse," I murmured. The sky was a clear blue with a few scattered white clouds, the sun lower in the sky now.

Jacques nodded. "Indeed it is." He had set both elbows on the parapet, and he was obviously quite at ease up here.

How I envied him! I tried to slow my breathing, and I told myself it wasn't so terrible. The touch of the cool air up so high on my face was rather consoling, and I sighed softly.

"Feeling better?" Holmes asked.

I nodded. "Yes. It is quite beautiful. So different from the view from Sacré-Cœur or Eiffel's new tower."

Jacques blew out his breath. "You can keep your great cities—especially your Paris. This is the true treasure, the land of Creuse itself. Its abundance, its beauty, are spread out before us all. Gold and jewels, riches, cannot compare to this. They are the toys of man. This is a gift from God."

Beautrelet stared at him, his eyes inquisitive behind his spectacles. "You are a philosopher, Monsieur Tambourin."

"Philosopher enough to know what is valuable in life. Philosopher enough not to go chasing after wealth, which if it even exists, can only bring trouble, and never happiness." He hesitated. "The old baron knew better. He was a wise man. He was not obsessed with fantastical treasures. He loved his home and the countryside around it. How I miss him!"

Holmes's smile was muted. "You are a wise man, Monsieur Tambourin. Tell me, were the old baron and his nephew close?"

Surrounded as they were by all the white hairs of his beard and mustache, I could not see all the tiny muscles about his mouth contracting, but I could recognize from his lips a certain muted anger, and you could see it clearly in his dark eyes. He was silent so long, I thought he was not going to answer, but he spoke at last.

"They were never close, and after Monsieur Frédéric's father died, we did not see him for many years. But as my master's health began to fail, then Monsieur Frédéric reappeared. As the old baron grew sicker and sicker, Frédéric circled about like some eager carrion bird. Oh, he pretended great sympathy, but his falseness was obvious enough to me. My master wanted to believe the best of his nephew, but in the end I do not think he was fooled." He sighed and lowered his gaze. "I should not be telling you this. It is stupid of me. If you were to relate what I have said to the baron, he would dismiss me in an instant. He would dismiss me though I have served his family faithfully for over fifty years."

Holmes touched his wrist lightly. "You need not fear. None of us would ever betray your feelings. I can see this is not a pleasant subject for you. One last thing, however—was Monsieur Frédéric here when his uncle died?"

Tambourin's dark eyes glowered. "Yes."

"And what exactly did your master die from?"

"He died in his sleep. Heart failure, they said." His voice had an odd timbre. He and Holmes exchanged a look which did not require further speech between them. I knew well enough what my cousin thought of that particular diagnosis.

Beautrelet sighed softly. "It is beautiful up here. Almost enough to make one renounce fame and riches."

I stared at him. "Almost?"

His grin was roguish. "Come now, Dr. Vernier, can a humble valet not have his dreams? Can I not wish to be as rich and famous as Sherlock Holmes some day?"

Holmes laughed. "'Famous' is questionable, and 'rich' is definitely overstating things."

"Ah, but perhaps if you find the treasure, Monsieur Holmes… If you turn it in to the Republic, they will pay you a commission, I am certain."

"Don't expect anything from the baron," Tambourin said.

We stared out at the countryside, quiet for a while, and I felt the butterflies in my stomach gradually stop fluttering about and come to a rest. At last Tambourin turned back toward the doorway. "I should also show you my brother's workshop."

"I am most interested in that," Holmes said.

We went back down the winding stairs, through the hall into another wing. Tambourin opened the door to another large room with high ceilings; but it was plain, lacking in elaborate cornices or flourishes of gold and white of the rest of the château. The floor was stone rather than parquet, and three large work tables covered by thick cloths dominated the room. Two tall windows cast light over their surfaces. Antoine was sitting on a stool, his morning coat replaced with a sturdy canvas apron, and spread before him on the surface of the center table were bronze wheels and cogs of various size. Close by was the empty clock case, as well as several screwdrivers, tiny wrenches, two magnifying glasses, and various tin oil cans. On the wall shelves were clocks of different sizes, in various states of disassembly or repair, and a longcase clock about five feet tall stood nearby, its case made of beautifully burnished, inlaid woods. A loud chorus of ticks and tocks of various pitches and rhythms filled the room.

Antoine swiveled about on his chair and regarded us from over the square lenses of the reading-type glasses perched low on his long nose. "Ah, welcome to my workshop, gentlemen. Let me show you a few things. I think there is just enough time before supper."

"Come to the dining room when you are finished," Jacques said. "No doubt you will want an aperitif after your long journey."

Holmes nodded. "An excellent idea, but you and your brother must join us."

Both men were surprised. "Are you certain of that?" Jacques asked.

"Indeed I am. And I hope you will join us for dinner as well. We have much to talk about."

Jacques smiled. "It would be an honor."

Antoine bustled about showing us various clocks, their cases, their mechanisms, and explaining the differences. Beautrelet and Holmes seemed fascinated by this, but I found it rather dry. I had never had a mechanical bent, and clockwork and machines of every variety remained a mystery to me. Antoine finished with the most valuable piece, the tall-case clock; he opened the back to show us the long metal pendulum with its disk at the bottom, then pointed out the elaborate design of the different colors of inlaid wood.

Holmes touched it gently, with reverence. "It is a beautiful creation." He gazed at Antoine. "I hope, monsieur, that you can spare me a few minutes of your time either before dinner or afterwards."

Antoine's brow creased, his eyes suddenly wary. "What for?"

"You are the expert on the clocks of the castle." A smile flickered over his lips. "They are, so to speak, your children. I have some questions."

Antoine sighed softly. "Alas, Monsieur Holmes, much as I would like to, I cannot. It is part of the tradition: the horologist of the Château de l'Aiguille is sworn to secrecy. He cannot discuss his clocks with anyone."

I stared at him in disbelief. "Are you joking?"

"I assure you I would not joke about such a thing." He was indignant.

Holmes gave a slight nod and smiled. "I understand. And I am not surprised."

Beautrelet was also smiling. "Just as we would have expected."

Antoine took off his apron, hung it on a hook, and took down his morning coat from another hook. "Come, gentlemen, let us go have that aperitif."

We had a drink of some Creuse wine in a small sitting room, then went to the dining hall for dinner. Jacques sharpened a long knife with a steel, and cut fragrant, steaming slices from the roast pork. The meat from the *cul noir* pig was truly exceptional. Both brothers were at the table, and Holmes also insisted Madame Tambourin join us for the meal, but she didn't have much time to savor her cooking, because she was always popping up and rushing back to the kitchen to check on something. Jacques apologized profusely about not having enough servants to serve us properly, but we assured him we were only too happy to eat such a superb country meal informally.

After an excellent tart for dessert we retired to the nearby sitting room for an after-dinner drink. Jacques poured small glasses of some local liqueur from a monastery, a thick dark brew, pungent, with a faintly bitter aftertaste. The flames of a big log fire leaped about in the fireplace. We sat and talked a long while with Antoine and Jacques, and I realized the two men were probably starved for company. Clearly they were more intelligent and well educated than typical servants.

At last Holmes glanced over at the clock on a nearby table (yet another spectacular antique, this one with golden trim that contrasted with the dark walnut case) and said that after such a long and busy day, it was time to retire for the night. Jacques insisted on accompanying us to our rooms. The castle's interior was hidden now, all in massive black shadow, with only candles faintly flickering, or the subdued light of lamps, here and there. Our footsteps and our speech echoed faintly in the vast emptiness of the great hall. The silence which settled about us was heavy, visceral almost: it never seemed so still or quiet in London or Paris.

We stopped before Beautrelet's door, number 18, and he put his hand over his mouth to stifle a yawn. "I know I shall sleep well. Goodnight Monsieur Holmes, Dr. Vernier." He smiled. "Thank you again for allowing me to accompany you. It has been a day I shall not forget!" He stepped inside, and the door swung shut.

Jacques soon bid us goodnight and started back down the hall. Yellow light jumped and danced about on the walls from the motion of his candle in its holder.

I yawned. "I am tired, but somehow not exactly sleepy."

Light coming from the lamps in our rooms and on through the doorways, lit up that far part of the hallway. "Would you join me for a moment, Henry?"

"Of course."

We went into his room, which was even more spacious than mine, with a sofa and chair near the fireplace, and by the window, a big antique desk which matched the vanity, the chest of drawers and the wardrobe. Holmes had set a pouch of tobacco and a pipe near the table with the lamp, and he began to carefully pack tobacco into the bowl. Soon he lit it, drew in a few times, then released a cloud of smoke. From the fragrant odor, I could tell it was a better grade of tobacco than the foul shag he often smoked.

He glanced at the clock near the pouch of tobacco, then lightly touched its glass front with his fingertip. That made me aware of the loud ticking of its internal works. "About two hours until midnight."

I stared curiously at the clock, then over at the fireplace where a lump of coal glowed red-orange. "I wonder why they didn't put the clock on the mantel over the fireplace. That would seem the best place for it."

Holmes smiled and shook his head. "Henry, Henry—that would be the very worst place for a fine clock! Both the internal mechanism and the fine wood of the case are sensitive to heat and temperature changes. You would not subject a valuable clock to such extremes by setting it on the mantel." He took an ashtray over to the sofa, set it on the end table, then sat. "I am going to take a stroll about this wing of the castle just before midnight. Would you like to accompany me, or would you rather sleep?"

"I shall gladly accompany you, but why go walking about at that time? What are you looking for?"

"I don't quite know. We shall see what we shall see."

"But why midnight?"

He shrugged. "Remember our clue: *st. s. 138?* Have you not figured out what that might mean?"

"You know I am dreadful at puzzles, riddles, and all such nonsense."

"Forget about the *st* for a moment. What might *s* before a series of numbers signify?"

I thought he was giving me a hint: "'Series?' Could it signify 'series'?"

"You are getting warmer, but there is a simpler choice."

I frowned. "Oh just tell me!"

He shrugged. "As you wish. It could stand for *somme*."

La somme is French for "the sum of," the words nearly identical in both languages, especially the pronunciation.

"Oh yes, that is rather obvious, I suppose."

"So what does *s 138* get you?"

"If you treat it as three separate numbers, 1, 3, 8, it gets you 12. I'm better at arithmetic than riddles. Oh, so that explains why you want to go exploring around midnight."

"Exactly."

"And the room—you wanted to look in room 12!"

He laughed. "Very good. But at first glance I didn't find what I was looking for."

"Which was?"

"Something to do with clocks. I think it is abundantly clear now that the secret of the château has something to do with a clock."

I was frowning again. "I still don't understand what *saint somme* might mean."

"The *st* does not stand for saint."

"What then?"

"Think about it for a while, and it may come to you."

"But have you figured it out?"

"I think so, but we shall soon see. And now we must while away the time for at least another hour and a half. I have some ideas which I would like to mull over."

"I suppose I could take a look at the recent issue of *The Lancet* which I brought along." I soon sat in an armchair with the journal on my lap; however, the warmth of the fire, my belly full and heavy from the big meal, and the text before me, all had an overwhelming soporific effect, and I fell fast asleep. Holmes had to shake me and repeat my name twice to wake me, and it took me a few seconds to remember where I was.

"Do you still want to come?" he asked.

"Oh yes." That was not exactly true—what I really wanted was to retire to a warm comfortable bed—but I extended my arms in a long stretch, then rose.

Holmes had set a dark lantern on the desk. He opened the front and lit the oil lamp, then swung shut the cover with its bulbous glass lens. He used the small protruding lever at the bottom to turn the shutter and cover the bright light. His suitcase was open, and I realized he was staring at the blue-black revolver which lay on top.

He gave a slight shrug. "I think not. The lantern takes two hands to open and close."

"I could take the lantern, you the revolver."

"We should not really need it. Our likeliest adversary has said he does not kill."

"Lupin, you mean? But we saw him in Paris just yesterday."

"And here we are in Creuse today!"

The coal in the fireplace had died down, and Holmes turned the lamp on the desk as low as it would go. We stepped out into the dark hallway. Only two candles were lit now, one at either end of the hall, and the flickering flames were feeble in the heavy darkness. Again I was struck by the great silence, all encompassing, somehow almost solid. It had grown much colder: my shoulders hunched briefly, fighting a shiver, and I considered going back for my overcoat.

Holmes went down the hall to room number 12, opened the door, and briefly cast a beam of yellow-white light inside, illuminating the covered furniture and the loudly ticking clock on the bureau. He closed the shutter again, plunging us into darkness.

We went to the stairs at the end of the hall, and Holmes paused to look back the way we had come. We went up to the second floor, which was equally dark, and traversed it. Next came the third floor, which was more brightly lit, but equally silent, all its occupants most likely fast asleep. The walls here were unfinished stone, and they radiated a chill which seemed to want to penetrate to the bone. I certainly should have worn my overcoat. Along with the cold was that heavy quiet, somehow more obtrusive, more overwhelming, than some sound would have been. How could silence be almost deafening? We walked to one end, then retraced our steps.

Holmes turned to me, the candlelight on a nearby stand giving his face an orange cast. "The floor below, I think."

I shrugged. I had no idea what he hoped to find.

We went downstairs and again stared out at the dark narrow expanse before us. Holmes set the darkened lantern on the table next to the candle, then removed his watch from his waistcoat pocket. "Almost midnight. The witching hour, so to speak. Let us wait for a bit, Henry."

"What are we waiting for?"

"I told you earlier—I am not exactly sure."

With both of us still, the silence seemed to gather round us, seeking to make its ominous presence felt, and I was only too glad for the soft murmur of Holmes's breathing. Old castles often had a gloomy ambience. This one was over two hundred years old, and many people must have lived and died within its walls. I was reminded of my own mortality, something that occasionally struck me in the early hours of the morning, and kept me from falling back asleep. Houses, clocks, and treasures might span the centuries, but never people. I felt a muted sort of ache, a tightness, in my chest, and I clasped my arms, trying to ward off the chill.

Abruptly, I heard a faint chime in the distance, then another similar peal with a lower pitch, and yet another. Clocks were tolling the hour with their twelve sounds in succession. Some were bongs, others repeated brief melodies. This went on for two or three minutes, and then the last of them grew silent. Holmes eased his breath out in a long sigh.

I yawned and put my hand over my mouth. Despite my nap, I was tired—and rather uneasy. This all seemed foolish. I wanted to go to bed, but Holmes generally knew what he was doing. It was a relief when he finally said softly, "Come along."

We walked slowly down the hallway. In the lead, Holmes was obviously trying not to make any noise, and I did the same. Again the silence was somehow resounding, something you could sense. We had nearly reached the end of the hallway when a faint clump sounded from behind us. Holmes froze, then turned back the way we had come.

A sudden harsh cry rent the darkness and the silence, making me start, and was followed by some much louder thumps. Holmes opened the light of the lantern and strode forward. The noise had come to our left, but it was impossible to know from which room exactly, so Holmes stepped into doorways and swept each room with the light of the lantern. Two were empty, but in the third, on the floor next to a bureau, upon which was a table clock, lay a sprawled figure.

We rushed inside. "Turn him over," Holmes said. I stooped and did so. The lantern's beam showed Beautrelet's pale face and gaping mouth.

A tall window was ajar, and the night air was even colder than that coming from the walls. A thick rope was tied to the leg of the bed and formed a straight line to the open window. Holmes held the light on Beautrelet, and I touched him lightly on the cheek. He didn't make a sound. My fingers probed about and found the pulse in his throat, strong and regular.

"Well, he's alive, anyway," I said.

"Look at this." Holmes nudged a cosh on the floor with his foot. The club was leather-wrapped and nearly a foot long with weighted bulbs on either end. "Wicked-looking."

"Someone must have hit him."

Holmes frowned ever so slightly. "So it would seem."

"And then they went out the window."

Holmes turned about and went to the window. He shined the light out into the night, sweeping it about.

I tapped Beautrelet lightly on the cheek. "Isidore? Isidore?" I shook my head. "I have some smelling salts back in my room." I probed gently about his head with my fingertips and soon found some swelling on one side. "He has a goose egg starting up here."

Beautrelet groaned softly. "Oh… my head."

Holmes set the lantern on the bureau, and he stood over us with folded arms. "Did you see anyone out there?" I asked, and he shook his head.

Beautrelet's eyelids fluttered, his eyes struggling to focus on me. "Dr. Vernier?"

"Yes. How are you feeling."

"Not so well. Why… why am I on the floor, anyway?"

"Someone hit you on the head."

"Someone...? I..." He tried to sit up, groaned, and winced with pain.

"Easy, now–no sudden moves."

"We must stop him. We must go after him."

I helped him sit up. "Don't think of standing–not yet. Who was it? Did you get a good look at him."

"It was Lupin."

"Lupin? My God!" I could not believe it. "Are you sure it was him? Did you see his face?"

"No, but I know that voice well enough–that mocking voice."

I shook my head. "How could he get here so quickly?"

"The same way we did," Holmes said. "By train."

Beautrelet stared up at him. "You believe me, then, Mr. Holmes? You believe it was Arsène Lupin?"

"Oh yes, I believe you."

"Perhaps–perhaps you could still catch him."

The idea of stumbling about in the dark after someone as potentially dangerous as Lupin certainly did not appeal to me, so I was relieved when Holmes shook his head. "I am certain it would be a futile endeavor. Besides, we have all three of us had enough excitement for one night."

Chapter 5

The next morning we were up for breakfast by eight, since Holmes wanted to get a fairly early start, despite our being up so late the night before. The three of us sat around an informal, rough-hewn wooden table in the kitchen, which was much warmer than the great chilly dining room. Rather than a hearty English breakfast, we had the usual French fare: bread and butter and jam with coffee and milk. The butter seemed freshly made, and Madame Tambourin told us she had bottled the strawberry jam last summer.

Before breakfast, I had given Beautrelet a brief examination, and he seemed none the worse for wear, save for that swelling on his right forehead near his short brown hair. Now, in the light from nearby window, the bluish-purple color was evident, and the sight made my stomach lurch slightly. I shook my head.

"What is it?" Beautrelet asked.

"You're lucky Lupin didn't cave in your skull. That cosh was certainly wicked enough to do so."

Holmes's eyes narrowed ever so slightly. "You forget that Lupin does not kill."

"Are we really so sure of that? I don't know why we should trust him."

"What do you think, Monsieur Holmes?" Beautrelet asked.

"Oh, I think he can be trusted on that point."

Beautrelet smiled faintly. "Well, that's a good thing for me. All the same, even if he did not cave in my skull, that's the second time he has left his mark on me! I'm not looking forward to another meeting. I wish... I wish we might have pursued him."

I shook my head gravely. "You were in no condition to do so last night. All the same..." I gave Holmes a puzzled look. "I am surprised that you did not make the attempt."

Holmes sipped at his coffee. "Believe me, Henry, I am certain it would have been futile."

Beautrelet's shoulders rose in a sort of shiver. "I don't like the idea of him lurking around here somewhere in the castle. With all these rooms, we could never find him."

"Oh, he must have gone down that rope," I said. "Then he probably made for the woods."

A brief smiled flickered over Holmes's lips. "I wouldn't be so sure of that." He set down the mug. "He could have just slipped back into the castle."

"That was foolhardy of you last night to go looking around on your own," I said to Beautrelet.

Beautrelet shrugged. "Mr. Holmes and I must have arrived at the same conclusion. The sum of 138 is 12, so it seemed possible something might happen at midnight. Lupin also must have figured that out."

"But you were on the second floor, and after all, room 12 is on the ground floor."

Beautrelet smiled. "Ah, but that is easy enough, is it not, Mr. Holmes?"

Holmes looked amused as he nodded.

"Well, it isn't easy for me! Would one of you please explain?"

Holmes took a quick sip of coffee. "What do you get if you add the letter *t* to the end of *somme*, Henry?"

I tried to visualize the letters in my head. "Oh Lord! Of course. *Sommet.*"

Holmes nodded. "Just as in English, from *sum* comes *summit*–the height, the top. So *st. s. 138* is… the summit of the sum of 138, or over or on top of 12."

"I tried to count off footsteps down the hallway of the second floor to get me to the corresponding room," Beautrelet said, "and I must have had it right, since Lupin showed up at the same place."

I was frowning. "And he was hiding there?"

"Yes. He must have been in the wardrobe. He was stealthy, but I heard him. When I turned, he bowed and said 'Bonsoir, Monsieur Beautrelet.' He must have hit me then. The next thing I remember is waking up on the floor with you looking over me, Dr. Vernier."

Holmes finished his bread, swallowed the last of his coffee, and set down the brown earthen mug. "Well, gentlemen, we have a busy day ahead of us. Shall we set to work?"

Beautrelet was somewhat pale, but his lopsided grin was enthusiastic. "I'm none the worse for wear, and all the more eager to get started!"

I hadn't slept well in the huge unfamiliar room, too worried about Lupin reappearing, but I tried to muster some energy. "What is on the docket, then?"

"We shall have a close look at room 12, then at the two rooms above it. That should not take too long, and we can examine the secret passageway before we return to one of the rooms just before noon."

"Noon?" I asked.

Holmes and Beautrelet shared an amused look. "The sum of 138, Henry," Holmes said.

"Oh, yes—12 o'clock, or midnight and noon."

"Do you really expect to find anything in the passageway?" Beautrelet asked.

"No, but we might as well inspect it while we have the opportunity."

Madame Tambourin came back into the kitchen along with her husband. She wore a black dress with a heavy white apron, and was rosy-cheeked as ever. "Finished up, are we? Or would you care for more of anything?"

Holmes stood up. "No, thank you, madame. Your bread and jam were both most excellent. I have never tasted better."

Beautrelet and I also congratulated her, and she smiled. "It's only simple fare. Nothing like what they make in Paris."

"Yours is better by far," I said.

Jacques Tambourin had on his black morning coat with a sparkling white wing collar, but it and the black tie were mostly hidden by his white beard. "Can I do anything for you today, Monsieur Holmes, or will you be about your business by yourself?"

"Thank you, monsieur, but I think we can make do on our own."

Jacques nodded. "I hope you find what you are looking for." He hesitated, his forehead creasing below his bald freckled pate. "Do you really think you might find the treasure here?"

"I doubt it. But I hope to find the key to the treasure."

"There is a key?"

"Most likely a figurative key, monsieur, not an actual one. Perhaps some... instructions."

"Ah, that makes more sense. They ransacked the castle so closely a few months ago. They couldn't have missed an actual treasure. When they found the secret passage, they were all excited, but of course, it didn't amount to much."

"Ah, that reminds me—perhaps room 12 can wait. We must, after all, be thorough, although I doubt we shall discover anything. Can you show us the way into the secret passage?"

"Certainly, monsieur. It is just off the baron's bedroom, the most spacious bedchamber in the entire castle."

"I shall just fetch my lantern, and then we can have a look."

Holmes and I both put on our overcoats and had our hats in hand. The castle was quite cold, and one could only imagine the frigid dampness in an underground passage. Holmes also took the dark lantern, and we met Beautrelet and Jacques in the great hall. Beautrelet still had on his usual rumpled brown tweed suit complete with waistcoat, and was chatting amiably with the older man.

"Don't you want to fetch your overcoat?" I asked Beautrelet.

He shook his head. "I am not terribly sensitive to cold. I shall be fine."

Jacques led us down another hallway with the usual elaborate decorations and flourishes of gilt carved wood, along with another black-and-white tiled floor. Soon we were in another wing of the château, and off the hallway through two large doors, was an enormous room with a great window overlooking an expanse of green lawn and beyond, a segment of the gray stone wall. The room had beautiful period furniture, including an elaborate poster bed with draping purple velvet fabric hanging from its top. Another of the huge tapestries, again with a hunting scene, hung on one wall, and a multicolored carpet took up most of the floor.

Holmes looked about. "This room is kept up, I see. For the baron, I suppose."

Jacques nodded. "Even so, Monsieur Holmes."

Along one wall stood a built-in bookcase of dark oak with both books and *objets d'art* on its shelves. Jacques stopped before it, and raised his hands, palms up, in a sort of welcoming gesture. "Here is your gateway to the underworld, gentlemen. Shall I show you the secret, or would you prefer to exercise your talents, Monsieur Holmes?"

Holmes shrugged. "There is, no doubt, some sort of latch within the bookcase. I could find it, but I would prefer not to waste any time when the answer is readily at hand."

Beautrelet was grinning again and nodded eagerly. "You needn't show us, Monsieur Tambourin. I have seen a similar bookcase before. If I am not mistaken..." A middle shelf was about three inches thick, and he gripped its sort of wooden lip with both hands at either end, then gave the whole shelf a tug. It came out perhaps a half an inch, and a muted sound could be heard from within the wall. Beautrelet grasped one end of the bookcase, then swung the whole thing open about a foot, the entire case behaving like a monstrous door hinged on one side.

Holmes gave an appreciative nod. "Very good, Monsieur Beautrelet. I have not seen that particular variation before."

"Well, I wish you gentlemen luck," Jacques said. "The dampness and chill down there do my rheumatism no good, I can assure you."

Holmes and I put on our hats, and he took the latch to open up the dark lantern so its light shone forth. Beautrelet stepped back and extended his hand. "After you, messieurs."

Holmes went first, and I followed. Both of us had to stoop to get through the opening. The bookcase might be ten feet high, but this aperture in the wall was only about five feet tall. Holmes's yellow-white beam danced about some broad stone steps, and the dampness was apparent at once, along with a musty mildewy smell.

"One moment, Monsieur Holmes."

We stopped, and Holmes swung the lantern around. Beautrelet was still standing atop the stairs by the bookcase door.

"Would you shine the light on the back here?"

Holmes and I went back up some steps, and he turned the lantern to illuminate the long flat wooden back of the bookcase. Beautrelet crossed his arms and stared at it for a long while. At last, he bent over, then knelt. At the very bottom, was a horizontal piece of wood perhaps four or five inches thick. It was only an inch or two above the stone floor. Beautrelet probed about underneath it with his fingers.

"Ah." He pulled hard with his right hand, and a drawer about a foot wide came out. "One always tends to ignore the entrance portal itself, but sometimes it has its own secrets." He reached inside, then withdrew a small heart-shaped silver object by a thin chain.

"What on earth?" I murmured.

Beautrelet held it up before the gap where the bookcase door was still open, letting the daylight from the room illuminate the piece.

"It's a locket, I think. You can see the tiny hook holding it shut. One side has a floral design, the other a pair of lovebirds. I wonder..." He carefully undid the hook. "Nothing inside any longer."

"Odd," Holmes said. "I would have expected a lock of hair. It looks like genuine silver."

"I think perhaps we may find an explanation. If I'm not much mistaken..." Beautrelet slipped his hand into the drawer again and withdrew a brittle, beige envelope. Opening it, he took out a piece of paper and carefully unfolded it. His eyes narrowed behind the lenses of his spectacles as he read. "Ah." He gave his head a shake. "Have a look."

Holmes took the letter. We stood together on the top step where the light would fall on the paper. The neat cursive script was written in French.

To whoever finds this locket, I leave you the dearest memento of my late and much beloved wife Jeanne. She wore this locket for over forty years. Curiously enough, it contained two locks of hair, one, dark brown, from me, the other, blond, from her. The two joined together were a symbol of our union and our love. I shall go to my grave soon, and those hairs, put in an envelope in my jacket pocket, will accompany me.

I am a humble man, only a high-ranking servant, and how I discovered this secret drawer is a story not particularly worth the telling. Jeanne and I had no children, and I have no one to leave this locket to. All the same, it is the most precious thing I own, and I would not have it buried with me. I shall leave it in this secret drawer in the hope that perhaps someday, somehow, it will find a worthy owner who can put it to good use. Perhaps God or Fate will see to that, regardless of how many decades or centuries must pass. Thus I cast this my message in a bottle into the great sea! Guard it well, my discoverer, and may it help you prosper in love, as we two did.

Jean-Louis Galamar
January 14, 1701

"How very odd," I said. "But rather touching, all the same. Here was someone who knew what really mattered in life."

Holmes nodded. "And his note was cast adrift for nearly two centuries. It is a sort of miracle it was ever found. Bravo, Monsieur Beautrelet."

Beautrelet said nothing, but only stared at the two-inch silver heart resting in his palm. He slowly eased out his breath, his eyes shifting to us. "Would either of you want it?"

Holmes sighed softly. "I think not. It would be more appropriate for Henry."

"No thank you. Neither Michelle nor I like anything hanging about our necks." I did not mention that I already had a small, beautifully carved ebony box in the top drawer of my dresser at home which contained a precious lock of red-brown hair.

Beautrelet stared at the locket again. "Might I have it, then?" It was a question he seemed to be asking himself as much as we two.

Holmes nodded. "Of course you may. After all, you did find it."

"I don't know." He seemed almost hypnotized by the locket. "Perhaps I should put it back. Let someone more worthy find it."

Holmes shrugged. "It has been hidden away long enough. If you don't take it, no one may ever find it again. Someday the château around us will all fall to rubble, and it will be lost forever."

I smiled faintly. "I suspect you know a young woman who might like it."

Enough light was coming in from the room that I could see Beautrelet's cheek turn quite red. I had never seen him blush before, and it made him seem somehow more human, less the eccentric prodigy than a normal young man with many confused longings and feelings to sort out. His fist closed about the locket, and he put it in his trouser pocket. "I shall think about it." He bent over again to shut the drawer.

Holmes folded up the letter, put it in the envelope, and gave it to Beautrelet. "You might as well keep this as well. Now, let us have our look at the passageway."

The steps led down to a narrow corridor with walls of grayish brick stained black and a packed dirt floor. The lantern's light bounced off the path and walls ahead of us. Holmes paused once or twice to look at sections of wall.

"I wonder if there could be a secret passage within the secret passage," Beautrelet murmured.

"It's certainly a possibility. Let us hope the first search was thorough. I want to examine the clocks more carefully before spending hours down here."

I gave a shudder. I wasn't terribly claustrophobic, but all the same, I was aware of being enclosed in a dark narrow space with all the great weight of the Château de l'Aiguille above me. I didn't like to think about what it would be like if Holmes's lamp went out. I tried to reassure myself that we could make our way back, and that the door to the bedroom was still ajar.

Eventually we did come to another doorway at the end of the corridor. Holmes pulled it open, and we were flooded with welcome daylight which dazzled our eyes and left us blinking for a few minutes. We stepped through some green vines into the woods, and the fresh smell of pine and earth was a wondrous relief after the moldy stench of the labyrinthian tunnel. We all looked about, our relief apparent enough.

I was the one to say what we were all thinking. "Can we go back through the trees? I don't relish the idea of more time underground."

Holmes shrugged. "As you wish."

Beautrelet had his shoulders slightly hunched; he must have been cold in there, despite what he had said earlier. "I share the doctor's sentiments."

We walked a short way round the mound where the opening was hidden, and there, through the dark tree trunks ahead of us, stood the château. It was a beautiful day, the sun out and shining through the greenery to form an elaborate pattern of shadow and yellow-green light. From somewhere nearby came the irritated chatter of a jay. We walked to the gateway in the fortification wall and soon stood before the great double doors into the castle.

I drew in my breath, savoring the clean cool air. "I had no idea the Creuse was such a beautiful part of France. A shame we have to go inside on such a fine spring day."

Holmes smiled faintly. "Duty calls."

We went back inside, and Holmes traded his dark lantern for a small bundle of tools wrapped in a cloth. The door to room 12 was slightly ajar. Holmes pulled open some draperies, letting in light, then went to the ebony clock sitting on a dresser top and turned it so the back faced toward the window. The front and back of the clock both had a glass door, and at the back you could see an elaborately engraved brass plate with swirling flourishes and a name in cursive, Warwick, or the like. The small pendulum swung back and forth in time with the ticking.

Holmes had taken out a magnifying glass, and he opened the rear door and peered closely at the back for a long while. At last he turned and smiled up at us. "Very good. It is as I suspected. We are on the right track."

Beautrelet grinned. "Excellent."

"What is it?" I asked.

"Have a close look in that lower left corner."

I took the magnifying glass and stooped to look through the lens at the clock. There was so much engraving it took a while to find the tiny cursive script: *v. e. chaud.* "V. E. That must be '*vous êtes.*' '*Vous êtes chaud.*' I wonder."

Beautrelet laughed. "A child's game when you are looking for something. You are getting warmer, *chaud*, or you are getting colder, *froid*."

Holmes closed the back door, half-turned the clock again, and opened the front door. Now he peered closely at the front of the clock, looking at each of the roman numerals set in a gray circle. He touched the number I lightly with his finger. At last he closed the door, then looked at a small glass opening in the side where you could see the gears turning.

"It is as I expected. This is not the one."

"We must look *au sommet*," Beautrelet said.

"Exactly. But first I want to make sure of something. Beautrelet, will you stand in the window here, and Henry, will you go upstairs into the room where we found him last night? 43, I believe it was. I am going outside to have a look. I want to make sure that the windows align, that 43 is exactly above 12."

"What about the third floor?" Beautrelet asked.

"We shall have a good look at the clock on the second floor first."

Holmes and I went into the hallway, and he started for the outside while I went upstairs. The door to 43 was still ajar.

I went to the window, and Holmes soon appeared out on the lawn. He stared up at me, then made a pointing gesture with his hand to my left. I nodded and turned back toward the hallway. I started forward, then noticed another door just to my right. I hesitated only an instant, then grasped the brass knob. The door was unlocked and led into the adjacent bedroom.

"Convenient," I murmured, with a smile. Ideal for any couple wishing to have a romantic tryst.

A man standing before the window turned to face me, his arms folded before him. With his long white beard and bald pate, Antoine certainly looked like his brother, especially as he was wearing the same type of black morning jacket rather than his work apron. "Good morning," he said.

I gave him a puzzled look. "Good morning." I went over to the window, and he moved aside. Holmes was waiting for me, and he gave an exaggerated nod to signal I was in the right room. I raised my hand and also nodded. He started back to come indoors.

My brow furrowed as I gazed at Antoine. "Were you waiting for us?"

He smiled briefly. "I suspected you would be coming here." He nodded toward the longcase clock standing nearby. "This beauty is my pride and joy."

The tall freestanding clock was quite spectacular. It was taller than me, well over six feet, probably of walnut, with beautiful inlaid panels along the front of light and dark woods, which formed designs of flowers and leaves. There was a kind of block-like pedestal, then a narrow long sort of tower, making up the greatest portion of its height, and finally the larger square part with the clock face and its internal workings. Like the other clocks, it had a small glass door protecting the face. The time was twenty-five minutes to twelve. Through a long sort of front window you could also see its pendulum swinging.

I gave an appreciative nod. "It is truly a work of art."

"It also dates from the late seventeenth century, about the time the château was built."

Holmes and Beautrelet soon came into the room. Holmes smiled at Antoine and the clock. "Getting warm, indeed. Come to watch, monsieur? I take your presence as another good sign." He stepped up to the clock and gave the glass cover over the face a tug. He turned to Antoine. "Could you open it, please?"

Antoine took out a key ring, found a small key, then turned the tiny lock, and opened the glass door. The ticking grew louder. Holmes had set his tools on a nearby table, and now took up the big magnifying glass. The one-foot-square face was of yellowish brass with a narrow grayish silver circle some two or three inches thick with twelve roman numerals set at five-minute intervals. A smaller solid circle of brass had the darker patterned hands set in its center. Holmes looked very closely at the space between the number 1 and 2. A small circle with a black fleur-de-lis design was set in the gray metal. Similar circles were between all the numbers. It was not immediately obvious whether these circles were merely engraved or whether separate round pieces of metal were actually set in there.

Holmes looked up at last, his delight obvious. "It is looking better and better." He pressed the circle between the 1 and 2, then proceeded to check all the other circles with his forefinger. He looked very closely with the glass at the circle between 3 and 4, and then at the one between 8 and 9. At last he glanced over at Beautrelet. "Care to have a look?"

Beautrelet shrugged. "It seems obvious enough. But I might as well." He took the glass and peered at the clock face.

Antoine's mouth was hidden by a bushy white mustache, but his eyes showed a faint amusement. He was standing again with his arms folded.

"I don't understand," I said.

Holmes nodded toward the clock. "You will see the answer in about seven minutes, Henry."

"Ah. At noon, you mean."

"Exactly. And I shall perhaps have you assist me."

"I shall gladly do so."

Holmes looked at Antoine. "I suppose you are still sworn to secrecy."

"Indeed I am." But Antoine appeared rather delighted.

"Tell me, monsieur, when they searched the castle, did anyone think to speak with you about the clocks?"

"They did not."

Holmes shook his head. "Imbeciles. They had only the treasure fixed in their minds, but not the key—whatever that may be."

"This key... what do you think that might be?"

"We shall see, I hope, in about four minutes."

All of us were staring now at the clock and watching the minute hand slowly advancing toward the XII at the top. The ticks went on as time, in its usual inexorable and unfathomable way, flowed on. I realized that soon this instant would be a memory, and even being in this room would be a memory, as all of my life was a memory, and there was only time, cascading forward and that vague promise of the future always just beyond reach. My temples began to throb slightly, and I clenched and unclenched my fists.

The hand seemed to jerk the last tiny distance, and then a deep chime sounded, the first of twelve. Holmes put the finger of his left hand on the circle between 1 and 2, then pushed. "Ah, yes!" he exclaimed. He did the same with the one between 3 and 4. The clock had chimed four times. "Press the one between 8 and 9, Henry—quickly, quickly!"

I raised my finger and pushed on the circle, and it did go in a tiny way. I felt something faintly engage beneath the sensitive skin of my fingertip, some inner mechanism. So the circles were not mere engravings, but devices which acted as push buttons of a sort.

"Keep pressing, Henry—do not let up!"

When the last chime sounded, there was a sort of clunk from inside, and then a small drawer just below the clock face popped out some two inches.

"Now we can let go." Holmes lowered his hands, and I did the same. He pulled out the drawer, fumbled about it with his long thin fingers. "Empty!" His gray eyes showed first dismay, then resolution. "Perhaps…"

Beautrelet was smiling faintly. "Think it through."

Holmes stroked his chin lightly. "*Sommet de somme.* Of course." He raised his hands and set them on either side of the square board which formed the very crown of the clock, then tugged slightly in each direction. He swung it up, and I had to stand on tiptoes to see the small compartment atop the clock and all its workings.

"Bravo, Monsieur Holmes!" Antoine cried.

Beautrelet nodded. "Bravo, indeed."

I was smiling, and I shook my head. "What craziness this all is."

Holmes reached about inside with his fingers. He withdrew what appeared to be a gentleman or a lady's small visiting card. He gave it a quick glance, then a sharp laugh burst free. "Oh yes, well played!"

"What is it?" I asked.

He gave me the card. Beautrelet peered over my shoulder. On it was written: *Arsène Lupin, Gentleman-cambrioleur.*

"But how… ?" I mumbled.

"Damnation!" Beautrelet cried. "He has beaten us to it! He must have opened the clock last night, before he clubbed me."

"Who is this Lupin?" Antoine asked.

"He is, as the card states, a gentleman burglar," Holmes said. "You need not concern yourself with him."

"But you did not find what you were after, Monsieur Holmes."

"No matter. Do not trouble yourself. We are finished here, I think. You may leave us."

"But the clock!"

"Oh yes." Holmes lowered the top, then pushed in the drawer. Again, interior cogs turned, and something seemed to seize up.

Holmes shut the glass door, and Antoine locked it with his key. He gave Holmes a slight bow. "You and this Lupin are the first, I think, to have discovered the secret of this longcase clock of the Château de l'Aiguille. We horologists have known about it, but that secret was always ours to guard. My congratulations."

"Did you know how to open it, monsieur?"

"No. I knew it contained a secret compartment, but I was not sure how to get to it—not without taking the clock completely to pieces. In other words, I did not have the combination: your 138 at noon."

"Well, thank you for your assistance, monsieur."

Holmes watched him leave, then he turned again to Beautrelet and me, that sardonic smile tugging at his lips.

I gave my head a shake. "What do we do now? Whatever Lupin found, he has probably fled with it to Paris by now. You will have to tell the baron that we have failed. The secret is lost."

Beautrelet looked grim. His pale brownish eyes behind the lenses of his spectacles swept the room, even as he ran his fingers back through his short hair. He winced slightly as he touched the livid bruise. "If only I had fought him. If only… I blame myself, Monsieur Holmes. I should never have come with you. It would have been better, indeed, if you had forbidden me, although I probably would not have listened."

I shook my head. "You are too hard on yourself, Isidore. He was too clever for us all." I saw that Holmes had hardly moved, his lips still frozen in that odd smile. "What is it? Why don't you say something?"

He turned to Beautrelet. "You have done well enough, but it is time now to show me what you found." He hesitated only a second, the white of his teeth showing. "Monsieur Lupin."

Beautrelet and I both stared incredulously at him. I thought somehow I had misheard. "What did you say?" I asked. Holmes had not taken his eyes off Beautrelet.

The young man looked completely baffled. "I don't understand. What are you talking about?"

"You are very clever, *mon ami.* It is one thing to put on a disguise with exaggerated features—perhaps a big nose, bushy eyebrows, a grand mustache—but another thing to make the disguise a part of you—to become another character. It is not merely a matter of makeup and gimmicks, but of inhabiting a role completely. It takes a great actor. And you are such an actor, Monsieur Lupin."

Beautrelet stared at him for an instant, and then he smiled. Even as he did so, his face, his bearing, were transformed. It was indeed as if an outer mask just fell away like the husk of some insect, or somehow dissolved entirely. The metamorphosis was instantaneous and complete: Isidore Beautrelet was gone, and another man had taken his place. His eyes squinted faintly, and that smile was one we had not seen before. He was standing very straight now.

"Bravo, Monsieur Holmes." His voice was deeper than Beautrelet's reedy tenor. He hesitated, then repeated Holmes's earlier words with a tinge of irony. "'Well played,' indeed."

I stared at him, my mouth agape. "I cannot believe it. I cannot… But who attacked you? Who is your accomplice?"

Lupin was still smiling at Holmes. "Monsieur Holmes?"

"He hit himself with the cosh, Henry."

"What?" I could not repress a shudder. "How could you do such a thing? How could you knock yourself out?"

"I did not actually knock myself out. That was feigned."

"Even so… that bruise is real enough."

His smile became something of a grimace. "I may not have knocked myself out, but it did hurt. And it certainly made me dizzy."

"All the same…" I thought back and realized no one, us included, had actually ever seen Lupin and Beautrelet together. "That time in the bar… Lupin–*you*–left before the police arrived."

He nodded. "And became Beautrelet just in time to join them in rushing in. I had a friend send a message at a pre-arranged time, supposedly from me, telling the police that I had followed Lupin to the bar, and of course I made sure to depart well before the earliest time they might get there."

I shook my head. "And you have the police and Inspector Ganimard convinced that you are a sort of… nemesis to Lupin."

Holmes smiled. "A nice touch, that."

Lupin smiled in return. "I think so, too."

I turned to Holmes. "But how did you know? With that black–wig, I suppose–and the black mustache, and in evening dress… Beautrelet looked nothing like Lupin. And those spectacles… Are they only clear glass?"

Lupin shook his head. "Unfortunately not. I am somewhat near-sighted, but I can get by without them."

"When did you figure this out?" I asked Holmes.

"Oh, it was obvious enough the first time we encountered Lupin."

"Obvious! How can you say that? Tell me how you knew."

"Come now, Henry, you know my methods well enough. You should be able to figure it out yourself. What is the one part of a person that is not easily disguised, one also that most people would never think of trying to disguise in the first place."

The creases in my forehead scrunched as I stared at him.

"Remember how I recognized Signor Rafaello Pozzolo in his disguises?"

"Ah—the scar on his ear." I turned my head to and fro, glancing at each of Lupin's ears. "But he has no scars."

"All the same, each individual's ears are unique and quite distinct. If one accustoms oneself to examining them closely, it becomes easy enough to distinguish a person by his ears. Also, Monsieur Lupin here…" He turned to Lupin. "By the way, which do you prefer, Beautrelet or Lupin? Both, I suppose, are most likely assumed. What is your real name?"

Lupin shrugged. "You must allow me a few secrets, Holmes. Either Beautrelet or Lupin will do. As you prefer, although I must admit a fondness for Beautrelet. He is much closer to my true self."

"Anyway, Henry, there is something unusually distinct about his ears which makes him easily recognizable. See if you can discern it."

Obviously, I had never made it a habit to stare closely at people's ears, but had instead spent my life ignoring them. Peering at Lupin's, I could see nothing unusual. They were just… ears, the usual two of them.

"All right, just tell me."

"In general, for about half the population, the ear lobes are completely attached to the face, while the other half has detached lobes which curve up and around before connecting to the face. What do you notice about Monsieur Lupin?"

It took only a few seconds to see what he was getting at. "The right lobe is completely attached, while the left one is separated."

Lupin grinned. "Bravo, Monsieur Holmes! That was something I did not really notice myself until I began my career in the theater. One day while making up and putting on a wig, that same oddity struck me. I never dreamed someone else might remark it."

"Oh Lord." I shook my head. "So you recognized Lupin was Beautrelet by his ears."

"Yes, but I was suspicious of him early on. The fact that Beautrelet had supposedly had several encounters with Lupin with no other witnesses present was simply too convenient."

"But why on earth did you allow him to accompany us here! You must have known…" Holmes said nothing, but his mouth still formed an amused smile. "I'm being an idiot. You wanted him to come along so you could keep an eye on him."

"Very good, Henry. Very good. But enough of this—and enough games." He turned to Lupin. "Now can you show us what you found? I am most curious to see this key to the treasure."

"I shall gladly let you have a look." Lupin reached into his jacket pocket, then shrugged. "I had to make sure, after all, that you were not overrated."

"I take it, then, that I have passed my examination?"

"You have indeed—with flying colors."

From within a brown parchment envelope, Lupin withdrew a folded scrap of paper and opened it up. The page was about nine inches wide and had cryptic writing:

$$2.1.1..2..2.1.$$
$$.1..1..2.2.\quad.2.43.2..2.$$
$$.45..2.4...2.2.4..2$$
$$D\ \overline{DF}\ \square\ 19F{+}44\ \triangleleft 357\ \triangle$$
$$.13\ .53..2\ ..25.2$$

Holmes looked closely at it, even as I gave a weary sigh. "I suppose it was too much to hope for something simple and direct, rather than more mysteries and puzzles."

"Come now, Henry, it is not that bad. The numbers vary from one to five. Their meaning is obvious enough."

"It is?"

"Yes, of course. We need some paper and a pencil. Let us…"

"Allow me." Lupin took out another folded piece of paper, this one obviously new. "I think this much is clear."

$$e . a . a . . e . . e . a .$$
$$. a . . a . . . e . e . . e . oi . e . . . e .$$
$$. ou . . e . o . . . e . . e . o . . e$$
$$D \overline{DF} \square 19F{+}44 \triangleleft 357 \triangleleft$$
$$. ai . ui . . e \qquad . . eu . e$$

Holmes nodded. "Yes, I agree. The numbers correspond with the five vowels. And of course, the missing letters for that last line are also obvious."

I was frowning again. "*L'aiguille creuse*, you mean. But that tells us nothing. We are already in Creuse at the Château de l'Aiguille."

Holmes shook his head. "No, I do not believe that is it. I think this note must be explaining the real meaning of *l'aiguille creuse*—note that there is no *de*, no 'from,' between the two words. I suspect we are supposed to take it more literally: the hollow needle."

Lupin smiled. "I agree wholeheartedly. The entire thing with the Creuse and the château was meant to muddy the waters—to hide the real meaning of *l'aiguille creuse* and the treasure's actual location. That secret must lie hidden in those first three lines.

Indeed, it could well be in that first line—the initial e could be *en* or 'in' some place."

Holmes's face had tensed with concentration. "Needle, needle? What other ones are there in France? Mountains with that name must abound. There is the peak near Mont Blanc, l'Aiguille du Midi, but a mountain wouldn't make much sense unless some hollow cave…"

"*L'aiguille,*" I whispered softly and slowly to myself. "*L'aiguille.*" I closed my eyes, and the vision came clear and abrupt: the cry of gulls, a cool wind, and a blue, blue sky with the swath of emerald ocean, and rising from the waters and tapering to a point near the towering limestone cliffs… "Can it possibly be? Let me see that." I seized the paper and stared hard at the first line. "Of course! That's it!" I was grinning broadly. "I cannot believe I have actually figured out something before you two geniuses!"

My zeal amused Holmes. "Explain yourself, Henry."

"The last part of the first line, just here. You have *e*, then two spaces, then *e* again, then space, then *a*, then space. The word must be *Étretat.* It fits perfectly—and *Étretat* has a rock formation offshore called the Needle which rises seventy meters high."

Lupin had also caught my enthusiasm. "Oh very good, Vernier! That makes perfect sense—and it is so far from Creuse, about half of France away. The castle here is a diversion so distant that you would never get anywhere close to the real treasure."

"*Étretat,*" Holmes murmured. "That is in Normandy, is it not? Just across the Channel from England."

"Yes," I said. "My family generally spend some time in July or August at the beach there. It's a beautiful spot, and the bathing in the sea is first-rate, although the water never gets truly warm."

Behind the glass of his spectacles, Lupin's brown eyes had an odd glint. "The Needle must somehow be hollow, and inside…"

We were all quiet briefly, sharing our moment of triumph.

At last Holmes eased out his breath. "We should pack our things this afternoon and try to get the first train back to Paris tomorrow morning."

"And then it's on to *Étretat*!" Lupin exclaimed.

"In a day or two. But first, I must speak to the baron."

Lupin was dismayed. "Must you?"

"He hired me, and I must justify my fee. However, I shan't show him this piece of paper. Not yet, anyway. I would prefer to go on to *Étretat* alone."

Lupin stared hard at him. "By alone, you mean with Dr. Vernier and myself?"

Holmes smiled. "Exactly."

Lupin's smile returned. "Very good. And in the meantime, we can work on decoding the rest of this scrap of paper."

"We can indeed." Holmes glanced at me. "And we shall be certain to include Henry in our efforts!"

Part 2

L'AIGUILLE, ÉTRETAT

Chapter 6

After a late lunch, we went to the library, which seemed an ideal place, both quiet and spacious, to further consider the mysterious paper from the clock. Holmes took out the copy Lupin had made with the letters rather than numbers, unfolded it and set it before him. He placed a hand on either side of the page and spread out his long slender fingers. He was at the head of the massive table, I to the right, Lupin to the left.

"Now then, let us have a look at this first line. The end word is clear enough, Étretat, as Henry discerned." He filled in the spaces with a pencil. "The first word is probably *en*." He wrote that in. "We then have *a* space *a* space space, for a total of five letters. Do either of you have any ideas? Since French is not my mother tongue, you both have the advantage in our guessing game."

I squinted down at the page. "I think perhaps I have it. There is a rock formation near the Needle, called the Porte d'Aval. A sort of column of limestone comes out of the water and curves over to the bluff, forming a towering natural arch. *Aval* also has another meaning: *en aval* means downstream from, or below."

Beautrelet grinned at me. "Better and better, Doctor!"

Holmes nodded, then used the pencil again. "Very good. So our first line is '*en aval d'Étretat*,' and the last one is '*aiguille creuse*.' Progress is definitely…" There were a couple of raps on the door. In what seemed an automatic response, Holmes turned over the page to conceal the writing, and said loudly, "Yes?"

The door opened, and Jacques's white-bearded face and bald cranium appeared. His expression was that of someone who had swallowed some foul-tasting bug. "Do pardon me, Monsieur Holmes. I know you did not want to be interrupted, but Monsieur Bazin insists on seeing you."

The curl of Holmes's mouth showed his disapproval. "And who is Monsieur Bazin?"

The door opened inward, and a tall man squeezed past Jacques and into the room. His green velvet frock coat was jarring here in the country, so far from its natural habitat in Paris, and he had an enormous waxed reddish-brown mustache similar to the baron's, a style more popular during the time of Napoleon III in the 1860s. His hair was somewhat thin on top, but luxuriant on the sides. "I am Monsieur Bazin, Pascal Bazin, at your service, Monsieur Holmes. And what a great honor this is!"

"I am sorry, Monsieur Bazin, but I am occupied just now, as I am sure Monsieur Tambourin told you. I am not available to satisfy… idle curiosity."

"Ah, but I did not come here from idle curiosity! I am the land agent and lawyer in Creuse for Baron Chamerac. He notified me that you were coming and asked me to check in on you and see if I could be of any assistance."

Holmes gave a weary sigh. "Did he now?" He shrugged once,

then stood up and came around the table. He shook hands with Bazin. "A pleasure, monsieur."

"The pleasure is entirely mine, Monsieur Holmes. And how goes the search? I know something of your quest. The baron and I are united not only in business matters but in friendship as well."

"I am returning to Paris tomorrow, and I hope to speak to the baron late in the day."

Bazin's eyes opened wider. "And shall you report success?"

"I am not at liberty to say, monsieur."

"But as I said, the baron and I keep no secrets from one another. I assure you…"

"Then he will certainly be willing to tell you as soon as he finds out anything. I do not mean to be rude, but our work just now is most important."

Bazin sighed and stated the obvious. "So you do not trust me?"

"In this case, I trust no one but the baron. And since we are leaving early in the morning, I fear I haven't a moment to spare."

"I see, I see. I understand. You do not know me. Why, therefore, should you trust me? Your caution is prudent indeed. Very well, I shall just be leaving, but first, this must be…" He turned to me. I had stood up when Holmes had, but was still before my place at the table. "This must be Dr. Vernier? The baron mentioned he was your companion."

I nodded. "Yes." I stepped forward rather begrudgingly and shook his hand. "A pleasure, monsieur."

Bazin was staring past me at Lupin, a crease showing in his forehead. "And who is this?"

Lupin and Holmes exchanged a look. "Well…" Holmes began, but Lupin strode forward.

"Dash it all, old man! Wish I spoke froggy, but even though I understand it, I can't say a word of it!" Holmes and I both stared at him. We had not heard him speak English before, and although he had a very slight accent, he spoke quite well, if in an exaggerated and eccentric manner.

Lupin eagerly shook Bazin's arm, bobbing it up and down. "I'm the valet for these two gentlemen. Someone has to look after them, make sure their socks match their shoes, and that sort of thing. I do my best, you know."

Bazin stared at him, his gaze uneasy and faintly appalled. "I don't understand English." He glanced at Holmes. "But I heard 'valet.' So he is your valet?"

Holmes's mouth formed a sardonic smile as he nodded. "Yes. He is, so to speak, my *gentleman-valet.*"

Bazin was still staring warily at Lupin. "I see. And he's... he's helping you?"

Holmes hesitated a split second. "One never knows when one might need to send him out for tea or for cognac."

Bazin nodded slowly. "I see. Well, I'll just leave you gentlemen to your very important work. If you see the baron tomorrow, give him my warmest regards. Good day, then."

Bazin closed the door behind him. Holmes stared at Lupin. "Your English is quite good, if a bit preposterous! You must have spent some time in England."

"So I did, in London, as a matter of fact." The corners of his mouth rose upward. "There was a young lady. I was quite smitten. She helped me perfect my accent."

Holmes nodded, then switched back to French. "Well, since we are trying to decipher a French message, let us use that language."

We resumed our places at the table and Holmes turned the paper over again so we could stare at the second line.

"I would wager the first word is *la*," Lupin said.

Holmes shrugged. "That is likely."

We stared silently for a while. I was frowning. "Could the end word be *mademoiselles*?"

"There is not the required *a*," Holmes said.

Lupin drummed with his fingers at the table. "Not *mademoiselles*, but perhaps… Yes, *demoiselles*, plural. Yes, that would work."

Holmes stroked his chin. "That fits perfectly, but it seems an odd choice. We are seeking directions to the treasure, and suddenly young ladies–*demoiselles*–appear. I wonder…" He used the pencil to fill in the letters and spell out the word *demoiselles*. "And in front of *demoiselles* we have a solitary *e* with a space to be filled on either side. Certainly the word is either *les* or *des*."

Lupin nodded. "Yes. Probably *des*. *La* plus some noun, and then *des demoiselles*. The 'something' of the *demoiselles*. What could it be, and who are these young ladies, anyway?"

We stared at the paper silently for a long while. I was struggling to remember my stays at Étretat. Something about *demoiselles* was tantalizing familiar. "As I recall… there is a cave in the vicinity, a cave of the *demoiselles*."

Holmes nodded eagerly. "That would be perfect." His smile faded. "But *cave* does not fit."

Lupin smiled. "You have been in England too long, Vernier. *Cave* in French is not the same as in English. It is a wine cellar, not a cave in the sense of *caverne* or *grotte*. *Caverne* might work."

But it became immediately clear that *caverne* would not fit in the spaces. I was frowning, and almost uncalled for, a word popped into my head. "*Chambre*, try *chambre*."

Holmes hesitated, then filled in the letters. *Chambre* fit perfectly. "*La chambre des demoiselles*," he murmured.

"That's it—that was the name of the cave. There was some old story about some maidens pursued by a wicked nobleman who were trapped in the cave and perished there."

"Excellent!" Holmes exclaimed. "We are making much better progress than I would have thought possible. And now, on to the third line."

We all stared silently for a while. Lupin was the first to speak. "Since we are looking for directions, I'll wager the first word is *sous*."

Holmes nodded, then put an *s* before and after the vowels *ou*. "Under, under something," he murmured in English. "Most likely *sous le*, 'under the.'"

"*La maison, le château, la colline...*" Lupin shook his head. "None of those works."

Holmes and I remained silent for a long while, even as Lupin occasionally muttered a word or two. Before long it grew silent, and Holmes and Lupin both stared at me.

I felt the corners of my mouth rise into a smile. "I take it you both consider me the expert. Well, near la Chambre des Demoiselles was some ancient fortress. And in fact, *le fort* would work there. *Le fort de*—the fort of... But there I am stymied. I cannot recall the name of the fort. It was something that started with *f*, a rather long word with two or three syllables."

Holmes gave an appreciative nod. "But this is excellent, Henry! We all but have it: 'Downstream of Étretat, la Chambre des Demoiselles, under the fort of something—*l'aiguille creuse*—the hollow needle!' When we get to Étretat we can ask the locals for the name of the fort."

"But that fourth line– it is something else entirely," I said, even as I pointed with my finger:

$$D \ \overline{DF} \ \square \ 19F{+}44 \ \triangleleft 357 \ \triangle$$

"Utter gibberish!"

"Hopefully when we go to la Chambre des Demoiselles, it will make more sense," Holmes said.

Lupin smiled. "Between the three of us, it should be child's play to figure out, once we are there. I am certain we will be able to make our way into the Needle."

I shook my head. "And you really believe it is hollow inside, and that the treasure lies within?"

"If it is not there," Lupin said, "then someone has gone to a great deal of trouble for nothing."

Holmes leaned back in his chair, one hand still lying flat on the table. "We shall find out soon enough, Henry. We have been indoors for almost our entire stay in the French countryside–I suggest we take advantage of the splendid weather this afternoon and go for a long stroll."

"I'll second that motion!" Lupin said.

We went downstairs to the great hall, and when he saw us, Jacques strode forward appearing genuinely repentant. "Monsieur Holmes, I hope you can forgive me for the interruption. I tried to keep him out, but he was most insistent."

"You are forgiven, Monsieur Tambourin. I know you did your best." Holmes frowned. "He has left, hasn't he? Excellent. We were planning on a walk. Perhaps you could recommend some local points of interest."

Tambourin told of us a path which went through the woods of the park, then gradually rose up a rocky hillside, ending in a spring of remarkably fresh and clear water. Indeed, most of the drinking water in the château came from that spring. They called it la Source des Renards because one often saw the small animal with its bushy red tail nearby.

"The Spring of the Foxes," I murmured. "Rather quaint."

Lupin gave Jacques an odd stare. "La Source des Renards? Are you joking with me, Monsieur Tambourin?"

"Why ever would I joke about such a thing? And what is the joke in a fox, anyway?"

Lupin said nothing, but his forehead was still creased.

We all fetched ourselves a hat, and soon met near the front doors. Holmes had on his battered woolen tweed hat with the wide brim, while Lupin and I had on simple woolen cloth caps of the type newsboys wore. Holmes selected a gnarled blackthorn stick from an assortment in a metal stand, and soon we were outside, on our way, and savoring the clean fragrant air of Creuse, so different from the frequently smoky or dusty miasmas of London and Paris. Here, too, there were no fine particles of dried horse manure floating about from all the ambulatory equine residents!

We went through the gateway in the tall stone wall around the castle, following the main gravel road which soon became merely dirt. On our left was the greenery of the park: tall evergreens, scraggly rhododendrons and deciduous trees just starting to leaf out, a yellowish tint to their foliage.

I stared over at Lupin. He *was* Lupin, again, or rather, he was that stranger who was neither Beautrelet nor Lupin. Around Tambourin, he had clearly been Beautrelet. Among other things, his bad slouch was now gone; he had splendid posture. And he was no longer gawky, but self-assured. His eyes shifted to mine, and he smiled.

"Getting used to me, Doctor?"

I shrugged. "I'm trying to. I... I haven't quite figured out who you are."

He laughed. "If you do figure it out, let me know, by all means."

"I'm still wondering what I should call you."

He shrugged. "As I told you before, it doesn't much matter to me. However, I suppose 'Beautrelet' would be safest. We can't have you calling me Lupin in front of the baron or Ganimard!"

Holmes laughed. "Certainly not! Beautrelet you shall be, or even Isidore, if we are to be on cordial terms."

"I rather liked Beautrelet." My voice was faintly wistful.

Lupin grinned again. "Doctor, it is hardly as if he has died! He can appear at your command. Besides, as I think I mentioned, Beautrelet is much closer to the real me—whoever that may be."

Holmes pointed with his stick to our left. "This, I think, is the path Jacques told us leads through the park to the spring." We turned into the shade, and the temperature immediately dropped.

"Beautrelet seems much younger than Lupin," I said.

Lupin nodded. "He certainly is. About twenty, I think."

"While Lupin is perhaps thirty."

"Very good, Doctor!"

I shook my head. "And how old is the real you?"

"Twenty-five and a half."

Holmes was abreast of Lupin, while I was just behind them. "I suspect," Holmes said, "that these twenty-five years have not been uneventful."

Lupin laughed softly. "No. I have... kept busy."

"Ganimard said Lupin first wrote to him about three years ago. Was that when you turned to a life of crime?" I asked.

"No. It was rather earlier than that."

"You must have been one of those troubled adolescents."

Lupin was briefly silent. "Perhaps it is too much like boasting, but herein lies, in fact, a major key to my character. You have both heard, I am sure, of child prodigies in music like the young Mozart or Mendelssohn. Well, even if I do say so, I was a child prodigy... in crime."

"Were you now?" Holmes said. "And at what age did you commit your first major offense?"

"Oh, I assure you I never trifled with paltry crimes: my first offense was a major one. And would you care to guess my age then?"

I stroked my chin. "Twelve," I said.

A few seconds later, Holmes spoke, "Ten."

Lupin's laugh expressed his delight. "Wrong. I was six."

"Good Lord," I exclaimed. "Are you joking? And what did you do? Steal something?"

"Very good, Dr. Vernier. I did indeed steal something. Try another guess as to what it was."

I was frowning. "Another child's toy?"

"No, no. As I said, nothing minor, nothing so petty."

"Some bank notes," Holmes said. "You took them from either a wallet or a purse."

"No, no. I strove much higher than that."

"What on earth did you take?" I asked.

"The diamond necklace of the Comtesse de Dreux-Soubise worth several thousand francs."

"At the age of six? Come now, you are not being honest with us!"

Lupin turned to give me an indignant look. "I assure you I am."

"How on earth did it happen?"

"Do you want the true version, or the even more spectacular one I told my friend Leblanc to put in his chronicles of my adventures?"

Holmes replied with an implied question of his own. "You must have had an accomplice, an older person. A six-year-old on his own might steal a valuable necklace, but he would never be able to dispose of it, never receive any payment."

Lupin laughed. "Oh very good, Monsieur Holmes! As ever, nothing gets past you. In the story I told Leblanc, I had no accomplice, and exactly how I managed to redeem the necklace for money was never explained."

"Was it perhaps some relative? Certainly not your mother, but…"

"No, no, my mother was absolutely honest and respectable! And as for my father, he died when I was only four."

Lupin's story had taken such a dramatic twist, that we had all stopped walking. Holmes and I were staring at him. The lenses of his glasses slightly shrank his brown eyes, and his lips formed an ironic smile. Holmes stared at him a while before speaking.

"A grandparent—and not a female one, of course—your grandfather."

Lupin clapped his hands together. "Bravo, Sherlock Holmes! Bravo! Your sagacity never fails to amaze me. I am enjoying our time together so very much."

We resumed our walk, and I shook my head. "Your grandfather actually enlisted you in a scheme to steal a necklace? I cannot believe it."

"Actually it was rather the reverse, Dr. Vernier. I was the one who suggested stealing the necklace, but my grandfather was quite knowledgeable, and helped with all the details. He also had former contacts who could dispose of the necklace and give us a fair cut."

"I suppose," Holmes said, "it was what they call an inside job. Your mother must have been a member of the household, perhaps a servant of the countess."

"Another bullseye, Holmes! Of course, technically my mother was not a servant, but a friend of the countess from school days who had fallen on hard times and was given a small apartment in the Saint-Germain town house of the count. It soon became apparent that the countess's motives stemmed more from practicality than generosity. My mother was an excellent seamstress, and she was soon put to work. She also doubled as an extra chamber maid. The countess was very stern and severe with all her servants, and perhaps more so with my mother. Even as a child, it was very clear to me that the countess was not the friend and benefactor my mother considered her. My grandfather and I were in accord on that point.

"One time the countess interrupted my mother, who was helping me with my schoolwork, and shouted at her to come at once. I immediately shouted back, 'How dare you speak to my mother that way!' I don't know who was more surprised, my mother or the countess. My mother blushed and immediately hushed me up. I realized afterward that my behavior had been foolish. It did no good and, moreover, it revealed my true feelings toward our enemy. I resolved to come up with some better way to revenge my mother's ill treatment.

"I knew that the countess was very vain and that the prize possession of the family was a diamond necklace which had almost gone to Marie Antoinette. My mother often helped the countess dress for special occasions, and she told me afterwards how beautiful the necklace was, how the diamonds glittered, and how splendid the countess looked. There was such sadness in her voice. She had come from a noble family herself, but when she married my father, her parents disinherited her. My father was a poor man, but honest—unlike his father, my grandfather. I suspect that when they were two girls in school, my mother had been the pretty one, the one with jewels and dresses, and that the countess really took her in so she could keep her under her thumb and remind her how the tables had turned—how she had triumphed!"

"What a dreadful woman," I murmured.

"I suppose your grandfather must have lived with you and your mother?"

"He did. He had been a burglar, a very good one, but he broke his leg while making an escape, and it healed very poorly. He had to retire. He came to live with us before my father was killed in a factory accident. After his death, we had nothing. That was when my mother went to the countess.

"My mother was always generous even in poverty, and she insisted grandfather come along to the wretched apartment with us. She had the tiny bedroom, while grandfather slept on the sofa in the small sitting room. I was nearby on a little mattress which we rolled up and unrolled every day. How the old man snored! There was no fireplace, only a feeble stove in a minuscule kitchen, and in winter we were always cold. And we ate mostly leftover scraps from the count's kitchen. Little wonder my mother's health suffered! I wanted to get her away from there—I wanted to save her." Lupin's voice had an unusual gravity.

Somewhere nearby a squirrel chattered. I realized the path had sloped upward, the trees thinning out slightly, but I had been so engrossed in Lupin's story I hardly noticed our surroundings. A small creek had also appeared, the water running and foaming over smooth brown and gray rocks.

"I am most interested in the particulars of this crime," Holmes said. "Tell us about it."

"Gladly, but..." Lupin stopped abruptly and turned to Holmes and me. "I hope it is understood that this is strictly confidential.

The case of the stolen necklace was never solved: it is still open. You must not tell anyone else, especially Ganimard! And you must not—you will not—use it against me in any way."

Holmes nodded. "Certainly not. You have my word."

"And mine," I said.

Lupin turned again, and we resumed our walk. "The count was smart enough not to leave the necklace lying about the house. He kept it locked up in a safety deposit box at the Crédit Lyonnais and only took it out for special occasions. That night there was a grand reception for some visiting royalty, and as usual, after they got back, the count hid the case with the necklace on the top shelf in the big closet of their bedroom. The door to this cubbyhole was at the foot of their bed, and inside, at the opposite end of the closet, was a window, one floor up, which opened up onto a small courtyard. This window was partially blocked by a huge chest, but it had a smaller transom window just above.

"The next morning, the count intended to return the necklace to the bank, first thing, but to his utter dismay, he could not find it. Impossible! He had locked the closet door and was a light sleeper, and the window, blocked by the chest, was also still locked shut. Frantic with worry, he sent at once for the police. The inspector who arrived, Monsieur Valorbe, also did a thorough search, but found nothing. He asked if any servant knew about where the jewel was kept, and they mentioned my mother. She was the only one who ever helped the countess dress when she was to wear the necklace, and the countess had once mentioned that they generally hid it in the closet for the night. Also suspicious was the fact that the kitchen of our apartment faced the same small courtyard. However, the distance between the two windows was about ten feet, and they were also ten feet up from the courtyard.

"When I returned from school for lunch, the inspector was grilling my mother and grandfather. Luckily, they had no idea of his former occupation, and he had pursued his trade in Lyon, not Paris. Grandfather was then about sixty, but looked much older, and he could play the feeble, slightly senile old man very well. I don't think they ever really considered him a suspect. My mother was their main concern. She was quite upset by the theft, and they soon searched the house from top to bottom—and they ransacked our apartment. They found nothing."

I was frowning. "And it was actually you who had taken it?"

"Of course it was me. I've already told you that."

"Where on earth did you hide it?"

"You had gone to school as usual that morning?" Holmes asked.

"I had."

"So you took the necklace with you and hid it in your school desk."

Lupin laughed. "No need to fill in the gaps in the story for you, Holmes!"

"The police would never think of searching a child's desk at school."

"But how ever did you manage to steal it?" I asked. "Did you sneak into the bedroom or…?"

"The transom window," Holmes said. "It must have been the transom window. It was only large enough, I'll wager, for a child to get through it, and they never imagined a child could commit such a crime."

"You do truly have it all figured out," Lupin said.

"But the courtyard?" I said. "How did you cross it?"

Holmes scratched at his shoulder. "Some type of bridge, I suppose?"

Lupin nodded. "We took two long shelves from the kitchen and screwed the boards together at the end. It was rickety—it could have never supported the weight of an adult, but I was a small, slender child."

"How did you manage the transom?" Holmes asked.

"I used a small metal screw eye. I screwed it into the wooden frame of the transom, then used the round eye to push the glass inward and open it. Even for me, it was awkward getting in and out of that narrow gap. Once I had the necklace, and before I left, I actually unscrewed the metal piece and took it with me. I don't think they ever even thought of the transom. They were focused on the larger window below, which I never touched."

Holmes slipped the blackthorn stick above his left elbow, clamping it against his side, then raised both his hands to clap twice. "Bravo, Monsieur Lupin. Cleverly done indeed. And it was mostly your plan?"

"Oh yes. My grandfather figured out what we might use as a bridge, but I was the one who realized I could get through the transom. We practiced it together a few times before the night of the actual theft, so I knew I could manage it."

I shook my head. "And at the age of six, you were that obsessed with vengeance?"

Lupin half-turned his head in my direction. "It was not just vengeance, Doctor—not even mainly vengeance. I did think the countess was a bad person who deserved to be punished, but more than anything, I wanted the money—I wanted it so I could get my mother away somewhere warm and safe, where her health might be restored. And in that, I was somewhat successful." He gave a great sigh. "But only somewhat. We had to wait several months before leaving so as not to raise suspicion, but in the end, the countess helped by dismissing my mother. Then we could move somewhere pleasant in the country, far from the foul air and stench of Paris. Her health did improve, but she was only with me for six more years. We never told her about the theft. We said my grandfather had come into a grand inheritance from a distant relative. My grandfather and I made sure those were happy years, but she died when I was only twelve years old."

"Oh, I'm sorry," I said.

"And your grandfather managed to sell off the diamonds on the sly to pay for this new life?" Holmes asked.

"He did, although we discovered many of them were fakes. The count must have sold some himself and replaced them to keep up appearances."

Holmes laughed. "Oh, of course he did! You were not exaggerating about being a child prodigy, monsieur. You have led quite a life for one so young. What else have you done? I suspect some time in the theater, perhaps as an itinerant player? That must be where you learned to transform yourself into another person both physically and psychologically."

"This is uncanny," Lupin said. "You do seem to know me almost better than I know myself. I worked as an actor intermittently from about the age of eighteen to twenty-two."

"But what of your education?" I asked. "How did that fit in?"

"Well, once we moved to the country, I had—at my own request—a series of governesses. I did not want to undergo the boredom and strict routine of a country school. I could go at my own pace and follow my own instincts. I had a knack for languages even then and started with English and German.

"After my mother died, my grandfather and I decided that I needed to become a gentlemen, so we moved back to Paris, and

I went to a rather fancy school. I, of course, adopted a new name and a very romantic past for myself, my father being a chevalier smitten with a commoner, marrying her and then the two of them tragically dying young, leaving me in the care of my old grandfather. I was much better prepared for the school than most of my classmates; besides mastering the usual subjects, I learned how to comport myself as a gentleman and how to assume the air of the upper class, a talent that has proven useful.

"My grandfather died when I was seventeen, and I decided to leave Paris and my school. Why not be paid for my histrionic efforts rather than performing for free? I traveled all about and played a variety of roles, most often the youthful romantic lead. I also spent some time in Italy and England." He laughed. "It is true that young ladies make the best teachers of language! I perfected my English with Geraldine and my Italian with Francesca."

"But what made you turn to crime?" I asked. "I would think the proceeds from the necklace would have been enough to keep you and your grandfather well off for life."

"Ah." Lupin sighed. "They would have—and they did, for a long time. But my grandfather had grown up in poverty, and in his mind, one could never have enough money. He was old and quite sick near the end. He wanted me to be secure after he was gone, so he invested our money—foolishly. All was lost in some harebrained scheme."

"But couldn't you make a decent living as an actor?"

Lupin laughed at this, and Holmes spoke. "That is a notoriously unreliable sort of living, Henry. Even more erratic than being a consulting detective, often feast or famine."

"But a person of your talents... Surely you could have found an honest occupation?"

"Ah, but doctor, I have found such an occupation! I enjoy my profession very much. I steal only from those who deserve it, and I enjoy the intellectual challenge and the sheer adventure of it all. And in the end, who would not want to be Arsène Lupin? Mine, too, is a very creative life, almost as if I were a playwright—after all, are not Lupin and Beautrelet original and unusual personages? As an actor, have I not totally brought my characters to life in the most dramatic and convincing way possible? All the same, I must confess I am thinking of retiring. Twenty-five is the age at which one thinks of marrying and settling down. I am hoping my share of the treasure will make this possible."

Holmes laughed softly. "One does not need to be Sherlock Holmes to deduce who the young lady might be."

Lupin, for once, remained silent, but I could see his cheek flush.

I gave my head a shake. "I must confess that compared to you, Isidore, my life has been rather boring and uneventful."

"But as a physician you have saved lives and helped heal people."

"Not so much as I would wish. There are so few effective treatments."

"And also, you have accompanied your cousin in so many adventures!"

I shrugged. "Well, I suppose there is that."

Our path had become somewhat steep, and the stream of clear water running through the rocks made a constant murmur. Green moss covered some of the rocks, and ferns grew nearby. Holmes stopped, removed his hat, and fanned himself lightly. "It seems to be warming up, or perhaps I am feeling the exercise."

I also took off my hat. My hair felt damp from sweat. "No, it has warmed since we left."

Lupin suddenly stood up very straight and raised both hands, his fingers spreading apart. He lightly touched Holmes and me. "Do not make any sudden moves."

"What...?" I began.

"Hsht—softly now," he whispered. "Look up there."

Ahead in the path near a big fir tree was a small reddish-brown fox. He was standing sideways so we could see his complete torso, legs, and his long bushy tail with the white tip. He was staring at us, and the two large, pointed ears stood out above that narrow white muzzle with the black nose. The expression in those two eyes was oddly intelligent, almost human.

Lupin slowly drew in his breath. "Stay here," he whispered. "Do not move." He lowered his hands, then slowly started forward.

Holmes glanced at me, his gray eyes curious. With his hat off, the moist skin of his brow glowed white in the sun, and stood out against his swept-back black hair.

Lupin walked toward the fox ever so slowly. The animal did not move, but his gaze was fixed on the man. Lupin stopped on the curving path about six feet from the fox, and said a word so softly I could not make it out. The fox was still motionless, as were we all, frozen in a sort of tableau: Holmes and I side by side, Lupin ahead of us on the trail, his back to us, and the red fox standing somehow expectantly.

Again, Lupin spoke, the words unintelligible. He raised one hand very slowly, then lowered it. The fox turned and walked briskly up the trail and then swerved to the left, vanishing into the shade of the trees. Lupin gave a great sigh, then turned back toward us. We went to him. An odd, crooked smile twisted his lips, and his eyes had a certain liquid quality.

"He let me get so close." Lupin's eyes were puzzled. "Almost as if..."

"He seemed quite tame with you," I said.

Lupin smiled, even as water seemed to overflow from his eyes. He turned away from us. "Pardon me. I'm being foolish. It's only that…"

"What is it?" Holmes asked.

"I had almost forgotten. It's been such a long time. My grandfather's nickname for me was *petit renard.*" He laughed once. "He called me that when I suggested that we steal the necklace. And from then on, the name stuck." He wiped his eye. "I was always his *petit renard.*"

Chapter 7

When our train arrived in Paris the following afternoon, the rain had begun again. The din and bustle of the swarming crowd at the Gare d'Austerlitz and of the carriage traffic on the street out front contrasted sharply with the peace and tranquility of the countryside of Creuse. Holmes and I waited with our umbrellas up, the pouring rain falling in angled sheets, for a cab to take us to our hotel. We had agreed to meet with Lupin for dinner in the evening after we spoke with the baron.

At our hotel, a letter was waiting for Holmes. He ripped open the envelope, perused the writing quickly, then gave a sharp nod. "Most interesting."

"What is it?" I asked.

"I made some inquiries about the baron with an old friend in Paris. He mentions some interesting rumors."

"Really? What were they?"

Holmes shrugged, then stuffed the envelope and letter into his inside jacket pocket. "We shall see soon enough, Henry."

After getting settled again in our rooms, we set out once more for the mansion on the Île Saint-Louis. The butler greeted us at the door and took our wet overcoats and hats. He said he would announce our arrival, and after we had waited for a while, he reappeared to again lead us up the stairs and through the sitting room before the library.

Angelique sprang up from her chair, smiling eagerly at us. "You are back!" She strode forward. She was wearing a spectacular green silk dress this time. She set her tiny perfect hand on Holmes's arm and whispered softly, "He knows Isidore was with you at the château—be careful."

Holmes nodded, then glanced at me. "The baron must not learn Beautrelet's... secret."

"Certainly not!" I exclaimed.

We went through the tall doors to the library which the butler had opened for us. The baron sat at the head of the massive wooden table, his arms folded, brow furrowed.

Massier sat nearby, and he stood, smiling at us, his sloping bald pate catching the light from a nearby window. "Good afternoon, gentlemen." Massier gestured with his hand at the chairs across the table from him.

The baron's visage radiated disapproval. "Is it true, then, Monsieur Holmes?"

"I am not a mind reader, monsieur le baron." Holmes's voice had a certain edge. "Is what true?"

"That young Beautrelet accompanied you to Creuse."

"I suppose you must have heard something from your friend, Bazin. Yes, that is true."

"He may have pretended to be an Englishman, but the description fit only too well. How dare you involve him in this case! Did I not make it clear to you that I had dismissed him?"

Holmes gave a long sigh. "My reasoning was simple enough. How better to keep an eye on Beautrelet than to let him accompany me? He does not expect payment, but only wishes to work with Sherlock Holmes. Our time together has reinforced my initial impressions. He is harmless enough, an impressionable young man with some promising talent for detection."

The baron's face had grown flushed. "I will not have him pestering Angelique again. I will not stand for it!"

Holmes shrugged. "That is out of my control, but I might point out that if he is with me, he cannot be with her at the same time."

"You state the obvious, monsieur."

Holmes smiled. "Yes."

The baron was still glaring. He undid the buttons of his dark frock coat, letting it fall open to reveal a gray silken waistcoat. His shoulders were broad, but he had a certain stoutness, and his thick neck was fleshy.

"I want you to promise me you will have no further contact with Beautrelet."

Holmes hesitated only an instant. "I shall promise no such thing."

"I can always dismiss you, Monsieur Holmes! You are not indispensable."

"Ah, but then I could not tell you about my major discovery at the château. I have discerned the meaning of *st. s. 138* and found the metaphorical 'key' to the treasure."

Surprise replaced anger in the baron's face. "Is this true?"

"Yes."

"Explain yourself."

"Very well, but I must have your permission to let Beautrelet work with me if I should so choose."

The baron scowled again.

"As I told you, I can keep an eye on him for you, and when he is with me, he cannot be pestering Mademoiselle Chamerac."

Massier nodded, then glanced at the baron. "That makes sense, sir."

Chamerac slowly drew in his breath. "Yes, I suppose it does. Now, tell me what you found at the château."

Holmes told him about deciphering *sommet somme de 138* and how that led eventually to a longcase clock in a certain room at a certain time of day and the discovery of a paper with five lines of mysterious code. No mention was made of finding Lupin's card or anything whatsoever about the gentleman burglar.

"We have deciphered much of the code. The first line is *en aval d'Étretat*, and the last is *l'aiguille creuse*."

Massier's hand formed a fist and tapped the table. "So it is the Needle at Étretat—which must be hollow." He laughed. "A hollow needle, after all, and not the needle of Creuse!"

Holmes nodded. "Exactly. Le Château de l'Aiguille was built in Creuse by Louis the Fourteenth to create a false lead. Only the Chamerac family was given the coded directions to the real location of the treasure."

The baron was frowning slightly. "This paper you found. Let me see it."

Holmes set one hand flat on the table, even as he sat upright in his chair. "For now, it must remain in my possession. We will set out for Étretat in a day or two, and once there, we should be able to discover the way to the treasure."

"Need I remind you again that you are working for me, Monsieur Holmes? Show me the document."

Holmes turned his head ever so slightly to the right, then back again. "I think not. After we have found the way into the Needle, I shall be happy to let you have it."

"But this is outrageous! You said yourself that it belongs to the Chamerac family."

"I assure you it is in good hands and will soon be returned to you."

"I can always dismiss you from the case!"

Holmes smiled ever so faintly. "You can try. Although at this point, I shall not rest until I unravel the secret of the Needle."

The baron set both hands on the table and hunched forward slightly. His dark eyes contained an odd light. "Do you take me for a fool? I know what this means. The blood of the Bourbons flows in my veins, but you want our treasure for yourself! If you find it first, you will steal it from me! Well, I promise I won't let you take it—I shan't allow it!"

Holmes stiffened slightly. "I am not a thief, monsieur le baron. You have my word that I have no intentions of stealing the treasure. I promise I shall reveal its secrets to you, and you can then return it to the people of France—after taking your commission, of course."

"Blast it! I don't trust you!" The baron's face was flushed.

"Unfortunately, you have little choice but to trust me."

Massier had been listening intently, and he spoke. "Why not allow me to come with you as the baron's representative, Monsieur Holmes? I assure you, I am not a fool." He smiled. "I think I might help you. As they say, two heads are better than one."

"Thank you for your offer, Monsieur Massier. I certainly do not take you for a fool—to the contrary!—but I already have Henry and young Beautrelet to assist me. They will certainly suffice. Again, if I discover the way to the treasure, monsieur le baron, you will be the first to know about it. You can then come to Étretat and have a look in person."

The baron was still flushed. "I do not approve of your methods, Sherlock Holmes. I most assuredly do not. I wish I had never employed you!"

"Ah, but then you would not know about the hollow needle at Étretat. Be patient a while longer. I am quite hopeful that within another week or so I shall have uncovered the truth, once and for all, about the grand treasure of the Needle."

The baron glared at him. "I see little point in prolonging this meeting."

"Nor do I." Holmes nodded and stood up. "I have a few lines of inquiry to follow here in Paris before we leave, but we should certainly be in Étretat by the day after tomorrow. I shall keep you informed."

The baron nodded, but did not speak. He remained seated, while Massier rose and went to the doors, which he opened for us.

Massier's fingers disappeared into his thick black beard as he scratched his chin. "Good hunting, Monsieur Holmes." He added more softly. "I hope to see you soon."

Holmes and I went into the sitting room, and the doors closed behind us. Angelique was back in the burgundy velvet chair by a window. She looked warily about, then rose and came toward us, smiling.

"You seem none the worse for wear," she said.

Holmes shrugged. "I'm afraid the baron is not very happy with me just now."

"I am so glad you took Isidore with you, Monsieur Holmes! What made you change your mind?"

"Oh, I had my reasons."

"He is clever, is he not?"

Holmes gave a sharp laugh. "That he is, mademoiselle. He most assuredly is."

"Perhaps if he helps you, you can put in a good word for him with the baron."

"I certainly shall, I promise you."

"Have you found out the truth about the treasure, monsieur?"

"Perhaps."

"And where is it hidden?"

Holmes only smiled at her question. She touched his arm with her fingertips and laughed softly. "Of course you cannot tell me! Well, I wish you and Isidore luck in your quest."

"Thank you, mademoiselle."

Holmes and I soon stepped outside into the foggy mists and cold drizzle. We took a cab back to the hotel, and that evening, we met Lupin (still in the personage of Beautrelet) for dinner at the hotel restaurant. He questioned us about our visit with the baron and was amused to hear that the baron was outraged at Beautrelet's involvement.

"It was wise of you not to show him the document, Holmes. He could never figure out anything on his own, but that secretary of his is a wily sort of fellow. And Angelique—you must tell me of Angelique! I do hope to see her briefly before our departure for Normandy."

"Is that wise?" I asked.

"Ah, Doctor, one asks the brain to be wise, but never the heart!"

During the meal, he and Holmes discussed, in a leisurely manner, some memorable thefts in which they had been involved, Lupin in perpetrating them, Holmes in solving them. Finally, as we sipped some cognac after the meal, Lupin exclaimed, "A lucky thing for me that there is no Sherlock Holmes here in Paris, but only Ganimard! All the same, I propose a toast, gentlemen: to crime, which has kept both Sherlock Holmes and myself gainfully employed."

Holmes laughed, I shook my head, and we all clinked glasses.

Holmes told us that the next day would be a busy one. He was going to a bank first thing in the morning, the Crédit Lyonnais, to seek some information about the baron. Would Lupin like to come along?

Lupin nodded eagerly. "And would you prefer the company of Beautrelet or Lupin?"

"Neither exactly," Holmes said, "but some gentleman in the usual formal daytime dress."

"Black frock coat and gray-and-black striped trousers, you mean? Done."

"Oh, and one another thing, Monsieur Beautrelet. I managed to secure a box at the opera tomorrow evening for a special performance of Massenet's *Manon* with Sybil Sanderson. It will be agreeable to have a brief pause from the case of Needle, before heading off to Normandy the morning after. Would you care to join Henry and me?"

Lupin set down his glass abruptly. "Would I? Of course I would! As a devotee of the theater and an actor myself, I have always had a great love for musical drama. Regrettably, I never had any formal training as a singer, but Lupin has attended many an opera performance. Verdi and Wagner are particular favorites, but as a patriotic Frenchman, I do admire Massenet! But how ever did you manage to get a box on such short notice?"

Holmes smiled faintly. "Some time ago, I helped the management at the Palais Garnier resolve a problem with a certain Opera Ghost, so they are only too happy to oblige me whenever I am in Paris."

We chatted a while longer, even as the restaurant emptied out. Lupin finally pulled out his watch. It was well after ten. We all rose, and he shook hands with us both before departing.

I watched him leave, then glanced at Holmes. "He is a fascinating young man."

"Indeed he is. He is certainly the most charming burglar I have ever encountered."

The headquarters of the Crédit Lyonnais, also known as the Hôtel des Italiens because it fronted the Boulevard des Italiens in the second arrondissement, was a huge, grandiose, and slightly overblown construction in the bombastic Haussmann style of the Second Empire. Flattened stone bricks imitating columns lined the many square windows, and the main entrance had a grand stone arch, as did the window directly above on the second floor. Higher still was an ornate clock perhaps ten feet tall, with two sculpted damsels in flowing robes on either side. At the very top, set in relief below another arch, five figures (banking deities?) were sprawled about just beneath the gray-blue slate roof.

I was familiar with the building because I had banked there when I had lived in Paris. When we went inside, we could hear a sort of muted din caused by a great crowd of people all trying not to be too noisy as they went about their business. The vast interior hall opened up to the ceiling far above, and you could see the offices on the sides up two or three floors, while at our level, counters lined the two long sides of the rectangular space, counters staffed by employees working with clients. In the center of the hall was a long row of tall tables, along with benches, where people filled out checks, deposit or withdrawal slips in preparation.

Holmes, who had transformed himself into an old man, complete with white mustache and eyebrows, spoke to one of the attendants standing stiffly near the entrance. The man nodded, then led us down the great hall to a spectacular double spiral staircase supposedly modeled after the one at the famed Château de Chambord on the Loire. A plush red carpet covered the steps. We went up to the third floor, then halfway down a corridor.

The attendant paused before a formidable door of dark oak. "Please wait here for a minute, messieurs." He knocked lightly, then stepped inside.

"Remember," Holmes said sternly, even as he gazed at Lupin, "let me do the talking."

Lupin smiled, the corners of his mouth rising into the impressive brown fake mustache. He was dressed impeccably and might have been an employee of the bank himself. "Of course."

The attendant reappeared and led us into a huge office. A tall portly man in an immaculately tailored black frock coat with gold buttons came around a desk larger than my dining-room table. Only a few wispy strands covered his bald pate, but he had a thick full beard and mustache, salt-and-pepper colored. The round lenses of his pince-nez shrank his dark eyes, and the black cord on the right side of the silver frame dangled down to a shirt button. He extended a great paw of a hand to shake Holmes's slender one.

"Monsieur Smythe, a great pleasure," he said. "I am Yves Albret, the chief loan officer for the bank."

"The pleasure is mine, Monsieur Albret. These are my associates, Monsieur George Louve..." Lupin shook Albret's hand. "And Monsieur Henri Croquette."

Albret had a formidable grip. He gestured toward a nearby small table with sturdy wooden chairs with hefty arms, their curvy ends shiny with wear. "Please, have a seat, messieurs." We all sat, and Albret folded his burly arms. "Since you asked for me in particular, I assume this must be about a loan. Are you a client of the bank?"

"I am not, monsieur." Holmes gave his voice a certain raspy croaky quality appropriate for his age. "It is about a loan, but not for me exactly."

"Explain yourself, Monsieur Smythe."

Holmes stroked his chin thoughtfully, then lowered his hand. "First, let me ask, do you know the Baron de Creuse, Frédéric Chamerac?"

A certain wariness showed in Albret's eyes, and a few seconds passed before he answered. "I have that pleasure."

Holmes smiled. "Ah. And I suppose you know him professionally through your office here at the bank?"

Albret was frowning outright. "Monsieur Smythe, we do not discuss our clients with others."

"Come now, sir. The baron does business with the Crédit Lyonnais. A recent check from him has told me that much, and I know he must have come to see you within the last few months."

"And how would you know that?"

"Because he wants to borrow a very large sum of money from me."

"*What?*" Albret's dismay was obvious enough, but he did his best to quickly hide it.

"Yes, he wants to borrow half a million francs."

The blood drained from Albret's face. "Are you serious?"

"I am always serious when it comes to my money, Monsieur Albret. I am lucky enough to have a large fortune, and I don't wish to squander it on bad loans. That's why I came to see you."

Albret gave a great sigh. "Monsieur Smythe, as I said, I cannot discuss our clients with you. It would be most unprofessional."

Holmes raised one bushy white eyebrow. "Not even a hint or two?"

"No."

"I see. A pity. On a related matter... I suppose the bank does not generally make unsecured loans. You would demand something in collateral."

Albret was watching Holmes cautiously. He nodded. "Yes, that is certainly the case. Like most lenders, we want to know that, one way or another, we will be paid."

Holmes nodded. "Most wise! Most wise! And I, of course, feel exactly the same way. What would you say if I told you the baron has offered to put up his town house and the Château de Creuse as collateral?"

Albret was still very pale, and he almost seemed to wince slightly. "What?"

"You heard me. He said he would put up his town house and the château as collateral on the loan."

This time Albret's cheeks swelled up, and then he let out a puff of air. "Indeed."

"What do you say about that?"

"I cannot... I cannot possibly comment."

"Of course, if he has already used them as collateral on another loan, that would change everything. And if I loaned him the money, it could create an interesting conflict as to which lender truly had the rights to the properties."

This time Albret did not hesitate. "The first lender's right would take precedence."

"A court of law might not see it that way." Holmes leaned forward slightly. "Better by far to avoid the possibility of such an unpleasant situation and the ensuing conflict. We can end this conversation rather simply with a mere nod on your part. He has offered his town house and the château as collateral on a loan from the Crédit Lyonnais, has he not?"

Albret's face was scrunched up as if in pain, his lips tightly clenched.

"A simple nod will be enough, and will save us all a great deal of trouble."

Albret jerked his head spasmodically downward, then up, and drew in his breath.

Holmes grinned, then stood up. "I thank you for your time, Monsieur Albret. It has been a great pleasure. And be assured, in the unlikely event that I need a loan at some point in the future, I will surely come to the Crédit Lyonnais for my needs."

Lupin heaved a great sigh, which made Albret notice him for perhaps the first time. Lupin shook his head. "This is all something of a dreadful surprise. If only I had listened to you, Smythe! You tried to warn me. But I would not listen."

Holmes stared warily at him. "I did try to warn you."

"I was not so wise as you. I should have admitted all straightaway—that I foolishly trusted the baron and gave him half a million!" Lupin stood and gestured with one hand. "And he did offer up the château and his town house to me as collateral."

Albret stared at him with horror but could not seem to speak.

Holmes's brow had creased. "A good thing, Louve, that you are so incredibly wealthy. Half a million is only a pittance to you."

Lupin grinned, genuinely amused. "Indeed it is."

"You can easily absorb such a loss."

"So I can!"

"And you would never dream of contesting the rights to the château and the town house with the bank."

Lupin gave an emphatic nod. "Certainly not! Even if my loan were prior to that of the bank, which seems unlikely, I would not wish to make any unnecessary trouble for the Crédit Lyonnais, an institution for which I have the greatest admiration. Indeed I have been considering..."

Holmes seized his arm above the elbow. "We have taken enough of Monsieur Albret's time, and as you know, I have other urgent business to look after. Let us run along." He aimed Lupin for the door and started forward, hobbling slightly in an old man's walk, and I followed them. Holmes glanced back at Albret, and tapped twice at the side of his head with a forefinger, even as he nodded in Lupin's direction, the obvious implication being that Lupin was slightly daft.

Albret didn't say anything. He had come around the table and followed us to the door. He stared warily, perhaps considering whether or not to shake hands, but in the end, he only nodded, his voice rumbling, "Good day."

We started down the corridor. Holmes shook his head. "I thought I told you to be on your best behavior, Isidore."

Lupin grinned. "Oh, you must allow me to have a little fun with a pompous functionary such as our Monsieur Albret. I'll wager that's more excitement than he has had for a very long time. But well done, Holmes! It is a pleasure to see you at work, and quite instructive, as well. I had heard rumors that the baron was in debt, but I had no idea..."

"Why would he have needed so large sum of money?" I asked. "I don't understand."

"He is not a gambler," Lupin said. "I would have heard about that."

Holmes scratched at his chin. "I believe he wants the treasure of the Needle for some definite reason, and I intend to discover it."

We started down the spiral staircase, then went through the great hall with its crowd of bankers and clients, and back outside.

The sun had come out, some blue sky showing, and the cool air had a fresh tang.

Holmes withdrew his watch from his waistcoat pocket. "We can perhaps have an early lunch, and then I wish to see certain people this afternoon, on my own. However, I think someone needs to keep an eye on you, Monsieur Lupin—especially after your behavior at the bank! Perhaps I shall entrust Henry with the task."

I nodded. "Very well."

Lupin smiled. "You don't trust me, Holmes?"

"Let us just say I think someone needs to keep you out of trouble until we leave for Normandy tomorrow."

"Very well, but you will have to have faith in me during the dinner hour. Or rather, you can rely on my friend Leblanc to keep me out of trouble. He and I are to dine together tonight. And of course afterwards, I shall join you at the opera."

Holmes nodded. "Yes, but do not come as Beautrelet or as Lupin. I don't wish to be seen with either of them in so public a place as the opera house. Who knows who might be in attendance tonight?"

Lupin laughed. "I shall surprise you."

Lupin withdrew a key from his pocket and unlocked the door to his rooms. He pushed it open and extended an arm. "After you, Doctor."

I stepped inside, and he followed. He had picked up his mail, and he glanced briefly at two envelopes. "I think I recognize this writing." He eagerly tore it open. As he scanned the words, his mouth formed a smile. "Ah, excellent!"

"What is it?"

He handed it over, and I read the brief note: *I must see you about an urgent matter. I hope you will be home at three o'clock. Yours sincerely, Angelique.*

I shook my head. "The two of you are playing with fire. This is most indiscreet."

"It is, isn't it? How delightful! She has never come here before. It's not like her to breach the rules of decorum. It must be something important. You will have to leave us alone for that time."

I felt myself frowning. "I am not so sure about that."

"Come now, Doctor! I have the highest respect for her. Indeed, my intentions are most honorable. As I've said, twenty-five is a good age at which to marry."

"All the same…"

Someone knocked at the door. "Isidore?" It was a woman's voice.

"Good Lord," I murmured.

Lupin looked at the clock. "It's only two—she's an hour early! Quick." He took my arm and guided me across the cluttered sitting room toward a door. "You can hide in the bedroom."

"Are you serious?"

"You said you didn't want to leave us alone!" The room was in a certain disarray, the bed unmade. He pulled off the frock coat, then quickly stepped out of one pair of trousers and into another, and grabbed his usual worn brown coat.

I stared at him, frowning. "The mustache—don't forget the mustache."

"Blast it! You're right." He went to a mirror with a basin below, splashed water on his hands, then wet the mustache, and soon pulled away half of it. A tearing sound was accompanied by a muted yelp. The rest soon followed, and then he put the towel in the water and wiped vigorously at his upper lip. "That hurt. Remember—stay quiet."

He went quickly through the door, closing it behind him. I gave a great sigh and shook my head. I looked around the room, grabbed a chair near a desk, set it near the door, and sat down.

"There you are—oh, I'm so glad you are here! I was so afraid." Angelique's voice was easy to make out, only slightly muted by the door.

"Calm yourself, my dear. What is the matter?" Lupin's voice had the higher pitch and the slight wobble of Beautrelet.

"What's wrong with your upper lip?"

"I… I scraped it shaving. Now what is it that you have to tell me, and why have you come so early?"

"I'm afraid my uncle found out I was planning to see you. My maid has been spying for him, and I was foolish enough to trust her and confide in her. He was furious. He is sending some thugs to give you a good thrashing, as he put it. He hopes they will hurt you badly enough that you won't be able to go with Sherlock Holmes to Étretat."

There was a brief silence. "Not very original of him, after all."

"This is no joke, Isidore."

"No, I understand that."

"You must stay away from here until you leave tomorrow. It's not safe. Perhaps you could go to a hotel."

"I suppose that would be wise. I wish…"

"What do you wish?"

"I wish I were more… physical. That I was the type who might thrash these men instead."

"How can you even think of such a thing?"

"Don't worry, I'm not so foolhardy. I know I am a man of brain rather than brawn, but I do hate to appear a weakling in your eyes."

"Oh Isidore, I like you just as you are. I would not have you be a ruffian."

"I am glad to hear it, dearest Angelique. And I am glad to see that you care enough for me that you have come to warn me." There was a brief silence. "You do care, don't you?"

"Yes."

Another pregnant silence followed. At last: "Ah, I see that you do—your lips are a true paradise! Angelique, I am certain Holmes and I shall find the treasure, and my share in the reward will make me a wealthy man. If all goes well, why don't we marry when I return?"

"Are you joking?"

"Not in the least. I do love you, you know." The pitch of Lupin's voice had lowered, and he sounded grave.

"I… I must think about it. It is not that I don't care for you, but my uncle would… I hate to think what he might do. He might… he *would* say bad things about me. He would make up lies."

"I don't care what he says."

"Isidore, we don't have time for this. I must go—and you must flee before these men arrive."

"It is only a little after two. There's no great hurry."

"Please, I must leave. Go now—promise me you'll go—swear it!"

"Very well. I promise you Isidore Beautrelet will be long gone from here at three o'clock. These men will not find him on the premises. You go ahead and run along. I've only a thing or two to do, and my bag to grab."

"You promise you will be gone?"

"I do, although if you give me another kiss that would encourage me all the more."

After a silence, she murmured, "You are incorrigible."

"Goodbye, my dearest."

The door closed noisily. I put my hand on my forehead, then shook my head. The bedroom door swung open and Lupin appeared, beaming. "It's safe now. She's gone. You know, I do think she is coming around."

"She was right about one thing. You are incorrigible. You had better grab your bag, and we can get away before these men arrive."

"Oh, I don't plan on going anywhere. I want to meet these rogues."

"Now that is asking for trouble! Besides, I heard you promise her."

"I said Beautrelet would be long gone. And so he shall." He grinned. "But Lupin is another matter! And he *is* physical."

I shook my head. "Holmes was right that it would not be wise to leave you on your own for the afternoon."

Lupin seized the chair and set it before a vanity and a mirror. "There is no time to waste." He opened the top drawer and took out a black wig. After removing his spectacles, he carefully pulled it over his short brown hair, then fluffed at the sides a bit.

It took him fifteen minutes or so to transform into Lupin. He worked quickly, but with great skill. I watched him build up the black mustache gradually, adding a layer of hair to the spirit gum, then trimming it neatly. He did the left side first, then the right. Finally he used some putty and makeup to create the small scar on his right cheek.

He took off his spectacles, seized the monocle and fitted it over his right eye, scrunching the muscles around the socket. "There! How do I look?"

"Quite transformed. The mustache is a work of art. So you do not use the kind you can stick on all at once, which comes with a backing?"

"Those are cheap trash! Less than worthless. Only a rank amateur would use one."

Rising, he slipped off the braces to his trousers, and soon stood in his underwear. He quickly donned black formal trousers, shiny black shoes, a fresh white shirt, and white waistcoat, and then he fastened a fresh collar about his neck. Last came the white bow tie and black formal jacket with silken lapels. He bent sideway to grasp the slightly curved silver handle of his fancy ebony stick. Again, the monocle was set in place over his right eye, a black ribbon now attaching it to a shirt button.

"*Voici Monsieur Arsène Lupin!*" His voice had a baritone's resonance.

"Bravo, Monsieur Lupin. Well done indeed."

Some loud pounding came from the sitting room. "*Ouvrez la porte!*" someone bellowed.

Lupin smiled at me. "Well, we are ready for them, are we not, Doctor?"

He strode past me, grasped the door handle firmly and pulled it open. A fist and forearm arched downward through the opening, missing the door.

"Please, messieurs! What is this din? What is this impertinence? You do not pound on a gentleman's door in such a rude and uncouth manner."

There were three of them, two big men and one skinny one, in dark suits of rough wool and flat cloth caps. The tallest, burliest one, the apparent ringleader, had a cauliflower ear, a bulbous nose, and the skin of his face was a blotchy red. Clearly, he had done some boxing in his day. His forehead creased in puzzlement. "You don't look like Beautrelet. Where is he?"

"How very astute of you! I do not look like Beautrelet because I am not Beautrelet. He has left for the day."

"That's not him behind you, is it?"

"No, certainly not. That is Dr. Henry Vernier, a friend."

"Damnation! You're sure Beautrelet won't be back today?"

"Quite sure. He was warned you were coming, you see."

"Warned? Who told him?"

"I am not at liberty to say."

The burly man gave him a hard look. "You must be a friend of his."

"I am indeed. We are, so to speak, inseparable."

Despite the aura of menace from the men, this remark made me smile.

"Then maybe we can use you to send him a sort of message."

"Oh, I would happy to relay to him a message."

"I wasn't thinking about a message in words."

"I suspected that might be the case." Lupin gave a long, rather theatrical sigh, even as he stepped well away from the door. His right eye opened slightly wider, and the monocle popped out and flopped down, hanging suspended by its ribbon. "It's no doubt a waste of time, but I'm giving you a polite warning to leave now. It will not end well if you try to leave a *message* with me."

The big man laughed. "Oh dear, you're scaring me." He turned to the others. "Aren't you afraid?" He stepped into the room.

Lupin backed away slightly, twirled the stick, then lashed out and struck the man across the shins. The thwack made me wince. He screamed and instinctively bent over to protect his legs. As he did so, Lupin brought the stick down on his head. The man collapsed, sprawling across the floor.

His big companion came through the door, cosh in hand. Lupin retreated, raising the stick extended, almost like a fencing foil, grasped by the silver handle. The man stepped over his fallen comrade, then hesitated, suddenly wary. Lupin was smiling and tracing a small circle with the brass-shod head of the stick. "I would suggest you take your friend and return to the baron. You can lie and simply tell him no one was home."

The man frowned slightly, and you could tell he was considering the suggestion. The skinny man seemed frozen in the doorway, unable to move. The man with the cosh stiffened, then took a resolute step forward. Lupin moved incredibly fast. He lunged, then struck, hitting him first on the left shoulder, then on the right hand; the cosh dropped to the ground. Lupin twirled the stick in a blur of motion, tossed it and grasped the brass end, then used the silver hooked handle to pull the man's right leg out from under him. He toppled over backwards onto the one already down.

Wide-eyed, the remaining man in the doorway half opened his mouth, the fingers of both hands outspread. He was missing teeth. He gave his head half a shake, then turned and fled. The second man down rolled off the other, staggered to his knees and reached toward the cosh he had dropped, but Lupin used the stick to push it away.

"I think not. I'll keep it as a souvenir. I would suggest you help your friend up, and then take your leave. I mostly spared your heads—I only stunned him this time. I really do not wish to start breaking jaws or fracturing skulls, but I warn you, I shall be less merciful in the next round."

The man rose to his feet, then helped the other one stagger up. The leader with the cauliflower ear blinked dully, closed his eyes and gave his head a half shake. His companion bent over and recovered their caps which had fallen off; he put his own on his head, then took his friend by the arm and turned him toward the doorway.

"We weren't paid for this," he mumbled. "And you aren't Beautrelet, anyhow."

Lupin nodded. "Very wise of you."

They stepped outside, and Lupin used the end of the stick to swing around the open door, then gave it a final push with the stick to close it. He shook his head. "I must confess I feel rather sorry for them. They are the most common sort, only good at dealing with weaklings or dullards—and that when they greatly outnumber their opponents."

"You certainly handle a stick well. The only person I have seen who might compare with you is Sherlock Holmes."

"You flatter me, Doctor, but I am glad to hear it!" He set the tip of his stick on the floor, and leaned on the handle slightly with both his arms. He was not in the least winded. "Well, I have another hour or two before Leblanc arrives. Rather early for an aperitif, but perhaps we could sit outside and have coffee and a pastry?"

"Given the perfect weather, that seems an excellent suggestion."

"I'm a bit overdressed for midafternoon, but..." He shrugged. "It was good of Angelique to give me a warning. I don't know how Beautrelet would have handled them. I'm afraid I would have given myself away." He smiled. "It's as I said: I do think she is coming around!"

I frowned. "You actually proposed to her."

"So I did, Doctor. So I did."

"And do you... do you really love her?"

He drew in his breath slowly. "Oh yes, from the very first time I saw her. It was the veritable lightning strike."

We were speaking French, and he used the expression *coup de foudre*, which literally meant lightning strike, but which was used for "lovestruck" or "love at first sight."

"Interesting is it not, that *coup de foudre* contains the word *fou*?" *Fou* was "fool" or "foolish," but also could mean "mad" or "crazy." "That's appropriate enough—I am indeed *fou d'amour!*"

Chapter 8

Holmes and I returned together to the hotel shortly after five, and when we entered the large lobby filled with spacious leather furniture and those big potted ferns, Louis Massier looked up from a newspaper spread out before him. He gave us a slight nod, folded the newspaper and set it aside, then stood up and came forward. He wore his usual dark wool suit, a blue color almost black, with matching waistcoat and a black cravat. With his height, full black beard, and massive chest, his was an imposing presence.

"Here you are at last."

Holmes stared closely at Massier, a faint hesitance in his eyes. "Do you have a message from the baron?"

Massier shook his head. "I do not." The corners of his mouth rose ever so slightly into the hairs of his black mustache, and he stroked briefly at his full thick beard. "I have a proposition of my own."

Holmes gave a faint nod. "Ah, I see."

"Perhaps we could have an aperitif and discuss the details. There is a bar nearby which serves an excellent absinthe cocktail, Le Dragon Vert."

"I have already sampled its wares, and I don't think I would care for something quite so strong as absinthe. We shall be attending the opera this evening, so I want to remain alert."

Massier's head gave a slight twist. "*Manon?*"

"Yes. Are you attending as well?"

"No, I do not much care for grand opera, but the baron will be there."

"Will he? I shall have to keep an eye out for him. Perhaps we should simply have a drink in the hotel restaurant. Our time is limited, Monsieur Massier."

"As you wish. I don't think this matter will take long."

We were soon seated in a corner table. Holmes mentioned the quality of their Armagnac, and soon the waiter brought us three glasses upon a tray.

Massier took his, held up the bowl and turned it slightly. "Excellent color." He gave it a sip. "You were not exaggerating, Monsieur Holmes, it is very good indeed." He had unbuttoned his suit jacket, and the bright golden arc of his watch chain stood out against his waistcoat.

Holmes sipped, set down his glass and settled back in his chair. "What is this proposition of yours, Monsieur Massier?"

Massier turned the glass ever so slightly again, swirling the brownish liquid. "Well, let me be quite direct and to the point. Believe me, the baron cannot be trusted. He is… how can I put this delicately? He is unbalanced. You have not seen him at his worst. At times his insanity becomes quite obvious. And he has certain delusions—such as this obsession about the sacred Bourbon blood flowing in his veins. I propose that we form an alliance, you and I, to seek out the treasure. When we find it, we shall share the proceeds fifty-fifty."

Holmes's slight smile was bitter. "And nothing for the baron?"

"No. It certainly doesn't belong to him, and the French kings are no more. In the end, the treasure is just pilfered loot taken by royal thieves. And besides, the baron is already a rich man."

"Come now, Monsieur Massier, I think you know better. He has enormous debts."

Massier gave an appreciative nod. "Ah, you know about that! He can repay them even without the treasure."

"How?"

"He has certain... tangible assets."

"His town house and the château, you mean?"

"Not just those."

Holmes stared very closely at Massier. "Some other... constructions?"

Massier laughed. "Very good, Monsieur Holmes! But I must keep some secrets of my own. Let's forget about the baron for now. If you share that piece of paper with me, I'm confident we can discern its meaning together. I have certain analytical skills, and I also know Normandy rather well. Let me come with you. Why not join forces?"

Holmes's smile grew ironic. "I already have young Beautrelet helping me."

"Young Beautrelet!" Massier's tone was scornful. "He is overrated, I assure you, and he was not smart enough to leave Angelique alone. Besides, I don't think he will be in any condition to help you. Not after this afternoon."

"You must be thinking of the thugs the baron sent to beat him up," I said. "They were not successful. He will be joining us tomorrow."

Massier frowned. "Not successful? But how is that possible?"

I smiled. "I must keep some secrets of my own."

Holmes laughed. "Very good, Henry."

Massier shook his head. "Why work with a boy when you can work with a man? He is a rank amateur, highly overrated."

"Oh, I don't know," Holmes said. "I have found him to be quite clever. Besides, you forget that I gave the baron my word I would not keep the treasure for myself."

Massier's great black eyebrows came together. "You actually meant that?"

Holmes laughed. "Yes."

Massier shrugged. "Well, you will not be keeping it for *yourself*. You will be splitting it with *me*."

Holmes was still smiling. "I see you excel at sophistry. Unfortunately for you, my word is my word—it is my bond. I do not go back on it."

Massier shook his head. "Very well. The more pity you."

"You, on the other hand, obviously feel no loyalty toward your employer."

Massier laughed. "Let's just say I have grown weary of his antics! I have worked with him for five years, and he does not wear well. He has also grown more and more erratic and unstable. He can simply not be trusted. I hope you understand that—you may keep your word, but if he gets the treasure, neither you nor I are likely to receive any share at all. And certainly the people of France will not get a penny! That is why keeping your word in this case is foolish."

"When I give my word, it is not conditional." Holmes stared closely at Massier, his gray eyes intense. "Five years is a long time."

"Yes—an eternity, I assure you, when you are with someone as innately boorish as him."

"So you were there when he took in his niece?"

"Yes, of course I was."

"Five years…" Holmes murmured. "I suspect you know all his secrets—including why he wants that treasure so badly."

"I do know them all—everything, all the secrets, all the skeletons in the closet—and I can share them with you, if you will agree to work with me and split the treasure."

Holmes sipped at his drink. "You already have my answer."

Massier shook his head. "Then there is little use in prolonging this conversation." He downed the last of his Armagnac. "Well, you have made it clear that the treasure must be inside the Needle at Étretat. And who knows? There may be another way in besides the one described on your paper." He smiled. "We shall see who gets there first." He set one hand on the table, preparing to rise, but Holmes raised his hand to signal that he should wait.

"Before you go, one secret is not, I think, the baron's, but your own. You arranged to have that potted plant dropped from the hotel window, did you not?"

Massier grinned. "Very good, Monsieur Holmes! I did indeed. Of course, I was quite precise in my instructions that you were not to be harmed. It was only meant as a warning. I was, so to speak, trying to test your mettle, and I wanted to see if I could scare you off. I did not want any useless competition in the search for the treasure. Getting my share already seemed problematic enough. But in the end you did far better than me at Creuse, and I am glad you do not frighten easily. I apologize for unnecessarily disturbing you."

Holmes nodded. "Apology accepted."

I was not so easily placated. "Well, I don't accept it."

"Sorry, Dr. Vernier." Massier had stood and had his hat in his left hand. "Good day, gentlemen, and thanks for the aperitif. I am sorry we could not reach an agreement, but I am sure I shall see you again soon—at Étretat." With a slight bow, he strode away.

I shook my head. "I don't think he can be trusted any more than the baron. They are both scoundrels."

Holmes smiled. "I must agree with you there, Henry! After a meeting with a person such as Monsieur Massier, one feels the need to thoroughly wash one's hands with hot water and soap."

Holmes and I paused at the foot of the grandest of grand stairways, that of the Palais Garnier, the Paris Opera House.

The steps before us were made of white marble, the balusters of the railing a dark crimson or even green marble, and to our side, two heroic damsels sculpted in dark bronze held candelabras with flaming candles. Indeed, one ornate candelabra with many candles had somehow sprouted from the upper figure's sculpted head! Over us were balconies and chandeliers, and a cavernous opening that rose a few stories to the ornate glass dome far above.

On the stairs thronged the high society of Paris come for this gala performance. While the majority of men were "crows" (mostly in black—formal black tailcoats and trousers, with either black waistcoats or white ones of silk, and bow ties, also in white or black), also scattered about were a few brilliant "peacocks" (soldiers in gaudy uniforms of red and blue, with gold braid or epaulets). The women, however, wore colorful silken dresses: shades of rose, blue, lavender, even a brilliant scarlet; and their shoulders and necks were generally bare. But jeweled necklaces or pendants—emeralds, sapphires, diamonds, rubies—or pearls, rested upon the exposed skin of their decolletages.

Holmes and I plunged into the crowd. Halfway up, the stairway divided in two, branching in either direction, and Holmes and I went to the left. Our destination was Box 5, the one which the "Opera Ghost" had demanded be reserved for him, but the Phantom was long gone and presumed dead. Holmes and I were the only ones present who knew that Eric, the tormented genius with the hideous face, had found happiness elsewhere at last. However, the opera management still generally left Box 5 empty, except when Holmes requested it. We two knew it was perfectly safe. We went down a carpeted corridor and opened the door with ornate carvings and the number 5 in brass.

The location was ideal, very close to the stage, now hidden by the great curtain. We were on the first floor up, the third box over on the left side. Above us rose two more floors of boxes, then the fourth floor with the *paradis*, or upper balcony. The fronts of the boxes and the occasional pillars, which formed a horseshoe shape, were all elaborately decorated in gold, while the interiors and the chairs were red. I glanced up at the domed ceiling with its paintings and the massive chandelier, and a shiver went up my spine as I recalled when its predecessor had come crashing down that time Holmes and I were investigating the Opera Ghost.

Someone rapped at the door. I turned and went to open it. Before me was a figure I recognized at once, a bent old man in a black soutane with an oversized black overcoat, a brimmed hat clutched in one hand, a cane in the other. Spectacles of blue glass hid his eyes, and his long white hair was all astray.

"*You*," I murmured. "What do you want this time?"

Behind me, Holmes spoke. "Come in, Isidore."

The old man smiled, briefly breaking character. "Thank you, Monsieur Holmes."

I sighed wearily. "I do hate disguises."

Lupin came into the loge, and I closed the door. He was back in character, bent over and perched on the cane. He advanced slowly forward, and I followed.

"Very nice, Monsieur Holmes." His voice was a raspy whisper. "A great view of the stage and—*mon Dieu!*—also of Mademoiselle Chamerac."

I glanced to the right where Lupin was staring. The boxes were separated by partitions covered with red fabric, partitions which sloped downward so that one's neighbors were only partly hidden. As our row of boxes curved off to the right round the auditorium, more and more of the interiors were revealed, and in a box about ten distant from ours, just before a pillar, sat the trio of Chameracs behind the golden railing. The Baron of Creuse was in the center, his wife to his right, his niece to the left.

The baron and his wife were in black, but Angelique wore an elaborately patterned ivory silk gown which left her shoulders and decolletage bare. The dress and her bound-up blond hair accentuated her long slender neck, and a jewel on her left ear sparkled as she moved. She wore a gold necklace with a pendant of gems which also caught the light. She was quite the vision of youth and beauty, especially alongside her aunt and uncle. The baron appeared almost fat and faintly comical with that enormous waxed mustache, while his wife seemed scrawny, and had what must be a perpetually weary, sour look. Her black dress was modest, and she wore no jewelry whatsoever. The faces of the baron and his niece showed a certain self-assurance, something so similar that I wondered if it might be a shared hereditary trait manifesting itself, although his expression veered more toward hauteur and arrogance.

"She is lovely, is she not?" Lupin murmured softly in his own voice.

I nodded. "That she is."

Holmes was staring at the baron's box, too, but he remained silent, his eyes stern.

"Can you blame me for loving her? With my share of the treasure I shall be able to shower her with jewels and the finest gowns." He must have noticed something in my look. "What is it?"

"A beautiful woman doesn't really need jewels and fancy gowns. In the end they are... superfluous." I was thinking of Michelle and how I found her the most stunning with nothing on at all. But of course, I could never say such a thing aloud!

Lupin shrugged. "Perhaps not. But you will never convince a woman of that! At heart, they are all like our Manon."

"Ah," I said, "so you have seen the opera before. Have you also read the book?"

"Certainly, as an adolescent. With its scandalous reputation you could not keep me from it."

I laughed. "It had the same sordid appeal to me as a youth, but I found it rather tedious and not in the least salacious."

Holmes smiled faintly. "I believe we are in agreement on the merits of the book."

From the pit, we heard the orchestra players begin tuning their instruments, and the three of us sat down in the plush chairs. The conductor with his corona of white hair strode to the podium, bowed to the crowd, and then, with a drum roll, the sprightly music of the overture began. In comparison with Verdi and Wagner, the two famed composers of our day, Massenet's music lacked true drama, but it had a certain Gallic elegance and charm. Soon the curtain rose on a pastoral scene before a country inn.

The opera *Manon* is based on the eighteenth-century novel, *Histoire du chevalier Des Grieux, et de Manon Lescaut* by the Abbé

Prévost. Both tell the same tale of the infatuated nobleman Des Grieux who falls hard for the country girl Manon. She is on the way to the convent, when they meet at the ripe old age of seventeen for him, sixteen for her, and both are smitten by the classic French *coup de foudre*. Des Grieux vows to save her from a life of celibacy, and they flee to Paris where they live in sin and quickly burn through his meager funds.

In the book, Des Grieux tells his own story, recounting the ups and downs of the relationship (and their finances), including Manon's occasional betrayals for richer suitors. Des Grieux is all overblown and hysterical emotion. He will lie, cheat, and do anything to keep Manon. He borrows money from a long-suffering friend with little intention of paying it back. He deceives several older men who trust him, including his father. He even shoots a man dead while helping Manon escape from prison and shows little remorse, blaming it on Manon's brother for foolishly lending him a loaded pistol!

The opera began with a raucous crowd coming and going before the inn, but soon a coach arrived and Manon made her first appearance. The soprano in the first *Manon* I had seen two years before had been close to forty and quite plump. The singer tonight was Sibyl Sanderson, supposedly the favorite of Massenet, and she looked more the part. Sanderson was still in her twenties, slender in her modest peasant's dress, and she had a lovely effortless voice. Soon Des Grieux made his appearance dressed in an elegant gold and white coat, brown breeches and a tricorn hat, and the tenor too was quite convincing in his lovestruck ardor. After the two rushed offstage together, ready to leave for Paris, the audience applauded loudly.

Holmes leaned toward me. "They are quite good, much more believable as youthful lovers than the last pair we saw."

I nodded. "I was thinking the same thing."

Lupin briefly turned toward the Chamerac box, then sighed softly. "Ah, I know just how Des Grieux feels!" His youthful voice was something of a surprise coming from so convincingly aged a visage. The blue glass of his spectacles hid his eyes.

I smiled faintly. "So you wish to run off with Mademoiselle Chamerac and live in sin with her?"

"Certainly not! Despite my profession as gentleman burglar, I am not lacking in moral scruples. I respect the lady too much to propose such a thing. Besides, I am not a foolish young nobleman and have no interfering father—I can marry whomever I wish. Once we have the treasure, I can make a respectable woman of her."

Holmes was watching Lupin closely. "But I wonder, would she take you without money?"

Lupin shrugged. "Perhaps. Perhaps not. But the treasure should make that a moot point. Besides, I need to be in a position to retire from my current occupation. She is far too proper to pardon it."

Act Two took place in a garret apartment in Paris. Despite her feelings for Des Grieux, Manon had accepted gifts from another admirer, de Brétigny. While her cousin kept Des Grieux occupied, de Brétigny explained that the chevalier's father was about to have him kidnaped and returned to his family. Manon need only keep silent, and de Brétigny would make her his own and shower her with jewels and riches.

Sanderson was very good at conveying Manon's inner turmoil as she struggled to choose. Her voice had a sorrowful intensity, a pathos, that made you believe she really did love Des Grieux, and yet, she could not bring herself to warn him. As the act ended with Des Grieux carried away offstage, Manon cried out twice, "*Mon pauvre chevalier!*"

The curtain came down, and again the applause was enthusiastic. She almost had me convinced, but despite the beautiful music,

Manon the character was hopelessly weak. She had to choose between love and greed, and she chose greed. All women were not fickle, all were not swayed by jewels and gowns, as I well knew—I had married one who would never in her life betray me.

In the end, one could simply not generalize about women. Certainly in my time with Sherlock, I had encountered women enough who were true monsters capable of terrible crimes. And indeed, greed was their usual motive. Lady Arabella had committed one murder and was about to kill her niece as well because she wanted the family estate, Diana's Grove. Worse still was Constance Grimswell, who had worked with her evil illegitimate son to kill off the legitimate heirs between him and the family fortune. In her case, it was not only greed at work, but a deranged sort of love for her devilish son. And yet I had also met many admirable and sympathetic women, true innocents like young Diana Marsh and Rose Grimswell.

Act Three began with the transformed Manon in an elaborate red gown wearing a white wig and savoring the delights of all her wealth. However, soon enough she was off to Saint-Sulpice where the repentant Des Grieux had become a zealous preacher who was about to take Holy Orders. Manon was the pleading temptress recalling their past love, and the tenor's voice conveyed Des Grieux's desperate, all-consuming passion for her. The act concluded with the two of them departing together, Des Grieux having abandoned all thoughts of the priesthood.

After the applause had died down, Holmes turned to me, a brief sardonic smile flickering over his lips. "Now the pair of them are even. Each has saved the other from a life of celibacy."

I smiled back. "I had not thought of that."

The fourth act took place in a grand hotel hall devoted to gambling. Since their money was gone, Manon tried to convince

Des Grieux to try his luck at cards. At first he refused, asking her if he must yield up to her not only his heart, but his honor. At last he yielded. Strangely enough, he actually won at cards, but old Guillot called him a cheat and stormed out. Soon enough he returned with the police, and Des Grieux's father also appeared, berating his son for dishonoring them both. The act ended with the two lovers each dragged away by the police.

After we finished applauding, I said to my companions, "Des Grieux never seems to learn anything; he is putty in Manon's hands. Massenet does his best to make her sympathetic, but in the end he has not won me over. She seems shallow and brainless. Des Grieux's father was right: he should have married some nice girl of his own class."

Holmes was smiling at me. "Ah Henry, so there is something of the pragmatist in you, after all! You are not a complete romantic."

Lupin gave his head a shake. "You are too severe, Vernier. You forget she is supposed to be only sixteen or seventeen years old, hardly more than a child."

"Not all children are captivated by shiny objects and beautiful dresses the way that she is. Children also do not offer up themselves to rich promiscuous gentlemen for a few trinkets."

"How harsh you are. Most women may guard their virtue, but I have yet to meet a woman who cannot be captivated by a beautiful gown or a diamond necklace."

"I know one."

"Ah, your wife the physician. She is the exception which proves the rule! Actually I find Des Grieux more reprehensible than Manon. A real gentlemen would not so easily forgive a woman's infidelity. She betrays him only once in the opera, but several times

185

in the book. I may not be a member of the nobility, but even once would be enough for me."

Holmes had been listening carefully, and he spoke to Lupin. "So you would not tolerate even a single infidelity?"

"Certainly not! And especially if the infidelity went... shall we say, all the way, as with Manon. A little flirting is harmless enough, but not *that*."

Holmes nodded. "I see."

"I think we can all agree on that," I said. "Faithfulness is essential between a man and woman—essential for both sexes. Some, especially among the nobility, think wives must remain faithful even while a man may keep a young and pretty mistress. I find that despicable."

"So do I!" Lupin exclaimed.

"Maybe you are ready for marriage, after all," I replied.

The curtain rose again, and Holmes sat back in his seat. "And now all that remains is for Manon to perish."

"She dies so conveniently," I murmured, "both in the opera and the book. Even as a doctor, I cannot diagnose what the exact malady was."

"How cynical you are," Lupin murmured. "I thought you were a romantic."

"And so I am—when it matters. You can ask my wife. But I cannot tolerate these stories of ridiculous lovesick puppies like Des Grieux or young Werther in Goethe's novel. Idiots, both of them."

Act Five took place at dusk in the countryside. Manon, along with some prostitutes, was being taken away to be deported to New Orleans in the New World. Des Grieux had arranged with Manon's cousin, Lescaut, to have a small band of men free her, but they had all fled. Des Grieux was outraged and in despair, but Lescaut told him that with a bribe he would arrange a meeting with Manon.

Soon Manon staggered on stage, dramatically changed, gone the fancy red dress of the previous act, replaced by a worn, dark blue one with a tear at the shoulder. She fell to her knees and begged Des Grieux to forgive her. He raised her up and took her in his arms, even as he sang how they would begin a new life together. Sanderson and the tenor were both quite affecting, their voices soaring as they recalled their first happy days together in the small apartment in Paris.

Manon's voice faltered, and she collapsed, then sang that she was dying. High above the stage, a bright light came on, representing the first star of the night. Manon called it a beautiful diamond, then smiled at herself, saying she was still a coquette. Again, they sang of their past joys. Finally, in a weak voice, Sanderson proclaimed, "*Et c'est l'histoire de Manon Lescaut,*" "And this is the story of Manon Lescaut." She slumped, her eyes closing. The tenor gave a dramatic sob, then bent over her, even as the orchestra played the final chords.

The curtain came down, and the applause began. That scene had been well done, but somehow it had not greatly moved me. The music was simply not so heartrending as that of, say, Verdi's *La traviata*. That opera had a similar final death scene, but Violetta, the reformed courtesan, was a much more sympathetic character than Manon, and Verdi the better composer.

As we applauded, Holmes leaned toward me. "What did you think of the final act, Henry?"

"It was well sung, but did not exactly grip me."

"I feel the same way."

Lupin had heard us, and he shook his head. "Unfeeling brutes, the two of you!" His voice was mocking but had a quaver of emotion.

The great red curtain soon rose, and the lengthy rite of final bows and applause began. The vast hall resounded with the steady sound of the many hands clapping. My eyes shifted from the stage to my companions. Holmes and Lupin had both turned their heads toward the baron's box. Lupin must be regarding his beloved, but Holmes?

In their box next to the golden pillar, the trio of Chameracs were all politely clapping, but none with real enthusiasm. Which of them was Holmes watching? The baron with his swept-back chestnut hair and that ridiculous mustache, the set of his mouth faintly arrogant; or his pallid wife with her almost lifeless, stolid expression; or Angelique, with her youthful sense of poise and self-assurance? One could tell she was aware of her spectacular beauty—aware of it and proud, glad to be alive, and confident of the future.

Again I was struck by her long slender neck. Some women had a certain plumpness in the throat, but not her. The line from throat, to jaw, to chin, was clean and well defined. Her nose was slightly turned up, and her full lips were certainly sensual. Her ash-blond hair was bound up tightly, and the way her tiny white ear with its flashing diamond stud was revealed in its entirety, was provocative, but hardly so much as that swath of white flesh below her collar bones, or that faint shadow where her breasts came together just above the silken lace of the gown.

I felt suddenly uncomfortable, ashamed even, and I turned my gaze to the stage. Angelique's beauty was unsettling, and hard to resist. Little wonder Lupin had fallen hard for her. *Coup de foudre* was certainly appropriate for what had happened to him. I bit my lip and wished Michelle was with me. It was curious. When I had first met Michelle, I had found her attractive, but it was only as I grew to know and love her that I came to realize how truly beautiful she was. And in her case, an inner goodness augmented outer beauty.

Holmes and Lupin were still staring at the baron's box. I wondered again about my cousin. I knew that he was not unmoved by the beauty of women, but unlike many men, it would never make him behave foolishly or impulsively. Could it be the two Chameracs, both the baron and his niece, who interested him? Was Holmes perhaps questioning whether Angelique could actually break free of the baron and marry Lupin?

At last Holmes turned to me. He knew I had been watching him. His dark eyebrows were slightly tensed, his lips set in a stern line. His gray eyes were faintly curious, but grave.

"Sherlock?" I murmured.

He shrugged, then looked down at the stage. Manon had come out for her solo bow, and the audience applauded warmly. For the first time there were shouts of "bravo." She smiled and bowed before the enthusiastic ovation. Sanderson was a beautiful woman, but I reflected that she could not really compare with the likes of Angelique Chamerac.

Chapter 9

W̲e arrived in Étretat late Sunday afternoon and went
to the small inn where my family had always stayed.
The owner, Monsieur Hubert, and I recognized each other
immediately, and he greeted me warmly. He was a short stocky
man, his hair and beard all of the same short length, the dark
brown now shot with gray. His left hand held a curving wooden
pipe which gave off a mellow fragrance.

I introduced my companions (Lupin as Beautrelet), then said,
"Tell me, monsieur, what is the name of that old fortress, a sort of
castle, up atop the cliffs near the Porte d'Aval?"

"Ah, you must be thinking of the Fort de Fréfossé."

I nodded. "Indeed I am."

Holmes eagerly reached into his jacket pocket for a paper and
into his trouser pocket for a pencil. "How is that name spelled?"
He wrote out the letters as Hubert said them, then smiled at Lupin
and me. "Perfect—*perfect*. It fits exactly. We have it all now: *sous le
Fort de Fréfossé* is the third line."

"The fort must be very near the Chambre des Demoiselles," I said to Hubert.

"It surely is."

"And why exactly is the cave called that? I vaguely remember some old story about the origins of the name."

"Ah, yes, the tale of the three demoiselles. And indeed, the Baron of Fréfossé is the villain of the piece! He was enamored of the three beautiful young sisters, *les sœurs* Jolivet. They were engaged to three soldiers away at duty, and the baron saw them out walking one day. He invited them to his château, but quite wisely, they refused. He was furious. After that, they remained secluded during the day, walking instead only at night. However, the baron heard about this and tried to capture them one evening. They fled and hid in the nearby cave, but the baron caused a rock fall which blocked the entrance and trapped them inside. Supposedly, some three days later, an old woman on the beach saw three angels carrying the souls of the girls up into the heavens. Henceforth their ghosts haunted and tormented the wicked baron until his premature death."

"As I recall," Holmes said, "this part of Normandy with its limestone cliffs is riddled with caves and caverns, many of which are only accessible when the tide is out."

"That is true, monsieur, and every year we lose some foolish visitors who wander into one of the caves or small inlets and are trapped when the tide comes in. When you walk along the beach, always have a care of the tides and where the waters are!"

I nodded. "That much I well remember. My parents were always very careful to keep an eye on the sea, and they never left us unattended."

"Quite wise of them! Some people are truly reckless and careless."

"Do you know the way to the cave, Henry?" Holmes asked.

"I do, but I am rather hungry. Would you care for an early supper, and then afterwards, we can go exploring before it gets dark?"

Lupin gave an enthusiastic nod. "I'll second that suggestion. I'm famished myself."

Holmes smiled. "As you wish. I would not be so cruel as to drag you two along while you are starving to death."

I turned to Monsieur Hubert. "Do you still prepare mussels Normand?"

"What sort of question is that?" the innkeeper demanded with mock outrage. "Is this not still Normandy? Is that not the plate for which our inn is famous? Certainly I can fix you some!"

I laughed. "Excellent. We shall stow our baggage in our rooms and then meet you at the table."

The dining area was suitably rustic, constructed of old beams of dark wood with a big log burning in the stone fireplace. Hubert gestured toward one of the large tables made of thick wooden planks, and within a few minutes, he and his stout wife appeared, bearing huge steaming bowls piled with the mussels. The odor was incredible and made my appetite soar to the skies!

I knew the recipe, since Michelle and I had made the dish ourselves. The broth was a mixture of water, local cider, some crème fraiche and butter, to which were added cubes of bacon, chopped onion, and parsley. In the gap between the dark shells, I could see the bright orange flesh of the late departed mollusks. Hubert uncorked a bottle of white wine in a green bottle and poured some into each of our glasses.

Lupin seemed dazzled. "*Zut*, this looks good!"

"This was an excellent idea, Henry," Holmes said. "We shall be well fortified before we venture forth."

Hubert set a basket full of crusty sliced French baguettes on the table with which to mop up the broth, and we set to with vigor. Soon the empty black shells began to pile up on the big platter in the center of the table, and by the time we had finished, there was an impressive heap.

Lupin swirled a heel of baguette in the liquid remaining in his bowl, getting the last of it up. "I see why this is the specialty of the inn. I cannot wait until tomorrow evening. I shall surely want the same dish again!"

Holmes dabbed at his mouth with his napkin. "So shall I."

I gave a contented sigh. "I think perhaps we should saunter along the beach for a while before we attack the path up to the cliffs."

"We are in your good hands, Henry."

We stepped out from the inn onto the narrow cobbled street. Many of the buildings had dark brown wooden cross-beams across pale stucco, the same construction one saw in certain older English villages. We started off in the westerly direction where the sky was more brightly lit.

Holmes raised his arm, pointing in the direction of a square tower which could be seen over rooftops. "Tell me, Henry, is that the local Catholic church there?"

"Yes. It's the Église Notre-Dame d'Étretat, a very old church. We used to go to Sunday Mass there during our holidays."

"Does it have a graveyard close by, as with our country Protestant churches?"

"Yes, indeed. On either side, I believe."

"Ah. Perhaps we could have a quick look before we head toward the sea."

"As you wish."

The church was easy enough to find, given that its tower's triangular top was by far the tallest point around. The stone walls were a faded brownish white color, and the different sections of the edifice each had their own roof of gray-black slate. As I recalled, the bulk of the church was very old, dating from perhaps the twelfth century. All along the side were the tall stones and monuments of the local cemetery. The French, more than the English, seemed to favor grandiose memorials to their dead.

Holmes strode forward and began to crisscross the rows of the interred. He was wearing a heavy tweed suit suitable for the country, and a battered walking hat, and in his left hand was a favorite gnarled blackthorn stick. Slung across his shoulders was a small pair of binoculars.

"Are you looking for anything in particular?" I asked.

"Not exactly. But I shall know it when I find it."

Lupin and I exchanged a puzzled glance, then followed him. I happened upon a small stone and saw from the dates that it commemorated a child who had lived for not even a year. Such markers always made me feel sad. These stones each told a story, often a very tragic one. Some were crumbling and very old, while the more recent ones were of polished granite of various colors. We seemed to head backward in time as we proceeded.

At last Holmes came to a sudden halt. "Ah!" He raised his stick. Before him was a battered gray-white monument at least six feet tall with a carving in relief of some rough triangular shape. The large block letters said *"LES GARDIENS."* I realized the carved object must represent l'Aiguille, the Needle. Below the massive memorial slab were various scattered gravestones, each with a different date. One could tell from their varying states of decay and the style of the lettering that they must span centuries.

"Gardiens... de l'Aiguille?" I murmured. "The keepers of the Needle?"

"In this case," Holmes said, "I think 'guardians of the Needle' might be a more apt translation." Holmes took a few steps amidst the stone markers underfoot. "They seem to be in chronological order, going from the sixteenth century to... Ah, here is the latest." He thrust at the stone with his stick: JULES BEAUFORT, MAY 1758 À 1840. "That would mean that there has not been a new guardian for over fifty years."

"And these guardians must watch over the treasure," Lupin said.

Holmes nodded. "Exactly. It is a solemn duty handed down over the centuries. This is more proof that we are getting very close to our goal. But enough, let us head for the seashore before it gets too dark."

Étretat had been a small fishing village, but in the latter half of the nineteenth century it became a popular vacation site for tourists in the summer. Set on a small bay with a long beach of shingle, massive limestone cliffs or *falaises* towered up on either side of the town. To the east of Étretat was a jutting promontory with a small arch, the Porte d'Amont, while to the west were two much larger arches: the Porte d'Aval, the ocean side of which had been compared to a giant elephant's trunk thrust into the water; and then further still, not visible from town, was the massive Manneporte, which dwarfed the other two arches, both its opening and its outer arch much larger than those of its two smaller brothers. The famed Needle, l'Aiguille, was a rock formation thrusting forth from the sea near the Porte d'Aval.

We walked through the small town down to the beach, and then went out onto the great swath of gray shingle. The tide was out. The waves made a low murmur as they swept in with a rush of foam, and as they withdrew, they rattled the small pebbles and left them black and glistening.

The beach was set at a slant to the southwest, and we started off in a westerly direction. Ahead slightly to the right, the sun was low in the sky, a yellow-orange orb behind some streaks of cloud, and we could clearly see the high bluffs and the elephant trunk of limestone from the Porte d'Aval plunging into the sea. However, the Needle remained hidden.

I had thrust my hands into my pocket. "A fine evening for a stroll. We are lucky to have such weather. April days are often all gray clouds, mists, and rain."

"This is a splendid place." Lupin was enthusiastic. "I only wish my friend Leblanc might have accompanied us. Like you, Dr. Vernier, he also knows Étretat well. He told me he vacations here every summer."

Below the brim of his woolen walking hat, Holmes's dark brows came together. "You did not tell him you were coming here?"

"No, no, of course not. I told him I was thinking of a trip to Normandy in summer, and I asked him if he knew the region. Imagine my surprise when he mentioned Étretat!"

We walked on in a companionable silence. The waves swept smoothly in and out, sunlight a dazzling glow on the water. A few gulls flew by, and I watched as two larger white pelicans glided along out over the sea, then plunged suddenly in search of supper, vanishing briefly.

We came at last to the cliffs. Ahead of us the striated *falaises* rose up some three hundred feet, all gray and white with a dark mossy strip at the base showing the high tide mark, and the beach itself changed from shingle to smooth rocky mounds with small, interlaced tendrils of water. A cave showed as a ragged black mouth at the bottom of a far cliff. You could continue along down by the sea, but we turned instead toward a rock-strewn sandy path which led up through dark green grasses and vegetation toward the top. Occasional rough stone steps were set into the dirt.

It was steep going, and I could feel all those mussels and that wine sloshing around inside of me! We paused occasionally for a breather. As we climbed, behind us we could see more of the panorama of the sea and the town bordering the curving bay. At last we reached the summit. The sound of the waves had greatly diminished, and just before us on a sort of detached promontory was the Fort of Fréfossé.

It was a small castle-like structure with two crenellated towers, each just over two stories high; and at each level, instead of regular windows, there were odd, cross-shaped openings. Between the towers were wooden doors with curving gothic arches. Higher still was a huge window with multiple panes of dirty glass. Jagged cracks ran vertically down the tower walls, and the square stones appeared rough and worn. The wood of the doors was faintly bleached, the hinges and a padlock rusty. A barred gate blocked the way.

"Shall we have a closer look?" Lupin asked, even as he managed to get one leg over the fence.

With a few misgivings, I followed my companions. We came up to the tall doors, and the lock appeared so badly rusted I doubted anyone could possibly open it, even with the key. Lupin started around the edifice, and I followed him. Before us appeared two limestone formations, rounded mounds, each about thirty feet tall with patches of greenery growing near their tops. They were on the very edge of the cliff, and behind them was the curving bay and Étretat. The left mound was the taller of the two, and a dirt path with some stairs led down the grassy slope to a ridge which crossed over to it. Wooden planks composed a sort of bridge, with a handrail, and it ended in the black gap of a door-like opening.

Another aperture, a smaller rectangular one, formed a rough sort of window to the right of the entry.

I felt a sudden thrill of recognition. "That's it! That is the Chambre des Demoiselles—just down there."

Holmes smiled at me. "Excellent! We are making progress indeed. Let us have a look."

We went down the path and started over the walkway. There was a drop-off to either side, not true precipices, but a downward slope of some thirty or forty feet. All the same I grasped the wooden handrail firmly as we crossed, even as I told myself this was not fearful enough to trigger my vertigo.

Holmes and Lupin went into the cave, and I stooped slightly to follow them. Luckily the cavern opened up inside, and orangish light from the sinking sun came in through the entry and the sort of window, providing illumination. Besides vertigo, I was also prone to claustrophobia and could not tolerate small dark enclosures. The cave was perhaps twenty feet wide, its jagged ceiling about twenty feet up, and its rocky sides appeared damp. Indeed, there was a distinctive musty smell. I saw that several foolish visitors had scratched their names on the wall, a practice that always irritated me.

"A pity there is not more light." Holmes ran his slender hand along one of the walls. "I brought along my small binoculars, but I should have thought to also bring a lantern. I am eager to begin, but our real investigation must wait until morning, I fear."

"One should at least allow one's supper to digest before commencing a major undertaking!" I said with mock gravity.

Holmes laughed. "Ah, Henry! Always the practical one."

Lupin had been peering carefully all about the cave. "There may be some sort of secret passage. We know the general route now: it begins at the Chambre des Demoiselles, then under the

Fort de Fréfossé, and out to the hollow Needle. Some hidden tunnel must go underwater all the way there."

Holmes nodded. "That seems likely. Well, for now, let us continue on to have a look at our real objective."

"The Needle, you mean?" I asked.

"Exactly."

We crossed the small bridgeway again, then went back around the castle and started uphill, with the sea off to our right. Some stone steps led up to a summit where the ground leveled out. The cold wind from the sea caught our faces, and the long yellow-brown grasses nearby were swept inward by the steady gust. The thin clouds were all aglow with red and gold. Holmes started forward. I followed.

The Needle rose up slowly before us as we advanced toward the edge of the cliffs: first came its jagged tip, like that of the monstrous sharp tooth of some creature hidden in the deeps; then, there was a gradual widening with each step, until at last I saw the entirety of the formation thrust forth from the luminescent sea, the foaming waters swirling all about the base. The general shape might be conical, but this was a thing of nature, not perfectly symmetrical or geometrical, but rough and uneven, with vertical slabs, cracks, and abutments, as well as a few splotches of green growth here and there. Seen so close, the striations, those strips of different shades of gray and gray-white, truly stood out. This was a creation of the ages, each of those layers representing many human lifespans. The Needle was some two hundred and thirty feet high, but was still below the prominence where we stood, which was nearer three hundred feet.

I gave a long slow sigh. For me, this was rather like seeing an old friend from my childhood, but I had forgotten how truly imposing it was.

Lupin made a soft whistling sound. "*Mon Dieu*, it is impressive, is it not? But can it really be hollow? Surely that could not be through some natural process."

"No," Holmes said. "The stories about the Needle go back to the time of the Romans and even earlier to the Gauls. Perhaps in primitive times, some tribe of men found a cave that led under the sea to the formation, and they labored over generations, slowly working their way upward toward the tip. They would have had to use primitive tools and haul out the debris as they went. Limestone is fairly soft rock. Even so..."

"But why do such a thing?" Lupin asked.

"Perhaps somehow it had a religious significance," I said.

Holmes shrugged. "Perhaps. The labors could have been divided. The Gauls might have started the project, but the Romans with all their engineering skills could have finished the task."

Standing there on the bluff in that cool wind with gulls circling all about, while observing the sheer mass and size of that great rock, such a thing seemed simply impossible. The sun had sunk into the swath of clouds, becoming a deep red as it neared the horizon and setting the clouds behind the Needle aflame with red, orange, and pink. Bluish-gray shadow muted the limestone striation facing us, tempering the contrasting stone layers.

I shook my head. "I cannot believe it. We have been deceived by a... sort of fairy tale. Someone made up all this nonsense about the hollow needle."

Holmes had removed his small binoculars from their leather case, and he turned them toward the Needle. We were all quiet for a while. Standing there at sunset before such a spectacle one truly sensed all the great power and the beauty of the natural world. At last Holmes lowered the binoculars as he made a muted sort of sound which I recognized as a laugh.

"It is not a fairy tale, Henry. Take the binoculars and have a look near the tip, to the left side."

I seized the binocular and focused them on the top of the rock. The color variations of the striations were even more apparent, as well as the bits of vegetation and some seabirds nested there. However, a whitish vapor drifted out from behind the top of the rock, curling in a way that mere clouds would not.

I lowered the binoculars, frowning slightly. "Smoke?"

Holmes gave a triumphant nod. "Exactly! Which means someone has a fire going. *Inside.*"

The next morning as we set out, a damp gray mist had settled over everything, and as we started up the hillside, I could not make out either the bay or the town behind us. Even the path before us was obscured. We had dressed warmly, and I was grateful for the woolen scarf wrapped around my throat. That sort of moist cold penetrates to the bones. As we trudged upward, the haze about us seemed to color slightly, a faint yellow showing.

Ahead of me, Lupin turned back toward Étretat. He wore a brown cloth cap and the lenses of his spectacles were spotted with droplets. "I think it wants to clear up."

"I hope so," I said. "If we are lucky, this will all burn off by noon."

"So much the better," Holmes said. He held his stick in his right hand, a satchel with various tools and accessories in his right.

When we reached the summit, the fort was only a specter, a vague apparition appearing and disappearing within the fog. Finding our way around it was certainly not as easy as the evening before. Soon we made out the bridge over to the Chambre des Demoiselles, but only the bottom of the two hillocks showed, their tops completely obscured.

I would not have thought it possible, but inside the cave seemed damper than outside. Holmes opened up his satchel, withdrew a small dark lantern, lit the wick, and cast the light all about us.

"The floor–the floor–look at that!" Lupin exclaimed. He grasped my arm and pulled me back slightly.

Holmes lowered the beam. Beneath us in the rock were two clearly carved letters, D and F, each about a foot tall.

"Very good!" Holmes exclaimed. "Just as in that fourth line of the paper. There was a D and F with a line over them."

Lupin put his two hands together. "The D must be for demoiselles, the F for… fort or Fréfossé. Either one will do!"

"I wonder…" Holmes said. He set down the lantern, then quickly knelt and felt about the floor. Lupin quickly joined him, but I stepped back. "Perhaps there is some opening."

"Or some sort of spring which opens something else," Lupin said.

Holmes picked up the lantern, then methodically shined the light on the rocky surface all around the two letters. At last he gave a sigh. "Do you see anything?" he asked Lupin.

"Nothing."

"They are, after all, just two letters carved into the rock, but perhaps there is the entrance to some secret passageway here in the cave. Let us have a look."

"Did you bring another lantern?" Lupin asked.

"I did. There is one more only."

"Good! Then I can search, too."

I smiled faintly. "I'm sure you both can do a much more thorough job than I ever could."

Lupin lit the other lamp, and then the two men began a painstaking examination of the cave. No nook or cranny of that interior rock was spared. Each man groped about with one hand, feeling for a pull or some hidden sort of lever, while his other hand directed the lantern. I grew chilled and trudged about some, trying to warm myself.

"I think I shall have a look outside," I said. "You certainly don't need my help."

They were both so busy they did not acknowledge my words. I smiled again, then went out through the cave entrance. The hint of yellow in the mist had grown, and the clouds had thinned. The Fort of Fréfossé seemed more concrete now, not so much a ghost, and I was fairly sure the afternoon would be a splendid one with bright sunshine, blue sky, and emerald seas.

I crossed the bridge and strolled about the fortress for a while, idly examining it. By the time I returned to the cave, it was almost noon, and some swaths of faint blue showed where the mist had dissolved. Holmes and Lupin stood in the center of the cave, both deep in thought. Holmes was holding the paper with the code.

"Find anything?" I asked.

Holmes shook his head. "No."

"We are quite certain there is no hidden passage," Lupin said. "We went over every inch in here more than once."

"Why not break for lunch?" I suggested.

"I have no appetite," Holmes said. "I would rather keep going."

"Come now, a pause and some nutrition might help clear your mind and suggest some other approach. It is early in the day. There is plenty of time."

Lupin smiled at me. "You are indeed ever the pragmatist, Dr. Vernier."

We ate some baguette sandwiches which the innkeeper's wife had prepared for us, thick slabs of brie cheese with walnuts, an unusual offering, and for dessert there were wizened sad-looking apples, which all the same, had wonderful flavor. All the while, the light gleaming through the openings grew more intense as the sky cleared.

Holmes sagged back against the cave wall, took a bite of apple, and chewed thoughtfully even as he stared down at the paper with the lines of code. "I am still looking at the fourth line. It is certainly the key. We have the DF here before us. Let us think. Next is a rectangle, with the representation of an angle in its lower left-hand corner. Is there any rectangle nearby?"

$$D \ \overline{DF} \ \square \ 19F+44 \ \square \ 357 \ \triangle$$

Lupin gestured with his hand. "Besides the entranceway, there is that sort of window in the side of the wall just there. The doorway is a vertical rectangle, but the window forms a rough sort of a horizontal one, like on the paper. It certainly doesn't appear natural to me. Someone probably carved it out to provide more light."

"Or to show us our way." Holmes stood up, went to the window, and bent to examine the bottom-left corner. "Ah. Look at this."

Lupin and I stepped closer. In the corner, an odd grayish piece of flint stuck out and curved slightly like a small bent finger.

"Excellent!" Lupin exclaimed. "Again, just like the drawing. But what is it for?" He tensed slightly, then bent over and sighted through the small gap formed by the flint.

"What do you see?" Holmes asked.

"The very old-looking remnant of some grayish wall set against a slope which is partly covered by green plants."

"Let me try something." Holmes glanced at the floor, then put one foot on the carved D, the other on the F. "Do you see!—I'm just on the right level for the window and that corner. I can see the wall you are talking about."

Lupin nodded. "That cannot be a coincidence. And after the rectangle is 19F. Perhaps that is some measure of distance—the distance from the corner of the window."

I frowned. "What unit of measurement begins with an F? If the note had been written by an Englishman instead of a Frenchman, it might represent feet, but we must be looking for a French measurement. Besides, that wall is obviously much further away than nineteen feet."

Holmes stroked his chin. "It could stand for fathom, which is exactly six feet. That might work."

Lupin's brow was furrowed. "The French fathom, the *toise*, is slightly larger than the English one, closer to two meters."

Holmes smiled. "So we shall try both!" He went to the satchel and pulled out a long coil of thin rope and a tape measure in a brown leather case. "Help me measure out nineteen fathoms. We can do it in six-foot units."

"Each of you hold an end," Lupin said. Holmes pulled out six foot, then gave the end to me, and I stood that distance away from him. Lupin had Holmes hold one end of the rope, then went back and forth between the two measuring out nineteen fathoms. He held up the rope, a spot pinched between thumb and forefinger. "Here we are. How can we mark it?"

"I have some wire." Holmes took out a piece of thin copper and wrapped it tightly around that point on the rope.

"Now what?" I asked.

"Henry, I would like you to stay here and hold this end with the marker wire just there by the flint. I shall head out toward that wall, and when I reach it, you shall sight through the gap and help me position the other end exactly. And we shall see what we shall see." Holmes took the small weight attached to the rope end and tossed it out the window in the direction of the bridge. He glanced at Lupin. "Come along."

"I wouldn't miss this for anything!"

Holmes soon retrieved the weighted end of rope, and the two of them made their way over the uneven slope to the ancient section of wall.

"Ah!" Holmes shouted in my direction: "We are short just a little. It must be the French fathom after all."

He and Lupin quickly returned to the cave. While Lupin retrieved the rope, Holmes took out a piece of paper, a pencil, as well as a small booklet with a black cover, which he thumbed through. "Let's see here in my conversion tables... While an English fathom is exactly six feet, or 72 inches, the French *toise* would be 76.73 inches. If we take 4.73 times 19, that would get us—" he scrawled some numbers on the paper "—89.87 inches, or... almost exactly 7½ feet more."

He had me hold the rope at the point with the wire, while he measured off the additional distance; then he moved the wire to the new spot. "Let us try again."

Lupin gave a fierce nod. "I know this is going to work. My intuition tells me so!"

Holmes and Lupin quickly left. I stooped slightly, squinting out through the piece of flint at the grayish brick wall. Again the two of them scrambled across the slope, and Holmes drew out the rope to the full additional distance. This time he could just exactly reach the wall. There could be little doubt the measurement was right. "That's it!" I cried, quite excited myself. "Perhaps a little lower."

Lupin pushed aside some plants, then shouted, "*Le voici! Le voici!*"

"Of course!" Holmes cried. "A perfect match!"

"I'm coming!" I exclaimed.

I strode out through the opening, crossed the bridge, and started across the grassy slope. I nearly tripped and realized that I could fall and that I needed to be careful. "What have you found?"

Holmes smiled up at me. "Have a look. I thought that was a plus sign after 19F on the fourth line, but it was a Greek cross—one with arms of equal length, just like this one."

Sure enough, there set in the worn gray bricks was a circular stone with a symmetrical cross carved into the exact center. Holmes grasped the circle and tried to turn it. "Perhaps if I press it…" We heard a sort of click like a bolt released, then the sound of a lock opening, and a section of the brick wall about a yard square swung inward, revealing a passageway.

Holmes smiled up at us. Lupin clenched his fists in delight, grinning broadly. "The rest should be child's play."

"We shall see," Holmes said. "Let's fetch our lanterns and my satchel."

Soon we were back at the entrance, and Holmes went first with his light. I had to stoop, then step down, to get inside. The passage opened into a vault, both floor and ceiling lined with brick. The back of the hidden door was made of solid iron, disguised by the worn bricks in front.

Holmes closed the door behind us and triggered a latch. "We want to keep this entrance a secret."

We started forward, the beam of light from the two lanterns dancing about here and there on the walls and floor. We came to some stairs and started down. The stone in the center of the steps was worn down: generations of men must have trod here. The stairs ended abruptly before a gray-black sheet of iron streaked with orange rust. "Is that a door?" I asked.

"It must be," Holmes said, even as he shined the lantern round its edges. The only break in the rectangle was made by two triangles of iron on the left side, one near the bottom, another near the top.

"But there is no handle, nor any obvious lock."

"So there must be a secret way of opening the door," Lupin said.

Holmes nodded. "Exactly. Remember on the paper there was the number 44 and a triangle after the cross. It must be one of those triangles there which seem to reinforce the door."

"But the number 44?" I asked.

"Perhaps... I wonder how many steps we have gone down."

"I thought it might be useful to keep a count," Lupin said. "The one just before the door is exactly 45."

"Ah, excellent!" Holmes exclaimed. "Let us all squeeze together above on step 44. Very good, although it is a tight fit." He knelt awkwardly, then grasped at the edge of the lower piece of triangular iron. It swiveled upward, and the iron door swung in, exposing a long two-inch gap.

"Bravo!" Lupin exclaimed. "I must say, this is great fun."

Holmes pushed the door open, and we stepped into a spacious cavern, the lantern beams shining upon the limestone. However, the whole interior was illuminated by the light coming from a long horizontal fissure some fifteen yards or so away from the doorway.

Holmes glanced overhead. "We must be directly under the Fort de Fréfossé now."

Lupin strode toward the fissure, and we followed. It formed a grand panoramic opening, and Lupin set one hand on the rock. "What a view."

Indeed, just before us was that jagged tooth of the Needle rising from the waters, and to its right, nearer still, the arching trunk of the Porte d'Aval. I took a step or two to the left, and further away, at the end of an inlet, was the third of the arches, the massive Manneporte which appeared much thicker and more solid than that of the Porte d'Aval. The murmur of the sea, the rising and falling of its swell, was constant and very loud.

I shook my head. "Could such an observation point as this possibly be natural?"

Holmes shined his light on the far end. "There was probably originally an opening here, but someone expanded it. You can see the marks of picks or chisels in the rock along the edges."

"Well, it is a quite magnificent view," Lupin said. "And that third arch. It is truly imposing."

"I believe there is a way out, just to the left here." Holmes aimed the lantern beam, and we could see more stone stairs leading downward. "You did such an excellent job last time, Isidore, that I shall ask you to again keep count of the steps."

"Gladly. And this time I suspect there will be 358, as the number on the line was 357."

We started down the stairs, which were steeper than the last ones. Occasionally a small opening in the seaward wall let in light, but before long, we had, no doubt, descended below sea level. Lupin was quietly counting to himself. Sure enough, when he was in the 300s, another iron door could be seen before us, this time with iron reinforcement slabs on the right side. We all squeezed together on step 357. Holmes tried the lower triangle, but could not budge it, so he stood and grasped the upper one. It swiveled neatly, and again the door popped open.

Holmes pushed it inward. A long tunnel through the limestone stretched before us, the walls oozing moisture, and planks had been set down on the floor, forming a path. We started forward. The beams from the lanterns bounced about on the wooden surface.

"We are obviously crossing under the sea," Holmes said, "and our final destination—the Hollow Needle—awaits us."

"Yes," Lupin replied. "And there will be no more doors in the way."

The tunnel was frigid and very damp. I had begun to shiver, and not just from the cold. I tried to reassure myself that if this passageway had held up for centuries, it would not choose today to come crashing down and bury us alive! I was mostly convinced, but all the same, glad when after a few minutes, we came to the end, and the tunnel opened up into the largest cavern yet.

Holmes and Lupin swept the vast space with their lanterns. Across from us was an opening with stairs which led upward, and to one side, was a vast dark pool of water, which glistened as the light struck it. The water rose and fell ever so slightly, and we could hear the faint lapping against the limestone walls.

Lupin raised one hand high and gave us a triumphant smile. "*Bienvenu, mes amis, à l'Aiguille Creuse!*"

Chapter 10

❧

We crossed the cavern and went up the curving stone stairway; again the steps were worn down in the center from the centuries of use. We came to a door which, this time, was not locked. Inside was a vast circular room, no doubt almost the width of the Needle, and a few limestone pillars stood spaced evenly apart, curving outward toward the floor and upward to the ceiling. They were clear evidence that indeed someone had, long ago, hollowed out the limestone to create this chamber, leaving the supporting pillars behind. It seemed to be a storage area, with packing crates, old pieces of furniture, oak settees, strong-boxes, and the like, what you might expect in the basement of a curiosity shop.

We wandered about in the direction of what must be another set of stairs, across from where we had come in.

"This looks like a rummage room," Lupin said.

I nodded. "I was thinking the same thing."

We started up the next set of stairs. Again the stairway curved around to the side, no doubt following the circular exterior of the conically shaped rock. Beyond a door was another round room with fewer limestone pillars, this one mostly empty, and again, the entrance to another stairway across from us.

"The plan seems obvious enough," Holmes said. "Circular rooms growing ever smaller in diameter at each level as one proceeds upward toward the apex."

Lupin nodded. "Yes, and they must be man-made."

"Good Lord," I murmured. "I wonder how many years of painstaking labor it must have taken."

We continued our ascent. The third floor seemed to be another storeroom, but when we opened the fourth door, a dimly lit room appeared before us, a long irregular opening showing along one side. We crossed over to this rough window and gazed outside. Perhaps thirty feet below, the dark blue waters of the sea swirled and foamed about the rock. The cry of a gull was very near.

When we reached the fifth floor, which was, of course, the smallest yet, things changed abruptly. Again a seaward opening provided illumination. The ceiling and the walls were bare limestone, but the floor was formed of worn oak. There were no pillars at this level. Hanging here and there, were elaborate tapestries with scenes from the Middle Ages or the sixteenth and seventeenth centuries. Many more tapestries were rolled up and piled on the floor, labels showing on their ends.

Lupin gestured toward one of the piles. "The beginnings of the treasure! These alone must be worth a small fortune."

We continued our ascent. The sixth level also had a wooden floor, as well as many shelves, all lined with clocks or timepieces of every size and shape imaginable. However, there was obviously no horologist here! The clocks were all sadly mute and still.

On the seventh floor were more shelves, row after row of ancient-looking books. Holmes pulled out one huge volume, opened it, and a cloud of dust was like an exhalation. "A botanical volume in Latin from the fifteenth century." He carefully put it back. "Trying to create a library here—or storing clocks—was a foolish idea. The damp sea air is inimical to both."

"We must be getting near the summit," I said.

Holmes stroked his chin. "I think so. But I am surprised we have not met anyone yet."

"Perhaps the place has been left deserted," I said.

"You are forgetting the smoke we saw."

Lupin's mouth formed a wry smile. "One would think the great treasure of France would be guarded."

Holmes nodded. "Yes."

Again we trudged up some steps, and Holmes opened yet another door. We stepped inside, and I immediately felt a welcome warmth. This room was, of course, the smallest yet, and tapered inward above us to a conical ceiling. Beautiful tapestries of hunting scenes covered the limestone walls, and the floor was an elaborate parquet of different colored woods. A bed with an iron frame was on one side of the room, and again windows faced toward the water, these actually glazed and shut up, which kept out the cold and somewhat muted the ever-present sound of the sea. Near the windows stood a massive square cast-iron stove which radiated the heat we felt; its circular chimney had curved segments directing the smoke outside.

Close by the stove, in a massive brown leather armchair, sat a very old man, and one need not be a physician like myself to tell that he was quite ill. His face was pale, the skin almost grayish, and his dark brown eyes were infinitely weary. A scraggly white beard covered his gaunt cheeks, and a few wisps of white hair still crossed the top of his head. His ears were enormously long, a sign of great age, the lobes very pronounced. He wore a dark woolen suit, a black shirt, and a brown woolen blanket covered his legs. We approached him slowly.

His eyelids blinked. "You have come for the treasure, I suppose."

Holmes, Lupin, and I exchanged a look. Lupin gave a brusque nod. "Yes," he said. Holmes half-shook his head in disapproval.

"You are too late. It is gone, hidden away where you will never find it. Only members of the Society know its new hiding place. But I congratulate you. I have been Guardian for decades, and no outsiders have ever found their way here."

"Gone?" Lupin sounded suspicious. "You *would* say that. How do we know you are telling the truth—how do we know there are not more secrets hidden here within the Needle?"

The old man's laugh was akin to a cackle. "You are correct. There were more secrets. Look at the floor beneath your feet. The design has six large circles set in wood. Choose one, then go to the smallest circle in the center, and step on one side. It will pivot, revealing a sort of handle, and you can lift open the whole thing."

I could see the pattern: six circles, formed by the parquet, each about five feet across. Lupin strode to one, put his foot on the center, then got his hand under the opening and awkwardly managed to pry up a circular panel some three feet across. Holmes and I stepped forward. Inside was a hollow space carved into the limestone rock, but it was quite empty.

Lupin quickly went to another circle, wrenched open its top, and then to a third. He was frowning, obviously growing more exasperated as each of the six empty spaces was revealed. He slammed the last cover back in place.

"What have you done with it!" he exclaimed.

The old man was smiling faintly. "Only three of those hiding places still had treasure. The last three kings of France were all spendthrifts who squandered the other half." His contempt was obvious. "But the treasure is gone now. We feared it was no longer safe in France. Over twenty years ago, the Prussians invaded our sacred soil and made it all the way to Paris. So very near! And then the Emperor Louis Napoleon, the last monarch, fell, and the wretched Third Republic came into being. So we sent what remained of the treasure abroad where thieves could never find it. You yourselves are proof of the danger."

I frowned. "But it belongs to the people of France."

The old man shook his head brusquely. "It belongs to the divinely appointed king of France, to God's representative on earth, and I am its guardian."

Holmes folded his arms. "This society of yours: I suppose it is an ancient one devoted to the safekeeping of the treasure of France. And are you the last of the guardians?"

"No—of course not. At least, I hope not. When I die, which will be very soon, old Bernard will find my corpse. He comes every week with supplies and news. He will tell the others, and they will choose a new guardian to stay here in the Needle."

"When did you have your attack?" I asked.

He stared at me, his white eyebrows coming together. "How did you know?"

"I am a physician. It's obvious enough. You look quite ill."

"It was three days ago, early in the morning. My chest…"

"Have you managed to eat and drink anything?"

He gestured toward a sort of cupboard near the big stove. Also close by was a metal coalscuttle half full. "I had a little bread and some water. I have no appetite. And I am cold, so cold."

Lupin's face was slightly flushed, and his hands had curled into fists. "But what is the point of having a guardian if there is nothing to guard?"

The old man gave him an incredulous look. "Is it not obvious? If the Republic were to end, if a true king were to return again and come here seeking his rightful treasure, then the guardian would reveal its hiding place."

Lupin seemed to ponder this, taking his lower lip between his teeth. Abruptly he removed his cloth cap, threw it down, then put his spectacles in his jacket pocket and stood up very straight. "And I am that king of France, come again to claim what is mine!" His voice resonated with authority. "Do you think mere thieves could have ever found the way here to the heart of the Needle? No, we discovered the secret of the clock, then untangled the coded note, and at last we have come—I, the true king of France, and these my faithful subjects."

I took half a step back, staring in disbelief at Lupin. He stood tall and ramrod straight, and his hands hanging loosely at his side, gestured expressively. I had to admit that he looked quite regal just then. The right side of Holmes's mouth twitched briefly upward.

The old man's dark eyes had opened very wide. "But who... who...? Explain yourself."

Lupin seemed to reflect for a second or two. "I am the grandson of Henry the Fifth, the last true Bourbon king of France. Sadly, as you must know, my grandfather was king for less than a week in August of 1830, just before that Orléanist pretender Louis-Philippe took the throne. Everyone thought that Henry was the last of the Bourbons, but he was secretly married, and had a son, Louis-Pierre, my father. My bloodline goes all the way back to Henry the Fourth. With a portion of that treasure which is rightfully mine, my allies and I can raise an army, overthrow the wretched republic, and claim the throne."

Lupin had crossed his arms, his expression quite stern, but now he lowered his hand and set it on the old man's shoulder. "My good and faithful friend, you have served me and your country well for all these years, but now your king has returned. Tell me where the treasure is hidden."

The old man raised both trembling hands. "Majesty… Majesty… I…" Suddenly he clenched his teeth. One hand dropped, the other clutched weakly at his chest. A low moan slipped free.

I seized Lupin's arm. "Let him be. The shock…"

The old man shook his head. "No, no, it is no matter. My time has come, but I feel such… joy." One feeble hand reached out, and Lupin knelt beside him and took it.

"The treasure is…" He was speaking French, but then he said in English, "White, white," and then, "*Les autres, les autres aiguilles… le phare… dessous.*" The translation was simple enough: "The other ones, the other needles… the lighthouse… below."

He winced again, moaned once, and his eyes opened very wide as he seemed to briefly freeze. Then his head sagged to one side, and consciousness slipped away from those dark eyes.

"What other ones!" Lupin exclaimed. "Explain yourself!"

I set my fingertips on the old man's throat, a mere formality. "He is gone. Your revelation was too much for him." I gently closed his eyes.

"Damnation!" Lupin exclaimed. "He was about to tell us everything."

I sighed. "And now we have more riddles. Why on earth did he switch to English and say 'white'? Whatever does that have to do with needles?"

Lupin shook his head angrily. "I must confess, I am completely at a loss. We are back where we started, with mysterious needles– we are going round and round in circles."

"I never suspected there were so many blasted 'needles' in France!" I said.

Holmes had been listening silently, a slight smile curving his lips. He appeared not to have a care in the world. "Not necessarily in France. This is a time when being a native-born Englishman helps. Spell wight for me, Henry."

I stared at him. "Spell it? What are you...? It's obvious enough. W-H-I-T-E."

"That is wrong. Think of an alternative."

I frowned in concentration. "Isn't there...? It is a very old word which means creature, I believe: W-I-G-H-T."

"Very good! That is the correct spelling, but it has another meaning besides 'creature.'"

"It does?"

"Try capitalizing the word."

"Wight." I was frowning fiercely, the answer just out of reach.

"Try prefixing it with 'the Isle of.'"

I shook my head. "How stupid of me. The Isle of Wight. That would be just across the English Channel from here, but needles– are there needles at the Island?"

"There are indeed. Three jagged chalk formations stand just off the westernmost tip of the Isle of Wight. They are less than half as tall as this Needle and more like rough-shaped rocks. However, there were originally four of them, and the tallest one, which was more conical and needle-like, collapsed sometime during the eighteenth century. Once after a stop at Osborne House, I made a tour of the Isle of Wight, and I have visited the location. Also, perched on the very farthest point of the last Needle, there stands a lighthouse."

"That's it!" Lupin cried. "That must be it! Oh bravo, Holmes."

"But why did he say *dessous*?" I asked. "Does 'below' or 'underneath' have anything to do with the lighthouse?"

"That we must determine when we get there."

"And we must leave at once!" Lupin exclaimed. "Le Havre is the nearest port. Perhaps there is even a ferry that goes to the Isle of Wight."

Holmes's triumphant expression changed to one of caution. "If I had a client whom I trusted, I would consult with him before pursuing this lead."

"But since you don't have that sort of client," Lupin said, "we can pack up and set off on our own at once!"

Holmes appeared amused, and gave his head a shake. "You are a most enthusiastic young man."

"That he is," I said, "and what an actor! I was almost ready to fall at his feet and become one of his partisans, joining in the struggle to return him to his rightful throne."

Lupin laughed. "Thank you, Dr. Vernier. I did think it was one of my better performances."

"You are very good at improvisation," Holmes said. "Anyway, I do share your inclinations about heading straight for the Needles, but I must give the matter some thought."

"Do so, and then let's get going!"

Holmes withdrew his watch and turned slightly toward the window. The sky framed in the squares was bright blue, the sun having triumphed over the earlier mists. "It is well after three now, probably too late to try to set off today. Besides, there is no real hurry. The treasure has waited for years and years; another day or two will not matter. We can leave in the morning. Let us start back for the inn, but in a leisurely manner. I would like to have a closer look at some of the rooms."

I gestured with my open hand at the old man in the chair. "And this poor fellow? What is to be done with him?"

"I don't mean to be callous," Holmes said, "but I think it would be best to just leave him here. When his weekly visitor stops by, he will discover the body and know what to do. That society of theirs will see that he is buried alongside the other guardians in the cemetery."

"Poor old man," I murmured. "To think of all the lonely years he has spent here inside this rock, guarding so many secrets."

"He must have thought that what he was doing was worthwhile," Holmes said, "and perhaps, in the end, that is all that really matters."

Lupin raised his shoulders in a feigned shudder. "It is not the life for me! I could not do without some adventures—or without the ladies."

Holmes headed back for the door to the stairs, and we followed. The floor below was the library one, and Holmes went over to one of the tall shelves. Earlier he had extinguished his dark lantern, but now he relit it, then shined it on a row of colossal leather-bound volumes. "There must be scores of real rarities here," he said, even as he pulled one out.

I wandered across the room to the window-like opening which faced out toward the sea. This one was at an angle such that I could see off to the south on my left, the massive third arch of the Manneporte. Directly below, the dark blue waters were calm, waves visible as undulations in the surface, but with no whitecaps showing.

"Ah!" someone exclaimed. "Good day, gentlemen! Imagine meeting you here."

Startled, I quickly turned. At the doorway stood the tall, bearded Massier, the sour-looking baron beside him. Accustomed as I was to seeing them formally dressed, it had taken me a second or two to realize who they were. The baron wore a navy-blue woolen jacket with two rows of four golden buttons down the front, as well as a peaked naval-style cap, an eagle insignia over the brim. For once, his bushy mustache was unwaxed. Massier had on a nondescript dark gray woolen suit, a black bowler hiding his bald crown. With them were two burly men in mariners' blue-and-white-striped shirts, rifles slung across their backs, lanterns in hand.

Holmes appeared completely at ease and not in the least surprised. "Good afternoon, messieurs."

"Are we almost to the top?" Massier asked. "All these steps are quite wearisome."

Holmes nodded. "Indeed you are. Only one more set of stairs."

"And is there finally someone here? Someone who can tell us something?"

"I fear you are trifle late. He was a very old man, and the shock of our visit did him in."

The baron glared. "Did you kill him?"

"Certainly not!"

"But before he died—the secret—did he tell you the secret?"

"Regrettably, no." Lupin had slipped his spectacles back on, and now his voice had the high-pitched whine of Beautrelet. He gave a melodramatic sigh. "We were too late."

Holmes stared at him. His lips formed the familiar sardonic smile. "That is not exactly true."

"He told you, then!" the baron exclaimed. "He told you? Where is the treasure?"

Holmes folded his arms, even as Lupin shook his head vigorously and said, "No, no!"

"They moved it because they no longer thought it was safe in France. It is at the lighthouse at the other Needles, rock formations off the west coast of the Isle of Wight. My companions and I shall depart tomorrow from Le Havre and sail for England to continue the search."

There was nothing pleasant about the baron's smile. "We shall see about that."

"How on earth could you possibly find your way in here?" I asked. "You could not have made it through the labyrinth without the coded paper–it was difficult enough even with that. Somehow you must have followed us."

"I doubt that," Holmes said. "I was careful to make certain no one was nearby before we went into the entrance near the Demoiselles. Besides, they would have never been able to get past those two iron doors. No, I suspect there is another way into the cavern below, perhaps other than by land."

Massier smiled. "Very good, Monsieur Holmes. I think we should have a quick look at the deceased on the floor above. Not that we don't trust you."

The baron assumed a stern assumption. "I shall give the orders–not you."

Massier shrugged, his smile faintly ironic now. "As you wish, monsieur le baron."

Chamerac gestured with his head toward the stairway. "Let's go see."

We went up the stairs and walked over to the chair where the dead guardian sat slumped to the side.

Massier glanced over at the windows. "A regular seabird's aerie up here." He gazed down at the man. "He does look very old. Do you have any idea how many years he has been up here?"

"A very long time," Holmes said. "Over fifty years."

Massier shook his head. "What a wretched way to spend one's life."

The baron reached out and touched the dead man's cheek with his fingertips. "And he told you the secret? He told you about these other Needles?"

Holmes's eyes shifted to Lupin, a flicker of a smile stirring his lips. "With a little gentle persuasion."

"If you didn't kill him, how did he die?"

"It was most likely his heart," I said. "He appeared quite ill. His skin had a faintly grayish tint, and then he clutched at his chest in pain. He probably had one cardiac attack two or three days ago, and the second one finished him. Our arrival was something of a shock."

"And are you certain he told you the truth? The treasure is not hidden, instead, somewhere in this maze of chambers?" The baron was clearly suspicious.

"I have no doubts," Holmes said, "and you are welcome to see us off at the harbor of Le Havre tomorrow morning, should you wish to ascertain that we are headed for the Isle of Wight."

The baron had a most unpleasant smile. "Henceforth, I am not letting you out of my sight! I do not trust you. I shall accompany you to these other Needles."

"We shan't allow it!" Lupin again used the whiny Beautrelet voice.

"Oh, you won't, will you not? Well, you can certainly remain behind, Monsieur Beautrelet, while Massier and I go in your stead."

Holmes raised both hands. "If you are to accompany us, I insist we remain together. Beautrelet has been most helpful."

The baron still looked angry. "Very well—but I don't trust him—I don't trust any of you. You will not act on your own any longer. I will be watching your every move."

Holmes shrugged. "As you wish. Again, we can go to Le Havre tomorrow and set out for—"

"That will not be necessary," the baron said. "I can provide faster and more secure transportation directly to the Isle of Wight."

Holmes gave him a curious look. "Such as?"

"Do you have any further work to do here?"

"No."

"Then come along, and you will see, soon enough."

We started down the great conical formation of the Needle, each stairway curving around and inward, an occasional small window providing light for the steps cut in the rock, and we crossed the hollowed circular chambers which gradually increased in size. Holmes and the two mariners had their lanterns lit, and the beams of yellow-white light jumped about on the floors. The air grew colder and damper as we descended, and the last three floors had no carven openings, so we were in utter darkness save for the lantern light.

At last we came to the great natural cavern at the bottom. The baron and his men started toward the expanse of water off to one side. The circles of light revealed the rough, uneven limestone, but then came to the fluid black waters, which moved ever so slightly, a faint swish audible. Suddenly a smooth metallic surface showed with square patterns formed by the round heads of rivets; and as we came closer, I could make out a curving oval shape floating in the pool. It had narrow windows at the front, and a smokestack rising in back. The vessel must have been thirty feet long, and most of it was underwater.

"What in the world?" I murmured.

"That looks like a modified torpedo boat," Holmes said, then turned to the baron. "Doubtlessly one of your own manufacture?"

"Very good, Monsieur Holmes."

"But how did it get inside here?" I asked.

"It must be submersible," Holmes said. "Quite an interesting design. It resembles more the early ironclad torpedo boats of the American Confederacy rather than the modern ones used by European navies. The newer ones resemble more regular ships, but then they are generally larger nowadays, and of course, they cannot go underwater." Holmes turned again to the baron. "Does it actually have a torpedo?"

"No, it does not. It is not necessary."

Holmes appeared puzzled. "Not necessary in what sense?"

"You will find out soon enough."

"Well, anyway, now we know how they got inside here," Lupin said. "There must be an underwater opening here in the Needle connected with this cave."

Holmes gave his head a shake. "I suspect it must be a tight fit."

The baron laughed. "So it is—as you will see. Prepare to come aboard, messieurs."

A gangplank stretched from the rocky shore alongside the boat to a hatch situated midway between the two ends. Massier and the baron went first, and we followed, the two armed men behind us. I glanced at the metal stairway leading down inside and repressed a shudder, hesitating. Again, I do not like enclosed spaces—nor did I like the idea of being completely submerged underwater.

Holmes must have read my thought. "Do not be alarmed, Henry. The design and construction appear first-rate."

The baron gazed up at me from below and gave an emphatic nod. "So they are! This boat is unique—and more technically advanced than that of any navy in the world."

It was a tight fit inside and smelled somewhat rank, a mixture of tobacco smoke, sweat, and something acrid. We went down a narrow hallway lined on either side with a giant rectangular metallic box, on top of which were small cubes, each capped with copper tubing and wires. Holmes raised a hand and touched the bank on the right lightly. "These must be batteries with multiple cells. I suppose that is to power the boat when you are underwater?"

"Exactly," said the baron.

"And when you are above water, the craft must be steam-powered. From coal?"

"I see again that you are quite knowledgeable about naval vessels, Monsieur Holmes."

"But if you go underwater," I said, "doesn't the smoke stack flood?"

The baron gave me an incredulous look. "We are not so stupid as that, Dr. Vernier. We can close off or open the smokestack."

We had reached the front, and the baron pulled a lever. Through the glass windows we saw a sudden illumination, no doubt from some type of electrical lighting. The water came about halfway up the glass. The vessel was swaying ever so slightly. One of the men had come with us up front, while the other had joined another at the back where the coal furnace and the engines must be. It was crowded with five of us there; the cabin had metal seats only for three.

The baron stood before a wooden wheel and a bank of instruments and gauges. He glanced over his shoulder and spoke to his men. "Seal the hatch and prepare for departure." He pulled yet another lever, a bigger one, and turned the wheel with his other hand. We could see the rocky bank of limestone recede slightly as we backed away, turning as we went. I could feel the dull thrum of the motor in the metal floor under my feet.

One of the men had stepped away and returned. "She's all closed up."

"Prepare for descent." The baron turned a knob, and the water level at the windows slowly rose as we sank. A large gauge in the center of the panel was marked with numbers and the letter M, and its needle slowly swung round clockwise. It was clearly a depth gauge, and we continued to sink, even as the boat swung around again, its lights raking the limestone wall. I tried to assure myself that the vessel was watertight, but my hands felt sweaty. The water was an eerie green, almost transparent, but wavery all the same.

To our right a jagged black patch showed, but as we came around, the light illuminated the opening, showing a sort of tunnel. "Now comes the difficult part," the baron said. He turned the knob again, and there was a whooshing sound which made me start.

Holmes set his hand on my arm. "Probably some ballast being let out. We must have overshot our mark." And indeed, we had sunk below the opening, but now we were rising again.

"Very good, Monsieur Holmes." The baron was turning a knob. "That should do it."

We started slowly forward into the rocky aperture. The light showed the curving sides which were covered with some sort of brownish-green lichen or other growth. A big fish appeared, then darted quickly to the side.

"I suppose this would be quite difficult during low tide," Holmes said.

The baron nodded. "Impossible, actually. That was why our arrival was delayed until this afternoon."

Happily, from my viewpoint, we were only within the rocky tunnel very briefly, and then we came out into the open ocean. The sunlight illuminated the waters all around us, lighting up everything a vivid blue-green, and I could see from the gauge that we were only submerged about three meters or so. A school of small fish swam by. I gave a relieved sigh, and another one, when we began to rise again. Soon the bobbing water at sea level appeared at the top of the windows, slowly descending as we rose up.

The baron turned to Massier. "Take the wheel, Louis. Ahead full speed. You know the coordinates."

"*Oui, mon capitaine.*" Massier's voice was ever so faintly sarcastic.

The baron took out his cigarette case, withdrew one, and put it in his mouth. He nodded toward a sailor. "Open the hatch, and let's get some air in here." He struck a match and drew in on the cigarette. "Would you care for a smoke, Monsieur Holmes?"

"No, thank you. It seems a trifle too enclosed in here for that. I don't suppose... You are not thinking of traveling all the way to the Isle of Wight in this vessel, are you?"

I felt a sudden sensation of dread at the idea of being cooped up in this tiny boat with seven other men for the hours such a trip would take.

"Of course not! I am a better host than that."

"Thank God," I murmured.

The baron glanced at me, then the corners of his lips rose, his expression faintly contemptuous. "Why don't we go above? It is rather cramped down here."

He led us back down the hallway between the battery banks. Ahead was an open door, and we could see a sailor shoveling coal. The thrumming noise was much louder now. The baron went up the narrow metal stairway, and we followed.

I did feel greatly relieved to step out into the fresh sea air and the bright sunlight; above us was blue, slightly yellowish sky with dark blue-green sea, all around us. Evening was fast approaching, and the sun was nearing the horizon. A metal railing curved across the front deck, and there was space enough for Holmes, the baron, Lupin, and myself to all grab ahold of the cold damp rail.

Holmes turned his head back toward the stern, then touched my shoulder. "Have a look. It's quite a view."

Behind us towered the jagged striated rock of the Needle bathed in yellowish light, and further back to its left was the elephant trunk of the Porte d'Aval. Then came the curving bay of Étretat, and at the end the smaller arch of the Porte d'Amont. To our right, we had a superb view of the massive bulk of the curving Manneporte. Clearly we were headed out into the open sea of the English Channel in a northwest direction toward the Isle of Wight. The waters were calm, and we were obviously moving very quickly, much more so than on the usual ferries I took. I could feel the vibration of the boat with my hands on the rail, and also on the deck under my feet.

Between the rumble of the engines and the rush of the wind, it was too noisy to try to converse, so we all stood silently staring out at the open sea. The waters grew a little rougher, swaying slightly, but thankfully, there were still no whitecaps. Finally, after several minutes, the boat slowed, and then the engine suddenly cut out entirely. Now the swaying sound and the motion of the water was very noticeable, and there was only a slight breeze. Streaks of cloud were off to the west, coloring slightly orangish-red as the sun descended.

Holmes turned to the baron. "What now?"

The baron had taken out another cigarette, lit it, and exhaled smoke. "You shall know soon enough."

We were still rocking slightly, and I glanced about. We had not completely left the coastline of France, and I could see rocky cliffs topped with greenery in the distance, but no human habitations. Nor were there any other boats nearby.

"This is the perfect spot." The baron seemed to be talking to himself.

Lupin smiled. "A pleasant enough evening."

I was staring at the coastline, but I heard Holmes draw in his breath. His hand grasped my shoulder. "Ah—look!"

I turned back toward the Channel. Ahead of us in the vast swaying expanse of water, a long silver-gray ellipsoid formed, slowly growing even as it rose up, clearly revealing its torpedo shape. Most of the thing was underwater, but whatever it was, it was enormous, well over two hundred feet long. I muttered the first thing that popped into my head. "A whale?" I shook my head, then more softly, "Obviously not." Its surface looked to be metal, not the skin of a fish or mammal, and a slight hump rose up near the far end. For a second, I thought I saw an eye, then I recognized round glass. "What on earth?"

Holmes's face beneath the brim of his hat, was faintly flushed, his gray-blue eyes gleaming in the fading light, even as a smile pulled at his mouth. "Incredible. So this is where all the money has gone. What is the name of your submarine, monsieur le baron?"

Chamerac looked pleased with Holmes's enthusiasm. "That should be obvious."

"Ah. The *Nautilus*, I suppose."

The baron nodded. "*Exactement.*"

Part 3

THE NEEDLES, ISLE OF WIGHT

Chapter 11

ℰ

O ur boat slowly headed nearer the center of the long vessel, where a flat expanse was visible, then came to a halt. A metal hatch was flung open, and two men came out. One of them threw us a length of rope. Massier and a mariner had come up from below, and the mariner caught the rope and drew us alongside the submarine.

The baron gestured with his hand toward ship. "The *Nautilus* will take us to the Isle of Wight. We shall be there by morning."

I glanced at the huge vessel floating there and felt a sudden queasiness in my stomach. This must be an experimental craft: we would definitely be putting our lives in peril. I could think of no worse way of dying than being trapped underwater and slowly suffocating or drowning.

I tried to speak lightly. "I hate to be a killjoy, but might we not use more conventional transportation to the Isle? Why not follow the original plan of going by ferry?"

The baron gave me an incredulous look. "This will be much

swifter and more comfortable."

Holmes glanced at me, then at the baron. "There is, in fact, no need for Henry to accompany us. Why don't you have your men take him and young Beautrelet back ashore, and we can go on without them?"

Lupin shook his head. "I wouldn't miss this for anything!"

"I'm not going to be separated from you," I said.

The baron's smile had a harsh edge. "Perhaps there is a slight misunderstanding here. I, and I alone, am in charge of this search. I meant it when I said I would not let you out of my sight. Don't force me to make threats involving my men and the use of force. Sufficient to say, I have chosen this submarine to take us to the Isle of Wight, and you will all accompany me without further ado."

Holmes stared at me. "I still think you might make an exception for Henry. He is not essential."

I forced myself to smile. "Not essential! I like that! No, as I said, I shall not be separated from you, Sherlock."

He set his hand on my shoulder. "Bravo, Henry. I think the vessel is sound enough."

"And so it is," the baron said. "Although quite new, having been launched only a month ago, it performed superbly during its initial voyage. The *Nautilus* went out into the deep Atlantic for some tests. They took her down to 200 meters without problems."

Holmes's mouth twitched into a brief smile. "*They?* I take it you were not on board, then?"

"No. I was otherwise occupied."

Holmes looked amused.

"Not that I had any misgivings! None in the least. As I said, she passed her tests with flying colors. Jules Verne has his submarine descending thousands of meters, but even with a double steel hull one cannot really go below two or three hundred without the pressure crushing the vessel. But enough of this—come aboard, gentlemen, and do consider yourselves as my honored guests."

"Rather than captives," Lupin murmured loud enough for everyone to hear.

The baron gave him a disapproving glance. "You should feel honored to be the first to see this submarine, which will truly change the history of the world. It is a technological marvel, and no country on earth has a vessel even remotely its equal."

We followed him across a gangplank, and as we came to the large open hatch, I drew in my breath and tried to ignore my fears, especially the thought that this could be my last time above water in the open air and the light of day. I wondered, too, if I would ever see my beloved Michelle again.

The baron descended, and we followed: Holmes first, next Lupin, then me, and finally Massier. The metal stairway down was very steep, almost closer to a ladder, and I clutched the rail tightly.

We gathered in small metal chamber with a hallway branching in either direction, and more stairs going down further below. The two men, standing nearby, were big and rough-looking. One had a long scar on his cheek, and his nose looked as if it had been broken. They wore uniforms modeled after those of the French Navy, dark blue blouses and trousers, as well as a beret-like blue hat with a pompom on top. The atmosphere seemed heavy and had even more of a stench than that of the other boat, a stale mixture of sweat and tobacco smoke. Technical marvel the ship might be, but the air circulation would seem to have room for improvement.

"Secure the hatch," the baron said.

One of the men climbed up the stairs, grasped about for a handle, then lowered the hatch. He used both hands to turn a metal wheel to secure it in place.

The baron turned to us. "I shall have the captain get us underway, and then, if you would like, I can give you a quick tour of the ship before dinner."

"Excellent," Holmes said.

Lupin grinned and spoke in the high-pitched theatrical Beautrelet voice. "Oh, this is all so very exciting!"

One of the sailors stared at him as if he were daft.

Both hallways were lit up by interspersed glowing white domes, no doubt powered by electricity, and the floors and walls were of some dark polished wood. We started down the corridor toward the front of the submarine, and passed several substantial doors of metal, which must be watertight.

Massier paused before one of them. "I take it you no longer need me."

The baron's lips twitched briefly. "No." He withdrew his watch. "We shall dine in an hour at the usual time, 7:30 P.M."

Massier nodded, then opened the door and stepped inside what must be his cabin.

We continued on, until we came to another stairway. We went up, one by one, and crowded into a small circular room with four round windows set at ninety-degree intervals. A thin, grim-looking man wearing a navy jacket with gold buttons and a peaked cap, both much like the baron's, clearly did not like having so many visitors in his domain. Nor did the stout sailor at his side. Besides the many gauges, dials, and various levers, a bulky bronze mechanism stood atop a metal shaft. Before the front window was a tall ornate wooden wheel with a brass center and eight wooden handles around the rim. Its purpose was obvious enough.

"Take her down, Didier, and then head northwest. We're going to the Isle of Wight. We can plot the exact course once we're underway."

Didier gave a curt sort of nod, then flipped one lever, then a second. He grasped a brass metal horn and spoke into it. "All hands prepare for submersion."

Again I could see a big dial with M marked on it for meters. It had gradations which went from 0 to 500. The interval between 300 and 500 was colored red. Obviously 300 meters must be the maximum advisable depth for the submarine. Once again, I saw the water rise up in the round windows as we sank, and soon there were only circles of wavery greenish-yellow at the ports, dimming even as we sank. Didier pulled down a lever, and the water at the windows was suddenly illuminated from some external light source. He stopped our descent at only about ten meters.

Again he spoke into the tube. "Battery room, bring us up to eight knots." At his side was a big wooden stand with an enormous compass, two large metal balls on either side of it. A distant rumble started up, something which could be felt underfoot as well as heard. Didier turned the wheel, bringing us slowly about until the compass dial pointed between north and west.

"Why is the compass set between those two large metal spheres?" I asked Holmes.

"That is called a binnacle, Henry, and those two balls compensate for the interference caused by the metal hull of the submarine." Holmes glanced overhead. "And unless I am much mistaken, that is a periscope you have there, monsieur le baron."

"Very good, Monsieur Holmes. Your knowledge of naval vessels is most impressive."

"What is the periscope for?" Lupin asked.

"It allows us to see above the water when we are submerged," the baron replied. His smile became rather gloating. "It also allows us to aim."

Holmes frowned. "Aim with what?"

"Ah, well, rather than answering that directly, let me show you. We shall commence our tour of the ship there—fittingly enough, at its most forward point."

We descended from the pilot house, and continued on down another level below the wooden corridor. "The ship has two decks, the second one being more well-furnished for the officers and passengers, while the bottom one is for the crew and operations." Indeed, the hallway was again lit up, but everything was of made of metal down here, a maze of pipes and wires lining the walls. The floor itself was a metal grate.

The baron opened a nearby door, and we found ourselves in a tall room with a narrow opening down the middle. On either side, rising to the ceiling high above, were stacked eight long metal tubes, each over a foot and a half in diameter and perhaps fifteen feet long, with fins and a propellor at one end. There was a sort of inclined plane beneath each of the two stacks where a tube rested, and at the far wall were two round metal hatches to what must be some sort of loading chambers. A large sign proclaimed in red letters, INTERDICTION DE FUMER—no smoking.

Lupin shook his head. "I'll be damned—torpedoes!" The voice was not quite right, but he added, sounding more like Beautrelet. "Who could have ever imagined such a thing?"

Holmes said nothing but looked grim.

The baron was smiling. "Nemo's *Nautilus* would ram ships to sink them. That was all well and good in the old days with wooden hulls, but to ram a modern naval warship with its thick armored steel hull would greatly threaten the integrity of this vessel. Instead we can remain at a distance and fire a torpedo. One of these can deal with even the thickest battleship's hull."

"What on earth do you intend to do with all of these!" I was dismayed.

"All in good time, Dr. Vernier. I shall tell you more about my plans at dinner."

"I suppose they must use gun cotton as their explosive," Holmes said.

The baron nodded. "Exactly. In a very dense configuration. But come along, let me show you the rest of the ship."

We started down the corridor. Unlike the hallway above, this was one was quite constricting. and I felt faintly claustrophobic. We went by two sailors, and in each case, they had to squeeze against the wall, and we could only pass by in single file. Both wore the same navy-blue uniform, and neither of them looked very happy to see us. As we proceeded toward the stern, the rumbling and vibration from the engines grew louder.

The baron paused before a doorway. "This is the crew's quarters." He gave Lupin a contemptuous smile. "You will be spending the night here, Monsieur Beautrelet."

The chamber was a long narrow one, and all was gray metal. Narrow bunks made up with brown blankets were stacked three high, and metal lockers lined one wall. Two men were lying on the beds.

Lupin laughed. "How charming! I cannot wait."

The baron was obviously irritated by this response.

We continued on. At the end of the corridor were big metal doors to either side, and the baron opened the one to the left. We saw rows of iron-gray metal rectangular cuboids about six feet tall; a jungle of wires connected all the units and then ran along the wall to disappear fore and aft. We stepped inside. A hum could be almost more felt, rather than heard, because the steady thrum of the nearby engines was so loud, and the air had an acrid smell.

"This is one of the battery rooms." The baron had to speak very loudly to be heard. "The other one is just across from this one. We have, in effect, two gigantic batteries, each with two hundred and fifty cells. They can power the ship for a maximum of about forty-eight hours at moderate speeds, but after that, we must surface. By then, our air supply is also compromised. The rotary electric motor which turns our propeller can then run off steam power from coal, even as the batteries are being recharged. As a practical matter, this means we typically travel submerged during the daylight when someone might spot us, and at night we voyage on the surface. That, in fact, is what we shall do tonight. Soon it will be quite dark, and the *Nautilus* will surface and make most of our journey to the Isle of Wight on the open sea."

Holmes glanced about the humming banks of battery cells; the air in the room was noticeably warmer than in the corridor. "Do these batteries employ an electrolyte of potassium hydroxide with electrodes of zinc and copper oxide? That, I believe, is the plan for the latest French submarine under construction."

"Very good, Monsieur Holmes! You are well informed, indeed, but no, that is much more primitive technology! Recharging would be impossible. These are lead-acid batteries, employing electrodes of lead and lead sulfate, with an electrolyte of sulfuric acid in water."

We went back into the corridor, and the baron closed the door, then went to the one at the end of the corridor. "Beyond here is the engine room. As I said, when the batteries are offline, a coal-fired boiler provides electric power for the rotary motor. Of course, in that case, we have to vent smoke and exhaust via a stack. It is rather deafening in here, I'm afraid. I can let you have a quick look, but I don't think we shall want to go inside."

He spun a metal wheel, then opened what was by far the largest door yet. A blast of heat struck us, and the thrum became deafening, and was accompanied by a rhythmic clanging. Inside the dimly lit room was another great maze of wires and pipes, often very thick pipes, running all along the walls and ceiling. A brawny bare-chested sailor stood with a shovel near a coal bin and a furnace, while another man was by a complex instrument panel. A huge shaft ran through one side of the room, and large wheels with gears and pulleys were all turning, buzzing, and whirring at different speeds.

The baron gave us an inquisitive glance, but even Holmes seemed unenthusiastic about entering the engine room. The baron closed the door and turned the wheel. The relative silence was a relief.

"Let us go up a deck, and you will see the more comfortable parts of the ship."

We went back down the corridor and followed him up a staircase. We started along the more spacious, upper deck hallway, and the interspersed ceiling lights brought out the dark wooden grain of the polished floors and walls. The noise from the engines became quieter. The baron opened another large door with a wheel, again, and we stepped into a dramatically different room, one appropriate for some elegant town house. A fantastical oriental carpet of many colors was on the floor, the massive sofas and chairs were of red-brown leather or velvet, the end tables and bookcases of dark oak, and to either side, two large oval windows gave a view of the ocean depths. A beautiful tall-case clock of inlaid wood, its pendulum swinging regularly, looked to be a close relative to those at the Château de l'Aiguille.

"This is the salon," the baron said.

Holmes looked about. "Obviously this is modeled after Verne's *Nautilus.*"

"Certainly, although the room is somewhat smaller. His took up two decks' worth, while mine is only on one deck."

"And what are the exact dimensions of your submarine? Do they match those of Verne's *Nautilus*?"

"Almost. His submarine was seventy meters long, with a beam of eight meters, while mine is sixty-five by nine."

"Close indeed. And tell me: what speed is this vessel capable of?"

"She can do ten knots submerged, and twenty knots on the surface."

Holmes was clearly surprised. "That is faster than the latest battleships. HMS *Victoria* will only do about sixteen."

"By now you should understand that this vessel has no equal amongst modern navies."

The baron went to one of the windows and pulled a lever. Immediately light illuminated the greenish depths, and we could see a school of big reddish fish sweep by. The water flickered and danced, undulating, as the submarine sped along.

Holmes gave a brusque nod. "Most impressive indeed."

Lupin was smiling. "I never thought I would live to see such a sight."

I said nothing. I was still thinking about those torpedoes at the front of the ship.

"Come along, messieurs. A few last rooms, and then we shall have our supper."

Next door, to our right, was the dining room, and a large table had been set with an elegant linen tablecloth, fine patterned blue and white china plates and silverware; to the left, in the steam-filled galley, a chef and his assistant were hard at work. We continued down the hallway, passing the central stairway up to the top deck. The baron showed us two cozy well-furnished guest rooms where Holmes and I would spend the night. Next came the captain's cabin, and finally, near the very end, was a huge room reserved for the baron himself. An oaken four-poster bed dominated the chamber, and nearby were a matching wardrobe and desk, and a well-stacked bookcase. It certainly seemed a world apart from the austere metallic quarters for the crew below.

We returned to the dining room to find Massier standing before the sideboard, a snifter of brandy held in one large hand, while the other stroked thoughtfully at his full dark beard. The glowing overhead electric lights set in a crystal chandelier gleamed on his broad sloping cranium. He had changed into his dark blue suit.

A big man in a blue sailor's uniform came into the room. He was nearly as tall as Holmes and me, but much brawnier, with broad shoulders and gigantic, powerful-looking hands. His reddish-brown hair was trimmed almost to a shadow over his ears, and only an inch or two sprouted up on top. His lips were very thin and pressed tightly together. He gave us a wary look.

"What would you like to drink?" he asked.

The baron frowned. "What would you like to drink, *messieurs.*"

The man scowled. "Messieurs. What do you want?"

We told him, and he poured us each an aperitif, then disappeared back into the galley. The baron shook his head. "I must apologize. He is only a coarse sailor, not an appropriately trained servant. I shall be bringing some of my regular staff along when I undertake a longer voyage."

"I have noticed," Holmes said, "that your crew are rather— how should I say it?—unsavory-looking. I suspect you did not hire regular mariners but men with a more checkered past."

"Very good, Monsieur Holmes! You are the master of euphemism. That is exactly the case. I wanted men who would absolutely follow my orders, come what may."

Holmes's faint smile was without humor. "Men, so to speak, without any moral scruples whatsoever."

The baron looked amused and gave a slight shrug of his shoulders. "You understand me, I see."

"All too well, I think."

The baron soon guided us to our places at the beautifully set table. I unfolded a large linen napkin and laid it over my lap. The big sailor soon appeared bearing plates with steaming pieces of meat, pork by the smell of it, as well as mashed potatoes and green beans. The chef in his white apron also came in and poured red wine into our elaborate goblets. After we had all been served, the baron looked about, then took up his glass.

"Rather primitive fare compared to what I would serve you in Paris, but my *Nautilus* is still not completely furnished. I hope to do better in the future! I give you a toast, gentlemen: to the great treasure of France. May it soon be ours!"

There was some clinking of glasses, but clearly none of us shared the baron's enthusiasm. We set to, and I ate rather mechanically, without much appetite. The pork was good, but hardly the equal of that we had eaten at the château only a few days past. Somehow it seemed an eternity ago. Holmes and Lupin asked the baron questions about the submarine, but I remained silent, as did Massier. He regarded the baron through languid half-closed eyes with a sort of faint contempt.

The baron explained how, as with the fictional *Nautilus*, parts of the submarine had been constructed all around the world.

Then it was assembled on a small island off the French coast, "whose location must, of course, remain a secret."

Holmes had finished eating and sat back in his chair. "It must have cost you a true fortune. You spent every penny you had and borrowed all that you could."

The baron swished his wine in its glass, admiring its color, then took a sip. "I'm afraid it has bankrupted me, but it was worth it, as you can see. The result is a masterpiece of engineering and technology, a submarine as far advanced for its time as Nemo's was for 1870. Fiction has become—as you have seen—reality."

"Of course, marvelous as your submarine is, the perpetually charged batteries of the novel are not possible. You can only be submerged for a day or two."

The baron shrugged. "True enough. Perhaps someday someone will find a truly perpetual power source, but until then... Besides, it does not exactly matter. If we surface at night, we can still remain hidden."

"And I believe you said that diving to the very bottom of the ocean is also not possible?"

"Unfortunately not. My top engineer and I did all the calculations. Even a double steel-alloy hull like this one cannot support depths much below three hundred meters. Again, I am certain that someday these problems will be resolved. We shall continue our research. Who knows what the future may bring?"

"And do you wish to circumnavigate the globe like Nemo?" Lupin asked.

"Eventually, yes, although because of the ship's limitations I don't think it will be possible to make it to the South Pole! All the same, messieurs, we live at the dawn of an amazing age of science and technology. Indeed, my *Nautilus* is proof enough of that! And *la belle*

France will be at the forefront of the new age. I shall see to it."

I regarded him warily. "And so you will share your discoveries with the world?"

"Eventually, yes."

Holmes and I exchanged a glance. We had both remarked his use of the word *eventually*.

"Nemo was content to have only one submarine," Holmes said. "I suspect you have grander plans."

The baron laughed. "Very good, Monsieur Holmes! This ship is only the predecessor of a fleet to come."

I was frowning. "But you said it cost a fortune."

"So it did, Doctor. But I hope to soon have another fortune—a much greater one."

Holmes swirled his own wine, then took a sip. "The treasure of France, you mean."

"Exactly." He laughed again. "Come now, Monsieur Holmes, you did not ever really believe I would surrender it, did you? That was only a polite fiction between the two of us."

Holmes smiled faintly. "Yes, I suppose it was."

"So you plan to steal the treasure?" I said. "To steal the treasure of the people of France?"

"Come now, Dr. Vernier—it is not the treasure of the people. It is the great treasure of the *kings* of France!"

"But that is outrageous! I would not have thought you capable of such a theft!" Lupin spoke with the high whiny Beautrelet voice, and while he might have fooled the baron, I knew he was only acting again.

"I don't much care what you think, Beautrelet. If you behave, I shall set you ashore on the Isle of Wight. If not..." He shrugged. "But you, Monsieur Holmes—if you would like, you could accompany me on the first extended voyage of the *Nautilus*. As I indicated, she passed her shakedown cruise with flying colors. You could see her in action. I've tried the torpedo on a stationary target of my own, an old ship destined for the scrapheap, but I haven't used them against a real warship. That will be one of my first endeavors."

I stared at him. "You want to sink a warship?"

"Of course! What do you think the point of the torpedoes is? Unfortunately for you English, Monsieur Holmes, you have the most advanced ships, so it is against your navy that I must prove myself. I hope to sink a battleship, either the *Victoria* or the *Trafalgar*. I have not quite made up my mind which one yet."

"And you—you would kill the entire crew?" My voice shook.

"That is the point of sinking a ship, is it not?"

"But why would you do such a thing!"

He stared at me. "That, too, is obvious, is it not? It is to prove that my ship is the master of the oceans, that none can stand against me." He was smiling amiably and looked about. "But I see everyone has finished eating. I have an excellent port there on the sideboard. And would you care for a cigar? I have some superb Cubans."

I could only stare at him, but Holmes said, "I would gladly sample one of your cigars."

"And I," Lupin said.

The baron gave him a contemptuous look. "I suppose you are old enough to smoke one." He stood up, then went to the sideboard and brought over a tray with the port and some glasses. Next came a wooden box with the cigars. He began to pour the port.

"Would you care for some, Dr. Vernier?"

"I don't want anything."

"A pity."

"I still cannot believe it." My voice trembled again. "That you would sink a ship just to prove... What is the point of it all? Why must you be the master of the blasted seas?"

The baron gave a mock weary sigh and glanced at Holmes. "Is he always this obtuse? I would think it is rather obvious, Dr. Vernier. You know that the blood of the Bourbons flows in my veins, do you not?" He lit his cigar.

I stared at him, then shrugged. "What of it?"

"What of it!" He was briefly angry, then smiled. "What of it? I was born into the nobility—into a royal tradition that goes back centuries." He sat up very straight. "Do you think I enjoy seeing my family humiliated and ignored, passed over by imbeciles? All these pretenders to the throne, worthless cretins, and this foolish Republic unable to do anything, a feeble reed swaying in the wind? And the Prussians—growing in strength, growing in dominance! Left unchecked, they will try again to conquer France—to humiliate us once more. No, no, I shall never allow it!"

He had grown quite red in the face. He drew in deeply on the cigar, calming himself. "You see, I do care about my country, after all."

Holmes and Lupin were staring at him. Holmes had just cut off the end of the cigar, and now he lit it. "I take it you plan on remedying the situation."

The baron sat back in his chair and tapped his cigar end on the edge of his dinner plate, knocking ash into some congealed pork fat. "Yes, certainly. France achieved greatness under Louis the Fourteenth and under Napoleon Bonaparte—and again, to a much lesser degree, under Louis Napoleon—but it has never lasted. My empire will be more permanent, a dynasty that will endure. My submarines will ensure its future."

I could hardly believe what I was hearing. "*Your* empire?"

"Yes. Once I rule the seas, it will be a simple matter to overthrow the Republic. The people will welcome me with open arms. The throne is rightfully mine, after all. France will be happy to have a king again, especially an all-powerful one. The Mediterranean will be mine, the Atlantic will be mine, and the riches I can command will make it possible to raise a great army—my army. My engineers also have ideas for new weapons of war. Soon we will be invincible. My conquests will surpass even those of Bonaparte. Someday soon the French flag will fly over every capital of Europe."

He was smiling happily again. "It is interesting. I have long reflected upon what flag I shall use. I considered abandoning the tricolor entirely. After all, it is associated with the Revolution and the Republics. All the same, it has a certain sentimental appeal to the French. I think I shall do what Napoleon did: keep the tricolor, but embellish it with my own symbol in the center. I'll bring back the crown and the three golden fleur-de-lis of the Louis. Yes, it will be a combination of the old and the new!"

Holmes and I exchanged another look. Massier had said almost nothing, but he was smiling faintly. He had not been exaggerating in his appraisal of the baron. I think we all understood that the man was quite mad.

"I suspect you have your campaign all planned out," Holmes said.

"Indeed I do! It begins—regrettably, I fear, from your point of view—with the subjugation of the British navy. But for her navy, England is a rather small and insignificant island on the outskirts of Europe. As for the Germans..."

The baron went on at length to describe his plans for conquest. Holmes and Lupin asked a few occasional questions, but I merely listened in disbelief at what I was hearing. Gradually I was caught up in what he was saying, and I had to remind myself that making yourself king of France and conquering all of Europe could not be quite so simple!

At last the baron withdrew his watch, then stood up. "It is after nine and time that we surfaced. I must see to it with the captain." He regarded Massier rather warily. "Come along, Louis. And you, gentlemen, you can retire to the salon and relax there until bedtime. I believe you all know where your sleeping quarters are." He smiled contemptuously at Lupin. "You can choose any free bunk in the crew's quarters. We shall make good speed on the surface, and even before dawn we shall be off the Isle of Wight by these Needles."

The two men left. Holmes, Beautrelet, and I regarded each other. I spoke first. "He is completely insane, is he not?"

"Not much doubt of that," Lupin said. "He sounded eerily like I did this afternoon when I made my claim to be the royal heir to the throne. I was a Bourbon too! He was practically quoting some of my best lines."

"Mad he may be," Holmes said, "but if he finds the treasure and manages to build a fleet of submarines like this one, he might indeed destroy the Royal Navy and command the seas."

I shook my head. "Let us hope we cannot find it—or that it does not amount to much."

We went to the salon, and we were there as the submarine gradually rose to the surface. Shortly after, the distant thrum of the engines increased in volume, and we knew we were well underway.

I was rather tired out—it had been quite a day—and Holmes and I soon went to our cabins. A large nightshirt and robe had been laid out on my bed. I undressed, put them on, and got under the sheets. Exhausted I might be, but I could not sleep. When I put my head down on the pillow, I could feel the faint vibration of the ship's hull, and the hum of the engines was louder. But that was not what kept me awake. I was only too aware that I was in an experimental vessel out for just the second time, and who knew how reliable it really was? At least we were no longer underwater, where it might be crushed by pressure and sink.

Also troubling me was the baron's obvious insanity. I have seen patients I thought were normal, who suddenly and casually revealed themselves to be completely crazy. Sometimes the line between madness and sanity seems very narrow, and one might easily slip across it. The fact that there are simply no effective medical treatments whatsoever makes such a diagnosis truly frightening. And asylums, by and large, are dreadful places.

Even more troubling was the idea that the baron might succeed in his objectives! If he did manage to build a fleet of submarines, he would truly be unstoppable. He could blackmail the nations of the world into paying him to keep the ocean lanes open, and with all that wealth, he might indeed manage to make himself king of France. The damage he might do seemed… limitless.

After tossing and turning for a while, I got out of bed and went out into the hallway. The door to Holmes's room was ajar, and light was streaming into the hallway. I glanced inside. He was seated in a chair near the desk, still dressed.

"So you cannot sleep, Henry?" he asked. "Come in and join me." He gestured at the other chair. "I wish I had my pipe and a pouch of shag. A good smoke always helps me think, but it is just as well. The air in here is foul enough without that."

"So it is. That was perhaps one reason I was restless. The air seems somehow inadequate, and faintly dirty."

"I can only imagine what it must be like if they remain underwater into a second day."

I ran my fingers through my hair, then lowered my hand. "Whatever are we going to do, Sherlock? We must somehow stop him."

Holmes's mouth twisted into a brief grimace. "Indeed we must. This truly is a marvelous vessel, and it is far beyond those of any European navy. All the same—if I could blow it to smithereens, I would gladly do so."

I smiled faintly. "Preferably when we are not on board."

He smiled back. "Yes. Preferably." His smile faded. "But if the opportunity arises to sabotage this ship..." He noticed my expression. "Don't worry, Henry! I would wait until you and Lupin are no longer on board."

"Would you actually accept his invitation to join him on his voyage?"

"If that is what it takes."

I shook my head. "Now I shall never sleep!"

He gave my forearm a quick squeeze. "Come now, somehow I do not think that it will come to that. This case has certainly been one surprise after another. I had surmised that he might have been spending money on some colossal naval construction, but all the same—never in my wildest imagination did I expect to be traveling this evening by submarine to the Isle of Wight! We shall just have to wait and see, Henry. The treasure is still a wild card. I am certain more surprises are in store for us."

Chapter 12

I did not sleep much that night, and I had vivid dreams involving the cramped quarters of submarines. The baron was smiling and talking incessantly, with a treasure chest on a table before him and a golden crown on his head, but he was ignoring the fact that icy seawater was pouring in through the open hatch.

I tried to yell that we were sinking, but the words would not come out. The water was a yellowish-green, and rose up over my head. I knew I would drown and that I could not breathe, and a terrible panic came over me. I swam toward the hatch, desperate to get out, but I seemed to be going nowhere despite all my efforts. All about me was that greenish water obscuring and distorting everything. Soon we would hit the bottom, and I would be trapped inside. If only I could move…

My eyes jerked opened, and it took me a few seconds to remember where I was. I threw aside the covers and sat up. Yellow-white light glowed faintly from the overhead, and a clock on the wall showed it was half past four. I rose, put on a robe, and went to Holmes's room.

The door was open, and he was lying on the bunk, still fully dressed in his tweeds, his head resting on his raised hands and the fluffy pillow. His eyes were open, and he smiled faintly. "Good morning, Henry."

"Have you slept at all?"

"A little. And you?"

"Also a little, but I have had such terrible dreams."

He lowered his arms and swung his legs around as he rose up to a sitting position. "Perhaps we should see if we can go up on deck. I believe we stopped moving a few minutes ago. We must have reached our destination."

"That seems a good idea. Perhaps some air would clear my head. I'll just get dressed." I gestured with my hands toward my robe and nightshirt. "For such a short night, it was hardly worth putting these on."

After I had changed, Holmes and I went down the wood-lined corridor to the central staircase. Dim light flooded in from the open hatch above, and the air was noticeably cooler and wetter, a faint pressure on my face rising and falling gently. A circular fragment of sky was gray, overcast, and featureless, but luminous—it was no longer night, but not yet day, either. Holmes started up, and I followed.

The wind felt much stronger outside, and the cool damp mist engulfed us and took the sharp edges off everything. We could see Massier and the baron a few feet away holding onto a railing, and further in the distance the white chalk cliffs could be made out, as well as the imposing structure of a lighthouse. It sat on the outermost and nearest rock, a tall pale gray tower with a thick black band painted around its middle, the contrast designed, no doubt, to make it more visible from afar. The iron frame of the glass-paneled and glowing lantern portion and its conical roof were also black.

The light itself shone not white, but red, dulled, and obscured somewhat by the mist. Mercifully, the dark seas about us were nearly flat, the submarine swaying ever so gently. The deck was only two or three feet above the water. Off to my right, to the east, the sky was noticeably lighter as dawn approached.

I frowned. "Is there some reason the light from the lighthouse is red?"

"It has to do with the angle of approach of one's ship," Holmes said. "There are fixed shades that can color the lamp's light, and one sees red if one is headed for rocks, or for the treacherous shallows with shingle. However, when you reach the right approach, the color will change from red to white."

Suddenly the distant, cavernously deep clang of a bell could be heard, no doubt an audible warning from the lighthouse to any nearby ships.

"Ah, there you are! Good morning, my friends." Lupin had come up the stairs, and I could tell from his tone of voice and his smiling countenance that he was in good spirits.

"Did you sleep well?" I asked.

"Like the proverbial baby. Oh, it did take me a while to fall asleep, what with all the thrumming and clanging, but once I had surrendered to the arms of Morpheus, nothing could wake me." He stared past me. "That's a very impressive lighthouse, isn't it? We must have made good time. I wonder how far we are from Étretat."

"I think it is about a hundred miles," Holmes said.

Again the deep bell sounded. "Is someone actually ringing that, I wonder?" I asked.

"Certainly not," Holmes said. "Typically, both the rotation of a Fresnel lens and the ringing of the bell are driven by clockwork mechanisms. In this case, it is true only for the bell. The lighthouse has a fixed lens, rather than a rotating one. You can see only the steady glow of its light, rather than a beam sweeping round and round. That is often the case with a first-order lens because they are so very heavy, over six tons or so, I believe."

"But what exactly powers the bell?" I asked.

"Typically a steel cable extends the length of the tower and has a very heavy counterweight on the end. One cranks up the weight and the cable using a winch with a lever. The weight then slowly descends, impelling all the various gears and cogwheels."

"How clever!" Lupin exclaimed. "And that lamp must burn oil, I suspect."

"Originally whale oil, and then lard oil, were used, but nowadays they have mostly switched over to kerosene."

The baron turned to us, one hand still grasping the railing. "I can tell you must know as much about lighthouses as you know about naval vessels, Monsieur Holmes. It is good to have someone so well informed aboard. Let us go below and have breakfast. Afterwards the sun will be up, and we can visit the lighthouse and begin our search."

Holmes gave him a questioning look. "Certainly we cannot go much closer by submarine. The sea is quite shallow near the lighthouse with dangerous shingle. In the old days, many ships ran aground there."

"We will only go a little nearer, and then we shall take the launch over." He gestured toward the front of the submarine. "It lies under some watertight doors just there. I'll have my men prepare it while we are eating."

We descended into the ship with the baron, and soon we were seated in the dining room, the surly seaman once again acting as our waiter. In honor of his guests, the baron had had his cook prepare a version of a hearty English breakfast, so there were scrambled eggs, bacon, sausages, toast, potatoes, and even some foul-smelling little fish that were apparently supposed to pass for kippers.

I didn't have much appetite and ate very little, but Holmes and Lupin seemed determined to fortify themselves for our upcoming enterprise, and they consumed a prodigious amount of food. The strong dark coffee was very good and revived me somewhat. I wondered what new surprises the day might bring—or, in a more cynical frame of mind, what new insanities! Certainly, at breakfast the day before in Étretat, I had never expected to travel to the Isle of Wight by submarine, and breakfast underwater the next day.

The baron, Massier, and Lupin were obviously excited at the prospect of finding the treasure. Holmes and I were more reserved, but even for me, a certain wonderment stirred. Would this be the day in which a centuries-old fortune was finally uncovered? Or would the whole thing turn out to be mere nonsense, a long-running hoax perpetrated by some French zealots?

Shortly after dawn, a few minutes before six, we gathered on deck. The mists had faded somewhat; the lighthouse, the white chalk of the three rock formations and the higher, nearby coastal cliffs, appeared more visible, more tangible. I could also make out the individual blocks of the lighthouse wall, each one a varying shade of grayish white, save for that black band painted in the middle, which covered perhaps a quarter of the tower. Those blocks must be cut from some massive rock, like granite, which could resist the winds and waters which often assailed the structure. The bell still clanged loudly every few minutes, the sound resonating through the fog and resounding off the waters. We must have traveled a way further in, because the lantern now shone white instead of red.

The launch bobbed up and down alongside the *Nautilus*. A wooden craft, it was about fifteen feet long with four oars manned by brawny-looking sailors in navy wool coats and berets. Another sailor, also in blue but with a crew cap, was at the tiller to the rear. Metal treads were set into one side of the submarine's gray hull, and we carefully stepped down. One of the sailors helped us in.

The boat was large and heavy, but I still didn't like the way it swayed when I stepped in. Thank God, however, that this was nothing like a rowboat, which a clumsy passenger could easily capsize! It was four or five feet wide, and Holmes, Lupin, and I sat together on one sturdy wooden thwart connecting the two sides. All three of us still wore sturdy woolen tweeds, Holmes and I with overcoats as well.

Lupin and I had our cloth caps, Holmes his familiar wrinkled walking hat of fuzzy blue-gray wool. He smiled at me from under the brim, gesturing toward the lighthouse with his head. "A rather exciting way to begin the day."

Behind us sat Massier and the baron. Chamerac muttered something, and a sailor pulled at a rope to withdraw it from a metal ring in the submarine hull. The oarsmen set to work, and soon the boat had swung around and was headed toward the lighthouse. The wind had picked up slightly, the water somewhat choppy, and I reflected how one always felt colder and chillier out in the open ocean.

"Do you know how tall the lighthouse is?" Lupin asked Holmes.

"About one hundred feet, I believe."

I gave my head a shake. "You seem very familiar with it."

"Lighthouses have always interested me, Henry, and this is one of the more famous ones. Also, I think I mentioned that I have visited this part of the Isle of Wight before. I stopped at Osborne House on business, then went on to make a tour of the island."

Lupin raised his hand in the direction of land and the rocks. "Are these cliffs the same sort of chalk as those at Étretat?"

"Indeed they are," Holmes said. "Chalk is a particular form of limestone composed from the shells of marine plankton which lived millions of years ago during the Cretaceous period."

Lupin smiled. "Perhaps it is only Gallic bias, but I find these rocks rather bland in comparison to those at Étretat. These—and their brothers at Dover—are more boringly and uniformly white, while the striations and the coloring are more apparent along the Alabaster Coast in France. Then, too, there are no elephant trunks plunging into the water to be seen here!"

The submarine had come in from the south, and the coast of the Island ran almost due east and west, so we could see the length of the three jagged rock formations jutting from the dark blue water and the adjoining shore of the promontory with its taller cliffs. The boat swung to the west, drawing ever closer, and soon we had come around so that the lighthouse and its rock were dominating the other two formations hidden behind them. So close, the outlines of the individual blocks were even more evident, and the structure seemed somewhat squat, but sturdy and unyielding. I could well believe that it could take any abuse the sea might hurl at it.

One could see that a landing and platform for the base of the tower had been cut out of the white chalk, and a sideways stairway descended into the waters. The boat drew closer, until finally one of the sailors, holding a length of rope, leaped about a yard to the steps. Iron rings were set above every other step, and the man put the rope through and pulled the boat abreast. Higher up on the platform was a stone bollard, and the sailor soon secured another rope to it.

The baron gestured toward the steps. "You three go first."

The sailor extended his hand and helped Holmes ashore. I was next, then Lupin. It was only a small sort of islet, but all the same, I was greatly relieved to be on solid ground again! The baron and Massier followed, then two of the sailors, each with a rifle slung over their shoulders.

We came to the top of the stairs and walked onto a broad landing of concrete. Where the white chalk had been cut away, there remained two sheer white walls forming an L-shape near the tower. An iron door was set into the one with the great mass of the rock formation behind it; some sort of cave must have been hollowed out for storage.

I glanced back out toward the ocean, but could not see the submarine. The mists had mostly cleared, the light was yellowish, the blue trying to show in the sky. I realized I had not heard the clang of the bell in a while. They must have decided it was clear enough to dispense with it.

The substantial metal door at the base of the tower swung open, and a tall man came out and descended the three steps. He wore a peaked cap and an open double-breasted blue jacket with a row of four golden buttons on either side. A wild bushy growth of reddish-brown beard and mustache hid the bottom of his face. He could not have had a shave or a trim in months.

"Here now! What do you think you are doing? This lighthouse is off limits to visitors."

The baron turned to Holmes. He wore clothing almost identical to the lighthouse keeper, but today his grandiose mustache was neatly waxed, the long ends curling slightly upward. Compared to the keeper, he appeared short and stout. "I think I shall let you conduct the search, Monsieur Holmes. After all, you are the expert and still in my employ." He had spoken in French.

Holmes nodded. "Merci, monsieur le baron."

"And you can deal with the keepers. Although… perhaps it would be best to simply tie them up for the duration."

"Certainly not. The lighthouse must continue to function normally. Otherwise we shall soon have visitors come calling to see what is wrong."

"Ah yes, I suppose that makes sense."

The keeper had said nothing, but beneath the brim of his cap, his thick eyebrows had scrunched together as Holmes approached him. "What was he saying? And who are you?"

"We have come to search the tower. Do you by any chance speak French?"

The keeper stared at him for a second or two. "No."

"This gentleman is the Baron of Creuse. And as you can see, his two associates are armed." The two sailors, hard-looking scoundrels, the both of them, had unslung their rifles and held them ready. "The baron is–" Holmes smiled faintly "–something of a blackguard. It would be best if you let us come into the tower and have a look about."

The keeper folded his arms across his chest. "And what if I say no?"

The baron obviously heard the word "no" which is nearly identical in French. "Tell him," he said in French, "if he does not cooperate fully, we shall simply enter and smash his precious Fresnel lens to pieces."

The keeper's eyes opened wide, the entire circles of blue irises showing against white, his horror obvious. "You could not!"

Holmes gave an abrupt nod. "Ah, so you do speak French?"

The keeper had managed to regain his composure. "A little, perhaps."

"What is your name, sir?"

"Martin. Joseph Martin."

"Martin. I see." Holmes smiled as he gave the name its French pronunciation with a nasal *i* at the end. Indeed, Martin was a very common surname in France. The man had no French accent, but he could well be of French descent.

"I regret this intrusion, sir, but it would be best if you went about your business and ignored us as best you can."

Martin's eyes had a grave expression. "What are you after?"

"I suspect you know."

His eyes changed every so subtly. "I have no idea what you're talking about."

"Joe? What's going on?" Another man's voice rose over the murmur of the sea. The other keeper stood warily near the open door. Wearing a similar cap and jacket, he was shorter with a black beard, curly, but less luxuriant than his companion's.

Martin hesitated. "They have come to do a search."

The other keeper stiffened. "We can't allow that!"

"We have no choice. You see those two thugs with rifles. And their leader threatened to smash the lens."

"What! Would they really do such a thing?"

"I don't want to find out."

We all started toward the doorway. Holmes stopped before the other keeper. "And what is your name, sir?"

He regarded Holmes suspiciously. "Bernard. Jack Bernard."

"*Bernard.* Of course. Another French surname." He glanced at Lupin and me. "So many English are descended from the French, no doubt because of the Norman conquest." A sardonic smile played about his lips, but the two keepers were definitely not amused.

Martin gave him a hard stare. "Who might you be, anyway?"

"My name is Sherlock Holmes."

"Sherlock Holmes?" Obviously Martin had heard of him. "I thought you were a detective—not a thief."

"Nor am I. My companions and I are here under duress. Is there something here worth stealing?"

Martin seemed to realize he had blundered. "Not at all." His eyes shifted briefly to the baron. "You are welcome to search the tower. What you might be after is a mystery to me. There is certainly nothing here of great value."

Holmes was smiling again. "Well done."

"Tell them to go about their usual business," the baron said. "And tell them my two armed sailors will be watching their every move."

Holmes did so, then turned again to Martin. "We shall be searching the tower, but we shall try to create as little disorder as possible. I doubt that there is much that is under lock and key."

Martin gave a brusque laugh. "What would be the point on a lighthouse with only two men?" His look soured. "And normally, no visitors whatsoever."

We all went through two doorways, the first heavy door made of metal, the second of wood, and found ourselves in a circular room dominated by a huge tank with pipes attached. Coiled ropes were stacked about, and a small rowboat stood on its end leaning against the wall.

"That must be the fuel tank for the lamp," Holmes said, and Martin nodded. Holmes turned to the baron and switched to French: "We may as well start at the top and work our way to the bottom."

His last word was *dessous*, and he gave Lupin and me a knowing look. It took me a second or two to recall that the old guardian had said *le phare* and then *dessous*.

"Bernard and I need to go up top to the lantern," Martin said. "Unless there is good visibility, even during the day we must keep the light burning." He added, grudgingly. "I can give you a sort of tour, on the way, I suppose."

Holmes nodded. "Thank you. That would be most gracious."

We started up a staircase that wound round the circular tube formed by the lighthouse wall. Martin explained that the second floor was a storeroom for various spare parts, and the provisions required for the two men. The third floor had a big round oak table with matching chairs, and off to one side, stood an enormous black cast-iron stove, which gave off a welcome warmth. A worn-looking brown leather sofa stood nearby.

"This stove is the main source of heat for the lighthouse," Martin said.

On the fourth floor were four bunks, two on top of each other. The beds were framed in beautiful varnished oak, sort of cubby holes, with a cloth curtain that could be drawn for privacy. Each floor, except for the ground storeroom, had thick square windows on opposite walls to provide light.

Martin glanced back at us before starting up the stairs. "The lantern is next up."

And indeed, when we stepped out, we could see that the upper part of the circular room was all of glass, framed in steel, which revealed grayish sky all around us. A massive iron pedestal in the center, which must support the lens, dominated the space. Charts and papers were spread out on a wooden table, alongside a glass-fronted bookcase, and instruments hung nearby. A tank was off to the side with pipes running up through the open steel grating which circled the lens.

"The lens itself is just above," Martin said.

Holmes glanced back at our group from the submarine and spoke in French. "I very much doubt anything could be hidden up there, but it is surely worth having a look at the lens. They have a gigantic first-order Fresnel, made in France, of course, by Henry-Lepaute."

"Oh yes," Lupin exclaimed eagerly, "we must have a look!"

Martin looked very stern. "I'll come with you." He raised one slender hand. "And please—do not touch anything!"

The other curving stairways had been enclosed within finished walls, but this one was an open construction all of metal with a metal railing. Martin climbed up first through the opening in the grate, then came Holmes, Lupin, myself, the baron, and Massier last. Before us, with the narrow metal walkway surrounding it, was a gigantic sculpted creation all of glass—something every bit as spectacular as a grand crystal chandelier—and lit so brightly that I could not stare into its center. Shards and diamonds of yellow-white light glowed and shifted along its circular bands as we started around it. The lens had sections vertically framed in metal, bronze by the look of it, but its core was a central horizontal band, with smaller angled bands above and below—prisms, no doubt, all of which helped amplify the light. The center portion was perhaps three feet high, with even more dramatically angled glass bands rising and falling below it. Both the top and bottom sections were about another three feet high, and their prismatic bands tapered slightly inward, so that the lens as a whole rather resembled a pine cone.

"Don't look into the center," Martin said. "You can damage your eyesight."

"Incredible!" I said. "I had no idea it was such a work of art. It is truly beautiful."

Lupin smiled. "It is grand, is it not? And so tall, almost three meters, I'll wager."

Martin nodded. "Yes, it's around nine feet tall and six feet wide, and it weighs some six and a half tons. A first-order lens is the largest size Fresnel generally available. This one has been here since the lighthouse was constructed in fifty-nine."

Holmes gestured toward the middle. "This is the beauty of Fresnel's design. Instead of a single massive nine-foot lens which might be three feet thick and very precarious, the lens is collapsed down into circular layers which function the same but with much less weight. Also, the additional glass itself would block some of the light, so a Fresnel lens is actually brighter. A rotating Fresnel lens is even more spectacular-looking: each section has a bullseye of circular glass which focuses the light into a separate beam."

Even the baron seemed impressed. "And this was, of course, made in France. We are the masters at this sort of construction."

"Indeed you are, monsieur le baron," Holmes said. "Indeed you are." He resumed walking around the curving platform, admiring the lens. He stopped to gesture at some sheets of red glass going from floor to ceiling on the seaward side. "Henry, this is what made the light appear red out on the ocean." He pointed toward the forward gap in the red glass panels. "And when one is at the correct angle from the bare space here, the light appears white, and you know you can safely head inland."

Martin gave an appreciative nod. "Very good, Mr. Holmes. I could not explain it better myself."

Lupin stared at Holmes. "You said it is unlikely that our... *object* is up here, but could some part of it not be hidden inside?"

Holmes shrugged. "One can open the lens to access the lamp itself, but there is not much room inside. Then, too, the chronology of the lighthouse's construction makes it unlikely. It was finished in 1859, but our... 'collection' was moved more recently, after the Franco-Prussian war, in the early seventies. Trying to modify this elaborate structure to hide something would likely put the lighthouse out of service for days, and the authorities would certainly notice the interruption. Moreover, it would require a great deal of technical knowledge and expertise. If all else fails, we might have a look—but at the end of our search, not the beginning."

"That makes perfect sense," Lupin said.

We all trooped back down the stairs to the lower floor of the lantern. Holmes turned to Martin. "Before we begin our search, might we have a look from the parapet? It is still hazy, but the view should be spectacular."

"Certainly." Martin led us to a door and opened it. The others went out, but I hesitated.

Holmes gave me a sympathetic smile. "Come now, Henry! I know your problems with vertigo, but that parapet around the tower should comfort you. Notice that it stands quite high and is made of solid granite, which, from the look of it, is nearly two feet thick. You certainly could not fall by accident over such a barrier!"

We went outside, and immediately I could hear the rumbling murmur of the ocean and the cry of gulls, even as the moist cool air touched my face. The door faced the landward side. Stepping slowly and warily to the parapet, I could see the rest of the white chalk rock formation upon which the lighthouse sat, then the sharp tips like jagged teeth of two more rock islands, and finally, off to the right, the high sweeping cliffs of the Island itself above a small sort of bay with the dark blue waters of the ocean sweeping in onto a beach.

We walked around the lantern, taking in the view from every angle. The breeze was strongest to the seaward side, cold and damp from the ocean. It had cleared somewhat, but out toward the west along the distant sea near the horizon, clouds were forming.

Lupin stood smiling out at the ocean, his hands resting on the massive curving parapet. "I think I might enjoy being a lighthouse keeper. To have such a view always at one's command!"

Holmes raised one hand. "Ah, but you forget that the lighthouse is often battered by storms with winds and crashing waves." He glanced at Martin. "How high do the waves actually reach?"

"Their spray sometimes splashes the glass up here of the lantern."

Lupin gave a theatrical shudder. "Perhaps not, then. There would also be the lack of female companionship to reckon with, although if your wife could accompany you...?" He was looking at Martin.

"That is not allowed at solitary lighthouses like this one. There is enough physical work to occupy two keepers. However, for some lighthouses situated on the coast rather than a remote rock, the keeper's family resides close by."

"Are there not three keepers, one of whom is always out on relief?" Holmes asked. Martin nodded. "And what is the surname of your other keeper?"

Martin stiffened. "Never you mind."

Holmes smiled. "As you wish. No doubt it is also one of French ancestry."

The baron stared sternly at Holmes. "We have wasted enough time with idle sightseeing. Let us be about our search." Holmes nodded, and we all went back inside. The baron spoke to his two men. "Duboeuf, Phillipe, you stay up here with these two men and watch them carefully. Make sure they do not try to do anything suspicious." He turned again to Holmes and gestured toward Massier. "Let us begin. Louis can assist you. He is very good at this type of endeavor."

Massier gave a slight bow. "It would be an honor to work with you, Monsieur Holmes."

Lupin had a certain lunatic grin. "I, too, am very good at this sort of endeavor. Before, we descend, we had best have a good look around this part of the lantern."

Holmes nodded. "And so we shall, although no likely candidates jump out at me."

Lupin lowered his gaze. "I shall examine this metal floor and make sure there are no suspicious cracks or fissures."

I smiled faintly. "And with so many experts at work, I shall simply try to stay out of their way!"

The three searchers set to, and after fifteen or twenty minutes, they were convinced nothing was to be found on that level.

Before departing, Holmes stopped by the work table and grasped a beautiful brass bullseye lantern by its wire handles. "Might I borrow this, Mr. Martin? I shall return it when we are done." Martin only shrugged in resignation.

We took the stairs down to the next floor with the bunks and the keepers' quarters. The many drawers and cupboards offered many possibilities. Holmes and Lupin proceeded to pull out all the six-foot wide drawers below the bunks, one by one. They went through the contents, and using the bullseye lantern, looked carefully inside the empty cavities. Meanwhile Massier opened the doors and carefully examined the closets where coats and jackets were hung. Holmes shone the light all along the ceiling, which was very high. One could see massive cross-beams which supported the floor above, so nothing could be hidden up there. I followed all this with great interest, but the baron seemed quite bored with it all, his earlier excitement dissipating.

Soon we descended to the kitchen and dining area. This seemed to me a highly unlikely place to store the great treasure of France! And indeed, the room was more open and had fewer hiding places.

Some cupboards were pantries stacked with brightly labeled cans of beans and tomatoes, larger glass jars of pickles, sauerkraut, or preserved meat in gravy, as well as tin containers of flour, sugar, and rice. There were also stacks of various dishes, plus pots and pans. A closet next to the warm stove was heaped with coal. Again, our searchers examined the floor and ceiling carefully with the lantern.

So more quickly this time, we went on to the floor below: the storeroom. It was even more of a jumble than the kitchen. Some shelves had still more canned goods. A great variety of tools, wrenches of various sizes and shapes, pliers, and saws, abounded, along with scrap wood and segments of differently sized, galvanized pipe. Some small chests contained various metal fittings and instruments. A huge assortment of flares and rockets stood well apart with a cloth draped before them which said DANGER, NO SMOKING. A curious assortment of furniture, chairs of different shapes and sizes, tables, and a desk, were also stored there.

The search went on, but they had to move things around to have a good look at all of the floor and the walls. Massier had thrown himself into the effort and was a hard worker. However, the baron was by now thoroughly bored and sat at the opposite side of the room from the rockets smoking one cigarette after another.

Holmes and I struggled to move aside a massive old oaken wardrobe, and then he smiled wryly. "Do you know Poe's story 'The Purloined Letter'?"

"Oh yes, of course. Isn't that where a missing letter is lying out in plain view, so obvious that it is simply ignored?"

"A pity that our conspirators did not follow that example and leave a casket somewhere in this mess for us to discover!"

Lupin sighed. "That would be agreeable, but I don't think it is likely. Given all that we have seen thus far, they enjoy hiding things!"

At last they had finished, and we trooped down to the ground floor, which was, thankfully, much less messy than the storeroom. The big storage tank of kerosene and an upturned boat were the two main objects, although ropes and life preservers were piled about, and hung on hooks on one wall were various forms of rain gear, including the classic hooded yellow slickers. I had begun to wonder if the dying old man had been merely raving. The same thought was obviously worrying the baron.

He stared gravely at Holmes. "Are you sure you have told me the truth, Monsieur Holmes? If you have led us here on—how do you say it in English?—"a goose chase" there will be a price to pay!"

"I do not make a habit of lying about important matters. Besides, I did not really expect to find the treasure in the lighthouse."

Massier looked surprised. "You did not?"

Now the baron looked angry. "You will regret this!"

"I did not say the treasure was not at the Needles, quite the contrary." Holmes and Lupin exchanged a knowing look.

"Enough of these riddles!" the baron explained. "Explain yourself."

"Did you notice the entrance to a cave set in the rock wall behind the lighthouse?"

The baron's frown became quite ferocious. "Cave? What cave."

"I think we are about finished in here. Let us go have a look."

Holmes opened first the wooden door, then the watertight steel one. Outside, the wind had picked up, and the clouds out at sea had thickened. We could hear waves crashing against the rocks near the landing. Just before us, opposite a bare expanse of pavement, was the sheer white cliff where the chalk had been cut away, forming two walls in an L, and set in the one with the bulk of the rock formation behind it, was an arched steel door. Holmes raised his slender hand and pointed.

"There, I suspect, we shall have better luck."

"*Dessous*," I murmured.

Holmes nodded. "Exactly."

Massier started forward eagerly. The door had a metal latch and was, of course, not locked. What would be the point on an offshore island with only two occupants? The entryway was at least a foot thick, cut, no doubt, like the entire cave, out of the white chalk of the rocky isle, and all of us except the baron had to stoop slightly to get in without bumping our heads.

Inside it felt even colder and damper than out. Some light streamed in from the doorway, but Holmes had the lantern, and he shone it all around the chamber. Two big metal tanks dominated the room, along with more ropes, and some shelves with stacked bottles, probably of beer or wine. The walls and ceiling were of rough-hewn white rock, but the floor was covered with planks of dark brown, almost black wood, no doubt soaked in creosote for preservation.

Holmes, Lupin, and Massier advanced in a row toward the back of the cave. The side walls seemed somewhat curved, but the back one was smoother and more vertical, forming near right angles at either side and at the top and bottom. The back was also rough and ragged, but the cuts had vaguely rectangular shapes.

Holmes tossed his hat aside, then went to the left side of the wall and brought the lantern very near the rock. Slowly he examined the surface, going from top to bottom. Lupin stooped slightly, obviously mimicking Holmes's inspections with the greatest interest. Massier also seemed fascinated.

After about ten minutes, only half the back wall had been perused, and the baron was obviously bored again. "I shall go outside and have a smoke," he said. No one acknowledged his comment.

A few minutes later Holmes was methodically sweeping the lantern from side to side when he abruptly froze. After a long pause, he murmured to Lupin, "Do you see it?"

"A crack, you mean? Yes, I do."

Holmes slowly moved the lantern downward. "I think it resumes just here." He pointed. "A door need not have straight sides. And notice there at the right side of the wall, at its corner—it appears different from the other side."

"There is a seam the length of the wall." Lupin sounded elated. "A gap. We have found the secret door, have we not?"

"I believe so."

"But how does it open?" Massier asked.

Holmes rubbed briefly at his chin. "That, of course, is the question. There must be some mechanism which activates at a press, a touch, or a pull." He set down the lantern and began to feel about the wall. Lupin immediately did the same to the right side where the back and side walls met, while Massier hovered about them eagerly.

However, half an hour later, I was despairing that we would ever find the secret of the blasted door. Massier had started poking about the rest of the cave. Holmes and Lupin were down on their knees examining the line between wall and ceiling.

"I would swear it is about a meter wide," Lupin said. "Again, there is a slight gap between the wall and the floorboards."

Holmes nodded. "I agree. But how…?" He stood up and went to lean against the wall, but some curled ropes were in his way. "Blast it," he murmured, then stopped abruptly. He raised the lantern and shone it on the adjacent wall. Someone had set a metal plate about three feet wide with three hooks into the wall, and the ropes and a jacket were hanging from them.

Holmes eagerly threw everything aside, clearing the metal plate, then tried moving variation combinations of the three hooks. Lupin watched briefly, then seized his arm. "Let's try pressing all three."

Holmes nodded, then took the first and second one, even as Lupin took the third. The hooks had thus far been unyielding, but now they all jerked downward, triggering a sort of clanking grinding sound from within, even as a section of the back rock wall swung inward perhaps three inches on the left side.

"Eureka!" Lupin cried.

Massier and I grinned at each other. "I'll fetch the baron," he said.

Holmes took up the lantern, then pushed the door further inward. It was clever sort of thing, constructed of metal, with a slab of rock all along the face. Three sides were straight, aligned with the floor, ceiling, and right wall, while the left side was completely uneven and followed the rough shapes of rock shards along that edge. Inside was another smaller cave—a cave within a cave—and dominating the space were three large, antique-looking, dark wooden chests reinforced with black metal, sitting upon the wooden planks of the floor.

"My God," Lupin murmured. "We've found it, after all."

Holmes smiled triumphantly at me. "Oh very good!" I exclaimed.

Nothing could have stopped Lupin. He stepped inside, yanked open one lid, then another and another, even as Holmes shined the lantern on the contents. The first two were piled with gold coins, and the third—the light lingered there on heaps of gems and jewelry—red rubies, green emeralds, clear glittering diamonds, blue sapphires, of every size and cut, alone and unadorned, or set in gold or silver bracelets and necklaces. It was like some fortune from the *Arabian Nights*, from the cave of Ali Baba himself.

"How beautiful!" Lupin cried.

The baron and Massier crowded in behind me. "You were telling the truth, after all, Monsieur Holmes." The baron sounded faintly surprised.

Lupin ran one hand through the jewels, then withdrew a large diamond and glanced at Holmes. "Let's have a look!" Holmes raised the light, and Lupin held the gem in its beam. He frowned in concentration as he turned it slightly, and behind the lenses of his spectacles, his eyes grew almost stern. He glanced up at Holmes, and some unspoken communication seem to pass between the two of them.

"Put that back, Beautrelet!" the baron exclaimed.

"In a moment. Don't worry, I won't steal any of your precious treasure." He and Holmes turned off to the side, and Lupin had his back briefly to us, blocking the light. I heard him sigh, and then he turned again. "I happen to know something about jewels, I can assure you that it is a perfect stone. It is flawless."

"I wonder…" Holmes murmured, even as he swept the light all about the smaller cavern. "Well, obviously the three caskets are the only thing in here."

Lupin made a grandly exaggerated bow toward the baron, cap in hand. "Congratulations, monsieur le baron. You can go ahead and build your fleet of submarines, and then conquer the world!"

Chapter 13

W hen we came out of the cave, the wind on our faces was colder and more forceful, and although the mists had somewhat cleared, dark clouds were massing ominously out over the ocean. Whitecaps also showed in the dark blue-gray water, rising and falling.

The baron grasped Massier's arm. "Fetch the oarsmen. It will take four to six men to haul those chests out of the cave and get them into the launch. I shall get the other two men from the lighthouse." He turned away and strode toward the tower.

Holmes, Lupin, and I followed him, and we all trekked up the many winding stairs to the lower lantern floor. Martin stood before the glass pane staring out at the sea through a pair of large black binoculars. He lowered them and turned to us, frowning slightly. "Is that a submarine out there?"

"Yes," Holmes said.

The baron gestured toward his two bored-looking sailors, who were seated with rifles across their laps. "Come. We're finished." They stood.

"Did you find what you were looking for?" Martin asked.

Holmes seemed to ponder the question before replying. "We found the three chests."

Martin scowled. "That treasure does not belong to you. It will bring misfortune to anyone who tries to steal it."

Holmes gestured with his chin in the direction of the baron. "I am not the one trying to steal it. Tell me, though: I suspect that you and Bernard are the traditional guardians just like the old man left behind at l'Aiguille near Étretat."

Martin's brow furrowed even more, but he did not speak. Bernard was seated in an oaken chair by the table, and he was watching us closely.

"It was clever strategy," Holmes said, "to infiltrate the lighthouse service with three Englishmen of French descent. You could then construct the chamber within a chamber, and eventually move in the treasure. By the way, I'm sorry to tell you that the old guardian left behind at Étretat has died."

Martin shrugged. "I never met him. Not that it matters."

"No, I suppose not."

The baron gestured toward us with his hand. "Come along. We're finished here."

We went back down the stairs. Massier was waiting with the four oarsmen. It required six men to awkwardly haul the two chests of gold out to the edge of the dock. The jewels would be more valuable, but they were lighter.

"It's a good thing they have that folding crane there," the baron said. Close by, bolted to the concrete of the dock, was a tall metal structure about seven feet high with a folded beam. The crane would be needed to help unload stores or machinery from visiting supply boats. "Especially with the seas so rough, it would be foolhardy to try to lower the chest into the launch from the steps. We certainly don't want to drop a chest into the sea!" The baron turned to his men. "Pascal, François, have a look in the storage area just inside the tower, there. I saw nets and ropes. Bring the largest rope and the sturdiest net you can find."

He turned to us and smiled sarcastically. "And now, I fear, it is time for me to bid you adieu, my friends. You have served your purpose, and you may remain behind here at the lighthouse. However, to show I am not ungrateful, you may each choose a gem or piece of jewelry. That includes you, Beautrelet. By the time you return to Paris, Angelique will be long gone and safe from your impertinent overtures. And also—" his smile intensified as he regarded Massier "—that includes you, Louis. I have finished with your services, but you may select a jewel."

Massier's mouth tightened, his jaw tensing, even as he slowly inhaled through his nostrils. His dark brown eyes assumed a dangerous gleam. "So this is how you repay me for my years of faithful service? I deserve a real share of the treasure—not a mere trinket!"

"Come, come, Louis—don't talk to me of faithful service! I am not blind or stupid. I know that you have conspired and plotted on your own against me. First, you tried to drive off Monsieur Holmes with that episode with the falling pot before the hotel, and then later I suspect you attempted to make a deal with him to steal the treasure and cut me out of the picture entirely." He glanced at Holmes. "That is true, is it not?"

Holmes looked faintly amused. "Yes."

"No, Louis—you don't want just a share—you want the whole thing. Well, you have failed. You can go ahead and select a piece from the chest worth a small fortune, and you can be grateful I am letting you off so generously!"

Massier was perhaps half a foot taller than the baron, much more broad-chested, and his hands hung at his sides, his fists clenched. His presence was quite threatening. He had gone very pale. "As God is my witness, Chamerac, if you do this to me—if you abandon me here and steal the treasure for yourself—I will have my vengeance. I swear it. I swear it."

The baron laughed. "Swear all you want." He went over and opened up the chest with the jewels inside. "Go ahead, gentlemen, choose your trinkets." His voice was mocking.

Holmes's amusement was gone, his look serious. "Monsieur le baron, I don't wish to interfere in your affairs, but in this case, I think perhaps you would be wise to take Monsieur Massier along with you. Abandoning him here may be a mistake."

"And why would that be, Monsieur Holmes?"

Holmes was silent for a few seconds before he spoke. "I think he means what he says about vengeance."

Massier gave a convulsive nod of his head. "*Yes*."

"Come, come, Monsieur Holmes, you take Louis much too seriously. I do not fear his vengeance. But enough!" He waved his hand at the chest. "Go ahead and choose something."

Holmes exchanged a look with me, then went to the chest. I followed along with Lupin. The other two seemed to take the first thing that caught their eye, Holmes an emerald necklace set in silver, Lupin a large diamond. He held it up to the light, then passed his other hand behind it. "Oh yes, how very impressive, so very clear. As a connoisseur of gems, I can speak to its superb quality!"

"Spare me your idle chatter," the baron said.

I selected a blue sapphire bracelet, since I knew Michelle liked those gems.

The baron waved his hand impatiently at Massier. "Hurry up, Louis! We need to load up and get away before the storm arrives."

Again Massier slowly drew in his breath through his nostrils. He stepped forward and selected a diamond necklace set round with small red rubies.

"Exquisite!" the baron exclaimed. "Whatever your other qualities, you do have good taste."

Holmes pointed at another chest. "Might we also have a coin or two as a sort of souvenir? They must be gold louis."

"Go ahead, Monsieur Holmes. Each of you may take two gold coins. As a souvenir."

"Curse your souvenirs," Massier muttered.

Holmes raised the lid of the chest, selected a gold coin, and turned it in the light. "Ah, Louis the Fourteenth himself. Even on a coin, one can see from his profile that he was not known for his good looks." He took another. "And his predecessor, Louis the Thirteenth."

Lupin dug about and picked out two coins. "I'll have one of each as well." He held up one of the coins before his spectacles and glanced closely at it. "Yes, what fine workmanship! Difficult to believe they are over two hundred years old, but then they have, no doubt, been preserved while safely stowed away in this chest." He was smiling, and Holmes gave a half shake of his head.

I had randomly taken two coins, and I put them in my trouser pocket.

The two sailors came out of the tower, one with a huge coil of rope, the other with a wadded-up net. Quickly, the men set about loading the launch. The beam was unfolded, the net secured to a rope, and soon the first chest was being lowered down into the launch, which rose and fell as waves swept against and round it, splashing up against the dock side. The second and third chest went more quickly, and all three were set in the middle of the boat, which at the end of the process was quite low in the water.

The baron glanced at the vessel. "A good thing the four of you are remaining behind. We can do without the extra weight. And a good thing the launch is large and well built. All the same…" He turned to Holmes. "A man of your abilities could prove useful to me. I mentioned before that you might accompany me in the first voyage of the *Nautilus*. If you could promise to set aside any inconvenient… scruples, you could still come along."

Holmes's mouth twitched in and out of a half-smile. "I think not."

"Oh well, more's the pity. And now, once more, gentlemen, I bid you adieu."

He went down the concrete steps, and one of the oarsmen helped him into the boat. Soon the baron was seated next to the treasure, the four men ready at the oars, another at the tiller. The boat swung out from the dock, made an awkward sort of half circle, bobbing and swaying all the while, then set out in earnest into the open sea. The baron raised his hand in farewell. In his peaked cap and dark jacket, alongside the crew all in blue sailor's uniforms with tasseled blue berets, he did look the very model of a naval officer.

A light rain had begun to fall, spattering against us as the wind gusted intermittently. Massier stared grimly out at the boat. Beneath the brim of his cap, his face was still very pale, his cheeks contrasting dramatically with his curling, full black beard.

Lupin was smiling as he waved back at the baron. "Well, farewell to our beautiful treasure. Thus are the hopes of men dashed upon the rocks of fate!"

I stared curiously at him. "You are taking this rather well."

"Look on the bright side: we no longer have to put up with the baron's arrogant company." His shoulders rose in a sort of compulsive shudder. "We had better get inside. The tide is rising, and a real storm is brewing. This whole dock will soon be awash in powerful waves."

Massier smiled ever so slightly. "It would be best that we remain out here. You will soon see something worth your while."

"Indeed?" Lupin asked. "Well, I'm freezing. You all are better dressed for this sort of weather. I have only a wool suit on."

The wind swelled, and Holmes's hand rose quickly to jam down his hat and keep it from blowing away. "I shall take Monsieur Massier at his word and remain here. I believe you will find this interesting, Isidore. However, if you are cold, you might avail yourself of one of those yellow slickers we saw hanging inside."

"Bravo, Holmes! So I shall."

He turned toward the door.

"If we are going to remain outside, I think we could all use one," I said.

Lupin and I walked across the landing, even as the biggest wave yet splashed spray across the expanse before us. Inside, Lupin and I each put on one of the slickers. I selected another one for Holmes, and Lupin took one as well. "I suppose Massier doesn't really deserve to be drenched."

We joined the other two men. Holmes gladly accepted the slicker, put it on, and raised the hood so that it covered the crown and back of his wrinkled woolen walking hat. Beautrelet and I also had our hoods up over our cloth caps.

Massier had taken a jacket, but his eyes were fixed upon the sea. The launch had grown much smaller in the distance, and the waves rising and falling occasionally hid it from our view. The rain began to fall in earnest, the watery gusts wetting our faces, trousers, and shoes below the shiny yellow fabric.

Lupin gave his head a shake. Water droplets covered the lenses of his spectacles. "This seems rather foolish, you know. I may call it quits. It is nice and warm there in the lighthouse."

I gave a wistful glance at the tower. "He does have a point."

"I am staying," Holmes said.

Lupin's shoulders rose in a movement half shrug, half shudder. "Oh very well. I suppose I don't want to miss anything."

We stood at the edge of the dock staring out at the open sea, being buffeted by the growing winds and rain of the incoming storm. At one point a particularly big gust made me turn away and crouch slightly, trying to shelter myself. "This is foolishness," I murmured.

Lupin's slight laugh was barely audible. "I agree."

Holmes and Massier stood, rock-like, staring out at the ocean. After some fifteen minutes had passed, I resolved that I would only wait another five minutes, and then go inside. I could not imagine what worthwhile thing Massier might be referring to. Would another submarine appear? Would the *Nautilus* come in closer? Would the launch return? Whatever it was—

A great flash of yellow-orange light appeared out at sea, a sort of false dawn, accompanied an instant later by a boom; the sound swept in upon us, and then more flashing bursts of fiery light flamed up, along with great spouts of dark water, accompanied by a blurred series of thunderclaps. All the sounds of the storm and its darkness were drowned out for that brief interval.

"My God!" I exclaimed.

Holmes turned to me. His blue-gray eyes were faintly angry, his lips tightly pressed together.

Massier was smiling triumphantly. "It was worthwhile, was it not?"

An icy fear stabbed at my chest. "That might have happened while we were traveling here. We had a narrow escape!"

Holmes shook his head. "That was not an accident, Henry."

Lupin gave an appreciative nod. "Ah."

"But how could such a thing happen?"

Holmes was glaring at Massier. "I suppose the *Nautilus* had some self-destruct mechanism built into it–probably one which ignited one of the torpedoes, causing all the others to explode as well. You were not so surprised by the baron's actions as you pretended. You must have thought he was going to betray you. You activated some apparatus before we left, which you could have disengaged if you returned to the *Nautilus*. If not... How was it set off? Ah, perhaps when the *Nautilus* submerged and reached a certain depth and pressure..."

Massier laughed. "Oh very good, Holmes. You are a clever devil."

Holmes was frowning. "The baron cannot have known of this device."

"He did not. Dombasie, the head engineer, and I had it built. We knew that the baron was unbalanced and, ultimately, quite mad. It was a precaution, one which has just proven its utility."

"But you killed the entire crew and blew up a technical marvel!" I exclaimed.

Holmes glanced at me and sighed. "His crew did not deserve to die, but the world is surely better off without something like the *Nautilus* in the hands of a madman."

"And the great treasure of France–lost forever, alas! All those jewels and gold, all fused and melted and gone to the sea worms!" Lupin seemed somehow more amused rather than disturbed by this loss.

"Better lost if I can't have my fair share," Massier said. "Besides, the important thing is the plans for the submarine. Dombasie and I can find investors and build another submarine. Who knows? Perhaps someday we can search out there for the scattered remains of the treasure. Regardless, we don't even need to build the submarine to become rich—we can hold a secret auction with the world's powers and sell the plans to the highest bidder. That would be an easy way to make our fortune. And unlike the baron, I have no wish to become emperor of all Europe."

Holmes eyed him coldly. "I fear it will not be that simple for you, Monsieur Massier. You have just admitted to us all that you blew up the submarine and killed the entire crew."

"What of it?"

"That is murder, and there are three witnesses here who have heard your confession. I intend to turn you over to the authorities to be tried for your crimes."

Massier's laugh was more surprised than amused. "You cannot be serious! Very well, I can pay you for silence, I promise." He took us all in with a sweeping look. "We can all be wealthy men. I am not so greedy as Chamerac."

"I will not be an accessory to murder," Holmes said.

"Nor I!" I exclaimed.

"Oh blast it," Lupin said. "I suppose I have some silly moral feelings after all."

Massier took a step back, regarding us all. "I cannot believe this—I cannot believe such foolishness." He shook his head, backing up to the edge of the landing near the stairs down to the water. Suddenly he reached under both his jacket and the slicker into his trouser pocket and withdrew a small gun, which I recognized as a two-shot derringer. "Stay exactly where you are. If you take one step toward me, I shall surely fire. I have two shots and can kill at least one, and possibly two of you."

"What is the point of this, Monsieur Massier?" Holmes asked.

"I shall show you. Come over here, closer, and Beautrelet, Vernier—step back." We all obeyed him. "Turn away from me, Holmes." Holmes did so, and Massier grasped his arm with his free hand, even while he pressed the derringer against the side of his head. "You two, go fetch the dinghy from the lighthouse. Mr. Holmes and I are going to take a trip ashore."

"Are you crazy?" I had to almost shout because of all the sound of the wind and the waves. "In this weather?"

"We shall chance it. You have forced my hand. Hurry up, and do as I say."

Holmes shook his head. "I would just as soon die here as be drowned."

"Do you want to see a bullet go through his head, Vernier? Do you want to see his blood spatter everywhere? Do as I say—go with him, Beautrelet."

Lupin stared at him, then his lips curved into an ironic smile, even as he stood straighter. He took off his spectacles and put them into a pocket of slicker. "Don't call me, Beautrelet, you idiot!"

Even amidst the storm, the transformation was remarkable. Lupin had been inhabiting the role of Beautrelet the whole time he had been around the baron and Massier. Now he had again become Arsène Lupin. The change in his voice, its deeper baritone quality, was evident.

"I am not Beautrelet—I am Lupin, Arsène Lupin. I believe you have heard of me. And I have not the slightest interest whatsoever in what happens to Sherlock Holmes—Holmes be damned! He has been my antagonist, not my friend. If you put a bullet through his head, you will be doing me a great favor. Enough of these silly theatrics. Shoot him if you will, but I'm going indoors." He turned and resolutely started for the lighthouse.

Massier was absolutely stunned, but finally he shouted. "Stop—come back here! Come back here, or I'll shoot you, I promise!" He swung the derringer away from Holmes's head toward Lupin's back.

That movement was all it took: Holmes's hands shot out and seized Massier's wrist, jerking his arm sideways even as the derringer went off, the shot going wide of its mark. Massier wrenched away one of Holmes's hands, even as a large wave hit the steps, dousing the two figures in the yellow jackets in spray. Massier stumbled, then fell back, teetered at the edge of the landing and seized Holmes's arm even as he slipped over the side. I rushed forward and grabbed at Holmes. I had hold of him, but with a sort of fearful clarity, I realized Massier was going to pull us over—that all three of us would tumble down the steps and plunge into the icy waters of the Channel.

But someone grasped at me from behind, even as more water doused us and then Massier screamed as he fell. Holmes and I half-turned, stumbled, and then we and Lupin all collapsed onto the wet concrete. We rose up on our knees, and Holmes was the first on his feet. He glanced over the side. I got up and looked down there, too. Dark gray waves crashed against the stairs, and below, the waters formed a swirling sort of maelstrom. Massier's hat briefly appeared, spun about, and was gone.

"Where is he?" I cried.

"Lost," Holmes shouted.

"There were life preservers. Perhaps if we threw one into the water."

"It's too late for that, Henry—and too risky. Even standing here we are in danger of being swept away. Let's get away from here—

let's get inside." He stared at Lupin who was standing next to him. "I must commend you again on your histrionic abilities, my friend. I trust that it was only theatrics when you said, 'Holmes be damned'?"

Lupin grinned. "It certainly was, but quite convincing, I thought."

"You had me worried for a moment," I said. I turned to Holmes. "He saved us both, you know—I think the three of us would all have gone over if he hadn't grabbed me."

"Thank you," Holmes said.

"You're quite welcome—and now let's get out of this storm before we are all swept away!"

And indeed, as we strode toward the iron doorway, another huge wave came crashing in just behind us. Lupin put one hand on the door latch and stared past me at Holmes. "All the same, I think we should have a last look, don't you?"

Holmes glanced at him, bit briefly at his lip, then nodded. He turned and strode off in the other direction. Lupin and I followed.

"Where on earth…?" I began, but it was obvious enough that he was headed for that other steel door set into the carved white cliff, the entrance to the cave.

I followed, and on the open dock, the wild wet wind swirled all around us, the storm briefly trying to swallow us up.

Holmes opened the door and stepped inside. I stooped to follow him. It was colder inside, but at least dry and out of the tempest. Holmes took some matches from his pocket and relit the bronze bullseye lantern which had been left there.

"What is this all about?" I asked.

"You will see soon enough, Henry."

Someone had shut the secret door, and Lupin and Holmes again pressed down on the metal hooks on the adjoining wall to open it.

We went into the smaller cave, and Holmes immediately focused the beam of light into a corner to his left.

"Ah, yes!" Lupin strode over, knelt down and grasped something, which on closer inspection must be the head of a bolt screwed into the wood. He wiggled his hand. "It's loose, all right. Move aside, Vernier. You are standing on the plank."

I glanced down at my feet, then moved to the right. Lupin pried at the blackish board stained with creosote: it was about six inches wide and some ten feet long, running the length of the inner cave. It rose an inch or so. Lupin struggled with it, then managed to get one hand under the end. He stood up, lifting the board as he rose, then he hoisted it up and over, then set it to the side. In the long opening, I could see the white strip of the rocky chalk in the lantern light. Lupin went to the center, then knelt and got his hands under the next plank over. He lifted it and also set it aside. And so it went, until he had pulled up the fourth plank. The light showed the edges of two sort of rough curves, probably the sides of holes or pits deeper into the rock.

"Ah!" Holmes exclaimed. He turned and offered me the light. "Would you hold this, Henry?"

I did so, and Holmes worked with Lupin to get the boards up more quickly. I smiled and shook my head at a sudden realization. "Of course—*dessous*. Underneath." Soon two pits were exposed with chests similar to the ones that had been hauled away. Lupin eagerly opened one, and I shined the light onto a heap of golden coins.

Lupin seized one. "Louis again! But this time the genuine article, I'll wager."

"No doubt," Holmes said.

The other chest also had gold coins. Holmes and Lupin continued to remove boards until a third chest in another pit was uncovered. Again, Lupin eagerly raised the lid.

"My God," I murmured.

It was filled again with jewelry and gems of every size and shape which caught the glow of the lantern and shimmered in the light: red, green, blue, yellow, some set in gold and silver. Lupin seized a big diamond and came quickly over to me. "Hold the lantern still, Vernier." He ran the diamond across the curving glass lens. "Yes! Yes! It is scratched! This time it's real, it's real."

Holmes was smiling. "Bravo."

I frowned. "So the others were fakes?"

Holmes nodded. "Doubtlessly. Mere paste. And probably the gold as well. I shall have the coins analyzed—perhaps there were a few real ones—but the other three chests were an elaborate decoy, meant to deceive thieves, who, unlike the guardians, would not know any better."

Lupin had put his spectacles back on earlier, and behind the lenses his eyes still had a look of wild ecstasy. "I cannot believe it. We're rich—we're rich."

Holmes gave his head a slight shake. "Come, now. The treasure does not belong to us. It belongs to the people of France. We really cannot steal it."

A faint smile pulled at Lupin's lips. "No?"

"No."

Lupin sighed. "Oh, I suppose you are right. Look where being greedy got Massier and the baron!"

"Now that we know what is here, let us put the boards back. We don't want the lighthouse keepers to know what we have found."

Lupin shrugged. "Oh, all right, but first... might I take a few trinkets, by way of... commission, for my assistance in this endeavor?"

Holmes stared sternly at him.

"Come now, you could not have done it without me. And I did save your life, after all."

Holmes's mouth pulled wryly to one side. "Oh, very well. I suppose you have earned a reward. Take a few things."

Lupin withdrew a diamond necklace, an emerald bracelet, and then selected some jewels: mostly diamonds, but a few rubies and emeralds. "This will allow me to marry and live happily ever after, you know. I can retire from the trade of *gentleman-cambrioleur*."

Holmes's dark eyebrows came together, but he said nothing.

"You will certainly be rich," I murmured.

"Indeed I will, Dr. Vernier. Indeed I will!"

Holmes and Lupin carefully set all the boards back in place, finishing with the one which had the bolt sticking out one end.

"Very good," Holmes said. "No one would ever know we had been under there."

"What are you going to do about the treasure?" I asked.

"It has been hidden away long enough, and it does not belong to kings or would-be kings, but to the people of France. I have certain contacts in the Foreign Office. I shall arrange to return here in a British warship, remove the treasure, then see that it is returned to the French Republic."

Lupin had a wary look. "But are you sure that the British government will not want to keep it for themselves, especially since it is technically on English territory? After all, thievery is not unique to the lower classes—it thrives in governing bodies."

Holmes stroked his chin thoughtfully. "You may be right, Isidore, but I shall let the diplomats squabble over it." He smiled. "You don't mind if I continue to call you Isidore?"

Lupin laughed. "Not in the least. Call me whatever you wish."

"I have contacts in the French embassy. I shall let them know about the treasure."

Lupin shrugged. "I suppose that will have to do." He glanced down at the blackish wooden planks forming the floor. "Pity, though. Through the ages, the conspirators were certainly good at puzzles and hiding things."

We went through the secret door and back into the larger cave. The main door was still ajar, and we could hear the howling and raging of the winds and the rains outside. When I pulled open the door inward, the storm appeared clearly worse than before. A huge wave crashed up onto the landing, then receded, leaving an inch or two of water swirling about. The doorway opening began about six inches above ground, or water would have come into the cave.

"I don't like that," I said. "After all we've been through, I wouldn't want to be swept out to sea."

Holmes stepped into the doorway, shielding me from the wind. "We shall have to make a run for it when there is a lull. Wait until I give the word."

But the winds and crashing waves seemed to grow worse still until, finally, it was briefly almost quiet.

"Now!" Holmes cried.

He leaped out onto the landing and ran toward the lighthouse. Lupin and I followed. It was only some twenty feet or so, but seemed much more distant, and indeed as we reached the door, icy water splashed about us, drenching my legs and feet. Holmes quickly lifted the latch, and we stepped inside to escape the cold gray water swirling all about. Holmes closed and secured the watertight outer door, and we stepped through the other portal with its wooden door, into the storage room. We removed our yellow slickers, shook them to get the water off them, and hung them back up. I hoped that the keepers could lend me a pair of dry socks.

Lupin stared at us through his droplet-covered spectacles and smiled. "Well, gentlemen, that is that, I suppose. I must say, it has been quite an adventure and great fun, indeed!" He had spoken in English, rather than the usual French.

Holmes was amused. "Yes, it has."

Afterword

A fine spring day in Paris truly makes up for the chilly overcast ones of fall and winter. Strolling one Monday afternoon in early May along the Champ de Mars, I felt that the season had truly changed at last. The sky was a vivid blue, the sun was out and shone on the beautiful pink flowers of the cherry trees in full bloom all along the way, and in the distance stood Eiffel's tower of dark steel, constructed only a few years past. Michelle and I had arrived on Saturday, and it was certainly different weather from my last visit only a month ago.

I paused before one of the larger trees with spectacular blossoms, the arching dark branches lost in fleecy clouds of pink. The rosy petals formed dense clusters, and a few small yellow-green leaves were just beginning to sprout from the branches. Curious, I stepped off the path onto the grass, then reached overhead to tug down a branch and sniff at some blossoms. Unlike the earlier blooming white ones on a different type of cherry tree, these had no smell.

A couple formally dressed, he in black top hat and frock coat, she in an extravagant purple silk, both smiled at me. "Does it smell good?" she asked. Her gloved hand loosely held her companion's arm just above the elbow.

I shook my head. "Sadly, no."

"Ah, *dommage*," she said in a mocking tone.

They proceeded on their way, while I touched a petal, ever so gently, with my fingertips. So soft. Almost like a woman's skin—but no, not really. The texture was completely different, and the firmness provided by the muscle and bone within was missing. There was certainly nothing fragile about Michelle. I had a vivid memory of her from the night before, which stirred a faint longing. Sometimes the more intimate we were, the more I desired her—I simply could not seem to get enough of her.

A faint smile pulled at my lips. We had not had a holiday together in a very long time, and it was wonderful to have her all to myself—or mostly to myself. I would have to share her with Holmes, Angelique, and Lupin for another couple days, and then the two of us were going off alone to Étretat. After all I had told her, she very much wanted to see the Chambre of the Demoiselles and the Needle itself.

First, however, there was to be a formal ceremony the day after tomorrow, Wednesday, during which Holmes and I were to receive a decoration and reward from the French prime minister in recognition of our aid in the recovery of the great treasure. True to his word, Holmes had contacted the French government, and after some frenzied back-and-forth diplomacy, a French ship went to the lighthouse at the Needles and reclaimed the chests. Lupin was certainly also worthy of a decoration, but he preferred to remain anonymous and was content with his "commission," that fortune in jewels he had taken.

I stepped off the grass back onto the pavement, and a portly man with bushy sideburns gave me a disapproving scowl. Certain Parisians very much believed in following the rules, such as keeping off the grass in the public parks. I strolled slowly, taking in the vivid pink and green of blossoms and grass, the blue and white of sky. The cool air on my face swelled and diminished in its own gentle rhythm. It truly was a perfect day, and I thought that I would rather be there on the Champ de Mars in Paris than any place in the world.

All that was missing was Michelle to share all this with, but I would be seeing her soon enough. I had no doubt she would rather be with me, but she had yielded to Lupin's entreaties that she join Angelique in a shopping trip to some of the grand fashion boutiques of the city. Michelle was quite gracious in accepting, although I knew that, unlike the vast majority of her sex, that sort of thing did not appeal to her—in fact, she actually loathed it. Of course, Angelique had rather gushingly implored her to come along, so politeness required that she acquiesce.

Lupin had rushed back to Paris and Angelique after our adventure at the Needles, and they were now formally engaged to be married and quite the lovebirds. While Michelle and I had some difficulty keeping our hands off one another in private, we were not given to obsequious displays of affection in public. Only rarely did Lupin and Angelique seem to have both hands free, one hand generally devoted to clasping the other's. Terms of endearment like *mon amour* and *ma biche* were also sprinkled liberally in their conversation. Given Lupin's comical and histrionic talents, this seemed somewhat out of character, but he appeared quite sincere.

He also confided to Holmes and me that he had told Angelique all about Arsène Lupin. Initially shocked, she had after some consideration declared that it made no difference to her. And indeed, he had dropped the assumed personality of Beautrelet, which I found quite confusing, since he had been Beautrelet for most of the time we had known him. He did keep his own chestnut brown hair—there was no black wig or false mustache—and he wore the same gold-rimmed spectacles. However, his voice had dropped down into the baritone range, and a certain eager silly manner had been replaced with a detached sort of irony.

I came to an empty bench, the classic sort with sculpted wrought iron painted black at either side, and a single long board forming the back. I took off my hat, then sat for perhaps half an hour enjoying the sunshine and watching the passers-by. At last I rose, and when I reached the street near the Eiffel Tower, I hailed a cab to take me back across town to a café near our hotel.

I sat down at a small round table a little before four and ordered a café noir from the waiter in black with a white apron. He was just bringing it when a tall red-headed woman in an electric-blue dress came through the door. Her eyes met mine, even as she smiled and started for my table.

She touched the waiter lightly on the forearm. "May I have one of the same, *s'il vous plaît*?"

She sat down, then gave my arm a quick squeeze, before she pulled off her gloves, revealing her large shapely white hands. Nothing off the shelf would fit her: all her gloves were made to order. She had been away from the physician's ritual washing with carbolic acid long enough that her skin was not so red or irritated. She also removed a blue hat with a wide-brim and a large swooping plume and gave her head a slight shake. Her long red-brown hair was pinned up, but as usual, threatened to go astray, one long curl in particular covering her white ear. Her eyes were a clear blue, her nose turned up ever so slightly, and already the Parisian sun had increased the dusting of freckles across her cheeks and nose.

Her broad full mouth formed a familiar smile with a certain trace of irony. "What are you smiling at, Henry?"

"You, of course. I am quite content to have one of the most beautiful women in all of Paris walk into a café and sit at my table."

"You are a hopeless romantic—and a shameless flatterer."

"Not at all." I was not exaggerating: I savored just having her close to me, the sense of her physical presence and her beauty.

"All the same, I am hardly in the league of Mademoiselle Chamerac. Parisian men are not subtle. Although not quite so extreme as the Italians, their ogling is rather obvious."

"I am sure they were ogling you and not her."

Michelle laughed and briefly gripped my hand. "You are sweet, Henry."

"And how did the shopping trip go?"

Michelle's mouth stiffened slightly, even as it straightened. "Well enough—for Angelique." She shook her head. "She must have spent a small fortune. She seemed to feel an obligation to buy something every place we stopped, either dresses or jewelry." Familiar creases had formed in her forehead.

I stared briefly at her. "I don't think you care much for her, do you?"

She gave her head a forceful shake. "I do not."

"Could this be a certain prejudice against small beautiful blond women?"

"It is true that I have a certain prejudice. I have told you before about the girl Agnes at the convent school. At twelve, I was the tallest in the class, skinny and awkward. Agnes was always the perfect little blond angel before the sisters while, in private, she was my tormentress. All the same, I want to like Angelique, and she did treat me as if we were the best of friends and old acquaintances. Nevertheless…"

"But you do like Lupin?"

She smiled. "Who could help but like him? He is quite charming and oddly… guileless."

I gazed at her curiously. "But Angelique, instead, has guile?"

Michelle's fingers spread apart, then she clenched and unclenched them. "Oh, I don't know. Perhaps… I don't like women who act differently around each sex: with men, they are all smiles and sweetness, while with women they assume a sarcastic or ironical mien. They seem to assume we women are all part of some grand conspiracy against the opposite sex."

"And that is the way she acted? I have not seen that before."

"Of course not. Also… I especially don't like it when the target of their mocking seems to be their husband."

"You must mean Lupin."

"Yes."

"What did she say?"

"It wasn't so much what she said, as her general attitude, although once she did say it was nice that the male of the species felt they had to prove their affection by giving the female a blank check."

"Speaking of that, did you find anything you wanted?"

She shook her head. "Oh Henry, I already have more than I need."

I laughed. "Little wonder that you and she did not hit it off." Michelle was still looking rather grave, and I squeezed her hand. "Luckily Lupin has enough money to keep her content, and perhaps once they are married and know one another better…"

Michelle grew stern. "You know that I do not approve of rushed marriages. It is not a decision to be taken lightly."

I smiled. "Well, everyone needn't wait as long as we did."

Her own smile was gentle. "But in the end we were quite sure."

"Yes, we were. And I have never had any regrets whatsoever."

"Nor have I."

I wanted to kiss her hand, but instead I stroked her knuckles gently with my fingertips. "It was the best decision I ever made in my life."

The waiter arrived with his tray and set down two small white cups of black coffee and two glasses of water. Michelle's eyes were still fixed on mine, even as she grasped the handle of one cup. "Let's drink up and go back to our room. We have over an hour before we need dress for dinner."

"However shall we pass the time?"

The corners of her mouth rose, along with one red-brown eyebrow.

Holmes, Michelle, and I went through the doorway into L'Exquis, among the most venerable and exclusive restaurants in Paris, and one normally far out of my price range. However, Lupin had invited us there for a celebratory dinner.

The maître d' dressed in a formal black suit nodded at us. "*Bonsoir, messieurs et madame.*"

"Good evening. I believe you have a reservation for–" Holmes faltered for a second "–a Monsieur Beautrelet."

The man frowned, then glanced at a paper on a nearby clipboard. "There is no one of that name."

"Perhaps, then, a Monsieur Punil."

"Ah, yes. He only recently arrived. This way, please."

We followed him into a grand dining room with a high curved ceiling decorated with paintings of gods and goddesses, similar to what you might see in a ducal palace. The pillars and the curved wooden supports overhead were covered with an elaborate golden frieze. Half the tables were occupied, all set with beautiful china, sparkling silverware, and immaculately white linen tablecloths. The low hum of subdued conversation filled the room, and everyone was formally dressed, the men in black tailcoats and white bow ties, the women in the sort of fancy gowns and jewels one might see at the opera. In a corner was Angelique, a true vision in a dress that showed off her bare arms and her decolletage along with a diamond necklace; and Lupin in evening dress, the variant who had black hair and a mustache, a scar on his cheek, and who sported a monocle.

Michelle looked briefly puzzled. "Who is that with Angelique?"

"That is Lupin—and that is how he usually appears in character as the *gentleman-cambrioleur*."

"Oh yes, I see now. I wonder…"

Lupin grinned at us and gestured at the table with his hand. "Here you are, at last! Join us in some champagne. We just ordered a bottle. Monsieur, could you fetch three more glasses and a second bottle?"

Michelle tilted her head slightly to the side, peering at him. "I had to ask Henry who you were. You look quite different."

He laughed. "And do you approve?"

She shrugged. "It is quite dashing. That scar is a nice touch."

"Thank you. I did this for Angelique." He glanced briefly at her. "She wanted to see the true Lupin about whom she has heard so much."

Angelique grasped his arm with her tiny shapely hand. "And I find him quite swank indeed! He does look much older, doesn't he?"

We sat down, and a waiter hovering nearby swept in and poured champagne for us all. Lupin raised his glass. "A toast to that most formidable duo of detectives—Holmes and Lupin, and to their essential colleague, Vernier!"

For the first time, a smile flickered over Holmes's lips. "Indeed!" he said, then joined in the clinking of glasses. To others Holmes might appear inscrutable, but I had learned to sense his moods, his emotions, and he seemed more reserved than usual that evening, somber even, for what was supposed to be a festive event.

After taking a big swallow, Lupin raised his glass again. "And to this lovely young lady soon to be my bride, my dearest Angelique!"

We clinked glasses again, but I think all but the happy pair did so with somewhat less enthusiasm.

Angelique set her hand lightly over Lupin's. I suspected that all the men present must have eyed her as she crossed the room to the table. Her dress was a pale glacial-blue silk which had puffy fabric covering her shoulders, but which left her arms and much of her chest bare. She was wearing a silver necklace with a big diamond, one of a faintly bluish hue, alongside which were placed smaller gems like carved bits of ice. Similar glittering diamonds were set in the lobes of her small ears, and her ash-blond hair was tightly bound up and secured in place—it was quite a contrast with Michelle's coiffure, from which all those errant red-brown strands and curls had escaped.

Michelle's dress was a much darker, more vibrant blue, the hue so different that it was hard to believe both qualified as the same color. She had on long white gloves, but as was de rigueur in a restaurant when dining, she pulled them off, revealing her long, shapely arms. Seated alongside Angelique, you could see how much taller and long-limbed she was, stronger, too—all of which I delighted in. I cherished Michelle's abundance, the fact that there was so much of her to love!

Lupin put his monocle into his left eye and peered at Michelle. "That is quite a beautiful sapphire ring you have, Dr. Doudet-Vernier. The blue is exquisite."

"Thank you. It was a gift from my husband." Michelle smiled at me. "He also gave me a beautiful sapphire necklace, but I rarely wear it in public. It is back home in London, safely stowed away. Bringing it to Paris would be foolish."

Holmes nodded. "Amen to that."

"Besides, I don't like…" She stopped suddenly and bit her lip. "I am… I worry it might be stolen." I knew she was going to say that she did not like to show off, but of course, that would be an implied criticism of Angelique with her spectacular diamonds. "I mostly only wear it… in private." Her lips puckered slightly outward as her eyes shifted to mine.

And little else, I reflected.

Angelique gave Lupin's hand a squeeze. "I don't think I have to worry about that with Arsène at my side."

Holmes smiled faintly. "So you call him Arsène now?"

"Yes. Isidore Beautrelet was only a make-believe name, and a rather silly one, actually."

"I fear he will always be young Isidore Beautrelet to me," Holmes said.

I nodded. "I feel the same way, but if you prefer…"

Michelle smiled. "Come now, Isidore Arsène Beautrelet Lupin, what should we call you?"

"How about Charles de Batz de Castelmore d'Artagnan?"

We all smiled, although Angelique looked briefly concerned.

"I always admired d'Artagnan, you know—and the Count of Monte Cristo, as well. Indeed, Lupin owes them and Dumas a debt. All the same, as we are all friends and I am not much for formalities, you might call me by a first name, either Arsène or Isidore, as you prefer. As for myself, I would not be comfortable taking such liberty: to me you shall remain Holmes, Dr. Vernier, and Dr. Doudet-Vernier. I have great respect for the medical profession, and you are, after all, my elders."

Michelle laughed. "How cruel of you to remind us!"

A blush appeared at Lupin's cheeks. "Oh, I am sorry—I did not mean…"

Michelle raised her hand, spreading her fingers apart. "Oh, do not worry, Isidore. I was only teasing. No offense taken."

"I am glad to hear it. Angelique was just telling me about your shopping trip." His eyes shifted to me. "How lucky for you, Dr. Vernier, to have a frugal wife who does not wish to bankrupt you!"

"Arsène!" Angelique exclaimed. "How can you blame me, when it was your idea, after all?"

"Come now, *chérie*, you must know that I, too, was teasing. I am sure you will look delectable in all your purchases. I can hardly wait to see them."

Holmes seemed to hesitate briefly. "And is that beautiful necklace you are wearing also a gift from Isidore?"

"No. It is a family heirloom of the Chameracs. My… uncle thought I should have it."

"That was most generous of him."

"Yes, it was." Her pale blue eyes filled with tears. "I know, Monsieur Holmes, that he may have turned out to be a bad man, wicked, even, but he was always most kind to me. I wish he had not had to die in such a terrible way. Blown to pieces!"

"He would have felt nothing at all," I said. "Given the agonies we doctors often see, a quick and painless death seems a blessing."

Lupin stroked his chin. "I suppose if it were not for him, we would have never met. I owe him that much, at least." He grinned. "All the same, I'm glad I didn't have to pay for that necklace!"

Angelique was definitely not amused. "I did not know you considered me such a profligate."

Lupin gave her hand a squeeze. "I was only joking. You must know I would deny you nothing, my love. But enough—let's not talk about money. Such a prickly and troublesome subject! Besides, I now have more than enough for us to live in style for many years to come. That is why I am retiring as *gentleman-cambrioleur*. As I have sworn, you shall have an honest man as your husband. And I shall pursue my grand dream: to become the greatest detective in… on the continent." He smiled at Holmes, who gave a slight appreciative nod. "And now, I think we should devote ourselves to a much more serious and immediate subject: the perusal of, and the selection from, the menu."

After lengthy consideration and some discussion, as well as a query or two to the waiter, we all gave our orders. The waiter scribbled on his notepad, while another poured us more champagne, and then both departed. We chatted idly, and again I noticed that Holmes seemed more reserved than usual. After a few minutes, the waiter returned with a platter of *escargot à la bourguignonne* which he set in the center of table. Next, he set before us each a small plate, along with two utensils: a snail clamp, or tongs, to hold the shell and a small thin fork with two tines to extract the flesh. When he came to Michelle, she raised her hand and shook her head.

About a dozen snails rested in the special plate with a concave depression for each one. The curving shells were a striated brown and white, with the black lump of the snail showing in the opening. They were swimming in yellow butter which smelled strongly of garlic, and sprigs of green parsley were sprinkled liberally about.

I ate one to be polite, and the butter and garlic did mostly disguise the pungent taste of the chewy creature. Holmes, Lupin, and Angelique ate the others with enthusiasm. I knew my cousin had a great fondness for escargot, and I had watched him consume them on many occasions in France. He handled the clamp and little fork with great skill to meticulously extract the tiny animal and pop it into his mouth. Next, he would pour the garlicky buttery juices from the vacant shell onto some bread.

Lupin also did quite well, but I was surprised that someone so youthful and inexperienced as Angelique seemed such an old hand at eating snails. Given the poverty of her upbringing, she would have had little access to such gastronomic delights. Perhaps the baron had relished them and had had them served often at his table. She handled the fork and tongs every bit as well as Holmes. All the same, something about the sight of a beautiful young woman wearing an elegant gown and a diamond necklace even as she extracted a baked gastropod from a shell, did strike me as absurd! All in all, she had an imposing presence, almost intimidating, much more so than Michelle. Perhaps, too... she was surely more conscious of her beauty and its power than Michelle. When she had finished with the escargot, she moved aside the plate, and again set her hand on Lupin's larger one.

Evaluations of beauty were always subjective, and as Michelle's husband, I was naturally biased, but I found her much more appealing. Partly it was because I knew her so well: her beauty and her ready smile with that broad mouth, her good humor and intelligence, her generosity of spirit, her basic goodness, were all inseparable, all part of that combination which made me love her so much. Somehow I was certain Angelique could never measure up to Michelle, but I hoped that she and Lupin could be happy together.

Lupin did most of the talking for a while, relating to the two women more of our adventures on the submarine and at the lighthouse. "I must admit," he said, "that I greatly enjoyed our time on the submarine."

I stared at him in disbelief. "Are you serious?"

He laughed. "Most serious. In fact... I know it is only an idle fancy, but someday I would like to have a submarine of my own! I could range round the Mediterranean, popping up here and there to right wrongs and help damsels in distress."

I continued to stare at him. "You are joking, after all."

"Not exactly. If I could wave my hand and have my own submarine, I would gladly do so."

"I also found our submarine voyage fascinating," Holmes said, "but Henry clearly does not care for being underwater."

I nodded. "Yes, if God had wanted people to travel about underwater, he would have given us gills like fish."

"It is a shame," Holmes said, "that such a marvel as the *Nautilus* was destroyed, and so many lives lost, but the world is a much safer place with it gone."

Shortly after the turtle soup (which Michelle also skipped because of her fond childhood memories of a beloved pet turtle), four waiters descended upon our table and fussed about, serving us each our main dish, and opening and pouring more wine into fresh crystal goblets. We had our choice of superb red or white French vintages. Michelle and I had ordered *gigot d'agneau*, lamb shanks; Lupin had tournedos of beef; Angelique, lobster; and Holmes, sweetbreads or *ris de veau*. Holmes was quite fond of this dish, which was some such gland as the thymus of the animal, but after my youthful days in the anatomy lab, I could not eat anything resembling an organ!

While we dined, Holmes and Lupin dominated the conversation, each telling some of their more notable exploits. Lupin listened to my cousin with rapt enthusiasm, his admiration obvious. I could also tell that Holmes was impressed with the younger man and his ingenuity. As we finished our main dishes, the two of them had an extended discussion about the art of the disguise: the various tricks they had used, the special makeup, the creation of false beards and mustaches. It turned out that Lupin's elderly priest was modeled after one he had seen at Notre-Dame.

I noticed that Angelique was as skillful at dealing with a lobster as with escargot, even though the crustacean was notoriously difficult to eat without making a mess. Her tiny fingers wielded the lobster fork to neatly extract pieces of white flesh, which she dipped into melted butter. Of course, the cook had helped matters by neatly cracking the shells of the big pincers. She was the last to finish.

She dabbed at her mouth with the napkin, then leaned back in the chair and grasped Lupin's hand. He paused briefly in his discourse, smiling reflexively, then continued on. When he was done, she spoke, staring at me and Michelle. "These two are both so clever—and brave, as well. How dull my existence seems in comparison. But I suppose that is a woman's lot."

Michelle and I exchanged a look. I knew she must be metaphorically biting her tongue, if not literally doing so.

Lupin squeezed Angelique's hand. "Oh, I shall see to it that we also have some adventures together. I know our two doctors there have not had idle lives." He glanced again at Holmes. "What an honor this has been, to—so to speak—compare notes with Sherlock Holmes." His smile encompassed us all. "This has been a wonderful dinner. I shall always treasure the memory of our time together here.

And dessert is yet to come! Their profiteroles are said to be the best in all of Paris. But first, a final toast—to all of us!"

He raised his glass, we did the same, clinked glasses, then sipped at our wine.

Holmes drank, then held up his glass again. "And a special thanks to our young host, who I suspect may someday—God help him—obtain the same notoriety as Sherlock Holmes!"

We all smiled, then joined in the toast.

Lupin set down his glass. "Before we order dessert, I have an announcement to make. Angelique and I have decided upon our wedding date—the day after tomorrow! Neither of us wants to wait, and that way you three can also attend the ceremony. Moreover, unbeknownst to her, I have something for her, a very special gift." He reached inside his jacket pocket and withdrew a brittle-looking old beige envelope, which looked somehow familiar. Next his hand slipped into his trouser pocket.

Holmes was sitting beside him, and his hand shot out and seized Lupin's wrist before he could withdraw it from his pocket. *"Wait*—just wait."

Lupin stared at him, astonished. He hesitated, then set his hand back on the table. "What is it?"

Holmes sat upright and sank back into his chair. His mouth formed a straight tense line, even as he inhaled through his nostrils. The sudden pallor of his thin face contrasted dramatically with his swept-back black hair and his black jacket. His gray-blue eyes were anguished.

"Well, what is this all about?" Lupin sounded annoyed.

Holmes raised both long slender hands, then clasped his fingers together. "I need to speak with you—alone." He dropped his hands and stood up. "Let's go outside for a moment."

Lupin was more puzzled than ever, but he rose.

Angelique grasped at his wrist. "Oh, do not go."

"We shall not be long–shall we, Holmes?"

"No."

"If this is serious, I must come, too," Angelique said.

Holmes gave his head a brusque shake. "No." He almost pushed Lupin away from the table, and then the two of them started across the room.

Angelique shook her head. "Men and their secrets." Her sudden smile was both bitter and ironic.

Michelle glanced at me. "Do you know what this is all about, Henry?"

"I do not. Not exactly."

I had remembered suddenly where the envelope came from: it must be the one we had found at the entrance to the secret passage at the Château de l'Aiguille. And along with the note, had been a silver locket, the memento to his beloved wife that a man, long dead, had left behind hoping that some future person might pass it on as a symbol of love and fidelity. Lupin had kept both. Obviously, he had been about to give the locket to Angelique.

Angelique raised her glass and nodded at the waiter, who quickly swooped in to pour her more white wine. She gave a nod of thanks, then took a sip and set down her glass. I noticed that her hand was trembling slightly. She sat up stiffly and forced a smile.

"Well, as Arsène was about to tell you, we hope to be married the day after tomorrow. It is to be a small wedding. Arsène's friend Maurice Leblanc will be the best man. I had thought of asking you, Michelle, to be my bridesmaid."

Michelle, like myself, seemed quite bewildered by the sudden turn in events. "I... I don't know what to say."

"It is true we have only just met, but I fear I have no real friends or old acquaintances here in Paris."

"Well, if you are certain, I shall gladly do so."

I knew Michelle did not really want to.

Angelique smiled. She had mostly regained her composure, but there was a certain expression in those pale blue eyes... She gazed out across the room, and her small full mouth suddenly stiffened.

Lupin strode across the room with long forceful steps. His eyes were wild, the monocle dangling from its chain and bouncing slightly as he came. He reached his chair and clutched at the back. His eyes showed a strange combination of dullness and wildness, the two opposing forces somehow mixed. Angelique stared up at him, her expression grave.

"Is it true?" Lupin's voice was ominously quiet, almost a whisper.

"Is what true?" she asked.

He hesitated, then spoke more softly yet. "That you were not the baron's niece, but his mistress."

The corners of Angelique's mouth rose briefly, then fell. "Does it matter so much?"

"It does."

She drew in her breath resolutely, then shrugged. "Yes."

Lupin grimaced as if he had been stabbed, then staggered around the chair and collapsed into it. "Oh dear God," he moaned. He started to run his fingers back through his hair, then stopped as he realized he had on a wig which he might dislodge.

"And you had no suspicions whatsoever? Not even an iota?"

"None." He shook his head wildly. "I was an idiot."

"So the famed Arsène is not so clever as he thought." The irony in her voice was bitter.

"I thought you were... I thought you were innocent. How could I be so stupid? And now I see... How old are you, anyway? Certainly not twenty, as I believed."

"I am twenty-five. The same as you." She drew in her breath in something like a laugh. "We are a match."

He shook his head. "I don't think so."

"Oh, Arsène, we each had our secrets. We each pretended to be someone we were not. You were Isidore Beautrelet, the insipid young man, and I was Angelique, the virtuous young demoiselle rescued from a hard life by her uncle. We each had our role to play. But underneath it... we are the same, you and I." Again she made a sound like a laugh. "We were made for one another."

He shook his head more wildly this time. "No, no, it's not true—I told you the truth about myself—I told you who I really was. You lied to me—it has been nothing but lies."

"And if I had told you the truth, would you have wanted to marry me?"

He stared at her, his eyes still wild. "Of course not."

"There! You see? You can have your false life and enjoy yourself as a man, but when it comes to marriage, you must have your vacuous virgin. Men are all the same. The baron could keep me around as his niece, but he could never divorce his wife and actually marry me. He was much too respectable for that! I went along with his silly game. It was a small price to pay to live like royalty. My story about growing up in poverty: that was not a lie. It was only too true. The part about the roaches and the rats... You made yourself into a thief as a boy to avenge the way your mother was treated; later, you became Arsène Lupin; and yet you blame me for becoming Angelique Chamerac. Can't you see that it was the same ingenuity at work, the same drive and determination?"

"I don't care," he murmured. "I don't care."

She made that sound like a laugh again. "I suppose this means the marriage is off?"

He stared at her a long while, then gave his head a single emphatic nod.

"You are a fool, after all. You will never find another woman so much your equal as me. But…" She shrugged. "As you wish." She glanced up at Holmes who had been standing silently behind Michelle and myself. "Are you happy with your work now, Monsieur Sherlock Holmes, the great detective?"

Holmes was still very pale. He said nothing. I noticed that our little drama had caught the attention of two nearby tables. Our waiter was also transfixed.

"Ah well…" Angelique—or whoever she really was—stood up. "I bear you no ill will. Perhaps, too, marriage would not have suited either one of us. Goodbye, my little…" She reached out toward his cheek with her hand, but he drew away. "That bad, is it?" She shook her head, then tried again. He let her touch his cheek with the fingertips of her small shapely hand.

"So in the end, you are not the clever rogue Arsène Lupin, after all, but only that foolish little boy, the insipid Isidore Beautrelet. Adieu, Isidore. Adieu." She drew in her breath, her chest swelling slightly, nodded to the rest of us, then started across the room. Most of the men paused in their eating or talking to watch her depart.

Holmes sank down into his chair. His eyes were still anguished. "I felt I had to tell you, Isidore. I could not let you give her the locket without knowing the truth."

Lupin nodded. "I understand. I can't say I'm exactly glad you did, but... I suppose it is always difficult to awake from a fool's paradise." He drew in his breath, gave a long sigh, then smiled weakly at the waiter. "Quite a spectacle, wasn't it? Could you please bring me a brandy?"

"I would like one, too," Holmes said.

"You had best make it four brandies." I glanced at Michelle, who gave a quick nod.

The waiter bowed slightly, then left.

Lupin wiped briefly at his brow, hesitated, then reached into his pocket, withdrew the heart-shaped silver locket, and set it on the table. The side with the two lovebirds engraved was showing. He looked at me. "I think you should have it, Dr. Vernier. That would best honor the old man's wishes. He wanted it to go to someone worthy, someone who had prospered in love. Clearly you two have done so. Take it."

I shook my head gently. "No. I do not need it, but I think you do. Keep it as a reminder that love is always possible. Besides, you are a young man. You will meet someone worthy of all your fine qualities and your affection. Almost every man has had at least one disastrous love affair. Lord knows, I did! And yet I am happier than I had ever imagined possible. You will meet someone who deserves it, I am certain."

He stared gravely at me. "You are quite sure you don't want it?"

"No. Keep it."

"Henry is absolutely right," Michelle said.

He regarded us both. "You are very kind, you know." He grasped the locket and thrust it back into his pocket. The waiter arrived with a tray with four brandies. Lupin took his and downed it in a single swallow. "Another, if you please." The waiter nodded. Lupin drew in his breath, exhaled, and his brow furrowed briefly. "I think... I think perhaps I shall live after all, although I still feel as if someone has diced up my heart and lungs into little pieces. My stomach, too, I think. Or maybe all my insides simply went through some grinder." He stared at Holmes. "I suppose you suspected her from the very first?"

"Yes, I did."

"Why, exactly?"

"There was her spectacular beauty, and then there was the baroness. Clearly something was gnawing at her. And what could be worse than having your husband's mistress live under the same roof with you? I made some inquiries among those who knew all the gossip of Paris, and there were rumors."

"Was there a moment when you were certain?"

Holmes swirled his brandy, then took a quick sip. "Yes. At the opera, at *Manon*. The way she was dressed, her bearing, those spectacular jewels she was wearing—it was obvious—she was no mere niece."

"Yes, it was obvious. And how appropriate that you realized it during *Manon*! But I did not see it. I saw only her beauty."

"If it's any consolation to you," I said, "I didn't see it either."

Lupin smiled ever so faintly. "I told you once, as Beautrelet, that Lupin had a weakness for the ladies. That was an understatement. They are my... blind spot. And I wanted to be a detective! I cannot deduce what is right before my nose."

Holmes shook his head. "You are too hard on yourself. Do you think I have never made any mistakes—especially as pertains to women? No, you have a great natural talent and a formidable mind. You will be a great detective. I am certain of it." His sardonic smile appeared. "And in the end, it is a better career than that of *gentleman-cambrioleur*."

Lupin stared at him, then nodded at last. "Thank you, Holmes."

The waiter set another brandy before Lupin, who reached for it. Holmes set his hand on his wrist. "Sip it this time, Isidore."

"Yes." He swallowed some, then drew in his breath. His lips pulled into a brief fierce grimace of a smile. "I'm afraid I've rather spoiled the party! I think... I think... perhaps we should have some dessert after all—perhaps those profiteroles I was telling you about."

Michelle smiled gently and set her large white hand on Lupin's. "Oh Isidore, I promise that you will have no difficulty at all finding some wonderful woman to love you."

After all that had happened, Lupin had thus far managed to hold himself together remarkably well, but his mouth contorted even as his eyes teared up. "Oh thank you." He wiped at his cheek, then turned toward the waiter. "Four orders of those famous profiteroles of yours, monsieur."

He sipped at his brandy, then stared more closely at the brown liquid. "This is very good, isn't it? I suppose now... yes, the case of the great treasure of France is truly and officially finished, the case of all the needles: the Château de l'Aiguille at Creuse, l'Aiguille at Étretat, and the Needles off the Isle of Wight. How would you rank the case, Holmes?"

"Near the very top—*au sommet*. It was very challenging, and took so many twists and turns. There was the submarine and the lighthouse, and perhaps most amazing of all, the ancient interior of l'Aiguille out off the coast at Étretat. It was a case I shall never forget."

"Nor shall I," I exclaimed.

Lupin smiled at us both, the raised his glass. "*À la prochaine,*" he exclaimed, which was a little tricky to translate, but "until next time" was closest, or perhaps more appropriately, "until the next case."

"*À la prochaine*," Holmes and I exclaimed in unison.

Michelle laughed. "And on that occasion you must bring me along!"

About the Author

Sam Siciliano is the author of several novels, including the Sherlock Holmes titles *The Angel of the Opera*, *The Web Weaver*, *The Grimswell Curse*, *The White Worm* and *Deathly Relics*. He lives in Vancouver, Washington.

For more fantastic fiction, author events,
exclusive excerpts, competitions, limited editions and more

VISIT OUR WEBSITE
titanbooks.com

LIKE US ON FACEBOOK
facebook.com/titanbooks

FOLLOW US ON TWITTER AND INSTAGRAM
@TitanBooks

EMAIL US
readerfeedback@titanemail.com